Before & After

Matthew Thomas is a young British writer, 29, who works by day as a flight simulator graphics designer. *Before & After* is his first novel. He insists he has nothing personal against sheep. It may not be mutual.

Voyager

MATTHEW THOMAS

Before & After

HarperCollins*Publishers*

Voyager
An Imprint of HarperCollins*Publishers*
77–85 Fulham Palace Road,
Hammersmith, London W6 8JB

www.voyager-books.com

A Paperback original 1999
5 7 9 8 6 4

A catalogue record for this book
is available from the British Library

ISBN 0-00-648302-9

Set in Goudy by
Palimpsest Book Production Limited,
Polmont, Stirlingshire

Printed and bound in Great Britain by
Omnia Books Ltd, Glasgow

Dedicated to N. G. Jones
and O. M. Jones

BEFORE

It was a beautiful summer day which, if anything, made events all the harder to take. The sun hung high in a clear sky. The birds indulged in an ornithological opera which would have made Pavarotti pack up in despair. Overhead, cotton wool clouds jostled for position in a cumulo-nimbus beauty contest lacking only sequinned bikinis. It was the sort of sickeningly happy day which weather forecasters and politicians dream about.

Or perhaps it wasn't. There was one black spot, or rather, red splat, on the horizon. Down in the meadow by the stream, the sheep were exploding once again.

'Baaaaahhhhhh!' said Colin.

'*KERBOOOOOOOOM!*' replied Kevin, from the spot three feet away where he had been busily munching grass. Short seconds later Kevin was three thousand feet away – straight up, and still accelerating.

Was there any significance to this strange behaviour? It certainly held significance for the sheep in question. It meant no more prancing about a quiet Welsh hillside and no more cold baths in vats of strange smelling orange cordial. It wiped out his one chance of immortality[1] – an appearance as an extra in *One Man and his Dog* – but perhaps most of all it meant no more staring at tufts of grass.

Colin looked down dejectedly at his lunch. It was hard

---

1 Relatively few world religions acknowledge the existence of Sheep Heaven.

to look at it any other way, apart perhaps from sheepishly. Colin had a natural bent for doing things sheepishly – sixty-five million years of evolution ensured it. The essential truth of all sheepy existence was that once you'd seen one tuft of grass you'd seen them all. Colin had learned this fact young. At least it was a conclusion he'd reached by himself, which was more than could be said for most of his siblings. By sheep standards, Colin was quite the intellectual. Sure, his mother had taught him the basics:

'Leg at each corner, woolly back – sheep. Leg at each corner, furry back – dog.'

She'd also taught Colin the ancient and sober tenets of sheep theology,[1] about which he had always harboured private doubts: that the pasture was created by THE GREAT SHEPHERD and watched over by his benign servant ROVER. Colin refused to believe that one day all good sheep would be rounded up for the mysterious ritual known as THE GREAT DIP, or that bad sheep would be reincarnated as an evil CARD-IGAN. This young lamb had long suspected there was more to life than that.

He was right.

Aimlessly, Colin wondered over to where, until a few moments ago, his friend Kevin had stood. He looked down at the four faintly steaming hooves and sighed. All was still once more. Somewhere, a grasshopper chirped self-consciously. Colin began to ponder the deeper mysteries of the universe. What did it all mean?

Slowly, a strange feeling enveloped the proud young sheep. It originated in his bowels and worked its way along his fluffy body until it ended in a not altogether unpleasant sensation in his loins. The nearest he'd ever come to this experience was the day Farmer Jones had mistakenly mixed twelve bags of All-Bran into the feed. That had been a

---

1 Known as Sheep Dogma.

very messy day, but this was subtly different – more cranial than anal.

For a dazzling second Colin's tiny brain caught hold of a concept both fleeting and dark. Its vast rolling blackness seemed to hint at ancient truths and bleak futures as yet untold. Like an overloaded jack, Colin's inadequate intellect struggled beneath the weight of his vision. Finally, his mind cracking under the unnatural strain, he went quietly mad. This great loss to sheep-based philosophy would never be known, because a split second later Colin, too, exploded. In his final moments he did at least write his name large in the annals of sheep history. At least in part, Colin was the first sheep to break the sound barrier.

ONE

September 1999

The sheep shall be the first sign.
Those that hop and frolic will detonate with great concussions,
The strongest glues will not hold them, their suffering will go
unheeded,
Until the Great Triangles depart.
Quatrain VII.5 The Lost Centuries of Nostradamus

One Dream Too Far

September should have brought some relief from that unnaturally humid summer. But as the months began their inevitable slide towards winter it had just got hotter and hotter.

The old man's sleep was troubled. Deep frowns creased his damp brow as he turned, muttering, arms flaying as if he were fighting off some pursuing nightmare beast. His bed sheets lay in a crumpled heap on the floor.

The cat watching him with impassive marmalade eyes had long since conceded that its best chance of safety lay away from the bed. It sat in the open window licking a paw. Outside, a bat screeched in the moonlight. The cat miaowed a threat then went back to grooming its thick ginger fur. For a moment it recalled better, cooler times before the oppressive heat had settled on the city. Then, with a startling display of feline agility, it succeeded in not falling out of the window with fright as the old man sat bolt upright in bed.

Suddenly not looking half as old, the man's eyes shone

with a manic intensity. He sat there for a long while, staring into space, hardly breathing, looking alarmingly like some crazed prophet of yore. Then he turned slowly to the cat.

'Well Aristo, they're back again. Better get this one down before I lose it.'

The cat said nothing in reply. They usually don't. It just watched as the shaking old man reached for a note pad on the bedside table and started to scribble furiously.

The Beginning Of The End

Early morning sunshine bathed the car park in bright yellow light as students shuffled along to their lectures. If some looked more bleary-eyed than others it may in part have been due to last night's Free Cider Promotion and Sponsored Snog-a-thon at the Union bar, in aid of Indignant Albanian Pea-Farmers – this month's favoured charity. Late for first period, some at least showed signs of haste.

The worst affected were still in bed, not all of them alone. Many would soon experience that *Oh my God, what have I done?* feeling. Some would soon know that *Why is my room so far from the toilet?* sensation. Several of the slower movers would soon fall back on that *With some hot water and a bit of bleach maybe I can clear it up* fuzzy logic. But fortunately only a select few would have to go through that terrifying *He/She didn't look this bad under artificial light. Maybe if I amputate my arm I can leave without waking them* panic.

Conspicuous amongst those who had made it into daylight was a figure neither youthful nor hurried. Professor Michael D. Nostrus seldom did anything at speed if he could help it. He was a law unto himself, and most often that law was: 'Thou shalt not get in my way, whichever random direction I may be taking.'

Though he wouldn't have admitted it, he was something of a hero to the more impressionable undergraduates. To the less impressionable undergraduates he was a weird old coot who should have been pensioned off with tank-tops and hoola-hoops – but few would have dared say that to his face. Professor Nostrus's reputation preceded him the way ball lightning precedes earthquakes.

He locked his battered old car and made his way across the forecourt towards the Department of History's main steps. Breathing deeply, he gazed up at the clear blue sky and smiled. It was the smile of a man who knew the simple joys of life and how quickly they could be snatched away – but thanks to last night's troubled sleep he had one more clue as to just how that might happen. Pondering that forewarned was forearmed, though perhaps not in the semi-automatic sense, Mike bounded up the steps.

He was a lean, white-haired figure, clad in an ancient tweed suit which had probably seen its best days before the British Empire turned from being a jolly good idea to a bit of a logistical headache. His face was etched with the cartography of life and showed more than a few detours. Beneath it a short white beard contrasted sharply with his sepia skin. But it was his eyes which stood out – not quite on stalks, though he had seen things that might have induced this in lesser mortals. They were ancient, out of place in this modern world – two twinkling sapphires which might have gazed out from a pirate prince on the Spanish Main, or a chief druid beneath glittering stars in the days when Rome was just a wagon stop on the Apennine Way.

Deftly sidestepping the most viciously spring-loaded swing doors on campus, Mike crossed the foyer. He wasn't in a rush, just eager as ever for his daily dose of the world's best informed receptionist.

'Morning Professor Nostrus.' Cyndi with an 'i' smiled as she looked up from *Hair Stylist Today!* [1]

---

1 This '!' was very important, and put an extra 20,000 on their sales figures.

Mike beamed back. 'Morning, my dear. What precious info-nugget do you have for me today?'

'Stand still and let me look you up.'

Like all good receptionists Cyndi was well aware of what went on around her. But while most of her colleagues could only claim to keep abreast of events in their building, Cyndi knew everything that went on in this universe and several others besides. A brave claim perhaps, but Cyndi was obsessed with astrology. If a gnat farted in Tibet she could tell what was on its mind. If one twelfth of the world's population was destined to feel queasy that day, she'd be the first to order in the Milk of Magnesia. Given a darkened room and enough Häagen-Dazs she would gladly have had Russell Grant's babies.

'Right then, Professor Nostrus – Pisces isn't it?'

Mike nodded. Cyndi never got it wrong. Her tangerine nail-varnished talon marking the spot, Cyndi let him in on his fate.

'Pisces – Thursday will be a good day for a henna rinse. Try to avoid a split-end situation encroaching into the weekend, as an unexpected guest from your past may arrive bearing news concerning a mutual friend . . .'

Mike did his best to look engrossed, which mainly involved grinning idiotically and nodding like a backseat plastic dog. Dazzling him with astrology was right next to the door marked impossible – the phrase 'bombs to Beirut' sprang to mind. He had dished out enough of it in his day to know the tricks, but that had been a long time ago. A very long time. Still, it was a harmless distraction. As with most religions it was of little concern in its early stages – it was only when some fanatic organized a crusade that the infidels would have to sit up and take note. Banishing from his mind the worrying image of Mystic Meg in a bulletproof vest, Mike smiled politely and asked pertinent questions re his impending follicular crisis.

Just as he was being told his optimum blow-dry parameters for the coming month, he caught a sudden movement out of the corner of his eye. Back at the department's infamous swing doors the Director of Studies was attempting a job an ambidextrous octopus would have found tricky. One foot was wedged between frame and hinge, in grave danger of being sliced off, as the flustered man navigated a vast pile of folders through the hazard. A sudden gust of wind was all it took to send the load tumbling to the ground.

Mike wasted no time. 'Fascinating talking to you my dear – but must dash – just remembered something very important I have to do upstairs.'

He hated to be rude, but he had no more desire to meet Dr O'Brian than Joan of Arc had to stand around with a group of French peasants discussing barbecue techniques. As he skidded past his pigeon hole Mike grabbed the mountain of junk mail it held. He didn't stop to check his lecture schedule, nor to admire the School of Modern Art's latest masterpiece entitled 'Mussolini: Was he really nice, or maybe just a git?' As he sprinted up the spiral staircase Mike could think only of the safety afforded by his office door.

Size Isn't Everything

If the size of a man's office reflects his power and standing in an organization then Michael Nostrus was not a powerful man. However, the magnitude of his office's contents bore no relation whatsoever to its volume. This rule can equally apply in reverse. Thus, a multi-billionaire property developer may possess a room the size of a small Middle Eastern country, containing nothing more than a desk, leather bucket-seat and a coffee table holding an oddly shaped statuette of a young lady with several interesting holes. Such minimalism in office design, when combined with an expanse of white carpet you could lose a bungalow in, has the undeniable effect of making a big room look bigger still. The only thing multi-billionaire property developers like more than owning a huge office is letting everyone know they own a huge office.

Mike's office was small in the way only adolescent amoebae and professional pygmy limbo dancers can be small. If it had been a breed of dog it would have been a Chihuahua stunted at birth. Even so, it was a Chihuahua that Mike certainly made the most of. The first question a visitor might ask would be 'Where are the walls?' followed nervously by 'How does the ceiling stay up?' Great piles of books obscured them from view, stacks of dusty leather-bound tomes that creaked when you opened them and looked likely to take off a finger as they thumped shut. Most of the world's languages were represented, including a few well past their sell by date – Ancient Provençal rubbed shoulders with rare Aramaic texts and scrolls of cuneiform. In the few places where there weren't books, and many where there were, lived notes, piled high to the ceiling or littering the floor like a giant's dandruff. As far as Mike was concerned, a filing system was what you used to trim your nails.

In one corner stood a dented suit of ceremonial Samurai armour, a large hole puncturing the chest piece. From the ceiling hung a mouldy old albatross, stuffed to the wing-tips. On the battered oak desk, next to a copy of *The Racing Times*, rested a dented brass astrolabe.

There was less free space here than on the last US chopper out of Saigon. But at least it wasn't full of sweating diplomats.

No, Mike was not a powerful man. He was an insignificant history teacher in an insignificant university in a sad, run-down London suburb. This had not always been the case. The suburb had always been sad and run-down, but Mike had led a life rich in experience, full beyond the wildest dreams of the most inventive biographer.

But then, anything less would have been a disappointment for a man nearly five hundred years old.

What's In A Name?

Professor Nostrus, Mike to his close friends – of which he had one, and that was a cat – was seriously old.

He had always thought there was an odd thing about age and names. In various cultures, of which Mike had seen his fair share, certain names were associated with a certain age. To accompany a zimmer frame and a bus pass you'd expect a solid, reliable name like Harold or George. 'Mike' was wrong for a geriatric. It suited DJs or football players, or the sort of children's TV presenter who could make sane parents favour compulsory sterilization. Nevertheless, the day would come when the streets were swamped by jittery old Garys and Waynes racing round in their meticulously restored Ford Capris and XR3is. Or perhaps the day wouldn't come, which brought Mike back to the present with a jolt.

The Professor looked down at the mountain of mail on his desk and sighed. How many letters had he opened in his time? The addresses changed but the name stayed the same – more or less. It had lost a few letters over the years, which had helped prevent the loss of more important things – like his head.

The assorted collection of envelopes and folders before him would reveal whether his survival plans were viable, or if it was time to start guzzling vodka and knocking back the pills. Was money even the answer? Not for the first time, Mike suffered a pang of doubt.

Over the courses of his multifaceted lives, Mike had observed that when the brown stuff seeped through the air-conditioning grate, it was nearly always the £2.50 an hour office cleaners who fared worst. Cash certainly hadn't guaranteed an escape from Pompeii, but it had helped. Mike didn't presently have money, but he had one advantage – he knew roughly what was coming. Somewhere out there in the black cosmic void the great snarling beast that forever threatens mankind's existence was brewing up a big one – it had eaten a Phall last night then corked its hairy bottom in preparation for the greatest stream of steaming kak it had ever let rip. Mike was determined not to be caught with his mouth open.

Despite its pressing urgency, for the time being Professor Nostrus left his mail where it lay. He had learnt long ago that there was no point in hurrying bad news. Whatever the damn things said it would keep for an hour or two. For the moment he had a lecture to attend – not unlike two people currently lounging in the 'Arafat Netanyahu Coffee-and-Bagel Reconciliation Bar', just a short drunken stumble from Mike's office.

Randy Andy And The Lasagne Of Love

'But Deborah – like yeah – how do you know you won't like my cooking until you've tried?'

'Look Andy, I just know okay? Anyway, I'm vegetarian.'

The foppish young man looked hurt. 'Since when have you been a vegetarian?'

'Since about five seconds ago.'

Andy was not only very randy, he was also highly frustrated. His cultured tones, paisley waistcoats and offers of Italian food usually did the trick by now. Flicking his long fringe from his eyes, he pressed on bravely .

'But like – you get what I'm saying don't you, yeah? I'm offering to cook you a meal and . . . and well . . . everything.' This was Andy's reasonable tone. Deborah could tell this from the sweaty palms he held out towards her and the sneer of disbelief on his suntanned face. In disgust, Andy's current primary target stood up from the plastic table and retrieved her pile of essays.

'It's the "everything" that worries me. Really, I'm touched by the lengths you're prepared to extend yourself to get me into bed, but you're not my type. I prefer my men minus the grease, though you could conceivably come in handy at the annual Department Barbecue.'

Nearby someone sniggered loudly into their coffee as Andy turned the colour of a sunburnt lobster. Deborah squeezed past the plastic ski jumps that passed for chairs, looking him in the eye all the while. 'I'm off to Nostrus's lecture. If you're coming, you'd better hurry up: you know how he treats late ones.'

Andy was acutely aware of eyes on him from all parts of the room as Deborah made her exit. Retaining as much cool as a dented gas fridge on a hot day in the Sahara, he called out after her, 'Right – yeah babe. 'Ll have to check my diary on that. Like er . . . catch you later.'

With nervous sidelong glances, he collected his things and scuttled after her.

We Don't Need No Education

The small lecture theatre was full to overflowing. The nervous shuffling of late arrivals was punctuated by a sharp squeal as some unfortunate sitting in an aisle had their fingers crushed by a stray Doctor Marten boot. Professor Nostrus sat impassively at the front, chin in hand, lost in thought. After ten minutes no sounds had broken the embarrassed silence. The third year class were well used to eccentric behaviour from their lecturer in Sixteenth-Century French Society and Politics, but even the most alcoholically dazed present could tell there was something different about today.

As the wait grew longer a few of the more fatalistic

students began murmuring amongst themselves. Andy had no objection to this state of affairs as it gave him ample opportunity to study the girl of his dreams – albeit over a thicket of unwashed hair and from an angle that presented a clear view only of her right ear. But it was a beautiful right ear. And it matched the rest of her. To tell the truth, Andy found her hornier than the massed ranks of the Hornechurch Municipal Brass Band, on the day they forgot their oboes and packed two dozen French horns instead. True, Andy found most girls horny in some way, but there was something different about Deborah. Maybe it was the way her golden hair glinted beneath the fluorescent strip lights in the library. Maybe it was the firm note of command in her voice as she ordered him to stop looking at her breasts. Or was it the way she completely ignored him at every available opportunity? Just as he was beginning to sense a pleasant stirring in his trousers, Andy's daydreams were rudely interrupted.

'PROGRESS!' Professor Nostrus bellowed. He rose abruptly to his feet and thrust his biro in the air like a lightning conductor. There was a zealous glint in his eye – the look Jehovah's Witnesses get when someone on the doorstep says to them: 'You know? I'd never thought of it that way before. Would you like a cup of tea?' But Mike's audience were rather less receptive. A doom-laden chorus of groans rose from around the room. This was a subject they'd all heard Mike deliberate on in the past.

'Where are we going?' asked the old man, rounding the desk and gazing intently into row upon row of bored faces. 'What are we going to do when we get there? Why are we going there in the first place? Who decides where to go?' Mike very precisely placed the biro on the lip of his lectern. 'And, perhaps most importantly of all,' he said with great deliberation, 'are we getting any closer?' The pen hovered for a moment, then clattered to the floor. Mike gazed questioningly at an ocean of blank faces.

Andy felt a nudge in the ribs and caught a whiff of stale sweat. The source of both, a leather-jacketed heavy metal fan, peered at him from beneath a greasy fringe.

'Madder than a shit-house rat.'

'Yah, and getting worse by the minute.'

There was no way Nostrus could have heard across the intervening space, but Andy got the nasty feeling the Professor focused the full weight of his attention on him. It was a most disconcerting experience. Rather like being hit by a turbo-charged steamroller, and then having it reverse back to finish the job.

Mike glared in Andy's direction. 'Is humanity's lot improving? If your generation's manners are anything to go by, clearly not.' He started to pace back and forth before the front row, occasionally stabbing the air with a wiry arm. 'Two thousand years ago the Roman Empire had the best system of roads any state has ever possessed before or since. Now we have crumbling motorways. Despite gangs of marauding rough-necks and more contagious diseases than you could shake a vial of penicillin at, medieval towns were safer than our modern cities after dark.'

He paused, then changed tack. 'We've come so far we've lost track of what's important. Let me ask you a question. How many of you could honestly cook a healthy meal?'

Whether through apathy or genuine lack of culinary talent the show of hands was not impressive. More might have claimed they could cook in private, but those few that now did belonged to a special breed. They wore clean clothes, did their essays on time and had fridges filled with bits of Tupperware bearing adhesive labels and correctly fitting lids. After a few furtive glances to judge the mood Andy kept his hands firmly down.

Mike wasn't put off. 'Right! Let me ask you this. How many of you can drive a car?'

This was different. No one wanted to admit they didn't even have the hand-eye co-ordination of a seventeen-year-old glue-crazed joyrider. Slowly, a forest of hands materialized.

'So what does that prove?' asked a denim-jacketed bruiser from the front row.

Mike looked at him pityingly. 'My dear boy, the very fact you have to ask that question *is* the proof. Our society has lost its way. The baby of humility has been thrown out with the bathwater of superstitious dread.' This got some strange looks. Mike's metaphors weren't mixed; they were pulped, ground, freeze-dried then reconstituted. 'So I ask you again, do any of you really think things are getting better?'

From where Andy was sitting he saw Deborah fidget apprehensively, as if trying to decide to speak or not. With a self-conscious brush of hair she raised an arm of such beauty it extinguished all thought of her right ear.

Nostrus's face lit up with this sudden show of interest. 'Yes, my dear?'

'Maybe it's just that our expectations grow faster than our ability to satisfy them. Wouldn't that give the impression that things were getting worse?'

I'd like to satisfy her expectations, thought Andy with a grin that could have lubricated the QE2 slipway. But his slimy smirk slid off his face as he saw the way Nostrus looked at his chosen one – the old man was beaming from ear to ear.

'An excellent point, young Deborah. I seem to remember you offering a similar opinion in my tutorial last week.'

Shit! thought Andy, the old fart's got the hots for her. That's . . . disgusting! One day he's going to get what's coming to him.

In Which Mike Gets What's Coming To Him

At that instant the lecture room door flew open and in blew the Director of Studies. Doctor Norris O'Brian did not look pleased; in fact he looked less happy than King Philip of Spain on the day his Defence Minister came and told him the Armada had hit a bit of a snag.

This was nothing new in itself. Dr No-Brain, as he was affectionately known throughout the department, was seldom in a civil mood, though at the moment he looked in a particularly foul temper. Students were wilting under the waves of heat emanating from the incandescent bundle of motion now storming down the central aisle.

'Nostrus, this really is the last straw! I want to speak to you in private – now!' It was clear that the No-Brain expected resistance – he was glaring at Mike like a boxer entering the ring.

Whatever the intention, Mike obstinately refused to be drawn into a fight. 'Aaah. Dr O'Brian, I was wondering when you'd track me down. We can certainly speak in private. If you'll allow me to fetch a notepad I can record any salient points for future reference . . . Half a sheet should do the trick.'

O'Brian looked like he might explode. 'I said NOW, Professor Nostrus!' Students close enough could see the arteries hardening beneath his bald scalp, and hear the gentle popping of fresh ulcers breaking out around his heart.

Ignoring the small throbbing man, Mike rounded the desk, retrieved paper and pen, then strode past the Director of Studies and out through the still swinging doors. Deflated by his opponent's refusal to rise to the bait, O'Brian blustered after him. He found Nostrus waiting patiently in the dimly lit corridor.

'Now,' said Mike in a completely level tone, 'do you mind telling me why you feel the need to interrupt my third year class? Those young people have received scant enough attention over the years without you curtailing my final chance to kick their slumbering minds into life.'

O'Brian's hairless head turned a strange shade of puce.

Mike tried hard not to notice the Christmas-ornament-style reflection the overhead lights created on its shiny surface, but it was a losing battle.

'Important lecture you say? Ha! I know for a fact you've been not so much straying from the syllabus as road-raging through it in a double decker bus. But, loathe as I am to admit it, that's not why I'm here.'

'Oh really?' said Mike, trying to sound surprised. 'You're not here for your health I trust, since I don't appear to be doing you much good.'

O'Brian ground his teeth in disgust. 'I am here,' he articulated very precisely and with immense personal effort, 'because last night this college received a visit from two acquaintances of yours. Do the names "Vinny the Weasel" and "Jacko" mean anything to you? I'm sure you'd remember them, they're not the sort of people – and I use that term in the loosest possible sense – one could easily forget.'

Mike looked thoughtful. 'Now you come to mention it, they do seem to ring a bell.'

'Oh, I'm so glad,' O'Brian seethed in a tone of mock conciliation. 'You must compliment "Jacko" on his interesting collection of tattoos: the rendition of that ninja garrotting the dove of peace, most original. But by the by. Once your friends had cornered me in the foyer – and pinned me to the wall – we had a nice little chat. Seems they are rather keen to speak with you. Seeing as you'd left for the night I sent them on their way.'

Mike started to show the first real signs of concern.

'Listen to me, Nostrus. You've been warned about this before. Keep your sordid gambling debts out of college hours and off college property. What you do with your salary is your own concern – you can spend it on hotel rooms full of baby-oiled urchins for all I care. Just don't let it interfere with this department. Have I made myself clear?'

'Certainly,' said Mike looking serious. 'I'm to supplement my meagre income in any manner of my choosing, I am at liberty to provide a roof over the heads of lubricated nubile waifettes – just as long as I don't drag any along this university's hallowed halls. After all – they'd probably leave a slimy trail. Someone might slip.'

The Director of Studies seemed about to reply then stared off into the middle distance, a strangely serene look on his face. Mike needed time to think, and that meant getting rid of his suddenly preoccupied boss, so he went for the about-turn grovel.

'Really, I'm most sorry for any embarrassment I've caused. Please rest assured that it won't happen again.'

O'Brian took a second to react, and when he did it threw Mike completely. 'Right,' said the Director of Studies, 'glad we've got that sorted out. I'll be on my way then. Lots of work to be getting on with . . . people to do, things to see.' With that he ambled off down the corridor, bumping into a set of lockers on the way.

Mike looked after him bemused, but with some relief. He had a lot of work to do himself, and he was going to have to start right away.

Spaced 1999

For his part, the Director of Studies' mind – or rather what was left of it – was currently far less focused than Mike's. As he had been speaking to Professor Nostrus he felt a giant hand reach down from heaven and take a tight grip of his spiritual scrotum. Then, with a slight twist, it had yanked his consciousness into an entirely new vector. All of which was a bit out of the ordinary for a Tuesday.

He saw his miraculous destiny so clearly, as if the angels had set up a widescreen TV inside his head and fitted a two-way mirrored contact lens to his bulging mind's-eye.

He was to be a part of THE MESSAGE, and it was a message that everyone would soon come to hear. With a dazed gleam and a speckle of saliva congealing on his chin he stumbled towards the Department of Archaeology's small museum.

In fact it wasn't so much a museum as a collection of glass display cases set along the corridor that joined the Department of History to its more earthly-based cousin next door. In his capacity as Head of Department, O'Brian had a set of keys to this modest collection of accumulated ancient clutter. Of course anything of any real value had been sold off long ago to pay for the Vice Chancellor's lavish corporate hospitality lunches, but there remained a few interesting pieces.

O'Brian, though, had not come to gawk like generations of bored students before him. He knew just the item he was after. Without stopping to check if he was being watched, he clumsily opened a heavy glass cover and grabbed the strange Hebrew relic – a short bronze tube which had been unearthed from a mound of ancient rubble near a small settlement on the West Bank. Without so much as a casual glance over his shoulder he marched robot-like from the building, not even pausing to reprimand Cyndi for crimping her hair during work hours. He had a long journey across town ahead of him.

He had to get off the Underground and take a bus the final leg of the way to Greenwich. Those tube lines under the river would be a bugger to finish on time, but O'Brian wasn't to care. Like Dr Livingstone the day he had rethatched his roof, O'Brian was a man on a mission. In no time at all (or so it seemed) he stood before the sleek space-aged lines of London's multi-million-pound monument to the Millennium. Like some 1970s idea of extraterrestrial architecture, dreamed up by an under-financed special effects designer, the huge dome glistened under the bright morning sun. This illustrious edifice, however, was not constructed from old egg cartons, washing-up bottles and enough sticky-backed plastic to make Valerie Singleton go weak at the knees – oh no. Like Kubla Khan's dome-based holiday home this building came with a far more hefty price tag. More, in fact, than any planner could have predicted. Hence the profusion of Japanese electronics firms' logos plastered across its surface.[1]

O'Brian could have stood at the entrance to the vast car park and taken all this in, just as he could have closed his eyes and imagined swarms of plastic-looking alien spacecraft, suspended on bits of wire, swooping down to bomb the site, but he didn't have time for such frivolous diversions. The former Director of Studies strode purposefully towards the saucer-shaped sanctum as if he had but a short time to live.

The dull-eyed security guards frisked him, just as they did all the visitors to this prime terrorist target. But what harm could a slightly mad-looking old man do with a dented brass trumpet? On the surface O'Brian appeared no nuttier than a broad cross-section of the dome's profusion of visitors and exhibits.

Once inside the vast auditorium he was not distracted by the multitude of diversions. He didn't stop to admire the multicultural stained-glass windows – carefully calculated to give equal prominence to each of the world's faiths, nor did he pause at the Baptist synchronized swimming demonstration. He took no notice of the Papal/Protestant Reunification seminars going on in the foyer, nor the Eighth Day Adventist infomercials blaring out from the banks of widescreen TVs. He just pressed on to his chosen

---

1 This association helps to explain why:

i) The Dome was finished ahead of schedule.

ii) It was smaller than expected

iii) It had a row of flashing LEDs down one wall.

iv) Batteries were not included, though 20,000 tonnes of polystyrene packaging was.

destination – slap bang in the middle of the giant hall. His new god was a jealous god, and He didn't like it when the opposition tried to muscle in on His turf.

With less ceremony than a Puritan preacher in a hurry, O'Brian drew the tarnished bugle from beneath his jacket and pressed it to his bloodless lips. At first nothing happened; he blew with all his might but no sound emanated from the arcane instrument. Then, as if a cow with gastroenteritis stood somewhere in the next field, there came a faint parp. Nothing seemed to change. Nearby a group of 'Musical Curates for the Millennium', who had been entertaining a party of well-fed school children, paused their tambourine playing to gaze questioningly at their new rival, but quickly went back to their song. As regular as clockwork, the building's vast intercom system sprang to life telling of the departure of another guided tour round the Dome's premiere exhibit – 'World Religions – How Much They Really *Do* Have In Common'. But those with keen hearing might have noticed something subtly different about the huge auditorium – a sound almost out of human range. It shook your teeth, as if the huge arching dome had been struck by a mighty hammer and was now ringing like a Perspex bell.

It took several minutes before the first cracks appeared. Far above, the vaulting roof turned into a mole's eye view of a crazily paved patio. By the time the first debris was falling lazily from the ceiling, the crowds were in a mad scramble for the exits, the exodus accompanied by a blood-freezing sub-audible groan that threatened to shatter bone and cartilage alike. Not since Samson had his bad hair day had the world seen anything like it. O'Brian stood in the midst of it all and watched, a happy smile on his face, as this temple to modern gods crashed to earth about him.

Unfortunately for what was left of O'Brian, the roof didn't just come down around him. It came down on him, through him and from underneath him. Boulders smashed into other boulders, creating a shower of deadly masonic shrapnel. By the time the mayhem had subsided, he was in more pieces than the One True Cross. The emergency services would later claim it to be a miracle that only one of the dome's visitors was unaccounted for, and of him there was no trace amongst the rubble. They had no idea how apt was their choice of words.

But in this modern enlightened era there was no time for such simple gratitude. There were more important things to do, like the ritual apportioning of blame. Somewhere not too far away, hastily packing as if his life depended on it, was an architect with some tough explaining to do.

Things Can Only Get Better

Ten minutes after his unsavoury meeting with O'Brian, Mike sat in his office studying intently the long letter he held in both hands. A hot cup of very sweet tea, perched precariously atop a pile of correspondence, provided an aid to concentration. His mood was brightening by the minute; occasionally he laughed out loud. Perhaps his plans stood a chance of success after all.

Admittedly, the news that there were two Neanderthals on his trail had come as a bit of a shock, though perhaps he shouldn't have been surprised. Maybe Big Jack's Honest Bookmakers wasn't used to taking the sort of bets Mike had placed: that the entire field would get electrocuted by a freak fault with the starting gate.

With a wry grin Mike made a mental note that he'd have to be more careful who he dealt with in future. Surely the more established financial institutions would have to pay up without a quibble? With this thought in mind, he turned back to the pages of the neatly typed letter.

It really was amazing the absurd lengths to which people's greed would stretch. And there was nothing as absurd or as greedy as that great bastion of capitalist corporate ethics:

The Insurance Business. The Professor planned to make use of that greed and in the process would become obscenely rich in a very short space of time.

Not just comfortably off, the sort of unbelievably rich which acquired yachts and filled centre spreads in *Hi!* magazine, although Mike would not be seeking publicity – that was the last thing he wanted. This undertaking needed publicity the way a lifeboat full of starving sailors needed Hannibal Lecter. Mike planned to use the cash to save himself from the dark days ahead, and that required more secrecy than an entire submarine full of civil servants.

As with all plans, there were several details that needed ironing out. Mike's early probings into the world of turf accountancy had been indiscreet, to say the least. He already had a pair of thugs sniffing around. The scale of organization necessary to pull this off might be beyond even his great talents. What he needed was an assistant, someone he could rely on in a pinch. But how to go about finding such a helper? You couldn't just advertise in the local press:

> Help wanted in plan to escape from DOOM OF ALL MANKIND. Must be able to type, make tea and tread water for long periods of time. Patience with obstinate cats a necessity. No previous experience required.

He'd have to table that one for now. People like that didn't just fall into your lap.

Synchronicity

Deborah paused outside the Professor's door, her fist half-ready to knock. Was she doing the right thing? Perhaps he just wanted to be left alone. When Professor Nostrus had returned from his impromptu meeting with the No-Brain he had seemed highly preoccupied. After some aimless pottering about, the class had been dismissed with the excuse that he was not feeling well. Deborah was not easily fooled. Though not entirely understanding why, she was worried about the old recluse.

With a slightly rueful smile she took her courage in both hands and knocked boldly on the door. After a suspiciously long pause a muffled reply bade her enter. Deborah was forced to use all her weight against some unseen obstruction, finally opening the door enough to squeeze breathlessly through. The Professor looked up briefly from the great mound of papers on his desk and absent-mindedly motioned for her to sit.

By the time Deborah had cleared a chair of its wide selection of books, (*Probability Mathematics for the Expert Gambler* and *SAS Survival Guide: Learn To Kill Squirrels the Way the Professionals Do*) Professor Nostrus was back at his notes. While she waited for him to notice her, Deborah studied her surroundings.

At best it could be described as 'cluttered'; at worst, as the odds-and-ends cupboard of a Karachi bric-a-brac shop in the midst of a major earthquake. Deborah coughed nervously. When her gaze returned to her host he was staring back at her with piercing eyes. It was an unnerving experience, rather like being covered with 'Trill' and locked in London Zoo's budgie enclosure at feeding time.

Mike broke the uneasy silence. 'Was there something specific you wanted to ask or are you just curious to see if I'm really cracking up?'

Deborah turned pink. 'Er . . . of course not Professor Nostrus, I mean yes there was – I mean . . . I'm sorry, perhaps I shouldn't have come.'

Mike smiled kindly, produced a large box file from beneath his desk and balanced it on his knees. Despite the fact it was already full to overflowing, he swept the contents of his desk into it and forced it shut with an elbow. Written on the side in bold black marker strokes were two words – THE PLAN.

Turning his attention back to his guest the Professor raised his eyebrows questioningly. Not wanting to appear any dimmer than she had already, Deborah hurriedly flicked through the ring binder clutched close to her chest. Acutely aware of the calm blue eyes fixed levelly upon her, her mind went suddenly blank. It was with considerable relief that she finally found her scribbled page of notes.

With a faint cough she cleared her throat and did her best to sound authoritative. 'With regards to your last published paper, "Social Aspects of the Great Plague of 1544" – I found it an incredibly detailed and informative piece of work.'

'I'm glad to hear it. Flattery will get you everywhere.'

'Well . . .' said Deborah, beginning to wonder how she got herself into these predicaments, '. . . it's not that I have a problem with it as such; it's just you always told us to be as objective as possible.'

'Right.'

'Well this paper isn't. It's the most subjective piece of work I've ever read. It almost reads like a first-hand account in some places.'

Mike seemed to go quite pale. 'Does it, my dear? Whatever gives you that idea?'

Deborah gulped. 'For instance,' she said, furiously consulting more notes, 'you suggest the outbreak amongst the French Royal Household wasn't the plague at all, but rather a nasty case of a common social disease. How can you be so specific?'

Mediaeval Gallic Hypochondria

Mike had every right to be specific. He was there at the time.

In sixteenth-century France the Black Death reached a social status on a par with 'being in therapy' today in polite dinner-party society. It was the height of fashion. If you'd never caught it you simply had nothing to talk about at the formal social occasions where the French chattering classes spent most of their time. The fact that without advanced antibiotics 99.9% of those who caught the plague died in a way too horrible to contemplate didn't come into it. There's no snob like a medical snob.

'Ooooooh yes, boils the size of bread rolls 'e 'ad. And when they took the leeches off they found they all had it too. Don't listen to my brother-in-law though, he never had it properly, not The Black Death anyways, more The Grey-Slight-Discomfort-Down-Your-Left-Hand-Side if you asks me.'

'That's nothing though. I heard tell of a man in Montpellier – when they took the poultices away they found the entire lower half of his body had been eaten away by the tiny worms every respectable surgeon knows carries the malady.'

The only thing more fashionable than contracting the plague was discovering a cure. They were all at it, even Louis XII, or 'The Turnip King' as he became known. Much to the disgust of the court physician, the famed Dr M. Nostromo, His Royal Madness maintained that strategically placed root vegetables were the key to a healthy life. For once the strange bulges to be seen beneath the clothing of the French aristocracy were not due to severe congenital deformities brought about by prolonged in-breeding, nor was the rancid smell due to festering open wounds or an aversion to soap. The quackier the cure the better. Few had time for the off-beat prescriptions of Dr Nostromo, with all his mumbo jumbo about regular baths and the extermination of rats.

Thus every minor sniffle, every 'I've got a bit of a headache. Think I'll take the afternoon off work' sort of feeling transformed into Le Charbon, The Great Pestilence. If you'd never had it, or couldn't at least give a grisly description of your imagined symptoms, it meant you had no friends to catch it from. As long as you'd had it at least twice it was a safe bet you were a well-adjusted, socially acceptable individual who would get invited to lots of dinner parties.

For those minor French aristocrats who were so successful in their attempts at social acceptance that they actually caught the plague, inclusion on dinner party guest lists soon became the least of their concerns. Death, no matter how fashionable, tended to get in the way of polite conversation.

Take A Chance On Me

'Let's just call it an educated guess,' said Mike, struggling to regain his cool. It was a constant strain, trying to remember what he should and should not know. After many years of practice, with the best incentive of all – staying alive – he was a skilled operator. Occasionally, he still slipped up. 'I was never really happy with that paper – long overdue for a rewrite if you ask me. Let me make a note.'

Deborah was about to press on when she noticed the odd way the Professor was looking at her. She'd been eyed up by lecherous old men in the past but this was subtly different. Professor Nostrus peered at her as if judging a racehorse. Deborah wouldn't have been surprised if he'd asked to see her teeth. Then, as if noticing her for the first time, his manner changed completely. He leaned forward in his chair and formed a steeple with his slender fingers.

'Tell me Deborah, do you like tea, and do you have a problem with awkward cats?'

An Offer A Girl Can't Refuse

Over the next ten minutes Mike confirmed what he had suspected all along. Deborah was a very cool, together person. Come World War III she'd be the one with the ten-year supply of baked beans and a full radiation suit. And she'd look good in it.

Mike wasn't by nature an impulsive man but drastic times called for drastic measures. With a disregard for consequences that comes from knowing that time might be very short indeed, and was relative anyway, Mike took the first big chance since suggesting to Louis XII that he might look more dignified minus the radish.

However, by the time Deborah had finished her tea, neither 'cool' nor 'together' could have been used to describe her mental state. It wasn't so much what her history professor had just told her – that he was a five-hundred-year-old retired prophet who knew the world was coming to an end – but the fact that someone who seemed so sane could secretly be stark raving mad.

Mike was looking at her expectantly, as if awaiting an answer to a question she had no recollection of being asked.

'I'm sorry,' Deborah said with a start, 'was there something else?'

Mike considered her for a long while. 'What I asked was, are you interested in a scheme to save yourself from the rough times ahead? A chance to batten down the hatches from the choppy, mist-shrouded future into which we sail. A way to secure your assets on the . . . ?'

Deborah raised a hand abruptly. 'Thank you, I get the general picture.' She had to hand it to him, he was almost convincing. When talented people flipped they almost always did it creatively, and Professor Nostrus was no exception.

'I think,' she said, standing up and backing towards the door, 'that you've been working too hard lately Professor Nostrus, and that maybe I should be leaving.'

Mike looked disappointed but made no move to stop her. 'Won't you sit down, dear girl? I do have quite substantial evidence to back up my admittedly outlandish claims.'

'Outlandish?' Deborah half-smiled as she reached for the door-handle behind her back. 'That's an understatement. It's not every day a girl gets offered the chance to save herself from Armageddon. You've been most kind Professor Nostrus, but . . . well, *but* will do. Thank you very much for the tea.'

Before Mike could round the desk and hurdle the pile of *Self-Sufficiency Quarterly* blocking his path, Deborah was gone. 'Wait until you see the next lottery draw if you want proof!' he bellowed after her but it was no use. She wasn't coming back. With a sigh he slumped down against the door and contemplated his predicament. How could he have been so stupid? This was becoming a worrying trend at this late date. It was ironic really that, in light of his former profession, Mike had completely failed to foresee Deborah's reaction. Morosely, he sank back into a mood of gloomy internal reflection.

Money For Nothing

It's a poorly documented fact that prophets, just like other creative scientists, do their best work young. Mathematicians at the cutting edge of their field rarely perform after the age of thirty – they simply lose that inspirational spark; and nowhere is the sudden intuitive leap more useful than in the much maligned art of precognition.

Mike had been a great prophet, possibly the best ever. He had been fortunate to be at his peak when prophecy was still a real money spinner. As a result he became very rich, very quickly. Thousands of people clamoured for his works. He became a household name. Had there been chat shows in sixteenth-century France his bottom would have been etched onto countless studio sofas.

His fame spread. But by the time he was well established and in his fifties, being regularly summoned to the royal courts of Europe to declare to awestruck royalty the destiny of their children, he'd lost the knack.

So he told them a load of bollocks. Ninety per cent of his prophecies were made up on the spot. The other ten per cent, if they held any vestige of precognitive power at all, were so diluted by dross as to resemble punch at a student party – virtually all flat lemonade. Mike's melodramatic mutterings lacked even the partially redeeming features of half a soggy apple and a thoroughly marinated condom that might or might not have been used.

It was all pretty ridiculous – the more outlandish Mike's claims, the more the punters lapped them up. When he wasn't improvising, or blinding them with razzle dazzle, he amazed them with good old-fashioned common sense.

'My Lord, if you invade the Grand Duchy many people will die. More even than that time your illustrious grandfather lined up the palace staff in an attempt to break the world long distance wagon-jumping record. Why not stay at home and declare a national holiday instead?'

In fact, during the course of his illustrious career Mike had prevented more wars than the threat of all the pre-emptive medium range Vera Lynn records put together. Unfortunately, he failed to remember one important fact. The only thing people like less than finding a plague victim face down in their privy is a clever bastard. Being a soothsayer was all very well and good but if your audience thought you got it right all the time they tended to get a mite stressed.

'What's the point in us working all day in the fields for a stale crust and a kick in the teeth,' one warty serf would say to another, 'when that clever twat tells us that next month the Duke of Burgundy's army will pass through these parts raping the animals and pillaging our daughters?'

'Aye?' the other warty serf would say. 'Haven't you got

that the wrong way round? I knows our daughters are ugly but they're not that bad.'

A third warty serf, who may not have known much but knew an ugly daughter when he saw one, would look confused. 'Well I don't know 'bout you, but I don't work all day in the fields for stale teeth and a kick in the crust. I don't hold with any of this modern Trade Union rubbish. A fair day's pay for a fair year's work, that's what I says.'

At this point in the conversation one of two things could happen. First, the exchange would break down into a long and utterly confused silence, sixteenth-century warty serfs not being renowned for their ability to spot a spoonerism when it hit them. Second, the Duke of Burgundy would turn up with his army, raping the animals and pillaging the daughters, Mike being well known for a rather vague grasp of time and self-fulfilling prophecies being inherently unpredictable phenomena.

Mike would be run out of town on a wheelbarrow, there being no SNCF in late mediaeval France. This pattern repeated itself time and time again. He was persecuted, pursued by the Inquisition, declared a heretic and generally made to feel like a Young Conservative wherever he went. All this for being such an accomplished liar that his lies actually came true.

This was all too much for a sensitive chap like Mike to take. When a psycho like the King of Savoy inferred from your wildest ramblings that he was destined to oven-bake every male child not called 'Gerald', it was enough to give anyone sleepless nights. In the end Mike's conscience got the better of him. Resigned to his fate, he moved far away, changed his name to Gerald, married a kind wife and practised his stupidest smile. Soon his prophetic powers dwindled away to nothing. Mike was quite happy about this. The meaningful stuff about the Apocalypse was all very handy, but was it any practical use to know there would be a shower of small purple frogs in Cracow next Thursday week? Mike didn't think so.

Fortunately, he was a man of many talents.

Renaissance Man

Michael D. Nostrus was a real Renaissance Man. Not because he could openly talk about his feelings, or change a nappy, or eat quiche, or appreciate light opera. He could do all of these things and more, but what made Mike a Renaissance Man was exactly what made Leonardo da Vinci, Christopher Columbus and Horace 'The Spike', Grand Duke of Moravia, Renaissance Men too.

Who was Horace 'The Spike'? Not quite as well known as the first two admittedly, at least not outside Moravia. In that locale he was very well known indeed – you could almost have called him a legend in his own lynchtime. Indeed you would have if you wanted to prevent him inserting one of his favourite accessories into your delicate bodily parts.

Horace didn't eat quiche, nor could he talk openly about his feelings. (His parents had split up when he was young and this may have been the cause of his generally unpleasant disposition.) He'd never seen a light opera, but if he chanced upon any tenors during his travels they'd invariably end up singing several octaves higher.

Fortunately for humanity Horace was dead. Mike on the other hand was very much alive, and intended to keep it that way for the foreseeable future. To maintain this happy state of affairs he learned some important facts. One – as near as damn it he was immortal. By the time he'd reached sixty he didn't seem to get any older at all. Two – if he intended to remain immortal and not become mortal very suddenly, he should keep quiet about his troubled past.

When prophets retire they don't get a gold clock and a framed photo of them with the MD. They may get invited to a surprise party but not the sort with streamers, party hats, crates of Vietnamese sherry and people who sit on the stairs endlessly talking about God. Appalling as this fate is, the lot of a retiring prophet is far worse. The party they're likely to attend usually involves pitchforks, burning torches, a length of rope and several hundred pissed-off peasants. Mike was a resourceful type – he had no intention of attending a party where the main topic of conversation was whether the guest of honour should be medium-rare or charcoal-grilled. Using the skills he'd picked up as a doctor he was able to fake his death, then run for the hills. Carefully he carved out a new life, escaping the ravages of the Inquisition and generally trying to make himself as inconsequential as possible.

Unfortunately, he had a talent for being inconsequential the way blue whales have a talent for hang-gliding. Things happened to him. Not small things like losing wallets down the backs of sofas, or meeting old friends on crowded streets, but big things. If Mike moved to a new town it inexplicably got sacked by hordes of screaming barbarians. If he passed through a province there would be a famine. Revolution followed him like an over-friendly puppy. Krakatoa had been an insignificant south-sea island until, assuming he'd finally escaped the hurly-burly of everyday life, Mike took up residence.

Now, quite suddenly, Mike's prophesying powers were back and as good as new. The dreams had been a bit non-specific, beating around the bush in a most infuriating manner as usual, but what they did give him were future echoes of a few specific events, an inkling of mankind's precarious future. He was unaware of the form the shake-up would take, but he knew it would be big and he knew it would be soon. Anyone else carrying this immense burden would have been reduced to the level of togetherness of a partially exploded jelly. Not Mike. So there were dark days ahead? No reason why a resourceful individual with the means to protect himself shouldn't survive. Unfortunately, the means he needed were of the small green papery variety, something he presently lacked. Mike certainly saw no possibility of mankind being wiped out. *Homo sapiens* was far too bloody-minded for that. Even if he bombed his planet out of all existence (and this wasn't something Mike had dreamt), levelling its surface to the state of a radioactive desert, some obstinate sod would insist on surviving. Where one survived, others would too, and then the whole process would begin again.

Mankind was a terminal disease the universe would just have to learn to live with.

Rebel Without A Clue

Mike shook himself out of his nostalgic daydream and looked down once more at the sea of paper.

The letters from insurance firms all said much the same thing. None were going to meet his undeniably offbeat demands without at least taking a look at him in person. Amongst the thick white, prepaid envelopes from insurance agencies, along with their obligatory mounds of unconnected publicity bumf – 'Week by week, this incredible publication builds into a priceless chronicle that you and your family will want to keep, detailing the fascinating development of mediaeval Hungarian broad bean cultivation' – were a selection of plain utilitarian envelopes. These were from bookmakers. They told exactly the same story – no bets covered without a face-to-face.

It seemed to Mike that gambling and insurance were essentially the same thing. When you take out an insurance policy you're placing a bet with the company that something bad is going to happen to you. Then, when a narcoleptic lorry driver takes a short cut through your living room and decides to transport your legs to Dunfermline but leave the rest of you watching *Coronation Street*, you at least have the satisfaction of cashing a fat cheque. In light of this, it had always amused Mike the way society treated these two identical professions. A job in insurance was seen as the height of respectability while turf accountants were viewed with unwarranted suspicion. Similarly, investing all your money on the horses and paying for saturation life insurance were regarded as existing at different ends of the sensibleness spectrum.

Anyone could see this for the arbitrary snobbery it was. Both professions existed solely to con money from the public. The only real difference was that the insurance industry was bigger and more efficient at taking your cash. This was Mike's chance of going some way to redress the balance. He wasn't so self-righteous as to think of himself as a crusader for the common man. After all, he was doing it for the most selfish reasons, but in some small way he was a champion for all the little people in history who had ever had sand kicked in their face by Trans-Continental Fat Cats Inc.

Taking a pen and notepad from his desk drawer, Mike picked up the phone and began to dial.

TWO

And I shall keep you from the hour of test, which is to come upon the whole inhabited Earth.
Revelations 3:10

All Around The World

Over the next few days Mike set up a string of meetings, each one immersing him deeper and deeper into a tangled web of financial chicanery. For the time being at least he was untroubled by world events – which was just as well since the news didn't make for happy reading.

The President of Latin America's major recreational talcum powder exporter became the ex-president very suddenly one night, when certain high-ranking members of that country's military decided that they could do a better job. The nation's former leader was last seen hurriedly boarding a plane for the US, dragging a bulging suitcase behind him. The free-style Democrats now at the helm were reportedly very keen to repatriate their ex-Head of State, along with as much of his luggage as possible.

At a massed rally in Revolution Square, North Korea's new premier officially declared his dead father a living god, despite the fact that his illustrious predecessor had spent the past twenty years dribbling onto his spring rolls, only breaking the routine to order the execution of political prisoners. The boy king went on to deny his country possessed a stack of hydrogen bombs twice as tall as he was; and anyway, what was the UN going to do if they did? Later that same day the 'Glorious Insane Small One', as he was lovingly known by his people, declared his poodle Vice President and decreed hats and whistling on a Tuesday to be punishable by death.

Back in Blighty, Ted Trundell's 'Church of the Eloquent Announcement' descended from heaven, via Heathrow Airport, to announce the New Revelation. An army of smart-suited young men, and no less smartly suited young women, quickly set about launching their long-awaited evangelical mission to the 'Godless Lands'. Ted Trundell, the New Messiah himself, would soon be flying in from the States to personally oversee the operation. A spokesman for the organization told the massed ranks of the world's press that; 'All you lost souls in Engle-land have yet to bow to the good news. We're here to save y'all from the dark forces of international communism, rock'n'roll music and chlorinated water.'

Acts Of God?

Mike sat alone in a small office, patiently gazing up at a pastel pink wall. The office belonged to Kestrel Alliance Insurance's Junior Accounts Executive of the Year – Mike knew this thanks to the lovingly framed diploma hung carefully beneath a signed photograph of Archbishop Trundell. Just why an insurance executive would need the beaming face of America's foremost TV evangelist grinning down at him all day, Mike didn't like to imagine. Maybe in this business a good word from the Big Guy upstairs still counted for something.

Mike adjusted his tie uncomfortably and tried hard to think cool thoughts. The open window offered scant relief from the clammy heat, while at the same time admitting an unpleasant cocktail of traffic noise and fumes that rose from the high street. His absent host might have been Junior Accounts Executive of the Year but he certainly took his time. Just as Mike was beginning to feel like the last coffee cream shoved around a battered old box of chocolates, the door was thrust open.

'Sorry to keep you waiting, Mr Nostrus.' The shirt-sleeved young man beamed as he rounded his desk. 'I've just been conferring with my colleagues. I think you have to agree that your request is – how can I put this without offending you – of an unusual nature.'

Mike did his best to look offended and mentally tuned himself into old git mode. 'Now look here sonny, I was taking out insurance when you were still filling your nappies with second-hand Farley's Rusks! If you don't want my business I can always go to one of your competitors. I hear the Imperial has a special offer on pre-millennium property cover.' He stormed to his feet and grabbed for his briefcase in disgust.

For a brief instant the young man on the other side of the desk seemed about to choke. Then, recovering quickly, his best toadying expression sprang into place and he was at Mike's side in a flash, wringing his hands as he grovelled near-horizontally before the Professor's feet.

'Oh there'll be no need for that Mr Nostrus sir. Let me offer my humblest apologies on behalf of the company.'

Mike looked uncertain for a carefully calculated moment then, as a fresh bead of sweat broke out on the young man's brow, slowly sat back down. 'Well – we'll just have to see how co-operative you are from now on. Need I remind you of the size of the premiums I'll be paying on this policy?'

The salesman made suitably subservient noises and scuttled back to his chair. 'As I was about to say, I'm sure we can come to a mutually beneficial arrangement – despite the . . . uniqueness of this policy.' He held out two open-palmed hands. 'After all, unique policies are all in a day's work here at K. A. We pride ourselves on bending over backwards to give our business clients a helping hand.' The young man's smile revealed an Antarctic expanse of blinding teeth, worryingly reminiscent of the manic American on the wall.

'Just to recap, then. Your company – Pyramid Travel & Leisure – wishes to insure the Great Pyramid of Cheops situated near Cairo, Egypt, against destruction, disappearance or other catastrophic damage including flood, fire, earthquake, meteor impact, nuclear attack . . .'

There followed an incomprehensible monologue which Mike's conscious brain edited out before it impacted fully on his mind. If he heard one more reference to 'the aforementioned clause relating to the relevant sub-section', he felt sure he'd go quietly mad. He answered the human oil slick's interminable questions on auto-pilot. No, he personally didn't engage in any unnecessarily dangerous activities, yes was indeed sole director of PT&L. (He had been since registering the name and opening a bank account the previous afternoon. The company's assets might not have constituted anything more than his life savings, plus the winnings from a few recent bets, but that did nothing to lessen its legal standing. To all intents and purposes PT&L was a going concern.)

After what seemed like hours of this drivel, the young man's mouth ground to a halt. He sat forward in his leather chair and grinned like an idiot. 'Does that all seem to be in order, Mr Nostrus?'

Mike brazened it out. 'Well, you seem to have the general idea. My company could expect a considerable loss of revenue if anything happened to the Egyptian pyramids. As I stated earlier, we cater for the independent traveller wishing to visit the Nile Valley. Our company name and logo tie us inseparably to the only remaining wonder of the ancient world.'

'Great. Excellent! You value your business's association with these monuments at half a million pounds a year, is that correct?' Mike nodded and the young man's smile grew so wide it seemed for a moment that it might consume his entire face. 'Superlative! Then in that case I'm very pleased to offer you cover to the tune of that sum. I've run it past our Stats Analysis boys and the monthly premiums we'll require come to this amount.' A small piece of carefully folded paper was pushed in Mike's direction. He casually took a peek and had to fight to stifle a whimper. Despite the apparent safety of the world's most impressive ancient relics (five thousand years and not a sign of rising damp) Kestrel Alliance weren't taking any chances on a policy of this size. But Mike viewed the situation with cold logic. If things went as expected there'd be just one premium to pay before PT&L could expect a very big pay-out indeed. It was hard to imagine the Pyramids suddenly crumbling into dust – but Mike did possess a very fertile imagination. And fertile ground grew rich crops.

'It all seems to be in order,' he said briskly as he rose and made for the door. 'Get your people to fax my people the contracts and we'll have this deal tied up before you can say "Perfectly safe Pyramids".'

The young executive was now just teeth on a neck. 'Been a pleasure doing business with you, sir. Can I call you sir? Please, drop in any time you want any other man-made mountains insuring.'

The account executive held out a hand. The handshake began to turn into an embrace, the embrace into a full-body back-slapping primal bonding hug. Mike untangled himself before he drowned in grease, and slipped out of the door. Before he'd gone ten paces he could have sworn he heard a youthful cheer from somewhere behind him, shortly followed by a bout of hysterical laughter. Someone reckoned they were having a very good day.

Mike left the humid confines of the building and strolled down the busy high street. He preferred walking to going by car; it gave him time to think. Like many people he'd often wondered about the origins of the Great Pyramids. They were a feat of engineering unrivalled to this day. What had inspired the ancient Egyptians to devote such a national effort to their construction? It was hard to believe they were simply a resting place for the Pharaohs. Mike had no better answers to these questions than anyone else – all he had seen in his nightly visions was a future without them. In fact the origins of the Great Pyramids, and all the other pyramids on earth for that matter, were far stranger than even Mike could have guessed.

Pyramid Power

Q'almn sighed. It wasn't just the usual stress of being the youngest Advertising Executive in Dolman Corporation history, nor was it the inconvenience of travelling sixty-four thousand light years to this hell-hole of a planet to close the deal. Pharaoh Khufu, with whom Q'almn was negotiating to obtain concession rights, was being, to put it mildly, a pain in the Horse Head Nebula.

'Anywhere but there. That land is sacred,' Khufu proclaimed from his jewel-encrusted throne, as scantily clad slave girls massaged his toes. 'Not next to the holy Nile, which everyone knows provides the vital bodily fluids that allow me to pilot the Chariot of Ra across the firmament each day to its resting place in the Land of the Dead.'

This guy was definitely several pulsars short of a star cluster, thought Q'almn. The alien's elaborate headcrest turned a slightly deeper shade of mauve – a display indicating mild annoyance amongst creatures of his race. But these creatures weren't to know. ECX-762954/B, or Soil to the touchingly prosaic locals, had only been discovered sixteen standards ago. Consequently, contact between the hairless bipedal natives and the races of the Galactic Consortium had been strictly limited by the Bureau of Cultural Affairs.

Q'almn didn't have anything against the Bureau. He could appreciate the need to protect young civilizations from the shock of exposure to the greatly advanced races of The Hub. There were plenty of documented cases that showed how quickly tragedy could ensue. Put simply, there was nothing more disheartening to a primitive race who'd just put the finishing touches to their new pressing machine for extracting a practical hair dye product from the kidneys of some unfortunate grazing animal, and who were beginning to think they were the bee's knees as far as technology went, than for some vast alien ship to put down on top of the new device and some smug bastard with more legs than a millipede to ambulate out and say: 'Listen boys, you're doing it all wrong.'

The worst possible scenario was if the locals fell down on their knees and started worshipping the first cosmic travellers. This was the sad pattern which this planet seemed about to display. The next stage usually involved the locals cutting each other up in your honour and feeding their former friends' still-beating hearts to wild dogs as a sign of their devotion. Q'almn shuddered: this lot were so barbaric they hadn't even developed TV game shows.

For these reasons contact was strictly limited to a few Cultural Investigation Teams and a controlled number of very rich VIPs. But all that was set to change. The discovery of precious metals on a moon of the system's largest gas-giant would mean a huge influx of miners – together with their family groups. The newcomers would be housed in orbiting space habitats, but to facilitate their leisure needs a wide range of day-trip destinations would have to be lined up. Tourism to the sickeningly beautiful third planet was about to become very big business indeed.

However, Q'almn didn't have time to meditate on galactic sociology – he was here for the hard sell.

'But Your Majesty, we don't intend any harm to your sacred river,' his translator unit croaked. 'We only require the specified quantities of raw materials for the structure, together with space to display our new advertising campaign for Pyramid Protein Snacks – the snack that leaves you in good shape!' (Q'almn was very proud of that line.) 'We'll use our sky ships to transport the blocks of sandstone from your quarries. Your people need not lift a finger.'

Despite the close family relationships that were the defining feature of his ancestral line, Pharaoh Khufu was not as loopy as he seemed. He may not have understood the concept of the TV game show, but he had rapidly picked up the basics of advertising. He knew that these strange visitors from beyond the stars had a deep fascination for his land and people. Some merely wished to come and look around; others, such as these he currently entertained, were in the business of selling various chattels to their kindred. To achieve this they required large eye-catching displays in prime locations. For the privilege they were prepared to pay all the market would bear.

'Still, the proposed site is not good,' said Khufu, cracking a walnut on the Chief Eunuch's head. 'If you wish to build there it will cost you twice as many camels. In addition, there will be one further requirement.'

Q'almn was happy to oblige on the camels front – they could be genetically engineered in batches of two hundred aboard his Executive Star-Yacht (a spanking new 24,000-valve, metallic aquamarine limited edition Star-Slug. It had all the mod cons, even an n-dimensional coat-hanger suspended in the rear window.) 'You have the camels, no problem there, Great Ruler. But, this other condition . . . ?'

Khufu drew himself up regally, and adopted his most impressive living god-incarnate voice. 'I have perused the plans for this structure and it pleases me strangely. Seeing as it is to be constructed next to our sacred Nile, when the time comes for my divine soul to journey to the Garden of Osiris, I desire my earthly body to be laid to rest inside this edifice.'

Q'almn was stumped, though he couldn't see any problem with the request – anything to please the locals. 'I'm sure that can be arranged Oh Mighty Hawk of the Desert. So we have a deal?'

Before Khufu could reply, the negotiations were cut short by a noisy commotion from the hallway entrance.

'Let me through, let me through I tell you! If you stick that spear there again, Mister, you'll be in big trouble.'

Forcing his way through the assembled throng of guards and court sycophants was a small bald man wearing a look of intense outrage on his bloated red face. Like certain breeds of miniature dog, Prolduk, Head of the Slaves' Guild, was able to bottle anger out of all proportion to his size.

'I demand an audience with the Pharaoh!' he cried, planting his feet wide in a confrontational manner. There was an awkward moment as everyone waited for the Whip Master to go on. When he eventually did his voice cracked into a piercing whine. 'I demand an audience with the Pharaoh!'

'In case you hadn't noticed,' said Khufu with monumental dignity, 'we are present.'

'Er . . . I did know that Your Majesty, but I would like to do this properly – if it's all the same with you.'

'Oh very well,' Khufu said in a tone of pained indulgence. 'Someone announce this tiresome little man.'

The Chief Eunuch stopped rubbing his bruised scalp and stepped forward, banging his ceremonial staff three times on the marble floor.

'The attention of His Supreme Majesty Khufu, Pharaoh of all Egypt, Hawk of the Desert, is respectfully requested by Prolduk, Head of the Slaves' Guild and First Royal Whip.'

Like petty bureaucrats throughout the universe Prolduk was a fine exponent of the art of monumentally pissing people off. What made his brand of small-minded, small-bodied officialdom all the more irksome was the fact that the Slaves' Guild could wield considerable power – as only the main labour organization in a society without knowledge of the horse-drawn cart could. So he had to be indulged. But only to a degree. Disembowelling was always an option – if you were prepared to accept a touch of civil war here and there.

Khufu was getting impatient. 'Prolduk, I don't have time for this. I'm in the middle of some very delicate negotiations here. If you don't get to the point sharpish I'll have you brought to a sharpish point.'

'Apologies, Great Lord, but the betentacled monstrosity soiling your floor is the reason I am here.'

Had Q'almn possessed a nose he would have stuck it in the air in defiance.

Puffing out his chest, Prolduck bleated, 'It has come to my attention that your guests intend to use their high magic to construct a "promotional" display.'

'That's true,' interrupted Q'almn. 'All we require of your Mighty Ruler is the sandstone and the five-thousand-year lease on the site. We'll be able to complete the building using our ships and chemical lasers in less than the time it takes your planet to rotate on its axis. All we request is that you allow it to be displayed to the many alien tourists who wish to visit your beautiful planet. In return we will provide two thousand camels . . .'

'Four thousand,' corrected Khufu.

'. . . Four thousand camels,' continued Q'almn, beginning to wonder if he'd ever get this deal closed, 'and a final resting place for your Dread King's physical body. What's the problem with that?'

The Slavemaster looked at the alien with pitying contempt. 'The problem,' he said very slowly, as if talking to a small child and not a ten-foot translucent jelly fish with a four figure IQ, 'is that my members will not stand for it.'

Khufu and Q'almn exchanged bewildered glances, or at least Khufu gave a bewildered glance, Q'almn swivelled his eye-stalks and allowed his headcrest to turn a peculiar shade of orangey-brown. After this rare moment of inter-species empathy they both looked back at the flustered bureaucrat.

The small man continued with an insolent air of authority. 'If there are any major building projects to be done around here they'll be undertaken by my Guild.' Then, in the twinkling of an eye, his manner about-changed to open-palmed reasonableness. 'Your Majestyness, what you propose would set a very bad precedent. I have to consider my members' livelihoods, you know. I've just come from a mass meeting and I've been instructed to threaten strike action if our demands are not met. All slaves everywhere, from the fig farmers to the shit-shovellers. The kingdom would grind to a halt in a matter of days.'

This was Khufu's worst nightmare. He could call in the army, or stop the slaves' food supply, but that would only make things worse. A bolshie slave could be talked around with offers of increased date privileges or a little whip work. Some of them liked that. But a dead slave was good for nothing except fig fertilizer. Without the slaves the economy would be in big trouble.

Khufu pondered his predicament for a moment, then came to the only decision left open to him. Drawing himself up to his full height he announced, 'I, Khufu, Pharaoh of all Egypt, do thus declare that my designated mausoleum shall be constructed on the agreed site, and that all work must be carried out by the Slaves' Guild, using traditional Egyptian methods of construction.'

Prolduk looked smug, Q'almn looked like he'd just swallowed a barrel of creosote – a feat not beyond the realms of possibility for one of his race.

'How long, exactly, would you expect this to take?' the alien enquired, trying hard to remain calm.

'Ooh,' said Prolduk, taking a piece of charcoal from his top pocket and scribbling a few cartoons on a sheet of papyrus. 'Well, now you're asking. It's not the materials you see, it's the labour. My initial calculations suggest . . . that I could have it ready for you . . . by the end of the century after next?'

Q'almn shuddered. However, this was a prime site and he supposed the lease was long enough to withstand the delay. 'Very well Your Greatness, if that is how it must be . . . Payment will be made at your first convenience.'

Q'almn sighed, metaphorically – not possessing the local lung arrangement. It had been a pretty bad day, all told. Maybe he could relieve his tension by flying off to some quiet corner of the planet and putting the willies up the natives. Besides, he heard the planet's other main continent group was gaining in popularity with visitors. Perhaps those Aztecs would be easier to deal with.

A Hard Rain's A-Gonna Fall

'Well, obviously, I don't just mean one or two. Shall we say five tonnes or more?'

The girl behind the glass screen looked at Mike as though he'd just landed from another planet and was asking for directions.

'And when I say mysterious,' he continued, 'I mean originating from no obvious source – if they fall out of the back of a van, obviously it doesn't count. Let's say that if their origins can't be traced we'll define them as "mysterious".'

The betting shop assistant was not used to serious-looking old men wandering in off the street wanting to place bets on showers of fish. She had a nasty feeling this was all part of some silly TV stunt and that any minute Jeremy Beadle would climb out of a pot plant, remove a false beard and ram a microphone in her face. She scanned the floor for dubiously bearded customers before replying as best she could.

'Uuurh?'

Mike took a deep breath. 'Do you think I could possibly speak to the manager.'

Not much later he was introduced to a smart young man dressed in a shirt and tie.

'Good morning sir, I believe you wish to place an unusual bet?'

Mike had given considerable thought to his tactics in just this situation. As usual he felt sure the direct approach was best. 'I'd like to place a bet on there occurring a mysterious shower of fresh fish somewhere in the British Isles next week.'

'Any particular type of fish, sir?'

'Non-specific. Dead. Eventually. The type that tend to live in aqueous solutions, saline or fresh.'

The Professor rattled it off with a completely straight face. He was walking a narrow line here – if he was too specific, even the greediest bookie would suspect a set up. On the other hand, his one chance of getting someone to cover such a bet was to appear utterly mad. Mike was in fact aware of the precise time and place of the shower, the species and exact number of piscine life-forms that would perish.

He needn't have worried. The young man didn't even bat an eyelid.

'Certainly sir, we can cover that. I'm authorized to offer you very generous odds of two thousand to one. There is however an upper limit on the stake of two hundred and fifty pounds.'

Mike was a little taken aback at just how easy this was getting. In fact he was almost as shocked as cinemagoers would have been if in the midst of *Death Wish XVI: The Search for More Ammunition*, Charles Bronson had taken his finger off the trigger and cried, 'Bugger this for a laugh, I'm off to Devon to join a commune.'

'Oh – right. Jolly good then,' Mike managed to say. He managed to hand the money over without laughing.

The Professor was unaware that large high-street betting chains were only too happy to accept bets of this nature. There was always some mad granny wanting to place her life savings on the Messiah turning up at her house next Thursday afternoon in time for tea. The market had been growing steadily over the last few years like a well-fed cyst. If the silly season lasted longer this year, so much the better. Soon, however, they were going to wish it had never started at all.

The Numbers Of The Beast

Three days later not much else had happened. Actually, that's not entirely true. World events, as ever, rolled on like some vast, out-of-control beast.

The warm spell broke in a way both catastrophic and faintly tragic. Weathermen, who had been predicting a continuation of the blistering Indian summer, went into hiding along with the rest of the population, as hurricanes lashed Britain to a pulp. Once the storms had abated, mobs of irate homeowners went on the rampage through the debris-strewn streets, seeking out meteorologists with revenge in their hearts and murder in their eyes. Numerous Met Office weather centres were burned to the ground by torch-bearing posses of rioters egged on by armed gangs of Lloyds Names.

Two of the small Balkan states which hadn't existed until the world suffered a sad outbreak of geography severed diplomatic relations with each other. Not a problem most weekends – which was about as frequently as this happened – but this time things were aggravated by the upcoming presidential elections in Russia and the US, prompting candidates in both nations to throw their weight behind the Christian of the two countries. In response the Muslim world united behind their Balkan brothers. Throughout the Middle East brightly coloured headbands were dusted off and tied around the heads of the faithful, in the hope of attaining the fast track to paradise.

For a moment Mike fondly remembered the days when 'Ji-had' was just something the Lone Ranger had shouted to his horse. Quickly, he changed channels. World War III[1] could be awfully depressing, especially if you were involved. Anyway, it was almost time for this week's Blotto-Lotto prize draw – Britain's favourite pastime after breathing and sex.

The Professor was not a regular player, not that he had anything against the lottery in principle. As a form of voluntary taxation it was enormously effective – and Mike always preferred his taxes served that way. This version of the oldest con in town just proved there were more optimists around than mathematicians.

But this week the Professor wouldn't have missed it for the world, and it wasn't because he had bought himself a ticket. He had given up on finding a way to make money from such a public spectacle. Correctly forecasting tonight's numbers would have got him nowhere, except maybe locked up. It might still have its uses though – with luck, back at her student dorm Deborah would be watching.

Mike settled down with a bottle of red wine to watch the show for pure entertainment value. Tonight, of all nights, he felt sure it would be a more riveting spectacle than usual.

With a breathtaking camera pan, the director, who obviously had ideas above his station, pulled back to reveal the massed ranks of the St Winifred's School Formation Spacehopper Team. Just as the little ones were reaching the

---

1 To give each its full title –
World War I: A Crowned Princes of Europe Production
World War II: This Time It's Really War
World War III: Return of The Dead-Eyed Fanatics

finale of their carefully choreographed routine, the show's hostess – Miss Harriet 'The Chariot' Hastings – stepped into shot wearing the sort of smile only attainable through regular use of powerful mind-altering drugs. As the last of the brightly coloured orange globes bounced from the studio, piloted by their eager young riders, Miss Hastings bobbed excitedly on the spot like a well upholstered blonde pogo stick.

'Welcome to the two hundred and sixty-third National Blotto-Lotto draw – LIVE! And this week's a triple rollover week, with an estimated jackpot of FORTY MILLION POUNDS! Yes, tonight someone's going to get VERY lucky indeed.'

'Ooooooooooooh!' cried the studio audience, long since whipped into a frenzy of anticipation and now egged on by the wholesome Miss Hastings.

'And just to remind all you happy people out there in television land, your Blotto-Lotto Big Night Prize Draw is brought to you in association with Yummy Tum's tasty Soya-based Snacks. Mmmmmmm! Yum, yum in my tum. I think I'll shuffle down a whole pack right after the show. I can hardly wait!

She paused for a second, making a great show of holding her finger to her earpiece. 'Ladies and gentlemen . . . I've just been informed that we're ready to go over live to our very own prophetess. Maybe she can tell us exactly who that lucky punter will be. Can you hear me, Psychic Sue?'

The camera cut to a mist-shrouded scene lit from below by eerily flickering fairy lights. The smoke cleared to reveal a woman in a black cape polishing her crystal ball like her life depended on it. At her side a huge black cat did its best to look bored to death – and very nearly succeeded. Slowly, the camera zoomed in to give a close-up of Pyschic Sue's crazed eyes, framed beneath lashes thick with industrial-strength mascara. When she spoke it was like a bat's wing brushing a crypt door at midnight.

'Tonight, I see an old man, ladies and gentlemen!'

'Ooooooooooooh!'

'Though he be of woman born, his life has been a strange one. He carries his years as a heavy burden, but he will share them with none. I see the letters M and N . . .'

At home Mike almost choked on his Burgundy. Either she really was psychic, or breathtakingly lucky, or, and this Mike found most disturbing of all, there was more to this astrology lark than he'd ever given credit. With a frown he looked on with heightened professional interest. Psychic Sue was looking rather distracted.

'He is a keeper of great secrets, but they trouble him not. Wait . . . let me focus. Yes – very dark secrets indeed. I can barely . . . Hrrrrrgh!'

Sue went rigid from head to toe and keeled onto the floor, as her cat was transformed into a rocket-propelled mass of teeth and claws. At first the studio audience thought it was all part of the act and cheered all the louder. When the floor manager and camera crew rushed to her assistance the viewers realized her seizure was for real. Hastily, the director cut back to a rather flustered Harriet Hastings.

'Errr, Psychic Sue seems to be experiencing a few . . . technical difficulties, folks. But not to worry because we're just about ready to go over to the big draw itself!'

The scene cut to a close up of 'Ball-Filled Bertha', Blotto-Lotto's famed bingo-ball selector. Meanwhile, a drummer whose only other source of income involved providing the backing track for firing squads and state executions, set about earning his pay. Miss Hastings' voice cut in as the first ball trundled down the chute. 'And your lucky numbers are . . .

'Five . . .' Scattered cheers from the audience. The drum roll continued as the second ball came into view.

'Four . . .' Miss Hernia gave the camera her best surprised look, raising two perfectly formed eyebrows. But there was no time to delay, the third ball was ready.

'Three? Well, well . . .' Suddenly she seemed a bit less sure of herself. All too soon the fourth ball appeared.

'Two!'

Her carefully pampered complexion turned a greenish shade as the fifth ball popped out with ominous inevitability.

'One.' She gulped, almost resigned to her fate.

Harriet didn't have the heart to call the last number. It didn't matter as every camera in the studio was focused in on it, magnifying to monstrous proportions the tiny black ball. Yes, black – unlike any of the others. But its uniqueness didn't end there, in fact it barely began. In homes across the nation, Britons stopped whatever they were doing to stare on agog. It wasn't only the colour that was wrong with this pagan ping-pong perversion. The number it bore glowed a malicious red like the embers of a recently torched church. It was a three digit number, and the number was:

Six, six, six.

All hell broke loose in the studio.

If Miss Hastings hadn't been huddled sobbing on the floor she would have been hit by the plastic chair hurled by a burly member of the front row. 'Fix! I want me money back!' he screamed, as he advanced on a cameraman intent on reclaiming his investment. No one did anything to stop him, mainly since most of the audience, not to mention millions of viewers at home, were thinking along very similar lines. The situation quickly developed from bad to worse, then went downhill from there. The studio's handful of security guards were in no way equipped to deal with a full-blown riot. Miss Hastings barely escaped a lynching as she was rushed from the fast-escalating battle.

With a philosophical shrug, Mike reached over and

turned off the TV. The last image he saw before the tube faded to black was of paramedics fighting a valiant rearguard action to rescue Psychic Sue, along with her cat, before the mob, chanting 'Fry the witch . . . fry the witch . . .' could burn her at a hastily improvised stake. It was truly amazing how well even the most synthetic studio furniture would burn if you tried hard enough.

For a man who had just seen the chance of forty million pounds slip away, Mike didn't seem overly concerned. Over the coming weeks there'd be plenty of other winning chits in plenty of other games of not-so-chance. Mike had his sticky fingers in many juicy pies – and pretty soon he'd be pulling them out to give each a good lick.

The Times They Are A-Changing

Old Mad Megan peered out of the window of her tiny cottage and frowned. Down in the pasture by the stream the sheep had stopped exploding, but she wasn't sure if even this was a good sign. Earlier that day, while picking ingredients for her lethally alcoholic herb tea, she'd found a five-leafed clover. Megan had sprinkled the area thoroughly with stream water she'd quickly blessed, but she hadn't had the nerve to check for others.

Shuffling hurriedly back home, her basket empty of berries, she'd spotted a flock of geese flying backwards. Such was her panic she'd barely made the sigil to ward off the evil eye in time.

As if this wasn't enough, while retrieving her washing before the storm clouds broke, an albino jack-rabbit had streaked across her lawn, run seven times around a hawthorn tree, looked at her sternly, then died on the spot. When she'd salvaged the poor animal, thinking of her evening meal, she found its internal organs had mysteriously been replaced with four ounces of cheddar cheese and the condensed works of Chairman Mao. Not anything to be overly concerned with you might think – but then you'd be wrong.

If you were as old, or as wise, or as mad as some people said Megan was, then you'd know that these events held great significance. They told this old girl their own story – and it was a story unlikely to have a happy ending. Most of all they told her that it was almost THE TIME – and that the time was almost TOO LATE.

But there was no sense worrying about that now. With a Gallic shrug which would have corralled a herd of snails, she waddled over to her kitchen to check on her baking. Megan was pretty as a picture (sadly, it just happened to be Whistler's 'Mother' – and not the final version at that. Old Mad Megan resembled an earlier draft the artist threw away for being too gloomy). But fortunately for this dried old raisin of a woman, not to mention the villagers down the valley, her looks were not a drawback in her everyday life. Because Megan kept herself to herself. There were hermit crabs off the coast of Alaska who had better social lives than she did. In fact, she mused to herself warmly, had hermit crabs ever developed singles bars, a conversation overheard in one might develop as follows:

'Haven't seen much of you recently, Jeremy. Where you been these last twenty years?'

'Oh, here and there, round and about – you know how it is, Veronica. Fell off the continental shelf the year before last. Reorganizing my sock drawer the past eighteen months – the usual, you know. Anyway, you can talk. You haven't exactly been coming out of your shell lately.'

'At least I get out more than that lunatic old bat who lives in North Wales. Fancy a shag?'

'Yeah, all right then.'

Megan cackled to herself gummily. She was very good at cackling: she got plenty of practice on the long winter evenings when the spirit world was unresponsive, there was nothing really good on TV and her imagination was her only entertainment. Her grin brought to mind Stonehenge on a wet and windy night – grown dentists would have fled screaming from her path. Not that you'd ever get Mad Megan near a dentist – she didn't hold with none of that modern rubbish. As she often said to anything that would listen, 'If God had meant us to travel in cars, She'd have given us six buttocks and no legs.' There was seldom much of a reply – Megan's conversations tended to be rather one-sided, mainly because the small flock of very fat birds she fed in her garden were too busy stuffing their tiny faces to offer an opinion.

With well-practised efficiency Megan drew out the tray of piping hot Welsh cakes and placed them on the table to cool. She was about to put her ancient black kettle on the stove to boil when she froze. Something unnatural had happened in the oven, and it was far, far worse than a comeback tour by Brotherhood of Man. Trembling slightly, she peered at the array of cakes. No mistaking it, all her fears were confirmed. There in the cakes, spelled out before her very eyes, was proof if proof be needed that in the near future mankind was in for a major change of course.

Within the small round patties of dough the currants and sultanas had rearranged themselves into four terrible letters spelling out S-O-O-N.

Megan grasped the iron tray in her oven mitt and hurried outside. She scuttled over to her ancient unused well and brushed the snacks of Satan down the hole with a disdainful shudder – she didn't want the birds or other wild things having any part of those unnatural perversions.

Overhead a black cloud slunk over the sun. As she looked up a huge dark raindrop hit her squarely in the eye. She beat the tray against the well wall until certain every crumb had been removed, then turned and hurried back inside, latching the heavy oak door firmly behind her. Once inside, her fear subsided a little, and she went through to the kitchen where a grease-stained calendar hung on the wall above her ancient New World cooker. She'd not looked at it in a long while. No need. She'd rather be blind behind the times than clear-eyed before the future. But the day's events had left her no choice. Turning the leaves as fast as her arthritic fingers could manage, she finally reached the correct month. And the moment she did, the nail holding the calendar to the wall gave way, dropping it into her trembling hands.

October already. So not long now.

The End was coming.

Carnival 2000

With a furtive glance over her shoulder Deborah increased her pace along the well-lit college walkway. It wasn't that she feared some unseen mugger lurking in the shrubbery (from his hospital bed her kick boxing instructor said she was a match for any assailant, trained or untrained. Nice man, Deborah hadn't meant to hurt him. She was just so eager and fast, and, well, *accurate*. The doctors said he'd be out in a week or two, once they'd removed as many of the pins as they thought safe. There'd be no long-term scarring, at least not on the surface. In fact, he'd gain one useful ability from the unfortunate incident – from now on he'd always know the direction of magnetic north.). No, muggers were pussycats compared to this. At least they surprised you. At least they pissed off after they'd nabbed your handbag.

Andy, of course, was capable of neither. He wasn't put off by Deborah ignoring his friendly call; nor was he in any way disheartened by his target's near-sprint away from him – because his dictionary placed 'Yes' right next to 'Up yours, arsehole.'

'Like, Debbs yah – wait up. I've got a great idea for banishing this winter chill.'

Deborah didn't even turn to look at her pursuer as he jogged alongside her. 'Unless it involves setting fire to your boxer shorts with you still in them I don't want to know. And while we're on the subject, I lost track of the last person to call me "Debbs" back in primary school – I believe he lost track of his teeth.'

'But like, hey babe, you've already started a fire in my shorts – and only you can put it out.'

Deborah halted in her tracks and stared at Andy in open-mouthed disbelief. Talent like that deserved an extra special response, one she was currently unqualified to give in her state of near speechlessness. The only reply that sprang to mind was physical in nature and would have made even her kick-boxing instructor wince. No matter what a turd, this leech didn't deserve that. So with an inarticulate howl, Deborah stormed off once again.

Despite what anyone could have said about Andy (stuck up supercilious twat was always an option), no one could have accused him of defeatism. His forte was persistence. Like the Light Brigade at Balaclava after the Russians had taken the piss out of their cardigans, he pressed on bravely.

'So hey my dear, what gives? Where'll you be spending Christmas this year? Curled up in front of a roaring fire with me I hope.'

Deborah turned sharply into the quiet tree-lined avenue that led to her dorm. 'Same as ever, I'll be spending it by myself.'

Andy looked alarmed. 'What, no family?'

Her face remained expressionless. 'My parents died in a car crash when I was a baby. Apart from them I have no family.'

At least he had the good grace to look distraught. 'I didn't know. Like hey, I'm so sorry.'

'Don't be, you didn't kill them. Anyway, orphans enjoy a really cheap holiday season – no presents to buy. There are other advantages too – from an early age you learn how to cope. Though at the moment I'm having difficulty coping with you . . . Don't you ever give up?'

Andy was about to give a glib reply, something along the lines of being a real long stayer – and in more ways than one – when he paused, the words not yet past his perfectly capped teeth. Deborah had suddenly halted her headlong advance and was staring up at the starry sky, a faintly bemused expression on her perfect face. Andy stood beside her and followed her gaze. Several hundred feet up an orange light bobbed and weaved; suspended beneath it, two smaller green lights formed a triangle.

'Helicopter,' Andy declared, then returned his attention to Deborah's smooth neck.

She shook her head. 'Can't be – no sound. And anyway, what would a helicopter be doing hovering above this clapped-out place? This probably sounds ridiculous but it almost seems to be following us . . . Now that we've stopped it's stopped too.'

Inspired suddenly, Andy pressed home a brilliant new line.

'Hey Deborah, you must be a thief!'

She looked at him with utter confusion. 'Whatever it is you're on, remind me never to take some.'

Andy looked her squarely in the face. 'Deborah, you must be a thief – because you've stolen the stars, and put them in your eyes.'

With a heroic effort she managed to gag back the vomit before she pebble-dashed his suede shoes. Degenerating into gales of laughter she turned on her heel and marched off into the night. Andy blushed like a Chernobyl victim but quickly followed after her.

'Slow down Debbs – sorry, Deborah. What about New Year's Eve, what've you got planned?'

Once again, Deborah refused to look at him. 'Oh, probably much the same as Christmas.'

Once again, Andy looked shocked. 'You can't spend NY by yourself. Not this one at any rate. It's not just a new year this time but a whole new century. An event like this doesn't happen every day you know.'

Deborah glanced at him pityingly. 'For your information it's a brand new millennium as well, though it all depends which expert you listen to. There's a good case for arguing the Age of Aquarius won't begin until January 1st 2001. And when you take into account that Jesus was most likely born some time in March, 5BC it makes the whole hullabaloo seem rather foolish, don't you think?'

Andy was finding this party-pooping disdain rather hard to deal with. 'But it's going to be a Beano on a truly worldwide scale, Debbsie. Jemima's parents are spending the hols in their Swiss ski chalet, so their pad in the country'll be free. She's throwing the biggest bash since we smashed Toxteth Poly on *University Challenge*. Want to come? There'll be a laser show and a buffet dinner and what's more . . .'

Deborah would never know what was more, what Dionysian treats she would be missing, because at that exact moment Andy was picked out by a pencil-thin spotlight from directly above. 'What the . . . ?' he gasped as the blinding white light was joined by a thinner beam of sickly green. This second ray scanned across his trembling body before fixing on the middle of his forehead.

The same unearthly craft which they had earlier observed now sank slowly towards the university's communal gardens, maintaining the piercing ray on Andy as it did so. 'Run for it!' Deborah screamed, grasping Andy by his clammy wrist. But Andy was going nowhere.

Deborah looked on in horror as the glowing craft settled gently on a low mound amidst the carefully landscaped grounds. It was no more than thirty yards away but details were lost in its shimmering ball of radiance. She could now see that the two smaller lights slung beneath the main body comprised some sort of undercarriage which flexed as they took the craft's weight. No sooner had it landed than a dark hatchway opened at one side. Two stocky children ran from the gaping hole and made for Deborah.

She quickly revised her initial assessment. Though small in size the figures were no children spawned by man – not unless Quasimodo and Mother Theresa had got together and kept it quiet. They were grey, and had the sort of bulbous eyes normally reserved for particularly unpleasant deep-sea fish. The things moved like inebriated puppets, their stubby legs pounding across the turf as long gangly arms swung by their sides. Within seconds they were upon the frozen students. Two pairs of multi-jointed hands grabbed for Andy and held him in a steely grip.

With a jolt Deborah snapped out of her panic-induced inertia and flew into action. Or at least she would have done had she been the star of a Kung Fu B-Movie. In reality, concluding that cowardice was the survivable subset of the valour Venn diagram, at least when facing species of doubtful origin, she resolved to make a run for it with or without Andy's help. She was all set to knock him out cold, intent on carrying him away from the scene fireman fashion, when a second green beam struck her in the forehead.

The sensation was indescribable. The closest she'd ever come to it was the night she'd downed nine tequila slammers quickly followed by an undercooked kebab.

Paralysed, she watched as the two goblins lifted Andy with unearthly strength and carried him high above their deformed heads back to their ship. Fighting against an invisible forcefield Andy stared back with bulging eyes. 'Deborah – help meeeeeee!'

But all she could do was watch as her hapless suitor disappeared behind the hatch. The ship became immersed in a surreal purple glow, then slowly and silently edged off the grass. For a moment it hovered a few feet above the turf, finding its bearings, before accelerating vertically at a phenomenal rate. Seconds later it was nothing more than another star hanging in the cold night sky. Deborah watched it go in disbelief.

It was a long, long time before she realized she could move again. But when she did, she made the most of it and sprinted home at Olympian speed.

She would keep her door locked that night, and more than once peer up at the newly terrifying firmament. There was only one man who might make sense of what she'd seen. Deborah resolved to pay Professor Michael Nostrus another visit. First thing in the morning.

Until then, she needed something simple, something normal and mundane to ground her. And she needed company. In a wide-eyed daze she drifted into her dormitory's communal kitchen, where her housemates were settling down to watch the lottery draw.

THREE

A man revives the infernal gods of Hanibal,
the terror of all Mankind,
Never more horror,
nor do the papers talk of worse things.
Quatrain II.30 The Centuries

Red sky at night, Arms Dealers' delight.
Red sky at morning, Four Minute Warning.
Professor Michael D. Nostrus

You're So Vain I Bet You Think This Chapter's About You

'Bugger bollocks bastards!' Not for the first time that day Adam MacArthur stifled an urge to smash his fist through the glowing computer screen.

'Why does this bloody machine always *do* this to me? Just when I'm at the end . . . Stupid, useless arsing fu –' Adam clamped up his invective to smile disarmingly as Sally the office temp pushed her mail trolley past his desk. He was good at disarming smiles.

Sally's perspective was a little different. As his lecherous eyes swept over her, she felt more nauseous than a pâté de foie gras goose on a trip to Alton Towers. She paled at the prospect of having to go any nearer to him.

Adam was not up to spotting such subtle reactions from a fellow human being. 'Darlin',' he said with all the sincerity of a conger eel, 'could you get someone from Maintenance to look at this thing? It crashes more often than Dago 747s in the week the Air Traffic Controllers have their annual piss-up. Course, you could take a look yourself, love. Always room at my desk for two.'

Sally, who had heard it all before, didn't even bother to roll her eyes (he didn't deserve such lofty recognition) but breezed past, careful to keep her body safely out of Intermediate Range Groping Zone. Adam gazed after her longingly, all the while making a primordial sound reminiscent of the monkey house at a major zoo. Then he grinned like a Prozac-laced pensioner, his AWOL word processor momentarily forgotten.

The young man's tender display of affection went largely unnoticed by the room's other occupants. They sat glued to their keyboards busily typing away like their livelihoods depended on it – which they did. This sad collection of sweaty, small-minded, middle-aged men were well used to each other's tantrums and idiosyncrasies. Snide glances and sarcastic sniggers were all Adam got for his amorous efforts. Not surprising, perhaps, since the young man was sitting in a room full of tabloid journalists, which was not an unusual place to find him, as he too was a member of that much put-upon profession. And at the moment Adam was wondering why he bothered.

Sod it, he thought. That highbrow investigative piece he'd been hacking out on the 'Vice Ring Vicars of Vauxhall' would just have to wait. If the Editor couldn't provide decent equipment how could he expect professionals to do their job? Who'd ever heard of a Russian-built computer anyway? Probably made with sliced beetroot, he wondered moodily.

He liked to wonder moodily from time to time – it seemed in keeping with his assumed persona. 'Adam MacArthur, ace reporter, man of the people and all round good bloke.

Get me New York on the blower pronto, and hold the lettuce on mine.'

The truth was that Adam became a tabloid reporter for two reasons only. Firstly, it was a chance to meet people; more specifically, it was a chance to meet young female people – often in an emotionally tender state. Secondly, it was the result of an embarrassing mix up in a video store during his frustrated, hormone-drenched adolescence.

Under Pressure

One rainy Sunday afternoon, quite a few years before Russian PCs hit the marketplace, the teenage Adam had found himself at a loose end. All his mates were away on a character-building school orienteering trip in the Faeroe Islands (sleeping under the stars with your only pillow a smudged hand-drawn map with OBJECTIVE scribbled all over it was not his idea of fun) and his parents were bowing to the statutory Least Favoured Uncle annual visit – the one who smelled of piss and forced him to eat rhubarb. Caught between a rock and a hard place he decided to opt for the marshmallow option of doing neither and staying at home. Surprisingly, his parents hadn't minded. Perhaps they'd finally come to the conclusion that he was no longer two years old and could put food into his mouth all by himself.

Even so, he was feeling a bit left out, sorry for himself, at a loss generally as to how to fill his time. Wandering around the streets of his grey hometown, he found himself outside his local video rental store. He flirted briefly with the idea of catching up on the *Driller Killer* series, but ruled that option out due to a lack of cash. It was pointless just getting one out, which was all he could afford. They were all pretty much the same – you needed to watch one after the other until the horror built up and consumed you and you realized just how adaptable masonry bits could be.

Then he had a dazzling idea. In fact he didn't so much have it, as it had him. Once this idea had slunk between his synapses and made a bed of his frontal lobes Adam knew he couldn't back out, otherwise the drill-toting, macho half of his personality would denounce the rest of him a wimp for all eternity.

Furtively, he checked the inside of the shop. All clear. Only Mr McGoldrick serving behind the counter and no sign of his daughter Jenny, the lead role in many of Adam's less angelic daydreams. With his parents away there might never be a chance like this again. Steeling himself, Adam strode purposefully into the store. Coolly, he made a show of considering the other films on the shelves. A meaningless montage of *Alien Zombie Swamp Fiends* (parts I and II), *Chaos Ninja Otters* and *Zen and the Art of Golf* passed before his eyes as, all the while, he edged closer to his real target.

Why couldn't he just go up and take it? Why did he have to feel racked with embarrassment and guilt? Because Adam had received a good British upbringing, that's why. He'd been taught to snigger at sex and, when he couldn't snigger, to experience a sickening, ball-tightening paranoia that threatened to drive him mad. The weight of a thousand *Carry On* films bore down on him, and it was a heavy load to bear. What made it worse was the fact that this heavy monkey on his back looked like Sid James and had an irritating chuckle that made Adam want to take a cold shower. It was this particular simian version of Sid that whispered in his ear at parties that all the girls were dying for it, and that if he only had the bottle to 'go for it' they'd let him sample their sweet delights. It was this mischievous monkey that told him he was a sex god when he was fortunate enough to catch himself in the mirror from that one angle that didn't make him look like a sad, boring little nobody. It was the voice that would soon come to dominate his life.

Finally reaching his destination, desperately trying not to rush it, to make it appear a spur of the moment decision, Adam reached up to the top shelf. He could feel Mr McGoldrick's eyes on his back, could taste the disapproval in the air. Turning around casually – and nearly falling over himself in the process – Adam was surprised to find the proprietor staring down at his accounts oblivious to his predicament. The young lad let out a deep sigh of relief. Everything's cool he thought to himself as he strode purposefully up to the counter.

Placing the case down under McGoldrick's nose, along with the money and his membership card, Adam felt the warm swell of success sweeping his body. Absentmindedly, the shopkeeper looked up from his calculations and lifted the box. He held it at arms' length, squinting for a second, his eyesight not being what it used to be thanks to many hours studying freeze-frames from *The Lovers' Guide*. After a moment of recognition McGoldrick half turned to the back of his store and called in a clear voice, 'Jenny dear, see if you can find *Busty Brenda's Bubblebath Bonanza* for young Adam here. Seems like his parents are away for the day.'

Suddenly Adam wished he could be away too; somewhere else, like on the surface of another planet for example, preferably one without an atmosphere – that way no one could hear his scream of shame. After what seemed like an eternity of eye-smarting embarrassment Jenny's lithe form appeared clutching a cassette. She sniggered as she handed it to her father who placed it in the case and gave it to the faintly glowing Adam.

Once he'd run all the way home the young man thundered up to his room and collapsed in a state of emotional exhaustion, his hard-won video clutched to his pounding chest. But when he'd finally recovered, reasoning he might as well at least make his public shame worthwhile by watching the bloody thing, he soon realized that as well as possessing the body of the little known Greek goddess of Step Aerobics and the face of an adolescent angel, young Jenny had the brain of a dyslexic armadillo. Combined with her father's failing eyes, this had resulted in a bit of an oversight.

After half an hour Adam was resigned to the fact that neither 'Busty Brenda' nor 'Pneumatic Pauline' were likely to put in an appearance. In his desperation he would have made do with 'Flat-chested Phillipa' or, at a push, 'Utterly Ugly Ulrika' but even they seemed a forlorn hope. The film was about two American reporters, a tall blonde one and a short dark one, uncovering all sorts of dodgy dealings in 1970s Washington DC. Despite the conspicuous lack of flesh of any sort (unless you counted hairy arms poking from rolled-up shirtsleeves, which he didn't), the story captured Adam's fertile imagination in a way he never would have guessed possible.

When term resumed a week later Adam immediately got involved with the school magazine, ignoring the near-universal reluctance to admit him on the grounds of his lack of tact, empathy, or personality. He'd win 'em over.

The seeds of an illustrious career at the pinnacle of investigative journalism had been sown.

36D, So What?

To tell the truth Adam rather fancied himself as the new Robert Redford. When he looked in the mirror, he smiled knowingly. The thought that he'd just got out of bed with the love god in front of him often got him quite excited. But sadly reality, as perceived by any of the other five billion inhabitants of this planet who had the misfortune to chance upon him, was rather more down to earth.

That day in the video store had done more than set Adam on the road to his lifelong career. Standing there wishing he was dead, something really had died inside him. That most underrated of social talents, his ability to feel embarrassment, had gone belly up, twitched its legs momentarily and died amid great spurts of shame. He'd used up his entire reserves in that one defining moment and Adam MacArthur now had no conscience to speak of.

As a young boy he had been shy and retiring, with a single curl on his forehead and a shine on his smart new shoes. Old ladies had felt the urge to kiss his cheek and wipe his mouth with spittle-damp hankies. Nowadays, females of any age risked an unanaesthetized tonsillectomy if they so much as lived in the same country as him. He had become an unmitigated poser, the saddest sort of poser of all – the sort that is actually quite good looking in an everyday sort of way and who, if he had even the vestige of a personality, would be well liked by all.

'Adam MacArthur? All round good bloke really, salt of the earth that one,' colleagues would have agreed. Instead what was usually said was: 'Adam MacArthur? All round git really. Owes me a tenner. Decent journo though.'

It was true. The one rider to an otherwise dismal genetic and social CV was that Adam was actually pretty good at his job. What really let him down characterwise was the fact his head was the size of a cross Channel ferry, but thankfully without the frontal swing doors. He referred to all females without exception as 'ladies', spiking the word with suggestion. When Ethyl, a grey-haired grandmother of four who brought the tea around the office every morning, pulled up next to his desk with her trolley of cakes she'd receive the same greeting each day.

'And how's my extra-special lady today?' Adam would ooze, Old Spice seeping from every pore.

Ethyl might have been sixty-two but she knew the score. 'You know something?' she'd sigh, gazing up into his glistening granite eyes. 'You're full of shit, you are.' And she was right. Adam was more full of shit than King Kong's colostomy bag. But he didn't care. He was at his worst while swaying in the middle of a wine bar after an unfeasibly long lunch break, holding forth on the troubles of the world and how he'd put them right given half a chance. He was at his best while unconscious, this second state following the first rapidly and with monotonous regularity.

Fortunately for Adam and his career there were usually large numbers of his colleagues present at the same establishment. After he'd hit the deck they'd scrape him off the floor, drag him back to the office and prop him up in front of his word-processor to come around in his own time.

It was in this dazed condition that Adam had created some of his finest masterpieces. Stories that sprang to mind included the exclusive exposé on 'Ronnie the Rotweiller', the nationally infamous hell-hound who'd won the hearts of millions by his ability to say 'Sau-sag-es', then gone for the chat show host live on network television. And who could forget the poetically titled 'Orca Porker Snorkelers', a meticulously researched piece on sexual proclivities of a bestial leaning at a well-known dolphinarium?

All things considered Adam had created quite a name for himself in the shit-shovelling world of sewer journalism. Editors loved him for his ability to conjure astonishing, readable pieces plucked from the ether. His male colleagues looked up to him (admittedly from an extremely low social platform) for his (much-cultivated) reputation as a ladies' man. The ladies themselves just ignored him – if he let them.

All this – the panoramic vista of opportunity and respect he now surveyed – he owed to Mr McGoldrick's chaotic filing system. Though, if he were honest with himself, which he found psychologically impossible, he'd have to admit to just a bit of a difference between the pages of the *Washington Post* and the *Daily Trumpet*.

Hold The Front Page

Adam returned to his blank computer screen, and spent the next ten minutes thinking up increasingly ingenious ways of destroying it for good so that they'd be forced to give him a new one. It teetered precariously on the edge of his desk. Every time he sat down, it wobbled. Perhaps euthanasia was the best tack. One small push was all it would take and he could go to Winslow saying, 'He just made a leap for it Guv. I tried to stop him . . .'

The rest of the office was getting on with its daily routine, though there was nothing routine about this particular day. Bouncing off the world's communications satellites and seeping from every fax a whole host of alarming news stories was cooking up into a mind-blowing current affairs vindaloo. What was more The Great Waiter In The Sky had been beckoned over and was on his way with sixteen pints of lager and a tray of lime pickles. The only piece of nan bread on the event horizon which seemed capable of mopping it all up was the hastily convened meeting of the United Nations Insecurity Council, which was now in permanent session – the phrase 'Pissing into a Force Twelve hurricane' would not have been inappropriate.

And if the foreign news was bad events in Blighty were no better. In a shock move Linda Lumps, 52, the much loved 'Queen of the Quadrangle' announced she was quitting *Squabble Square*, the nation's favourite soap. Ms Lumps denied she'd been pushed after claiming in her autobiography that the show's producers had been kidnapped and replaced by identical space aliens intent on subverting British culture from within.

If it went on much longer this year's 'Silly Season' was going to spill over into the next millennium – as if that fateful date wasn't enough of a worry in itself. As the century came to a close, this tired old Earth seemed to be spinning ever faster on its wobbly axis, until it threatened to throw its poor bemused passengers off into the cosmic void once and for all.

A sudden noisy commotion in the outer office derailed Adam's train of thought from such weighty matters as the Russian civil war, the Chinese famine and the sexual preferences of some of London SE1's more religiously liberal parsons, and brought it skidding to a halt just inches from the station's safety rail.

A large group of ostrich-necked people were milling about in the foyer with that air of ghoulish voyeurism which can only accompany a fatal accident. With mounting curiosity Adam realized the agitated crowd were straining to see out of the wall-sized window and down to the main street below. Suddenly, from behind the throng, the office lift doors flew open and out rushed the vast round bulk of Bill Winslow, the *Trumpet*'s Editor in Chief. The iridescently scarlet man seemed highly flustered as the ever-growing crowd parted before him like the Red Sea on the day Moses went for a paddle in a bad mood. None present dared get in the way of their radioactive boss.

'Who here ain't doing nothing?' he bellowed in his lyrical Aussie accent, causing the windows to rattle and the floor to shake. 'Forget that – ANYBODY! There's the story of the century breaking beneath our very noses and we ain't even got a reporter at the scene. Strewth, even Cyclops with an eyepatch could spot what's going on out front!'

Adam nearly fell off his chair with fright. He'd been relaxing with his feet up, contemplating whether or not to pop out and doorstep some of the unwilling subjects of his latest story when his boss stormed in. Spotting the reporter lounging in his chair, Winslow homed in on the young man like a heat-seeking missile. Adam briefly knew how a startled bunny must feel when a juggernaut thunders towards it. He was just on the point of volunteering his services when his boss beat him to it.

'You there, MacArthur. On the street pronto! Something big's going down and I don't mean me pants. Looks like a bomb scare. The police are cordoning off the area – though if you don't get through, as sure as I ain't a dead dingo, I'll roast ya balls on me barbie for Christmas.'

But Adam was long gone. Before the echoes of Winslow's cultured tones had finished reverberating round the office, he was out of the door. This is more like it, he thought to himself as he ran down the stairs two at a time. He'd had enough of perverted preachers anyway. This was real news – whatever it was. This was why he'd gone into journalism in the first place. This was professional stuff.

For the first time in his life he felt a warm anticipatory glow spreading through him that had nothing at all to do with what went on in his trousers.

2000 To 1 – A Plaice Oddity

Adam sprinted down the front steps of Trumpet Towers and hurtled himself through the mêlée of a rapidly growing crowd. Not far down the road the police were diverting traffic and forcing back the onlookers. Several flustered officers were hastily cordoning off the area. As he arrived at the scene, Adam realized his boss's guess at a bomb scare wasn't even close to the mark. The straining crowd were being held back sure enough, but the few coppers present were making no effort to clear the street.

Behind the police lines there was a great deal of activity. A small army of street cleaners and council workers, not to mention a fair few firemen, all seemed to be paying particular attention to the ground. Jumping on the spot like a demented grapecrusher, Adam did his best to see over the throng. When a small bespectacled old gentleman went down in the crush before him MacArthur grabbed his chance. As a harried policeman rushed to the pensioner's aid, the gallant reporter dashed for the gap left in his wake. The bobby barked an order to halt but Adam was through and still running before the words left his lips. A worried-looking fireman was next in his path. But, 'Don't get in the way of the clean-up operation!' was all that Adam heard him say. Before the reporter could ask, 'What clean-up operation?' the situation came crashing home like an overfed carrier pigeon. Something wet and slimy, not to mention flesh-creepingly wriggly, gave way beneath Adam's designer slip-ons, sending him flying through the air to land on his back with a resounding slap. In a confused daze he staggered to his feet and looked around.

Scattered over the street, several feet deep, was a silver sea of pathetically flapping fish. Adam gazed up the road to the junction fifty yards further on – same over there. In fact, the squirming mass stretched as far as the eye could see in both directions. Standing there, for once in his life truly lost for words, Adam caught the eye of one of the myriad maritime mavericks. It looked up at him sadly, its mouth desperately sucking at the thick London air as it slowly died of suffocation. It held a questioning look in its pearly eye, seeming to say: 'What you gawking at? Never seen ten million live fish fall on a city centre street before?' It was a mark of Adam's sense of unreality that he heard himself answer with a mumbled, 'No, not really.'

Half the London Fire Brigade were shovelling vast piles of the things onto great flat-topped trucks which, when full, drove off and churned up a sicking fish pesto beneath their wheels. For a while Adam just wandered about in a waking daze, doing his best not to break an ankle on the slippery surface, and repeating, 'I don't believe it. This is the most unbelievable thing I've ever seen – and I've seen *Mambo Warriors from Venus III*.' Finally, he gathered his wits, and reminded himself he was on a mission – got to get the story.

Carefully, he picked his way back toward the police lines to find the man in charge. He wasn't hard to spot – you could almost watch as the years ticked by on his face. Not long before the bloke could be conning his way into getting a free bus pass. Adam arrived intent on ageing him further still. Unsurprisingly, the officer wasn't too keen to talk to the press. It took all of Adam's persistence and diplomatic skill to get any information out of him at all. It seemed eyewitnesses had reported the fish falling from a clear blue sky. The shower had lasted for several minutes and was limited to a few nearby streets. No, the officer in charge was not at liberty to divulge information regarding whether there had been any other fish-falling incidents reported – he was too busy dealing with the here and now to worry about anywhere else. Information was still sketchy due to the fact that many eyewitnesses were being treated in local hospitals for a range of serious fin-related head wounds.

The cause? The officer refused to speculate, though Adam was only too willing to provide some suggestions. A publicity ploy by a frozen food company that went horribly wrong? A frighteningly subtle terrorist attack? Or maybe the fish weren't fish at all, but represented the advance guard of some super-intelligent alien race who'd mistakenly calculated that the entire Earth was covered with water? In the light of this last offering the policeman lost all patience and had Adam moved on.

Several bulldozers arrived on the scene and the clean-up operation now got into full swing. The large crowd had already begun to disperse. There was only a certain novelty value in watching dead fish being shovelled onto lorries. The hardcore remaining largely fell into three categories. There was the usual spattering of accident-site voyeurs, though many of these were losing interest for although a great deal of blood and guts was on display none of it was human. Next came a thick slice of society's ample cross-section of morons – people who just didn't have anything better to do with their time. They stood about slack-jawed and silent, as if witnessing the second coming. For some reason City bankers seemed to form a sizeable proportion of this group.

The third category didn't seem to be thinning at all; if anything they were increasing by the minute. From out of the arteries of the city, like pus from a festering wound, oozed the great British Press Corps. They came in all shapes and sizes, from all flavours of unpalatable rags. They came with TV camera crews and satellite uplinks, with notepads and pens, and most of all they came with common but divisive purpose – to get a jump on the competition. Only one of them was destined to succeed.

Adam noticed him first. It was his singularly odd behaviour which marked him out from the crowd. Seeing as the man was standing on a London street surrounded by news teams all trying to get better shots of a mountain of slowly rotting fish, this strangeness was strictly of the relative kind. Conspicuous amongst the milling journalists and TV technicians, not to mention hawkish agents driving hard bargains for exclusive interview rights to their pet eye witnesses, stood a smartly dressed man holding a pocket calculator and quietly sobbing to himself. He'd look down at the mounds of fish before him, tap a few numbers into the calculator, then indulge in a fresh bout of tears. Adam's curiosity was kick-started into life. Trying to remain casual, he strolled over.

'There, there old mate. No need to take it to heart. You some sort of aquarium manager?'

At first the man didn't seem to notice him at all. And when he did, it was only through a haze of tears. 'What you say? No, I'm no fish conservationist, though at the moment I almost wish I was.' A fresh bout of sobs ensued.

'If you don't mind me asking,' said Adam, beginning to get very curious indeed, 'just what line of work are you in?'

The man looked up at Adam with large bloodshot eyes, the sort exclusive to sick old Labradors and hard-drinking cabinet ministers. 'I am, or rather I was, a bookmaker's risk assessor. After this fiasco I think we can take it as read that I'm currently unemployed.'

Adam blinked. Sooner or later today was going to start making sense, but his best reckoning was that it wasn't going to start much before bedtime. With his unreality meter flickering way off the scale he pushed: 'But how can these fish cause you to lose your job?'

The man looked even more crestfallen than he had a few seconds ago, quite an achievement under the circumstances. His voice held a bitter twang of regret. 'It was my job to calculate odds for the loony bets. They've been getting really popular with the big M coming up. We recently covered a large wager involving a fall of fish – and I was the fool who advised on the odds. We're going to lose so much money, and I'm going to lose my job. I can't believe I could have been so short-sighted. I ask you, two thousand to one, what was I thinking of?' The tearful turf accountant covered his face with his hands.

For the first time since seeing his favourite TV weather girl that morning, Adam's mind went into creative overdrive. If he couldn't carve out a story from the fish themselves then here was the perfect opportunity. He could see the headlines now – 'BOOKIE BUST IN FISH FALL FIASCO! Another world exclusive by Adam MacArthur, all round good bloke.' Barely containing his excitement he drove in for the kill.

'Listen pal, we can't talk here. I know a quiet pub just round the corner. Let me buy you a nice little drink.'

Stone-Cold-Arse-Holed

The 'Nice Little Drink' is a finely honed journalistic ploy with a long and glorious history. In its classic form it involves taking your subject to a conveniently situated drinking establishment, getting them completely shit-faced, then waiting patiently for them to spill the beans. Adam was a past master of this particular manoeuvre.

On entering the dimly lit pub the reporter guided his guest, whose name he'd now gleaned between hysterical wails was Martin, to a secluded corner table. Adam then meandered over to the bar, taking the time to smile disarmingly at a couple of female business types locked deep in debate. They ignored him pointedly. Probably lesbians, he thought to himself smugly. Still, it was always worth a punt on the off-chance.

Taking into account that his guest had just received a nasty shock and that the weather had turned a bit chilly lately (he wouldn't want Martin to catch a cold at his moment of greatest trauma now, would he?), Adam ordered a pint of lager and a triple vodka.

Martin was well in the mood for drowning his sorrows. Adam handed him the vodka. Martin took the glass in both hands, downed its contents in one long gulp. With a grin, Adam pushed his pint across the table. 'Here, have mine, Martin. Think you're thirstier than me.'

Martin looked up, wiped a sleeve across his wet eyes. 'Thank you, that's most kind.'

'Oh it's . . . nothing.' He'd nearly said . . . *all in a day's work*, which might not have been conducive to further communication other than a swift fist in the face from a soon-to-be-dole-queuing risk assessor. Time for the nitty-gritty. 'So Martin, if you don't mind me asking, just how much money are we talking here?'

'Enough to get me fired,' Martin said hoarsely. 'The bet we covered will pay out close to half a million big ones.'

Adam whistled. 'Bad news. Any chance of finding out who placed the bet?'

Martin shook his head. 'Even if I knew, I couldn't tell you – client confidentiality and all that. Anyway, it's besides the point 'cos I don't know. It's all stored on our computer.' An edge had entered his voice.

Time to back off a bit. 'Fair enough, that's cool,' Adam reassured him. 'Let's not worry about that now. Why don't you tell me a bit about yourself?'

For the next four hours Adam listened to Martin's very boring life story. It's not that Martin had had an amazingly boring life, most people's experiences of everyday existence don't improve in the telling – the only person they're vaguely interesting to knows them only too well. Fortunately, most people realize this fundamental social truth and have the good manners to keep their preferred method of car-bonnet polishing to themselves. Unfortunately, alcohol loosens this inhibition faster than the sight of a freshly cleaned Ferrari loosens a pigeon's arse. Martin was no exception. It seemed all his problems could be traced back to an individual called 'Sharon', who, one night at a fifth form disco, had spurned his advances in favour of his best mate 'Gary'. Even Adam, a committed practitioner of finding the most outrageous links and coincidences to get a story, found it hard to conceive that Sharon's taste in teenage boys led to a career-wrecking fall of fish. But that was besides the point, Martin had made up his mind. And by the time Martin got to the stage where he was telling everybody and everything, including the half empty bottle of Smirnoff on the table, that he loved them 'very mush', Adam was beginning to lose patience. After a good deal of subtle probing, which mainly consisted of holding Martin by his lapels and shaking him violently, it turned out that he did have access to the database which held the name of the winner. As luck would have it Martin's flat was connected to his company's computer network, allowing him to work from home. He was almost certain to be traced as the source of any leak, but as Adam so tactfully pointed out Martin was almost certain to be fired anyway. So what did he have to lose? And there was always the fee for a story like this. It might just stretch his Giro for a month. Every little helps.

Even when on the brink of the greatest scoop of his career, Adam still knew how to bargain down to the bone.

Together In Paralytic Dreams

So it was that as the landlord locked up his pub at the end of the afternoon session, Adam dragged the semiconscious Martin from the bar. He found an address inside his wallet and retrieved his car keys from his vodka-stained trouser pocket. The flat was on the other side of town, so with Adam at the wheel and Martin flopping beside him at every right turn, they began their long journey through the heavy cross-town traffic. After an hour-long drive, made all the harder by that morning's unusual meteorological events, they finally arrived at a nondescript apartment block jutting like a cold finger into the bloodshot sky. With all the grace of Bulgaria's foremost female shotputter the two men stumbled up the stairs and into the bookie's simple home.

By the time he'd drunk three cups of coffee, Adam's host was at least able to sit up straight for periods longer than a nanosecond. With consummate professionalism, Adam endeavoured to press home this slender advantage. 'Come on Marty me old mucker, you can do it. All we need is one name. Just one little name – and maybe an address. You can do it for your old mate Adam can't ya.'

Martin's reply consisted of half a litre of second-hand vodka intermixed with his lunchtime spaghetti. As the torrent abated Adam fought back the urge to lash out. 'Come on Martin, just give us a name.'

'Uuuurgh?' Martin gurgled. 'No one likes me. I'm a failure. Just want to roll up 'n' die.'

Adam scraped a half-digested courgette off his lapel. 'No Marty, *I* like you and that's very, very important. But I'll like you a lot better if you just do this one little thing for me. Come on mate, come and sit by your computer.'

'Will Shrarun lurv me if I sit by my compuer?'

'Sharon will lurv you for evermore if you get the name for us. Look, she's sitting on your bed wearing not very much and telling you to help us out. Give me what I want and she'll give you what you want.'

Martin peered dubiously through his open bedroom door at his empty bed, but nonetheless Adam's words spurred him into life. Groggily, he staggered to his feet using Adam as a crutch.

'That's right, mate. No, not the bedroom, Sharon wants you to help me out first. Come and sit by your terminal – good, that's right. Now just get us the name.' This had better be worth it, Adam thought moodily, otherwise this ex-bookmaker would become an ex-ex-bookmaker very suddenly indeed. 'Okay Martin, how do you turn this baby on? No, wait – I got it, round the back here.'

The machine sprang to life. Martin did the reverse, keeling forward to rest his head against the nice, comfy computer screen. Adam gently pushed him back, positioned him securely against the back of his chair so that he couldn't fall over and pulled Martin's eyelids up till he was forced awake. 'What next?'

'Llggg on,' Martin mumbled.

'Can you manage big fella? No, use your fingers not your lips – that's better.'

Martin's PC might have been a clapped-out Robin Reliant parked in a lay-by off a side road of the Information Superhighway, but at least it was on the road. His company had been one of the first to offer a comprehensive programme of terminal installations in the homes of its middle managers. These allowed hard-working executives to do much of their work from the comfort of their front rooms, enabling them to access company databases and communicate instantly with the thousands of high-street betting shops.

Why this massive investment in new technology? Was it to allow employees an extra half hour in bed? No chance. Was it to give their stressed out executives the opportunity to spend endless hours locating the Net's most dubious sites for instant relief all on the sparkling new machines? Less chance than none at all (the PCs being blocked to all adult sites considered more than harmless fun by the Board of Directors who had spent a month's strenuous road-testing the most unsuitable links themselves for the good of company morale and productivity). No, the reason the company splashed out the cash was that they knew this new way of working got more done, by less people, in less time, and they didn't have to fork out for a coffee machine.

The attractions of the home/office of the future had been known for some time to any organization which had to meet a wage bill. It had become the semi-mythical holy grail of office managers handling a budget so small it couldn't buy a pencil from a car boot sale. Basically, an employee sitting at home had no one to chat to, took up no valuable floor space, required no heating or light and didn't guzzle tea like a dehydrated grandad. This dispersal also had more sinister aspects. Since all information was passed electronically it was far easier to keep tabs on workers throughout the day. If in a ten-minute period a key wasn't pressed or a mouse wasn't moved the fact would show up on the graphs of the newly formed 'Productivity Analysis Police'. Thanks to the wonders of electronic mail a redundancy notice would be whizzing down the wires before you could say, 'Low Wage Service Sector Economy'.

It was like building a tenement block bang in the middle of the Global Village – with none of the lifts working.

Another hour brought Martin and Adam finally into the Current Betting Database.

'Need to crsss refrenss against FISH, FALLS OF.' Adam was doing the typing, Martin was slumped by his side telling him what to type. It wasn't quick but they were getting there. After setting out the commands Adam looked to his host for confirmation, but the inebriated bookie had passed out once again. Adam held his breath as he hit the Return key. After a brief pause as electrons raced down phone lines like supercharged tadpoles, the screen flickered and a page of text appeared.

There was only one name on it, and it came complete with a west London address. Adam gave a whoop of joy and made a surprisingly successful attempt at giving himself a high five.

'The lucky bastard,' he declared to the world, though not Martin who was curled up foetally on the floor and sucking his thumb, 'is Professor Michael D. Nostrus.'

FOUR

But know this, in the last days critical times hard to deal with will be here.
Timothy II 3:1

Waiting For The Big One

October 16th, 1999 was the day that went down in economic history as Smokers'-Lung Friday. There had been so many crashes, bumps, blips, and slumps over the past few years that the financial press had run out of suitable adjectives with which to describe them . . . 'Murky Monday', 'Grey Thursday', 'Jet-Black Saturday' (when brokers had put in a massive overtime session in a vain attempt to recover from the chaos of 'Turbid Tuesday'), and of course the infamous, 'Noticeable-Absence-of-Light Wednesday'.

But SLF, as it came to be known, was different. SLF was the Big One, the Krakatoa of market eruptions.

Where did all the money go? Much of it went on overtime pay to the New York street cleaners whose job it was to hose down the blood-stained sidewalks of Wall Street, after hundreds of merchant bankers once again confirmed Newton's First Law of Gravity: don't jump out of a very tall building if there's something hard at the bottom. But not even this princely sum could account for the trillions wiped off shares in a matter of seconds on that fateful day. The story behind the final resting place of all those little coloured pieces of paper was far simpler and at the same time far more profound. The money had never existed in the first place, at least not in physical form. It had been held in the hearts and minds of mankind, and in the random access memories of their computers. Thus it was transient, subject to the eddy of electron and the vagaries of human emotion – and now it was all gone, lost like a fart in a jacuzzi.

The great house of cards that was the World Financial System had trust at its foundation – the surety that you could get your money out when you wanted it. Unless, of course, everyone wanted it at the same time. The effects of a sudden loss of confidence had been less severe back in the days when the fastest form of communication was the office boy's legs, but now everything was computerized. Dealers simply oversaw the Expert Systems which did the buying and selling and were all programmed along similar lines. When one spotted a run on a certain group of shares it started selling its stock faster than plutonium potatoes at a harvest festival for international arms dealers. The result: a grossly unstable system, subject to the sorts of swells and surges that could have inspired the Beach Boys to strike up a tune.

So when one zealous Sydney stockbroker overheard an influential colleague comment: 'Remind me not to buy any more coffee,' he raced back to his terminal and plunged the Brazilian economy into free fall without staying around to hear the rest of the sentence: 'coz my wife got two jars this month by accident. Can you believe it?'

That was all it took. By the time the other markets had snapped on their red braces, drunk their first cups of increasingly competitively priced instant and raced to work in their BMWs, it was too late.

As Mike sat watching the breakfast news reports he found it hard to believe people were surprised by this sort of thing anymore. Perpetual financial chaos seemed to be the one feature of contemporary life you didn't have to be a prophet to predict. This crash was large enough to stunt the Developed World's growth for years to come – that's if there was going to be any Developed World, or years for that matter, left – a subject on which Mike was still reserving judgement. If only the effects could be limited to those who'd caused this catastrophe. The perpetrators deserved whatever they got in Mike's book. Unfortunately, things were never that simple. As he got up to switch off his TV the Professor reflected sadly that the Third World had just got a whole lot thirder.

Even allowing for his pensive frame of mind Mike didn't look like a man who'd recently won the best part of half a million pounds. Standing in his flat, with a bacon sandwich and a cup of very hot sweet tea, he looked more like a kindly granddad than an international insurance fraudster and ruthless professional gambler. There were no buckets of champagne in evidence, no chorus girls posing for the cameras, no press headlines screaming – PISCINE PREDICTING PROF SAYS 'IT CHANGED MY LIFE'. Publicity was the last thing Mike desired; he wanted it less than he wanted having his tonsils removed by Vlad the Impaler with only half a glass of murky lemonade as a local anaesthetic.

He had collected his cheque the previous afternoon, straight after reports of the fish fall had come flooding in. The betting firm had been happy to comply with his request for privacy – they had no desire to make it common knowledge they'd just covered a huge loss. Mike had raced home and placed his winnings under his bed for safekeeping. Soon they would be converted into assets of a firmer nature – the sort that repelled bullets and came in a nifty, drab olive colour scheme.

Momentarily, Mike allowed himself an iota of concern over his Pyramid insurance policy. He was an optimist by nature but a pessimist by experience. If Kestrel Alliance folded there was nothing he could do about it, so why worry? The insurance policy was the only way he had come up with to make money from the disappearance, so he might as well wait and see what panned out. If the ruse didn't pay off it wouldn't cripple his plans – he still had more fingers in more pies than Sweeney Todd's formerly six-fingered cousin Sidney.

Conscientious as ever, Mike had filled his wastepaper bin with early drafts of a letter he'd sketched out the night before. The finished document simply required his signature to begin the lengthy process of claiming his money from the insurers. Then of course there was the minor matter of The Great Pyramid of Cheops obliging and sailing off into the Saharan sunset, or doing whatever it was departing pyramids do.

Banishing this disturbing image from his mind Mike looked at the envelope next to his plate. This was one piece of mail that didn't have to wait. It was addressed to the college and contained his notice of resignation. Why hadn't he done this earlier? Fifteen years was too long to spend in any job, even for someone on his timescale. Despite the circumstances, he found himself looking forward to a change of scene. It had been too long since he last felt that tingle down the spine, that breathless quickening of the pulse.

He was excited. He'd often observed over the years that he never felt more alive than when he was about to start running for his life.

Cool For Cats

Just then Aristotle sauntered into the room. With a flick of his long luxurious tail he ran across the floor, jumped onto Mike's lap and made it known he was not pleased at the absence of bacon.

'Sorry, old son.' Mike rubbed the sensitive spot behind Aristotle's ears. 'Don't I feed you enough or is it just attention you're after?'

The cat looked up at him balefully and said: *Despite*

what you apes seem to think, our lives do not revolve around the search for food and affection. The day I can no longer live without the puerile pamperings of one of you hairless monkeys is the day I pack in the cat-nip and put my paws in the air for the last time.

The words bypassed the space around Aristotle's head, took a little known shortcut through a place with way too many dimensions, pausing only to thumb a nose at the laws of conventional physics, before finally forming themselves in Mike's mind unbidden.

'My my, didn't we fall out of the basket the wrong side this morning? Maybe a full stomach will improve your mood.' Mike got up to fix breakfast, while Aristotle slalomed between his legs in a valiant attempt to break the old man's neck.

Over the years Mike had become used to his companion's moods. The cat was vain, supercilious, unbearably aloof, a terminal cat-nip addict and generally hell to live with – and they were just his good points. Most cat owners would be shocked to peek inside little kittie's brain – Mike knew Aristotle's only too well. To the usual stresses of feline/human cohabitation was added the strain of instantaneous two-way communication.

'Will his lordship lower himself to tuna-flavoured Kito-Chunks this fine morn?'

I ate better while I sojourned with the lice-ridden whores of fourteenth-century Lisbon, said the cat, wolfing the meat down like a lion in lambing season.

Mike smiled as he rubbed his old friend's back affectionately. The animal was a gigantic yet sleek ginger-and-white tom. A physique which matched his attitude – robust. When Aristotle went at them full tilt, adult timber wolves had been known to run for the hills. His muscled shoulders and paws akimbo stance would put you in mind of a bull-dog with a bad attitude – and one with razor-blade claws at that.

Mike and Aristotle had been companions for a long time, a very long time. Mike may have been old in human terms but Aristotle was ancient by cat standards. Despite this, the creature carried his years well. The only tell-tale signs of his extraordinary age were a few grey hairs on his pelt, a couple of nicks in his mobile, radar-dish ears, and the sort of ingrained cynicism that came from observing humanity close up for far too long.

They had first met when Mike was only a boy, back in a side street in the Jewish quarter of mediaeval Avignon. The regal animal had been sitting patiently in an alley-way, as if waiting for Mike to show up. The creature had fixed him with an inscrutable feline stare, said: *Hey kid, how'd you like me to show you a few tricks*, then followed the young Michael home. They had been companions ever since.

Wherever Mike had travelled Aristotle went too. The cat had accompanied Mike on his silk trading trips to China. He had inflicted genocide on the vicious rat population aboard the Caribbean privateer Mike had captained for a time[1]. He had slept in Mike's blanket on the frozen retreat from Moscow in Napoleon's shattered army. And to this day, in the Mississippi Valley, you might still hear tell of the laconic river boat gambler and his lucky ginger tom. In short, this was one well-travelled cat.

Going Underground

There was one place, however, that even Aristotle hadn't visited. It was a location colloquially known as DOWN THERE, at the very mention of which cowering peasants

---

1 Captain Whitebeard – scourge of the Spanish Main. Famed far and wide for having the right number of eyes/hands/feet and for the ginger tomcat which sat on his shoulder instead of the ubiquitous parrot.

would go into a frenzy of salt flinging and horse-shoe rubbing.

It was down deep. Past the worms and the tree roots, past the fossils put there by mischievous gods to confuse archaeologists, a group for whom they felt unbridled contempt. Past even that special Circle of Hell reserved for people who snog their friends then can't bring themselves to speak to them ever again. It was Infernity Central, the A1 Penthouse Suite in the Hotel of Lost Souls, and what's more once you'd moved in you couldn't get decent TV reception ever again.

This particular place was currently the venue of a high-level meeting, which isn't to say the participants were any nearer the surface. DOWN THERE the usual spatial dimensions did not apply. FORWARD was twisted around UP, which doubled back on itself in a fit of pique. RIGHT did an inverted barrel roll around DOWN, and, after wrapping itself twice around LEFT, shot off into infinity. BACKWARDS just gave up on trying to get a look-in and went off to do its own thing. If some bright young origami expert was ever able to build a model of this arrangement it would have sling-shotted him into another dimension.

Somehow denying the laws of geometry, the members of the meeting had gathered like a gangrenous infection.

'Right, before we start – drinks. Tea? Coffee? Liquid nitrogen on the rocks anybody?' The speaker was known around these parts as Young Nick. He was the gathering's genial host and undisputed Prince of Hell. The other two entities at the meeting declined his offer politely as best their idiosyncratic anatomies would allow.

Nick thumbed the intercom on his desk with one satanically curved fingernail. 'I'll have my usual please Helen. Oh – and bring in a plate of chocolate digestives if you'd be so kind. The Hob-nobs if there are any left.'

The office they sat in was plushly furnished. Great

bookcases covered two walls, leather-bound tomes reaching up to the distant ceiling. Nick lounged in front of his huge leather-topped desk, on his red leather swivel chair, somehow managing to move about without making it squeak. This absence of sound was perhaps the most disconcerting aspect of the entire place. The leathery motif was carried over to the neatly folded pair of wings resting in an umbrella rack by the vast leather-padded door.

'They're a bugger to sit down in,' explained Nick seeing his guests enquiring glances. 'I just pop them on for official business. Life's a bitch ain't she? But then I expect you two know that don't you?' His two guests nodded urgently. It wasn't every day they were summoned to a meeting with the boss and immediate agreement to all questions seemed the safest policy.

The dim reaches of the room contained an uncomfortable-looking leather settee, numerous potted plants, a large open fire and a tropical fish tank containing something part amphibian, part insect which sprouted a forest of legs and antennae that twitched at a frequency too high for the human eye to follow – not that humans ever got close enough to take a look. The carpet was deep and red (so as not to show the stains, it was said). The office had been decorated this way since time immemorial, Nick's predecessor's reverence for tradition being surpassed only by his hatred for interior designers. But things were set to change.

Almost apologetically, the new Lucifer peered about him. 'It's so depressingly . . . well, *dark* for want of a better word. First chance, I'll get the decorators in. There are going to be some changes around here, I can tell you now. We've got to introduce some modern work practices or we're in for drastic corporate downsizing: Total Quality Management, Time and Motion Studies, get on the Internet – that sort of thing.'

His two guests, whose idea of corporate downsizing combined with a Time and Motion Study involved watching the Chairman of ICI being turned on a spit through a vat of sulphuric acid, nodded all their heads in agreement.

The truth was that despite a radically different taste in wallpaper, the current Prince of Lies was dedicated to running the family business with the same care and attention to detail that his old dad had shown whilst cradling it lovingly between his own callused hands.

Before Nick could confide in his accomplices any further Helen slithered in carrying an ornate silver tray. It held a plate of neatly arranged Hob-nobs and a laboratory jar containing a bubbling blue liquid with two straws and a small paper parasol balanced on the rim.

'Thank you my dear,' Nick said as his secretary left the room with a squelch. Settling back into his immense chair, he nibbled on a biscuit and eyed his two employees.

'I suppose you're wondering why I've brought you here?' he asked, in the same tone of voice that an old bald guy with one eye and a fluffy white cat might say: 'Do not underestimate me, Mr Bond.'

Fixing them with a glare that could, and often did, shatter crockery, he went on. 'No sense in waiting for an anwer from you two. You're not exactly the sharpest tools left in my torture cupboard are you? Nevertheless, I have a very important mission for you.'

Dante Was An Optimist

The names of Young Nick's nervous guests were Guttlehog and Rubicante, both lowly field operatives for Forces of Darkness Plc.

In fact, Guttlehog's full title was 'Junior Assistant High Demon (2nd Class), Lord of the Warthogs and Arch-fiend of Washing Machine Motors'. Considering his station, he looked impressive, though his huge fur collar tended to wilt in strong heat, and his scorpion tail could be a bugger in the shower. The only part of his anatomy that bore any relation to his patron animal was his head. Which also had its drawbacks.

'Ve exhisht to sherve great Mashter,' he just about managed to say, creating a great cloud of vaporized saliva in the process. Tusks were great for scaring peasants shitless, but clear speech was another matter.

His companion could only agree. Rubicante possessed a far broader brief than his associate. His CV read 'Fire Demon', but then so did just about everyone else's around these parts. He looked like the product of a crazed design meeting between Johnny Morris and Aleister Crowley. Rubicante had the head of a locust and the ability to strip a cornfield in two minutes flat. Why, he'd often wondered as he chomped his way through yet another fieldful of shredded wheat, couldn't they be given useful anatomical accessories, like a bottle opener finger or a clock radio shoulder hump?

Nick glowered at Guttlehog's interruption. Somewhere far above a small child fell off her bicycle, badly skinning her knees. 'As I was saying. The reason you've been called before me is . . . A Number 47.'

'A Number Worty-Shevern Alva!' Guttlehog's vast bulk lifted several feet into the air with excitement. 'Ish'nt that vhere ve[1] ride in on the north wind, screaching like banshees and . . .'

'No no,' said Nick, rapidly losing patience, 'a Number 47 is a precision assassination. One where we ride in like butterflies on a night breeze, rip the living heart from our intended target, then flutter out again without so much as a hair out of place – apart from those on our victim's chest.'

---

1 I think you get the picture by now. Satansoft Translatomatic™ software up and running.

'Oh, that type of Number Forty-Seven. I was confusing it with the Sixteen series –'[1]

Nick ignored him pointedly. 'And you know who we aren't at home to on this sort of mission don't you?' He glowered. Guttlehog's forehead creased like colliding continents as he strained to recall the Standing Field Orders. Nick wasn't prepared to wait for the answer. 'We aren't at home to Mr and Mrs Collateral Damage are we? Or their close personal friend, Mr Cock-The-Whole-Thing-Up-Before-We-Even-Get-Started. If we are, we can expect to be banished to the very worst of our last remaining outposts Up Top. We can start packing our bags for a summer season touring Britain's seaside resorts doing *variety*, can't we? Get this wrong and the time will come when we shudder at the very mention of Bournemouth pier. Got it?'

As Nick let this dire threat sink in, he considered his options. He wasn't so much scraping the bottom of the barrel here as digging down to the bedrock. But then he had no choice. He grimaced and pressed on. 'As I'm sure you know, for the past several hundred years Head Office has been terribly over-staffed. Since the Middle Ages opportunities Top Side have been strictly limited. In fact, we've had quite an unemployment problem. You can't just pension off a Demon now, can you? More's the pity. Anyway, I'm sure even you've noticed the increased comings and goings recently. Suddenly, there's hardly enough cold bodies to fill the rotas, would you believe?

'Well it's all hands, paws, tentacles and mandibles on

---

1 *Hades Field Manual* V1.1 (As of October 1597AD)

1–13 General hauntings.

14–22 Mass murder

23–26 Rape

27–38 Pillage

39–44 Plunder

45–53 Precision assassinations

54–216 Supermarket openings and promotional appearances.

deck from now on, even yours. Because this is it, boys. The Last Battle is a-coming. The Ultimate Penalty Shoot-Out At The End Of Time. And whoever wins gets the lot.' He paused to allow his words to filter through centuries of built-up stupidity. 'It's in the interests of both us and *the opposition* that those unfortunate worms currently inhabiting the battlefield don't become aware of this fact. But don't get too full of yourselves, I'm only using you because we're so short of operatives. I've just been doing the work rosters and you're all that's left.' This wasn't entirely true, but there was no way Nick was sending Brillocrank – 1st Reserve Lesser Demon of Kitchen Cleaning Accessories – on a mission like this.

'Ssso, who isss the target Massster?' asked Rubicante, having a spot of resonance feedback in his gigantic thorax.[1]

'Well . . . A certain human has somehow become aware of the approaching Apocalypse. It's imperative that this information does not leak to the population at large. I've been on the hotline to my opposite number upstairs and, unsurprisingly, he's "agreed" to let us handle the situation. He always chickens out of the dirty work.

'I needn't tell you how important it is that we deal with this efficiently. Our professional pride is at stake.' Nick drew some comfort from the looks of terror on their faces. 'I want this human terminated with extreme prejudice. Imagine he's JFK and you're that Bolivian vice girl hired by the Pope.[2] Do I make myself clear?'

'Yes Master,' Guttlehog and Rubicante answered in unison.

'See Beelzebub on your way out for details and kit.' Nick gave them a dismissive wave of one taloned hand. 'Oh, and boys,' he called as they reached the door, 'I'll be very

---

1 Let's see if this thing can multitask.

2 For a full explanation see Appendix B.

unhappy if I have to pull Alastor off the Daytime TV Task Force to help you out. I'm sure he would too: I hear he's having a whale of a time.'

Guttlehog and Rubicante paled at the very mention of the Chief Executioner of Hell. It was said he did things with cocktail sticks that would make Jack the Ripper nauseous. With this worrying thought they hurried from the office.

Moments later, Beelzebub materialized in a puff of green smoke. He'd been listening to the conversation and now addressed his boss with concern. 'Are you sure they're up to it Chief? They strike me as even more hopeless than that agent we managed to install in the White House.'

Nick sighed. 'I know Zeb, but it was either them or Sonylante, The Spirit Of Temporarily Mislaid Video Remote Controls.'

Back To The Wild Frontier

Mike had plenty of other bets and policies waiting for fruition but his first big win would allow him to begin the second phase of his plan. Open in front of him was a large-scale road atlas of the British Isles. He had a rough idea of where the safest places would be, now all he needed were the details.

'There you go Aristo.' He pointed triumphantly at a barren area on the map. 'Looks like a safe bet. It's way above sea level, far from centres of population and not even a nuclear power station downwind. I think we've cracked it. They say Gwynedd is beautiful this time of year as well.'

The cat wasn't so impressed. *Wonderful. The only thing more stupid than a sheep is a Welsh sheep. And the only thing more stupid than a Welsh sheep is a Welsh local. And I hate mountains, bad for the complexion. They should be steam-rollered.*

'You'll love it when we get there,' Mike assured him. He placed the atlas on top of his open travel bag. He wasn't planning on leaving for a few days yet, but centuries of experience had taught him to think ahead.

He was about to clear away the breakfast things when the doorbell went. His heart beating, Mike silently checked the security peephole. After assuring himself his visitors weren't a pair of retro-evolved turf accountants he opened the door.

There in the hallway, looking rather preoccupied, stood an angelic figure with a frown. Deborah gave a sharp smile as she shifted distractedly from foot to foot. Mike hid his bewilderment and beamed back.

'Hello, my dear. This is a pleasant surprise. Can I invite you in for tea?'

Deborah was in no mood for niceties. 'Let's cut the crap, Professor Nostrus. Are you going to tell me what the hell is going on? How did you know about the Lottery? You didn't mention UFOs last time we met – are they linked? This is getting too much to take.'

Mike shook his head. 'I think you'd better come in.'

Deborah's jaw barely slowed down as she stumbled forward. 'You can hardly blame me for the way I reacted yesterday.'

'Who's blaming?' Mike soothed.

'I mean, it's not the sort of news a girl hears every day. This time I want the real answers, and none of that five-hundred-year-old prophet crap.'

Mike held up a reassuring hand. 'No need to explain, my dear. You were just worried that your favourite geriatric had flipped his lid. Let me assure you that there's nothing at all to worry about, at least not on that score. Why don't you make yourself at home while I put the kettle on.'

As Deborah sat down on a sofa that seemed to stretch the entire length of the living room she took the chance to look around. There were relics from just about every culture she could think of, and plenty she couldn't. One wall held a vast collection of gruesome war masks and a stuffed duck-billed platypus. There were thousands of books, covering every conceivable subject including titles like *Unarmed Combat for Beginners*, *The "Which?" Bumper Book of Bomb Shelters*, *Goat Rearing Made Simple*, and *Card Games for the Lonely*. They were scattered around the place in vast piles and wedged on, against and under a chaotic series of shelves.

Despite the bewildering clutter, Deborah's attention was almost immediately drawn to a large ginger tom sitting on an easy chair in the opposite corner. The animal looked at her in a most disconcerting manner. Its large, amber eyes seemed to be stripping her to her soul. 'Nice cat,' she called out, 'what's its name?'

'Him? That's Aristotle. We've been together quite a while,' said Mike, returning with a loaded tray.

'Cute. You named him after the Greek guy right?'

'Probably the other way around, actually.' Mike sat down and started pouring the drinks.

Deborah had had enough of this cryptic conversation. 'Look, Professor Nostrus . . .'

'Please my dear, call me Mike.'

'Mike – this isn't easy for me to say. I've seen things in the past few days that have made me doubt my sanity. You somehow knew about those lottery numbers didn't you? I keep coming back to that conversation we had in your office.'

'I'm glad to hear it. Mature reflection is so rare in the young these days.'

'Believe me, I've experienced very little mature reflection over the past forty-eight hours. Mike, what on earth is going on? Either fill me in or phone the funny farm right away. At least a nice padded cell might protect me from myself.'

'I wish I could give you a different answer my dear, but

I think I covered most of the pertinent points back in my office. I wasn't exaggerating with my *Book of Revelations*-style revelations.'

'And you stand by your five-hundred-year-old prophet story?'

'Yep. Hopefully soon-to-be-six-hundred-year-old prophet.'

'Fine – okay – fine. I suppose that's it then. I'm off to hand myself in to the relevant authorities. Do you know the number for Schizophrenics Anonymous? Maybe if you came along with me, we could get a bulk discount – four for the price of two.'

He took her hand gently in his. 'I'm rather afraid you'll find a long, long queue.'

Suddenly, the conversation was joined by a third party.

Oh, but if mere insanity was the extent of his personal problems! You've got it easy girl. You only work with him, I've got to live with the loopy old coot.

Deborah's eyes went wide. 'Who said that?' she cried. She jerked her hand out of Mike's, sending her teacup skidding across the floor.

Mike's heart jumped. He'd heard Aristotle's mental voice quite clearly as usual, but had what he thought just happened really happened?

'You just threw your voice!' accused Deborah. 'As if I need stupid bloody parlour tricks to impress me after what I've seen!' She felt her voice cracking, tears coming.

'I assure you my dear, I didn't throw my voice. But if you're capable of hearing what I just did, it becomes all the more important that we talk. Please, don't ignore this. The sooner you accept what your senses are telling you, the easier this is going to be for all of us. There's a lot to get through.'

Deborah stood up, opened her mouth and looked for a while as if she was going to say something that would make sense of it all. Gradually, this expression faded.

Sit down and listen, Deborah.

This time she was ready. Deborah was paying attention to the voice. With a sudden jolt of understanding that physically threw her off balance she realized that she wasn't hearing the voice with her ears at all. It was coming from inside her mind. Very slowly, as if any sudden movement could cause her head to explode, Deborah turned and looked at Aristotle.

The cat simply stared back as cats do. Then he jumped down from his chair, ambled across the room with a relaxed grace and climbed onto the coffee table in front of them. When the animal had steadied himself he looked from Deborah to Mike then back again.

Well old man, this is a turn-up. Are you going to break the good news or am I?

Now it was Mike's turn to look concerned. 'Tell me my dear, just to get everything out in the open, what is it you believe to be going on here?'

'Mike,' Deborah began very slowly, all the while hoping that something would happen to prove her wrong, 'I think your cat's talking to me telepathically.'

'Well isn't that the most amazing thing.' Mike's smile lit up the room. 'Perhaps now we can get down to business.'

It's The End Of The World As We Know It

Ten minutes later things were looking pretty grim, at least from Deborah's point of view. She briefly entertained the thought of running from the building screaming, but that wasn't in her nature. She no more ran from trouble than three-week-old milk ran from the carton. After their previous meeting she had begun to doubt Mike's sanity, now she realized he was no more crazy than she was. The possibility that they were both sane was even less attractive. Still, if you hallucinated a ten-ton truck thundering towards you, best get out of the way. You never knew when you'd get splattered on a psychosomatic front bumper. In the absence of any better explanations she'd just have to accept what Mike and Aristotle were telling her.

'So that's it. There's nothing we can do? It's the end of the world?'

Mike took a long sip of tea. 'Not exactly. If there were no hope, I'd be entrenched in a public house right now spending my sudden windfall in a valiant attempt to forget my problems. What we need is a safe port of call for the coming storm. Suitably equipped, we can surf out this tsunami and come out the other side whistling "Good Vibrations". And I've already got a fair idea of a good spot for our bolt-hole.'

'But if the world's going to end, what's the point? Nowhere on this rock is going to be safe if we get hit by a giant meteor, or gobbled up by some ravenous starbeast from the outer edges of the galaxy.'

Mike smiled patiently. 'I think you've been watching too many fifties B-Movies, young Deborah. I've been in this business a very long time. Forgive me, but I've got used to using a rather apocalyptic turn of phrase. I'm pretty sure the *entire* planet won't be destroyed. You have to account for the change in meaning of words since my day. "World" can mean a good deal more than just this planet, it can mean culture, civilization, our current way of looking at things.'

Human culture, ha! Isn't that an oxymoron? Aristotle had found a prominent perch between them on the arm of an easy chair.

Mike ignored him. 'You have to remember that I'm used to playing to an audience. One had to . . . you know . . . spice it up a bit. It was pure showbiz back in those days. Make 'em laugh, make 'em cry, but most of all make them believe that when they're gone the poor sods left are going to have no fun at all.'

Deborah watched Mike go all misty eyed. If this was some schizophrenic delusion, it went way deep. Despite her doubts, she found the idea of a shift in the world's power structure a little easier to swallow than a big flashing GAME OVER for all humanity. 'Shouldn't you take this theory of yours to the authorities?' she asked. 'Don't you have a duty to warn people?'

'My dear, what slightest bit of good do you think that would do?'

'Well, I'm sure the government has contingency plans, evacuation procedures, that sort of thing. They don't want people to get hurt. It's just a case of taking what you've got to the very top.'

Mike shook his head sadly. Oh to be young again and free from five hundred years of fossilized cynicism. 'Deborah, if I've learnt one thing over the course of my life it's that people only believe what they want to believe. Do you really think for one minute that the arrogant arseholes who run our lives would be any more accommodating? Believe me, I know only too well where publicity can get you, and there's not even a very nice view. If we let this cat out of the bag it's likely to stain the carpet. No offence, Aristo.'

None taken, I'm sure.

Deborah sat and thought for a long while. 'So, accepting for the moment that I am perfectly sane, that you have become very rich predicting showers of fish, and that this may or may not be the start of a chain of events leading to you-know-what, of which you say the next will be some famous Egyptian monuments going walkabout – what do you do now?'

Mike formed a steeple with his fingers. 'We-ell . . . I have been planning a little sightseeing tour. Want to come househunting?'

Only The Crumbliest, Flakiest Currency

That evening, as Deborah and her housemates crowded around their black and white TV on the kitchen table,

Mike briefly tuned in himself. She'd wanted first-hand, in-your-face proof of his powers, so he'd given it to her. Told her what was going to be on the news that night, happening live, so he couldn't have found out sneakily.

It was with an air of detached professional interest that he watched as the flustered officials from the Bank of England tried in vain to explain what could possibly have gone wrong. Not an easy task. As the Governor floundered before the world's media, the slow trickle of thick brown fluid that seeped out of the half open vault behind him bore testament to his outlandish claims. It seemed that sometime during the early evening Britain's vaulted reserves of European Currency Units, held ready for the day when we finally joined our continental cousins in glorious economic union, had somehow, inexplicably, metamorphosed into chocolate money.

Next morning as Mike hefted his travel bag down the apartment steps to his battered car, and Aristotle did his cheerful best to lend a paw, they got a pleasant if not totally unexpected surprise. Standing at the kerb with her obligatory student rucksack packed and ready, Deborah beamed back at them.

'Well, good morning boys,' Deborah greeted them, 'what are we waiting for?'

Throwing It All Away

Several hours later Adam sat eating lunch in the pleasant tree-lined street outside Mike's flat.

He was sitting in his brand new Japanese sports car – a car designed for the man who wanted a sports car but didn't quite have the readies ready; a car for the man who liked to wear the odd gold chain or six. The vehicle was made mainly of plastic and was hung lower to the ground than a gopher's gonads. It also bore a striking resemblance to a rather intimate part of its owner's anatomy – small, off-white, painfully ugly to look at and with a nasty habit of failing to start just when he needed it most. Despite these shortcomings, Adam loved it with a passion he normally reserved for televised snooker, take-away food and girls who felt claustrophobic in underwear. The main focus of this unconditional love was the fact that the electronic displays exactly matched the design of his wrist-crippling digital watch, which he was currently gazing at for the third time in fifteen minutes.

Whoever this Nostrus guy was, he wasn't at home to visitors. Repeated ringings of the foyer intercom system had established that soon after Adam's arrival. Knowing instinctively that he had to follow up on the fish fall story while it was still fresh in the public's nostrils, Adam had settled in for the duration.

He finished his hamburger and, after letting out a belch which would have done Moby Dick proud, carefully placed its cardboard container in the paper carrier bag, then wondered why he bothered. The car's interior already smelt like a mid-August abattoir. With hope springing eternal, unlike the world's oil supplies, he rolled down the window to breath in the refreshing London air.

Or rather he attempted to roll it down. In this vehicle things were rarely that simple. Accidentally, he thumbed a small joystick controller set close to the window-mode selector. This had the unfortunate effect of throwing the car's myriad air-flow spoilers out of the carefully calculated alignment that Adam had spent most of the previous weekend programming. With a quiet whirring a horribly ugly piece of white plastic rose from the horribly ugly white plastic bonnet, prompting howls of rage from the young reporter. Once he'd done his best to set things straight, Adam at last located the correct, and unnecessarily minuscule, switch. But even playing with the electric windows did little to lift his mood of growing despair. The entire incident had brought back painful memories of the frustrating hours he'd spent studying the car's weighty manuals in an attempt to find the ashtrays. Those cunning devils from the land of the rising sun might have been cruel to our boys in the war, he thought to himself, but they certainly knew how to make cars, or at least they knew how to give you complete control of your vehicle – right down to the refractive index of the windscreen glass.

It was whilst Adam was speculating on such weighty matters that he got his second life-changing event in twenty-four hours. First, the scoop of the century, then:

'How ya doing, me old mate?' came a cheerful voice from somewhere close to his left ear.

Presumably it had been a rhetorical question because what Adam was doing was very busily jumping out of his skin.

'Aaaaah!' he shouted. 'Who said that? Who said that?'

The voice fell silent as the reporter hurriedly checked the back seat for unwanted visitors, but the car was empty. It wasn't as if there were many places to hide. If you'd wanted to swing a cat in this car then it would have had to have been a very small kitten. The only possible source of the voice, Adam was loathe to contemplate. His car was talking to him?

'Na, I ain't your car. A bit closer to home than that.' The tone was disturbingly familiar.

With a shudder, Adam added mindreading to his vehicle's list of unspecified design features. 'Then . . . who are you?' he asked with a mounting sense of unreality.

The voice chuckled in a way that suggested specialist magazines in brown paper bags. 'I'm here to give you a helping hand. If you want to get some dirt on Nostrus why not take a walk round the back? It's amazing what you can find if you look in the right places.'

'But . . . but why are you telling me this?'

The voice seemed to pause. 'Let's just say I'm an

acquaintance from your past, and I don't mind doin' me friends a favour every now and then. Gotta be off now, don't forget to take that walk.' Then that chuckle again, fading off into the distance like some sex-starved hyena.

Adam put his head in his hands. He'd been working much too hard lately. The pressures of being such a young, successful, talented, not to mention handsome, newshound were finally getting to him. When you put it like that it almost sounded heroic. Now that he came to think of it almost all the old grizzled reporters he had ever known had possessed more than a slice of madness pie on their plates. It came with the territory.

Feeling better about himself than he had done in a long while, Adam gave an insane giggle. Then, perhaps for the first time since deciding not to proposition his fifth-form English teacher, he came up with a sensible idea. It was being cooped up in his much-prized vehicle that was doing this to him. Understandable really. The car was so responsive it *did* almost seem to have a life of its own sometimes – it just wasn't usually in the habit of coming up with helpful suggestions. With a relieved grin, Adam set about locating the small but perfectly formed door handle and got out.

Mike's apartment stood in a wide, tree-lined avenue, the sort of place you'd expect to find TV executives or 2CV-driving architects rubbing corduroy-clad shoulders with ambitious young art critics. Somehow, Adam didn't get the impression this was going to be a rags-to-riches story as he gazed up to the first-floor windows. There was no doubt that this was the address Martin had given him. Thinking what the hell, go with your instincts, he made his way round the back.

The smart block backed onto a rather-less-than-smart back lane. As Adam purposefully strolled up the alleyway he did his best to identify which of the rear windows belonged to his target's flat. He wasn't exactly sure what he was looking for. He gazed around for something worth investigating – not many options . . . apart, perhaps, from a pile of bin bags stacked on the rear forecourt. The local cat population had done its best to destroy them, scattering debris across the tarmac. Adam's attention was drawn to a trail of stained white sheets of paper escaping from the bottom of one bag in particular. Curiosity getting the better of his sense of smell, he bent down to retrieve a typed page of A4. It appeared to be a letter.

As he read it his expression went through a remarkable transformation. Over the course of several seconds his boyish face went from Sunday Morning TV mode to its Small War in Previously Unheard-of Country setting, through finally to its Female Full Contact Naked Karate World Championships ogle. The document he held in his trembling hands seemed to be a rough version of a letter from Nostrus to an insurance company. What was more, it seemed to be making an advance claim on some sort of policy dealing with the Egyptian Pyramids.

For a long moment Adam felt quite faint, and his condition had nothing to do with the putrid stench emanating all about him. When he'd steadied himself he took a deep breath and dived in amongst the rotting garbage to hunt for further evidence. This was shaping up to be one story well worth getting the dirt on.

FIVE

The sons of Genghis shall arise in the East,
As the Atlanteans make Uncivil War,
In Egypt much sorrow,
And elsewhere much mopping-up of fish.
Quatrain VII.11 The Lost Centuries of Nostradamus

Nowhere Road

That afternoon, while Adam ransacked a rotting pile of rubbish behind a West End apartment, Mike, Deborah and Aristotle sped along narrow mountain roads into the slumbering county of Gwynedd. Welsher than a slap in the mouth with a wet daffodil, the country seemed a world away from the frenetic rush of the seething metropolis. By late afternoon the winding highway had carried them over age-eroded hills and down sunlit valleys ground out by ancient glaciers, over picturesque bridges and through oak-shrouded hamlets where the craft shops were hung like honey pots to snare unwary travellers.

The news coming from the car radio was not quite so welcoming.

The State of California announced that its recent ballot of top-rate taxpayers proved the legitimacy of its secession from the Union and demanded its independence be recognized forthwith by United Nations mandate. To date, only Albania and Quebec had obliged. Federal troops continued to mass on the border but denied recent manoeuvres had carried them over the frontier. International Business Computers had immediately declared themselves extraterritorial from the new nation and surreptitiously begun to liquidize their assets. Many other major companies were expected to follow suit.

From the east came even worse news for atlas publishers. Russia's asbestos-like disintegration continued apace. There were now so many splinter and splinter-splinter states that even the woodworm were packing up and moving on. In an increasingly mediaeval atmosphere the Grand Duchy of Kazan demanded the repatriation of a top-secret military convoy it claimed had been hijacked by the resurgent horsemen of the Golden Horde. The Chief Khan of the Siberian Confederacy denied all knowledge of such an act, and what were the Kazans planning to do with so much weapons-grade uranium anyway?

Meanwhile, the radiant Bianca Butowski of Iowa was crowned Miss Galaxy at a glittering ceremony in the United Nations General Assembly Building. Later, she told the assembled world Press that she wanted 'To work with small children and animals, to experience other nations and cultures through first-class travel, and build lasting world peace through the healing benefits of Country and Western.' As a taster of what was to come, she proceeded to sing a song about a lost puppy.

Deborah leaned forward and put an end to the depressing catalogue of doom, disaster, and plain bad taste. 'So Mike, this bed and breakfast you've booked us into – you say you've stayed there before?'

The Professor smiled knowingly. 'That I have my dear. Though I wouldn't exactly call The Screaming Sword public house an ordinary B&B. It's an inn with a history as long as mine. The current owners practise my sort of hospitality – the sort that doesn't ask awkward questions and comes with big portions.'

Deborah looked at the old man quizzically. 'Would I be right in assuming then, that this isn't the first time you've laid low in this neck of the woods?'

Mike nodded. 'A life like mine has its inevitable ups and downs. I've often sought safety out here on the wild frontier. Maybe I'm just a creature of habit.'

Most of them bad, Aristotle muttered from a semi-conscious doze. Deborah rubbed the cat's ears affectionately as he lolled back into her lap. On the rear seat her travel bag bulged with the assorted mish-mash of clothing she'd thrown together at the last moment. The rest of their simple luggage comprised Mike's compact, yet extensive, field survival kit. This was by no means their entire inventory; the heavy equipment would have to be fetched from London another time.

'You certainly seem to have it all planned.'

'Merely the benefit of vast experience, I assure you. I've learned the hard way – it doesn't pay to be caught with your trousers down. I've already arranged for an estate agent to show us round some properties.'

'I never knew you had these hidden depths. I hope you don't mind me saying so but you rather had the reputation of being . . . well a . . .'

'A dotty History professor stuck in a back-water college,' he finished for her. 'I gave up worrying about what people thought of me too long ago to remember. It's the first step on the road to a happy life.' He smiled for a moment. 'But I did rather enjoy my recent persona. By far the most agreeable I've had over the years.'

Deborah looked at him for a long while. It wasn't so much that she didn't believe his wild claims – the rational part of her couldn't ignore the Everest of evidence – it was her irrational self which was clinging to the past, refusing to accept absolutely what was going on. The past few days had a misty dreamlike quality about them, seeming to coax her along with the turn of events. With an effort she reminded herself that facing up to unpalatable facts was never easy, and these particular nuggets of truth were like three-week-old haddock.

Despite her confusion, she was certain of one thing: the teacher she had thought she had known, the scatter-brained, mad professor stereotype was nothing but a cover. This new Mike was together in an alarmingly down-to-earth way. Whoever he was now, there was a delicate matter she felt duty bound to raise.

'Mike, assuming for the sake of argument that you are a five-hundred-year-old retired prophet, and that you were at your peak in sixteenth-century France . . .'

'Yes, my dear . . .'

'Would you be the same sixteenth-century French prophet who some claim knew about Hitler and that Corsican git? The one whose writings, on the surface at least, mean absolutely bugger all?'

'I was wondering when we'd get around to this.' Mike chewed at his lower lip. 'I *did* have more hair in those days and several more letters to my name. But I do stay reasonably close to the original – hopelessly sentimental you see.'

'Well, forgive me Professor, I don't claim to be an expert on your published works but I don't remember anything about vanishing pyramids, chocolate money, or falling fish for that matter.'

Mike gave a hefty shrug, almost swerving into the opposite lane in the process. 'Prophecy has never been an exact science. You only have to look at my published works to see that.'

Deborah scoffed. 'Yes, they do seem to err on the side of vagueness.'

'My point exactly. It saved embarrassing court cases when I turned out to be wrong. Any reasonably educated person can make them mean whatever they want to, that way everyone goes away happy. The skill in a good commercial prophecy is making it tantalizingly open-ended.'

'Perhaps you should have been a politician.'

'Never had the stomach for it. With any luck they'll be

at the sharp end of what's coming and I won't lose much sleep over the fact.'

I must have gone crazy long ago, thought Deborah as she rubbed Aristotle's ears. I'm sitting in a car with a man who thinks he's older than Shakespeare's granny, who believes Armageddon is just round the corner, and I'm accepting it all because it's the least insane explanation. Maybe exam pressure finally got to me or the strain of fending off advances from sex-starved anorak-clad electrical engineers has run me down.

And look what happened to him! You saw it with your own eyes, so for the last time woman you are not mad, just different from the usual herd of unwashed cattle inhabiting this rock.

With an effort Deborah managed to calm her jangling nerves, interruptions from sarcastic telepathic cats notwithstanding. Despite his unusual method of communication Aristotle had raised an interesting point. 'Mike, what exactly does he mean by different? Doesn't he talk to anyone else?'

The Professor rubbed his stubbly grey beard. 'Well, apart from you and me I've never come across another human being who could communicate with Aristotle. That's what makes us different my girl, and that's what makes us dangerous.'

Over The Hills And Far Away

By seven p.m. the sun was sinking behind the looming mass of Cader Idris. The mountain seemed crowned in a spiritual light, as if playing host to the sort of supernatural rave which could give Faeryland a bad name. Just as Deborah began to think she'd seen the best of the scenery the car breasted a small hill and, like an open-mouthed sky diver, her breath was ripped away. The valley stretched before them in the gathering dusk, pools of golden sunlight draining down to the distant sea like fluorescent treacle from a turquoise bathtub. At the valley's base stood a small lake, no larger than a mountain tor and fed by a sparkling stream. The sides of the hills were swathed in lush woodland, leaves shimmered in the sinking sun. And between the trees Deborah could just make out the whitewashed walls of a village nestling against the protective mountain side. Lights were coming on in the homes, hinting at open fires, clean sheets and freshly baked bread. A hand-painted sign on the roadside read:

NODDEGAMRA WELCOMES CAREFUL DRIVERS
POPULATION 17~~2~~ 1

'Odd name,' Deborah said, hardly able to take her eyes off the view below. 'Doesn't seem Welsh somehow.'

'No, it doesn't,' Mike muttered absent-mindedly. He'd seen most of the scenery the world had to offer in his time but even he was lost for words every time he came back here. 'It's very old, possibly pre-Celtic. Some say it goes back to the Ice Age.' The car seemed to pause at the brow of the hill as if taking in the sight itself. Then, finding top gear, Mike took them down the slope into the valley's waiting arms.

As the battered old vehicle sped down the hill, several heads turned to follow its progress. Six pupils and a thousand insectoid vision sensors stared unblinking at the diminishing car. The two entities, hidden in the bushes at the side of the road, sat on three sets of haunches atop six legs. David Attenborough would have been fascinated by the panoply of the animal kingdom represented in the anatomy of the two creatures, but his fascination would have been short-lived, because within seconds he would have been eaten.

Can't Stand Losing You

As evening fell over the silent valley Guttlehog and Rubicante skulked forlornly in a dark forest clearing. They were two creatures far from their natural habitat and they were hopelessly lost.

'I told you we should have taken that side road,' Rubicante muttered, illuminating their surroundings with his in-built thumb light. Contrary to popular belief, demons can't see in the dark, they just usually have access to sophisticated night-vision equipment. Needless to say Guttlehog had forgotten to fill out the appropriate requisition forms in time for this mission.

'Oh, that's very easy for you to say,' the Boar Demon spluttered around his monstrous tusks, his agitation doing nothing for his elucidation. Between them this crack assassination team represented a speech therapist's worst nightmare. 'I notice hindsight is a speciality of yours. Why don't you try making a decision for once?'

'My first decision would have been to bring a map. And call me a pessimist, but maybe a compass would have come in handy.'

Guttlehog looked hurt. 'You don't know what it's like these days at the Quartermaster General's Office. They make you sign for everything in triplicate. That red ink's a bugger to get off your hoof afterwards. And did you hear what happened to those imps on that agitation mission to the Middle East? Left half their kit behind and were skinned alive when they got back. Most of the lads prefer to buy their equipment topside these days. Better quality and no awkward explaining to do if it gets broken.'

Rubicante looked pained. 'Oh, well if we find a shop open maybe we can purchase a tourist's map.'

'Won't that blow our cover?'

'Nah . . . they'll probably just think we're from England.'

A *Darkness At The Edge Of Town*

Later that same evening Deborah and Mike lolled merrily in the lounge bar of The Screaming Sword. They had finished the sort of meal which would have had the Borgias reaching for the Alka Selzers and now they were almost ready for bed.

The pub's landlady, Crystal Jones, was famed far and wide for being a magician in the kitchen, and the intrepid pair of househunters would have been hard pressed to dispute that fact.

The pub itself was mock Tudor in style with black oak beams that threatened to brain any one over six feet tall. The collection of horse brasses above the fireplace would have weighed down an oxen. Mike had first-hand experience of real Tudor living conditions and he could testify that there was nothing quaint or homely about sleeping on straw, picking weevils out of last month's oat cakes, or dying at forty. Although it brought back sometimes painful memories, he liked this place. The proprietors were friendly, the food and beer were exceptional and despite the period touches the mattresses were from the twentieth century.

Clearly, the pub had plenty to recommend it, but Mike and Deborah were the only customers eating in the small dining area. The public bar, too, was near empty: just a few old men sat around the walls looking into their bitter and mumbling to each other in Welsh, and in a far corner a wild-eyed young lad in combat fatigues playing dominoes against himself with great enthusiasm, slapping the pieces down each time as if he was killing a wasp.

'Not many in tonight?' said Mike as Hywell, Crystal's other half, returned with their dessert. His round face took on a far away look.

'Things have been odd round here lately, Professor. Folks seem to prefer to stay indoors, even on these warm nights. And as for visitors, well, they just shoot on through like the devil himself were after them.'

'Things have been odd everywhere lately, my old friend,'

said Mike with a wink. 'Nothing odd about that, given the times we live in.'

Hywell's frown grew deeper. 'I know what you mean, Professor Nostrus, I watch the TV news. But this is different, things just aren't right round these parts at all. It's almost as if there's an air of hushed expectancy hanging over the valley, and we're just waiting for the signal from up above for the floodgates to open.'

'Go on . . .' Mike coaxed him.

After a surreptitious glance around the room, Hywell leaned forward conspiratorially. Just as he opened his mouth, he froze rigid. For a moment Mike thought he'd been struck dead in front of them. Then out of the corner of his eye he saw a black shape hovering menacingly in the kitchen doorway. With a half-smile Mike turned and waved to the mistress of the house. Crystal ignored the friendly greeting and continued to stare at her husband like a boa constrictor sizing up its evening meal. After a long second, in which Mike could almost hear the fear breaking out on their host's brow, Hywell broke the uneasy silence.

'That'll be two apple pies then, stranger. Breakfast at eight. I trust you'll have a pleasant stay.' With that he left like a man who'd just found he was shaking hands with a leper. Mike and Deborah exchanged bewildered glances then went on with their meal in silence.

After the dessert, which was as good as expected, the diners left their plates and helped each other into the hallway. They were both feeling rather bloated by this stage and Mike for one was looking forward to sleeping it off. After wishing her good night and stumbling into his room the Professor left Deborah alone on the landing. She opened her door to find Aristotle sitting by the open window gazing out into the dark still night.

'Hope you ate as well as we did, Aristo. We're both stuffed,' she said unpacking her travel bag onto the bed.

The cat didn't look around. *Rest assured that I feasted*

adequately, though I will hunt later – I need the practice. It's not often I get to travel these days.

As she went about preparing herself for bed Deborah watched Aristotle sniff the gentle night breeze. Suddenly, with less warning than an earthquake in Ealing the cat was transformed into a snarling ball of fur and fury. His back arched, his coat stood on end, and his tail swelled to twice its normal size.

'What is it Aristo?' Deborah rushed to the window and attempted to calm him. Under her soothing hands he slowly relaxed.

I don't know exactly. There's something out there. I can't place the smell. It's part insect, but it's . . . wrong. There's something with it too. If I could only just . . .

Deborah peered out into the darkness. She didn't get the impression Aristo was the sort who scared easily. All she could see beyond the car park and main road was a tangled hedge then darkness captured the fields beyond. Suddenly feeling the night chill she pulled her dressing gown tight and made to close the heavy frame.

'Are you sure you're all right to go out by yourself?'

Aristotle gave her a withering look. Deborah didn't need telepathy to know what he was thinking. But he told her anyway.

It's what cats do!

With a dismissive flick of his white-tipped tail he jumped off the ledge and into the blackness beyond.

Noddegamra Nocturne

As well as performing miracles in the kitchen, Crystal was also a magician on those special evenings when, along with like-minded friends, she got her apron off and pranced naked round a bonfire singing songs about Peter the Naughty Pixie. This strange rite was performed in an earnest attempt to save Mother Earth from the ravages of post-industrial Western society, but all it really did was add to Europe's fast-growing goosebump mountain. The title Crystal preferred for her role in these ceremonies was 'Grand High Priestess of Mathonwy, Druidess of Darkness' – which was odd, because most people would have just called her a witch.

The sleepy village of Noddegamra couldn't offer much in the way of entertainment during the hours of darkness. There was the Sword of course, but if your tastes extended beyond real ale, darts, or sink the toilet fag end its appeal was strictly limited. Harp recitals had been known to take place in the Methodist hall but since Esme Williams had turned ninety-two she'd found it difficult to get her fingers round the strings. Like an amputee before the days of general anaesthetic the people of Noddegamra were in desperate need of a distraction. Until some far-sighted entrepreneur opened a Roller-Bladerdrome Burger Bar or the world's smallest multiplex cinema, Crystal's informal covens were guaranteed a steady supply of initiates.

'We like to keep things informal here as well as infernal – Haaaaaa Haaa Haa Ha!' she'd honk at new members in a vain attempt to put them at their ease. Any self-respecting Demi-Elf[1] would by this stage be wondering just what they were letting themselves in for. Crystal had the sort of laugh the Royal Navy could have used for detecting Russian submarines. Her appearance didn't help matters either. Her wardrobe contained way too many black dresses with tassels on the hem; indigo nail varnish weighed down every finger; her hair was like a raven's wing at midnight, but thankfully lacking the feathers and parasitic tics. One forelock was died silver for mysterious effect, but all it did

---

1 Though no formal career path existed, Crystal would have been delighted to improvise one on the spot for anyone keen enough to enquire – Demi-Elf, Tree-Child, Shrub-Maiden (applicable to both sexes), Witch/Warlock, Assistant Druid/Druidess to the Goddess, and finally Major Wizard-in-Chief, Lord of the Garden Centre.

was make her look like Vincent Price's cleaner. But then, to Crystal that would be no bad thing.

The covens were indeed informal gatherings. Very much a 'Come as you are' sort of affair – usually a 'Come as you are when you step out of the shower' sort of affair. Black tie was not required. Undoubtedly this contributed to their popularity; unfortunately two things conspired to dampen the attraction.

(i) British weather, whatever the season. It was amazing the damage hailstones could do to exposed flesh.

(ii) Generally speaking, the reason a bank manager from Bala finds himself in that profession and not a world bodybuilding star or an Olympic decathlon champion is that his physique isn't up to it. The inhabitants of Noddegamra were no fitter than the typical modern Briton, i.e. not at all. Any passing Greenpeace activists would have made a brave attempt to drag the reclining participants down to the coast to resume a life of freedom in the open waters eating plankton and avoiding Japanese ships.

All things considered, these gatherings were about as erotic as a kick in the groin. Nevertheless, people still came, partly because Crystal undeniably had the body for it, partly because she knew just how to ham the whole thing up.

'Oh Mathonwy, Great Mother of the Universe and sister to all your daughters, return and guide your poor wayward children away from the path of male-dominated nastiness. Show us how to return to the bosom of your creation, how to be nice to small furry animals and how not to drop bombs on each other.'

Crystal was good, even if she did sometimes get carried away. The more respectable members of the community thought she should be carried away – and locked up.

Purity Roberts fell into this category. A stalwart of a thousand church jumbles, jamborees and tombola stalls, one stare from this blue-rinsed harridan could stun a New

Age Traveller at fifty paces. She would have cracked down on Oliver Cromwell and his gang of happy-go-lucky funseekers, if she hadn't been born just a couple of years too late. Fearing the wrath of God she'd even filed down the tips of her horn-rimmed spectacles in case of appearing too satanic. Along with her posse of self-appointed guardians of public morality, Purity would sit up all night when the bonfires lit the hillsides.

'Pass the binoculars, Betty . . . Quickly! I think I can almost see what they're doing!' There would follow a night of eyestrain, fruitless calls to the police and much self-righteous indignation.

Just lately, Purity had reached the end of her tether. The covens had been coming thick and fast, but there was more to it than that. There was something demonic afoot, and this time it had nothing to do with Betty's verrucas.

With the full force of her cast-iron will Purity had made herself a promise. Tonight would be different. Tonight she was going to stop the nonsense once and for all.

Tonight Purity Roberts was on the war path, and no goat-cavorting heathen was going to dance naked in her way.

Tonight, Tonight, Tonight

As Crystal left the Sword that evening to call at the homes of her coven members one by one, she was watched by the bright amber eyes of Aristotle. It was midnight and Indian summer stars sparkled through a low cloud scuttling off to the north as if there was somewhere else it would rather be. To the east, a bloodshot harvest moon shone across the hillside as Aristotle darted fleetingly from bush to bush. His progress was as silent as a shadow, and the night sounds carried easily on the warm breeze, hinting at a host of small trembling bodies nestling in the valley's overgrown floor.

Despite ideal conditions for the hunt, Aristotle had

little luck in the hedges and gardens of the village. The local rodent population seemed to have packed up and left town. If this was a ship there'd be cause for alarm. After an hour of luckless hunting, he took the plunge and advanced into a likely looking field that stretched up the hill. This was further than he'd intended to travel tonight, but as a Persian he'd once known had been fond of saying: 'You can't catch fish without getting your paws wet.' The countryside around Noddegamra was sprinkled with rich forest, the denser patches separated by lush meadow. Perhaps these would provide more fruitful territory.

He was still looking for his supper half an hour later. But at least now he had a plausible excuse: scattered groups of humans were blundering around the woods complaining in loud Welsh voices about the excessive number of thorn bushes and what they were doing to intimate parts of their anatomies. In the face of this *Homo sapien* stampede, any half-sane wild animal would be in Bristol by now and asking for the next boat out. Aristotle crouched on padded paws as two particularly vocal late night hikers stumbled past.

'This had better be as good as you said Emmyr – I'm bloody well frozen already.'

'Ah, stop your moaning you grumpy bugger and think of all the rampant totty that's going to be there – starkers too! Dick, you won't believe it when you see it.'

'I bloody well hope so. Whassit meant to be tonight anyway?'

'A summonin' of the Earth Goddess if I remember correct.'

'A summonin' aye? And what exactly does that involve?'

'Crystal Tips gets 'er tits out and dances round like she's havin a fit. Come on, let's see if we can get there before one of these gorse thickets makes Jews of us.'

'Why do they call 'ere Crystal Tips anyway?'

''Urry up and you'll see.'

Once they had passed him by, Aristotle resumed his hunt. But soon he had to admit that tonight was just not going to be his night. He heard the fire long before he saw it. At least now the great blundering hairless apes seemed to be congregating in one place, but the curiosity that killed his legendary cousin had got its claws into Aristotle's furry head and wouldn't let go. So he followed his nose, ears and eyes to the confused babble at the centre of a large forest clearing.

What he saw as he crept through the ferns at the edge of the secluded grove were fourteen shivering locals all trying to get as close as possible to a crackling bonfire. The female from the inn seemed to be in charge. She stood to one side wearing only a set of moose antlers, but somehow retaining her dignity. Like all cats, Aristotle had a well developed sense of propriety. He was constantly amazed by humanity's ability to act like idiots while maintaining an infuriating belief in their own importance.

The be-horned one waved a dagger around and cried, 'Oh Great Cernnunos, Lord of Beasts, Master of the Safari Park grant us a sign of your benevolent approval. Send us a portent, we beseech thee!'

If Great Cernnunos was listening and not down the pub or off cleaning his cosmic chariot, he chose a strange way of showing it. Just as Crystal finished her impassioned monologue a band of small and frail, yet highly irate, figures came bustling through the trees. They carried burning torches and heavily thumbed prayer books in their trembling hands.

Purity Roberts thrust herself to the fore.

'You'll put an end to this sacrilege this minute, Crystal Jones. We'll not stand for it in our valley a second longer, will we Betty!'

Behind her, Purity's sidekick made a great show of studying the local shrubbery. She'd never been in the presence of such a tonnage of exposed male genitalia and was never likely to do so again. 'Er – no, probably not,' she mumbled, paying particular attention to her sensible shoes.

Crystal was not one to back down in the face of adversity. Drawing herself up to her full height she was about to begin her counter attack when she was interrupted by a piercing scream from a coven member. In unison, everyone turned to follow the outstretched finger of the whimpering wicker worshipper. There for all to see, standing amongst the ferns at the side of the clearing, looking rather dazed and confused themselves, stood Guttlehog and Rubicante.

Over the next half second several things happened at once. Without exception, the humans present were not experienced at assessing the mood of a face with more than the usual number of lips. If they had been they might have realized just how scared the hapless Assassination Demons were. For their part, Guttlehog and Rubicante experienced a momentarily nasty recollection of certain decades from the late sixteenth century, a period when no self-respecting satanic servant wanted to be confronted in a dark forest late at night by a group of irate villagers carrying torches and screaming damnation.

The net results of this complex social interaction were subtle and manifold. Mr Trevor Griffiths, a retired school teacher from the village, was lucky he wasn't wearing underwear because if he had been, he'd have needed to change it. Mr Douglas Prichard, the previously mentioned bank manager from Bala, experienced an attack of mental turmoil in which his sanity finally packed its bags and struck out on a freelance basis to find a less eventful mind to inhabit. Psychiatrists and psychoanalysts could have found intriguing case studies aplenty in that half second, enough for countless books, endless papers and perpetual lecture tours of North America. So it was sad in a way that the only mental health practitioner present, Miss Gladys Graham – a psychiatric nurse from Dolgellau – was the first to go running and screaming off into the woods in the opposite direction.

Her lead was quickly followed by the others, except for Crystal who made a commendable effort to take events in her skirtless stride. Despite being on a par with a startled midje attempting to take a speeding Ferrari head-on, spirit like this just has to be admired. Redirecting her ire from Purity's fast-diminishing form, Crystal looked Guttlehog and Rubicante squarely in their multitude of glinting eyes and gathered her inner strength. Raising her arms above her head in the best theatrical tradition, she began her most formidable spell of banishing.

'Eye of eagle, badger's snout, give me the power of Hangar Lane roundabout.'

Rubicante turned to his companion in some alarm. He had no idea if this represented the opening line of some potent white magic spell, and he had a vague suspicion that it didn't even scan properly, but he for one wasn't taking any chances.

'Bugger this, let's make a run for it!' And they did, disappearing into the forest like an extensively mutated Hansel and Gretel.

Aristotle had remained crouched under a bramble bush while all hell broke loose around him, but when a ghostly white maternal figure came close to stepping on him he quickly shrunk out of sight.

Suddenly alone on the hilltop Crystal picked up her antler head-dress – half of which had fallen off in all the excitement – and followed them out of the clearing with some haste. Soon all was still and quiet once more. The only sounds breaking the cold night air were an occasional scream and crash as, far off in the woods, confused cultists bumped into each other.

Aristotle thought he'd recognized the one with the tusks, though he couldn't be sure. It was a long time since his path had crossed with the spirit world. Whoever they were, they'd made themselves scarce faster than a vampire at a garlic growing festival. But why were they here in the first place? It certainly wasn't due to Crystal's inane activities – you stood more chance of summoning a demon by phoning for a take-away pizza. Despite his best efforts, Aristotle kept coming back to the same worrying conclusion. He'd seen it too many times before to hope otherwise. As far as the cat was concerned the arrival of the multi-limbed ones must be connected with Mike's presence in the valley. Clearly, a bit of investigative work was called for.

Aristotle slunk off into the night in search of a lead, fearing not a little the demonic Rottweiler he felt sure would be attached to it.

Home By The Sea

The next morning Mike and Deborah stood outside what was described in the brochure as 'An imposing Georgian farm cottage'. The only justification for this description that Mike could see was that the owner of such a home might eat a lot of cottage cheese. It was a cottage the same way the *Titanic* had been a holiday yacht or Australia was your average Polynesian island.

'This substantial dwelling, known locally as Caer-Mathonwy Farm, sits in fifteen acres of ancient oakwood and commands impressive views of the valley below.'

Mike and Deborah were in the capable hands of Mr Jason Llewellyn, the youngest Llewellyn in Llewellyn Llewellyn Llewellyn & Goldberg, Aberystwyth's foremost estate agents and the local signwriters' most sought-after client.

Mike viewed their host warily. Mr Llewellyn Junior looked like he should still be at school, not selling houses for a living. Despite his gangly frame and spotty countenance their guide carried all the trappings of his noble profession. The line of his smartly tailored suit was broken only by the impressive bulge of his firm, young personal organizer. He wore his mobile phone like a Colt 45. And his sales patter was a little too rehearsed.

'The site enjoys a southerly aspect and celebrates many hours of daily sunshine throughout the year. The property's capacious grounds contain a number of well-restored outhouses including a fully operational water wheel on the entirely authentic and unique mountain stream.' Mike and Deborah exchanged a tired look. It seemed they were in for the full treatment today.

'If sir and madam would now care to interact with the main complex, access being available through the primary ingress/egress portal feature.'

'What did he say?' Mike asked under his breath as their guide bounded up the front steps.

'I think he invited us in through the front door.'

'This guy is so far up his own arse, he can taste his tonsils.'

When they caught up they found their escort waiting patiently at the stout front door. For a moment he looked far away, as if trying to remember something important, then with a faint nod of reassurance the young man continued: 'The main structure itself comprises stone farmhouse c.1792, a tasteful modern extension added by the last owner, plus a reinforced concrete basement containing its own heated swimming pool. The site was originally a working sheep farm but today offers a luxury retreat for the discerning country squire.'

'Certainly looks like a solid construction,' Mike said, giving the stone wall an inquisitive tap.

'Oh, yes sir. This building could withstand anything mother nature could throw at it.

'I wouldn't bet on that, young man.'

'Interesting name, Caer-Mathonwy,' said Deborah. 'What's the story behind it?'

Mr Llewellyn looked as pleased as a bishop in a brothel. 'A quaint local legend, Miss. The literal translation is

Mathonwy's Stronghold. She's said to have a special affinity with this valley, Mathonwy of course being the . . .'

'The Mother aspect of the Celtic triple goddess,' Mike interrupted. 'Representing the creative side of the tripartite deity. Along with the maiden and hag aspects she constitutes the embodiment of planet Earth and all its natural forces.'

'I see you're familiar with the story,' Llewellyn replied with a trace of annoyance.

'I was a Druid in a past life,' Mike said, no hint of a smile.

After an hour or so of 'spacious bedrooms' and 'commodious living quarters', Mike and Deborah had seen it all and heard the rest. During a particularly florid sequence Mike enquired if Mr Llewellyn had any thesaurus writers in his immediate family, for which Deborah gave him a sly dig in the ribs. Finally, after more 'colossal cooking cupboards' than they cared to remember, the pair found themselves in an 'ample family habitat space', looking down over one of the many 'beatific visual arrangements'.

'Nice view,' Mike agreed, following Llewellyn's gaze.

'It is indeed, sir' said the estate agent, sensing an angle. 'There're many people who'd be prepared to pay a small fortune for that impressive vista alone. Fortunately we at L L L and G can offer this property at a very reasonable price.'

'Tell me,' continued Mike, conspicuously ignoring the offer to talk money at this early stage of the game, 'what's the mean height above sea level of this house?'

Mr Llewellyn looked a little confused. 'Er, I could find out for you. Is it important to you, sir?'

'Well, put it this way: if I'm going to end up living next to a fjord I want to know which side of the waterline my bedroom window will be on.'

Their guide looked at Mike most oddly.

'I'll . . . make a note of it.' The young man retrieved his electronic organizer and made a great show of tapping away at the tiny keyboard. While he was attempting a feat that would have challenged a pin-fingered midget, Mike and Deborah wandered into the kitchen.

'Well?' Deborah asked.

Mike thought for a moment. 'Pretty good. The basement might come in handy. And we could rig a generator up to that water wheel – no need to rely on the national grid.'

Deborah felt the time was right for reason to take a stand. 'Mike, it's your money, your decision, but are you absolutely sure all this is necessary?' Without Aristotle around to constantly remind her that things were a little out of the ordinary, Deborah kept slipping temporarily back into reality mode and all its niggling questions.

'I thought we had this sorted out? You can't still believe you're imagining a telepathic cat and that I'm some mad old duffer wearing an "End Is Nigh" T-shirt?'

'Let's just say I'm withholding judgement, shall we.' As soon as she said it, she realized it sounded a bit pompous.

Mike looked ready to explode. 'What the hell is it with your generation and this non-committal attitude? You've seen the proof, what more do you want? Either start facing facts or sod off back to London to stick your head in the sand. But you'd better watch out, young lady, because the tide is coming in.'

Their discussion was cut short by Mr Llewellyn's triumphant return. 'Ah, here you both are. I can assure you Mr Nostrus that we presently stand a good 800ft above high tide. I trust that would suit your aquatic disposition?'

'Yes – yes it would,' Mike said after an uncomfortable pause. 'You can tell the entire male line of the Llewellyns and Mr Goldberg that I'll pay the asking price. We can close the deal immediately. No point in hanging around till Doomsday, is there?'

The young man's eyes lit up at his sudden good fortune. They seemed to spin around in their sockets, finally coming to rest on the images of two small palm trees next to a golden white beach. 'A superb decision sir. Let me fetch the paperwork.'

Talking About The Revolution

As Mike and Mr Llewellwyn shook hands on the deal outside the imposing 'cottage' they failed to notice the twitching shrubbery that lined one side of the wide gravel forecourt.

'Imperialist bastards!' declared a bush to the small tree next to it. 'They'll soon get what's coming to them and no mistake.'

The small tree made no reply. To tell the truth it wasn't quite so committed as its horticultural associate and was having grave misgivings about this entire undertaking.

Even a cursory investigation by a passerby would have soon established that this part of North Wales did not in fact boast a previously undiscovered species of communicative tree, but did provide an ideal habitat for two young men with a garage full of paraffin and a track record in radical home improvement on behalf of English second property owners. They didn't know it yet but Gwylym and Ivan – or 'The Gwynedd People's Liberation Army' as they liked to be known – were in for a very nasty surprise.

'You sure this is a good idea?' mumbled Ivan through his bruised upper lip. Being the inherently poetic one, he had wanted to rename their organization 'The Sons of the Flaming Sword'. After a two-hour emergency meeting of the senior staff officers of the G.P.L.A. (i.e. Gwylym and Ivan), in which it came to light that Colonel Gwylym's main objection was that the proposed name change made them sound like ponces, it was decided to retain the original title. A compromise proposal to rename themselves 'The Sons of the Gwynedd People's Flaming Liberation Sword Army' was quashed for being untranslatable into

Welsh – plus the BBC would be unable to fit it on the inevitably biased news bulletins when the brave Celtic crusaders got round to bombing the Houses of Parliament. The issue was finally put to rest when Gwylym put Ivan to rest with a playful slap, Colonel Gwylym being the inherently violent one.

'We'll come back in a few days and see if they've taken down that For Sale sign,' said Free Gwynedd's Commander in Chief, rubbing his boot-polish blackened jaw with thick stubby fingers. 'If they do, then we'll mount a courageous battalion-level tactical operation to liberate the target.'

'So, what do you mean, then?' asked Ivan wide mouthed. He'd taken to military matters like a duck takes to contract bridge.

Gwylym gave his second-in-command a long look. 'It means we'll come back when it's dark and fire bomb the bastards.'

Talking About The Revelation

Little did Gwylym know, but 'the English bastard' was not, of course, English at all. Like syphilis and the Eurovision Song Contest Mike was a truly international phenomenon, though at the moment he was having severe difficulty convincing Deborah of that fact. As they entered the main bar of the Screaming Sword the couple were still arguing.

'Look Mike, it's not that I don't *believe* what you're telling me. Each passing day there's yet more proof. It's just . . .'

'Just what? That you don't want to believe? You rate cynicism a virtue?'

Deborah looked weary. 'It's nothing to do with cynicism. It's just not so easy for me to completely switch my world view. Give me a chance to adjust at my own pace. I suppose I still haven't entirely given up hope that there's a perfectly rational explanation for all this.'

Mike scoffed. 'Such as?'

'Yes, well . . . admittedly that's not an easy one to answer. The only rational explanation that springs to mind is that I'm cracking up and hallucinating the whole thing. After all, no one apart from me saw Andy being abducted. No one apart from me and you can hear Aristotle. No one apart from me was told your lottery and banking predictions. Far too much of this is occurring just in my head. It's just all a bit too . . . *neat*.'

Suddenly, Mike stopped dead in his tracks, an intense look of concentration on his weathered face. Deborah followed his gaze as the Professor held up a hand for silence. Over in the corner the pub's battered old TV was tuned in to the one o'clock news. With a smile Mike checked the date on his watch and broke into a heartfelt chuckle. For Deborah, as well as the Egyptian Tourist Board, things were about to get a lot less tidy.

It seemed that most of the world's press were gathered on a small plot of desert near Cairo. Despite much hysteria and wailing, Deborah could just make out the Egyptian President lamenting last night's cataclysmic events. In the background a conspicuous absence of large ancient monuments and two very big holes in the ground told her far more than the multitude of bewildered TV reporters on the scene ever could.

Mike turned to his young associate with a wide grin. 'My dear, you seem to have gone quite pale. Would you like some fresh air? Perhaps a stroll to the post office would be in order. I've got an insurance claim I need to urgently post off.'

Deborah turned and looked him straight in the eye, shrugged her shoulders and held her palms up in defeat. 'Okay Mike, I give up on the rational world I once knew and loved so well. I'm convinced.'

SIX

> And to him that conquers and observes my deeds down to the end I shall give authority over nations. And he shall shepherd the people with an iron rod, so they will be broken to pieces like clay vessels.
> *Revelations 2:26*

The Yellow Rogue of Texas

Houston, Texas – a city where 'muggy' refers to more than just the weather. In any given year the police could expect to deal with over two thousand murders or, as the locals preferred to call them, 'unlawful killings'. As in: 'We were just sitting in our back yard Officer, when our neighbour unlawfully killed my entire family with that there rocket-propelled grenade-launcher of his.'

In any other country the words 'civil' and 'war' might be apt, but, as everybody with or without a gun licence knows, the right to bear arms is enshrined in the American constitution. Unfortunately, the constitution was written at a time when the only offensive weapon most people owned was a flintlock musket – a device that might just have been capable of bringing down an asthmatic squirrel at fifty paces.

These days some Americans saw it as an infringement of their rights if some pinko-bed-wetter stopped them buying laser-guided anti-tank missiles – they were essential for hunting the Federal Government's legion of over-zealous tax collectors, postmen, park rangers and their ilk.

The gun lobby had plenty of spokesmen – they needed them, since many of its grass-roots members had difficulty with the order of the alphabet let alone sentences of more than one syllable.

One of the lobby's most powerful allies was a man named Ted Trundell. He wasn't born-and-bred Houston but hailed instead from one of those rectangular states in the middle, where men were men, women were kept barefoot and Korean shop-keepers were constantly nervous.

Ted wasn't interested in the guns themselves; he just used whatever platform he could to reach his under-evolved target audience. Supreme Bishop Trundell was far more concerned with the parts of the constitution dealing with religious tolerance. Not tolerance of other people's beliefs, tolerance of his own. For Ted had plenty that needed tolerating. When your personal TV station owned more satellites than the KGB, heads of South American countries came to you for a loan, and you didn't pay tax on any of the earnings, you needed all the good will from your peers you could muster, and a small army of accountants to keep the cash moving.

And what use was any army if it wasn't properly equipped?

It hadn't always been this way. Ted, if not exactly born on the wrong side of the tracks at least came from close enough to them for passing trains to rattle the fillings in his crooked teeth. Ted's family were poor – but unhappy. Unhappy even though merriment in the face of abject poverty is usually a safe ticket to greatness – and Ted's folks had plenty of ground to make up. The nearest this early-seventies household came to floor covering was watching the carpet-bombing of North Vietnam. 'Irony' might as well have been a nutritious new breakfast cereal. And as for 'Tolerance', that was as unknown a territory as High School graduation day or trips to the ballet.

The Trundell home stood at the edge of a one-horse town. In fact it didn't so much stand as balance on blocks – it had been this way since Ted's mean old pawh pawned the wheels to pay for one final bottle of JD. The random collection of burger bars, cheap motels and chicken-processing plants half a mile down the dust-swept road didn't even measure up to its description, for it contained no horses.[1] A more accurate description might have been a one-pick-up-truck-several-shotgun town, but the inhabitants would have been confused by such a long compound adjective.

As Ted grew up in this insignificant place, surrounded by insignificant people, he realized that he had no desire to be insignificant himself. Some inhabitants could grasp the concept that there was a universe beyond the burnt-out oil drum at the end of Main Street, but they were considered with suspicion and shunned by the right-thinking majority. The percentage of the population who were ignorant or narrow-minded was no higher than in any other community or any other country, but to this day what sets the American ignorant apart from their ubiquitous brethren is that they are particularly good at it. Nowhere on the globe has ignorance reached such a pinnacle of high art as in small-town America – and it was into one such centre of excellence that Ted was born.

After an uneventful childhood, marked only by the inventive ways he found to torture soon-to-be-road-killed animals, Ted became the sort of '80s teenager who grew his hair long and listened to way too much heavy metal music. The sort of teenager that sometimes, after a particularly intense session of Speed Thrash gets depressed and makes suicide pacts with their best friend. The sort that sometimes carries out these promises – if they manage to drag themselves out of their drug-induced stupor long enough to get some of their head behind the shotgun. Ted succeeded in avoiding this particular fate mainly because

---

1 At least, not since the first burger bar opened.

when played backwards he found Judas Priest just as unintelligible as when played forwards, and the closest he and his best friend got to a drug-induced stupor was sniffing Mom's hairspray cans.

Ted's best, or rather only, friend was a be-pimpled evolutionary backwater called Dwayne, a soggy sticking plaster languishing at the bottom of the human gene pool. His name would have been handicap enough for most people, but Dwayne compounded his woes by his choice of companion. Dwayne's friendship was based on Ted's massive thrash-metal collection and his never-ending ability to think up cool things for them to do. Ted's imagination didn't stretch much beyond setting fire to used hairspray cans, saying 'The Lord's Prayer' backwards while staring into a mirror, or doing things to insects with kerosene, but hey, it was entertainment.

If anything, Dwayne's family were even poorer than his own, mainly due to the medical costs of treating little Bethany's extremely rare new strain of polio. Things had been tough since Dwayne's parents had lost their jobs last fall. They'd been unlucky all round, what with Elvis losing his arms in that thresher, and since the local abattoir got a machine to automatically stun cattle Trina-Jo had been out of work too. The best doctors they could afford informed his parents that Beth would never walk again – but they lived in hope of a miracle. At least they didn't live in a wheelless motor home up on blocks like those awful Trundells, whose gormless son always seemed to be leading their Dwayne into mischief, they would think as they prayed for divine intervention.

Smarter Than The Average Bear

The first tantalizing glimpse Ted got of his glorious destiny occurred one rainy Saturday morning round at Dwayne's house. After a particularly heavy session on the hairspray, which left Dwayne's bedroom filled with more CFC than the entire upper atmosphere, the only entertainment left to them was TV. They were just slobbing out on the couch when Trina-Jo thrust her big hair around the chip-board door.

'Just where does all that ha'spray go to? I'm shower they put less'n'less in each week. I'll have to drive down to the mawl and fetch somow. You all be good now.' Dwayne managed an uncoordinated wave as his mom left the house. Ted just slouched in a semi-conscious daze, a trickle of saliva running down his receding chinline. Soon they were alone, Elvis was out watching his old bowling buddies and Bethany was resting in bed across the hall. The boys had the house to themselves. So they made optimum use of it and stayed right where they were.

Poor or no, Dwayne's folks had the best TV set high-interest credit could buy. It took up one corner of the lino-floored room, the only decoration breaking its sleek lines a plaster cast diorama of Jesus patting the heads of some little children. Pretty soon Ted and Dwayne found themselves watching an old rerun of Yogi Bear. It was an episode with a startlingly original plot development – Yogi and Boo Boo dress up as Girl Guides to outsmart Ranger Smith and pinch all the picnic hampers. Ted had seen it before, that's why it came as quite a shock when Boo Boo suddenly turned and looked out of the screen, a golden halo shining around his fluffy little head, and said in a decidedly un-Boo Boo-like voice, 'Listen son, there's something I'd like you to do for me.'

Ted couldn't remember this ever happening before. He looked over to his friend for confirmation but Dwayne was dribbling away as usual, clearly oblivious of Boo Boo's new intimacy. Boo Boo continued, sounding more and more like Orson Welles as he went along: 'You've been chosen, my son, for great things. You're going to be bigger than the Rolling Stones.'

'Who're they?' Ted gurgled.

'They started off as one of mine, but I went a bit wrong somewhere. Never mind that now though . . . Listen up and listen good, 'cause thisy here's your destiny.'

The bow-tied bear went on to tell Ted of the great mission he must accomplish; to bring peace, light and understanding to mankind, to save sinners from the twin threats of flared trousers and international socialism. To spread tolerance and justice where before there had been strife and discord; and if anyone got in the way of this great message to have them quietly taken out the back and have seven sorts of shit kicked out of them by some big lads in suits.

To say Ted was rapt would be an understatement. He was more stunned than the cattle at the abattoir. Before this revelation he'd been under the impression that he was just another spotty American teenager with too many hormones and not enough deodorant. Now, he'd been told by no less a theological figure than Boo Boo that his life had meaning.

Boo Boo went on: 'Now, to prove that I'm for real and not some apparition brought on by Silky-Soft Hairspray™, the hairspray for the way you live today, sponsors of the US Olympic Ladies Gymnastic Team . . .'

Ted flinched with guilt; if Boo Boo knew about his propellant habit, it meant he was omniscient as well as cute and furry.

'. . . I'm going to let you perform a miracle. Go into Bethany's room, place your hands on her legs and tell her to get up and walk. I've got to go now, but you'll be hearing from me again. Errr – May the Force be with you.'

With that Boo Boo dissolved into the huge yellow shape of Big Bird. It seemed that while Ted was receiving his instructions Yogi had finished and Sesame Street had come on. But young Trundell wasn't interested in the letter D, so he got off the sofa and staggered towards Bethany's room, reeling under the twin influences of divine enlightenment and Silky-Soft Hairspray™. Dwayne stumbled after him, concerned at his friend's strange expression.

'What's up man? You confusin' me with all this moving.'

But Ted wasn't listening. He knelt beside little Beth's bed and placed his hands on little Beth's legs. Trundell could never remember exactly what happened next, his time sense seemed to stretch like an elastic hand-grenade. The next thing he knew, Dwayne's entire family were huddled round the bed as Bethany wiggled her tiny toes in delight. Everyone was singing hymns and crying as finally the little girl found the strength to fling her callipers out the open window and take her first weak steps. The only sour note was provided by the family mongrel, Himmler, who put up a frightful baying in the front garden as twelve pounds of stainless-steel shattered his skull. But nobody noticed – they were too taken up by that miraculous moment. Ted didn't think he'd ever seen a man the size of Dwayne's daddy cry so hard when little Bethany ran into his outstretched stumps.

So that was how Ted found religion, or rather religion found him. It wasn't quite the road to Damascus, not even the road to Dallas in fact, but the events of that day set Ted on the path to a personal fortune that would have made Judas blush.

Don't Mess With A Missionary Man

Ted might not have remembered the exact process but he did remember the press coverage resulting from his first venture into spiritual healing. The editor of the local paper was beside himself with glee: this was human interest with interest on top. Ted got a front page splash and lapped up the publicity like a true pro. What followed, the old Ted would have described as 'awesome', but Ted was changing as fast as his fame was spreading. He had his hair cut, took to wearing smart suits and disposed of his heavy metal collection, discreetly.'

After two years of revivalist meetings, where Ted displayed a natural ability for public speaking if not quite repeating his initial success as a faith-healer, he enrolled in a small-town Bible college to study Comparative Theology. It was the sort of university peculiar to North America, where the men wore crew-cuts and short-sleeved shirts and the girls smiled a great deal and took home economics courses. The classes did not come cheap, but thanks to another of Ted's hidden talents – separating the faithful from their money – he raised enough to put himself through school.

After five semesters of study, Ted split from his established church in a blaze of publicity and set up on his own. He wasn't short of backers: Ted could hold an audience in the palm of his hand, milking them for all they were worth. His rabble-rousing rants had to be seen to be believed, but then Ted could make his flock believe just about whatever he liked. Eternal damnation from purchasing the wrong brand of hairspray was a particular favourite of his, and the best way to avoid this terrible fate was to only buy church-approved products, digging deep with a glad heart in support of the One True Faith. Pretty soon Supreme Bishop Trundell was able to buy off his greedy family, there being nothing worse in later life than the tabloid press digging up the details of your rather-less-than-immaculate conception. Overseen by fervent units of PR midwives, accountant obstetricians, and a hospitalful of spin doctors, 'The Church of the Eloquent Announcement (Incorporated)' was delivered into the unsuspecting world.

Radio Free Andes

That was more than twelve years ago. Since then, Ted Trundell had come a long way. He had really made a name for himself as the founder of an evangelical mission to the upper Amazon, bringing the benefits of western civilization and caramel-based fizzy drinks to the poverty-stricken locals of the Peruvian Andes. Ted and his stormtroopers for the Eloquent Announcement brought other blessings to the awestruck Indians – microwave ovens, chicken-pox and Elvis Presley, to name but a few. They also brought truck-loads of small, battery-powered transistor radios set permanently to one frequency: Radio Free Andes. No prizes for guessing the station's number one DJ. The receivers were battery powered but when they ran out, which they often did, the Indians would come down into the mission complex to get new ones. Radio Free Andes was very clear on this point, between Bing Crosby and 'Songs from the Shows' there were frequent public announcements. The only condition on the handout of new units was that the eager recipients had to sit through four hours of Ted face to face.

Ted on the radio was one thing, Ted in person was a different kettle of worms entirely. First he'd woo his audience with the good news – that no matter how poor they were in this life, paradise awaited them if they'd just follow the way of Jesus, or at least Ted's interpretation thereof. Then he'd offer any headman who happened to be present the loan of a colour TV, and Ted's engineers would even fly out and set it up for them. Radio Free Andes became TV Free Andes. That was when the show really got off the ground. John the Baptist had nothing on this. Ducking people in a murky river could not compete with endless Dynasty reruns, interrupted only by ten minute sermons from Ted every hour, even if the viewers couldn't understand a word he said.

Ted's backers were ecstatic. They paid his church a set fee for every lost pagan soul he saved. The more money they gave him, the more TV sets he handed out, the more pagans he reached. The operation was a resounding success – but Ted wanted to go still further. There were fertile pastures much closer to the black bile-filled thing that passed for his heart just waiting to be ploughed with the trusty blade of Jesus' word, and Trundell was ready to spread the manure on good and thick. Leaving the Amazon to his young, crew-cut, suit-wearing disciples, Ted prepared for a heroic homecoming.

U.S. And Them

The mid-90s America that Trundell returned to was a Godless, whore-ridden, soulless pit of depravity. Like Moses returning from his hike, Ted was distraught at how low his flock had sunk without him.

The areas of this once great land that weren't owned by Japanese mega-corporations were crumbling, junkie-filled ghettos. Now, even gang leaders were too frightened to venture out in Los Angeles by night. All the while, the Federal Government was slowly losing control. Some of the richer states were beginning to wonder why they supported the ineffectual welfare programmes. California was looking west rather than east for its economic leadership – which may have been just as well, what with the San Andreas Big One still waiting to happen. The Golden State was soon likely to be moving into the Pacific Rim in more ways than one.

But every shit-heap has a silver lining, and it's an ill wind indeed that doesn't show someone which side his bread is buttered on. There's nothing that fuels a spiritualist revival quite like a good old-fashioned socio-economic crisis, and Ted for one intended to make the best of the situation. He had to modify his techniques slightly. The American people were unlikely to fall for the free one-station radio ploy which had served him so well in the past. Ted needed something more American. And so, GOD TV, 'The Satellite Station Bringing Salvation to the Nation', was born.

What Ted did wasn't particularly original, but the sheer scale of the presentation set it apart from its rivals. The nation's cathode-ray tubes were his pulpit, the electromagnetic aether his parish. As the countless unemployed lounged at home they were at least assured twenty-four-hour, non-stop quality entertainment. *The Good News Game-Show* was GOD TV's most popular creation. Contestants had the chance to win millions by answering challenging Bible-based questions. Reading the Good Book became America's leading pastime overnight. The schedules were crammed with such treats as *Morality Heights* – The Soap That Cleanses Your Soul. Who could forget *Aroma-Cast-PM*™, the world's first scratch'n'sniff news bulletin? And then of course there was Ted himself. All the shows were punctuated by regular visits to The Great Man at the Church's headquarters in Houston, Texas – or 'Mission Control' as he preferred it to be known.

'Well howdy folks, Supreme Bishop Trundell here to tell you that The Lord God and The Little Baby Jesus are watching over you night and day. They both know that the white Anglo-Saxon God-fearing population of North America, who made this country great, have it in them to make it great again. And no meddling "One World Government" bew-ro-crat can stop us if we put our minds to it. So brothers and sisters, why not take the first step on that glory road this very day. All you have to do to join the holy fight against heathen sinners and the International-Zionists-Marxist-Conspiracy is pick up your phone and dial toll free 0100-L-U-V-G-O-D. One of our crack team of telephonist Sales Angels will be more than happy to take the number of your major credit card. So stop milking that cow, phone right now, and help reinstate America as the Elvis in the Lord God's Hit Parade of Nations. And remember, all contributions are fully tax-deductible.'

Ted undoubtedly had screen presence, what with his blond hair, blond teeth, blond suits and hordes of blonde, swim-suited Angels dancing around in the background. His politics were quite blond too, though any opponents brave enough to say so openly were hit with a law suit faster than they could scream 'National Socialism'. And often it wasn't just a law suit that hit them. The methods Ted's henchmen used to put their political points across owed more to Goebbels than Ghandi, though naturally these acts of systematic thuggery never got traced back to the Supreme Bishop himself. God simply worked in mysterious ways.

You Can't Make An Omelette Without Breaking Legs

The despondent American population lapped up Ted's message. There's nothing like a good scapegoat to make people forget their own inadequacies – and Ted was offering a whole list. He got given so much cash, and built up so much influence, that eventually he was almost as famous as God himself, and he got a lot more media coverage.

But still he yearned for greater things.

Despite the fact he'd given Daisy-Jo's bra-strap more attention than geography lessons at school, Ted was dimly aware that there existed other countries apart from the two he'd fleeced already. Across the sea in Europe millions of unfortunates still lived their lives in sin, listening to that modern rock music, unaware of the benefits of a truly free-market, supply-side economy. How could a man like Ted rest knowing this? Slowly, he turned the might of his empire to a scheme for helping these poor people. For the past year a special task force had laid the groundwork for a mission to the Old World, and now it was almost ready.

The Russians were paid two billion beetroot to launch a shiny new telecommunications satellite that hung in the dawn sky like a twinkling malevolent eye. A massive greenfield site was bought in rural England to house the nerve centre for the new venture: EUROGOD TV: a *Songs of Praise* meets the Eurovision Song Contest hybrid. The remainder of the vast site would become the Wings Over Creation Theme Park, Europe's first open-air religious attraction since the Spanish Inquisition decided to hear cases outside, seeing as it was such a lovely day.

Finally, everything was in place. On the same day that Mike and Deborah drove to North Wales, Trundell and his entourage arrived at Heathrow Airport. The press were kept at bay by hordes of well-built young men, all wearing dark glasses and looking more menacing than the heavily armed airport security. This was just as it had been planned. Publicity would be built up slowly, reaching a peak at the park's grand opening in two weeks' time.

As Ted stood at the exit to Heathrow's VIP arrivals lounge, gazing out over the sun-drenched taxi rank where his personal limo took up three spaces, his personal aide, Casper P. Addleflower turned to him and grinned. 'Beautiful day, sir. A sign of the Lord smiling down on our heavenly mission?'

'You bet Casp!' Ted beamed. 'And he'll smile all the more once we've saved thisy here continent for Jesus.'

A Frenchman's Home Is His Castle

Mike stood at the living room window of his new home watching the furniture van accelerate down the drive. It would take months to fill the rooms, make the place feel lived in, but at least he'd made a start. Any hopes he might have entertained that Deborah was the domestic type had been scotched when he overheard her telling a door-stepping sales rep quite firmly what he could do with his textile samples.

Apart from such minor outbursts Mike's companion had been in pensive mood. The disappearance of the Pyramids, which had been headline news around the world for the past two days, had given Deborah more than a few things to think about. Mike now knew her enough to let her come to terms with events in her own time. The pair had come to an unspoken understanding, Mike didn't mention it and Deborah acted as if nothing had happened. A bit of peace and quiet would bring her round.

Unfortunately, at the moment peace and quiet were in shorter supply than volunteers at a Rottweiler wrestling competition. Around the farm's extensive grounds workmen were busy erecting a high steel fence. Builders were laying cables and wiring the perimeter to the spanking new generator house. The locally quarried stone that faced this structure concealed walls of two-metre-thick reinforced concrete. Why anyone should want a rustic water-wheel replaced with a cross between an air-raid bunker and the Hoover Dam no one had found it their business to ask. Mike had been particularly careful over this point. He'd rung around until he finally discovered a security firm that did this sort of job, then made it very clear he didn't want any awkward questions. Like: 'Is a mine-field really necessary to deter trespassers?' Naturally, a small fortune changing hands always smoothed the course of discreet business transactions.

That was all in the future though. Mike needed to phone some shady Middle-Eastern contacts before he could take delivery of those particular TNT-tulips. But already the hardware was beginning to build up. It was surprising, and rather depressing, just what you could get hold of these days if the money was good. On a flat section of the farmhouse roof stood a padded wooden crate. A sticker on the side read: UKRAINIAN VODKA – HANDLE WITH EXTREME CARE. A decoy purely for the benefit of H.M. Customs. The contents were equally lethal, but of a rather more direct nature.

The men contracted by the security firm went about their work with speed and efficiency. Soon they would be gone, replaced by another set of labourers who would start on converting the basement. Mike wasn't happy about this – it meant a good deal of coming and going – but at least no one group got the entire picture. It wasn't that Mike was paranoid, just careful like a cat at a Kennel Club Christmas party. Besides, now he had a house and the work underway there was no particular rush. If his calculations were correct, and they had been up to now, he and Deborah had two more months until the security measures would start earning their keep.

'What would you like in your omelette?' said Deborah, breaking his train of thought.

'What've we got?' he called, watching an electrician fitting a surveillance camera onto a long pole. There followed some brief banging of cupboards and a loud whirr as the brand new refrigerator door was opened.

'Eggs. This is not exactly a well stocked fridge, Mike.' The pair hadn't had time for shopping, not with Armageddon round the corner and arms shipments still to be ordered.

Minutes later, Deborah emerged carrying two steaming plates. They sat down at a huge mahogany table, still shrink-wrapped in plastic sheeting, and tucked in. After a few mouthfuls Deborah coughed hesitantly. 'There's some things I've been meaning to ask you Mike. What exactly is going to happen as we get closer to December, 31st? You've been rather vague up until now.'

The Professor smiled: so she really *was* coming to terms with events. Feeling more hopeful than he had done in weeks, Mike looked towards the window and the sunny valley beyond. 'I think that somewhere, quite soon, there's going to be a battle. A contest between two diametrically opposed forces. A decision once and for all on who's in control of this neck of the woods.'

'You mean a war? That doesn't make sense, there's no one left in the ring who could stand up to the Yanks – even with the mess they're in at the moment.'

Mike looked pained. 'I'm afraid, my dear, that these antagonists are, how can I put it, of a rather less worldly nature. Two fundamental philosophies are going to collide, and the results will not be pretty.'

Deborah's brown eyes went wide. 'What, good and evil? Are the men in white and black hats going to ride into town and shoot it out? Give me a break.'

'I don't think it's even that simple.' Mike rubbed his chin pensively. 'I've never been comfortable with the idea of absolute good and absolute evil. They're overused concepts, relying too heavily on fallible human emotions. No sane man ever thought of himself as "evil" – it's all subjective. History is nearly always written by the winners.'

'But what about . . . Hitler, for example? You're not saying he was anything less than evil?'

'Oh I'm sure he was, by my definition and by that of all right-thinking people. But who are right-thinking people? What makes our viewpoint any more valid than the millions who followed him? All I'm saying is that good and evil can't be natural forces since opinion can't be measured under laboratory conditions. Five hundred years ago, those same right-thinking people would have thought you unspeakably evil for daring to believe the Earth went round the Sun, or that stoning an adulteress wasn't a just thing to do. If they knew you talked to a cat and wore those shorts – well, they'd be piling the firewood high in the name of all that was good faster than you could say "hubble, bubble, toil . . . " and all the rest of it. If there's one thing living for five hundred years teaches you, it's that what goes around, comes around. Human morals are no more a natural constant than skirt lengths or the price of pork belly on the Chicago futures market.'

Deborah looked confused. 'But what else is there if it's not good and evil that'll be slugging it out?'

'You're clearly the victim of your early indoctrination, same as everyone else. The years simply give me a sense of perspective. My best guess would be, Order versus Chaos. They're far more fundamental agencies. Completely amoral, and in their purest form way beyond the scope of human understanding. Try thinking of them as political parties, and this is going to be the big vote.'

'But why here? If humanity's so insignificant on the cosmic scale . . . why on Earth? And, more to the point, *where* on Earth?'

'Two very good questions my dear, only one of which I can satisfactorily answer. My, you are having a good day aren't you? Perhaps we could phone your tutor and have your finals brought forward.'

Deborah's expression darkened. 'Mike, first of all you are my tutor, and second if you don't stop patronizing me, you'll be wearing that omelette instead of pushing it around your plate like it was Quatermass's last experiment.'

Mike grinned as he scooped a large forkful into his mouth. 'Who's to say? The Middle East is tottering on the brink again, though there's nothing unusual about that. My bet's on some madman launching a belated bid to kick the Children of Israel out of the land of Canaan. Always a good starting point. Historically.'

'Then why the elaborate precautions here?

'I have car insurance Deborah, but I don't *plan* to crash. Over the centuries I've found Baden Powell had it about right – and I don't mean the secret of a happy life lies in riding along on the crest of a wave when the sun is in the sky. The repercussions from these events will sweep the planet like a bad case of the clap. And I, for one, don't want to make any embarrassing visits to specialist clinics.'

Deborah thought for a moment, then looked at Mike slyly. 'If I didn't know you better, and perhaps I don't, I might think you very skilfully changed the subject just then. What about the first part of my question? Why on this Earth, and why now?'

Mike put on his most innocent face, the one he saved for young policemen and high-court judges. He wasn't being secretive. The truth was he didn't have a good answer. 'The why now part is easy my dear, I'm sure you don't need my help on that one.'

Deborah looked dubious. 'The end of the Millennium? Comets falling from the sky, dragons rising from the sea, talking horses and heavenly visitations? Mike, this isn't the Dark Ages.'

'I wouldn't be so sure, my dear.'

'But that doesn't tie in with what you've already said. Our own Western calendar is no more a 'fundamental natural law' than human morality. Why should the big milometer in the sky running up two-triple-zero have any bearing on events? It doesn't make sense.'

'Very little of what happens on this planet ever makes sense,' sighed Mike, 'and this business is going to make it ten times worse. Sometimes I feel like I'm fighting a losing battle just to stay one step ahead of events. Aristotle going missing doesn't help either.'

Deborah looked concerned. 'Yeah, where is he? Aren't you worried, we haven't heard from him in nearly two days now.'

'Aristo has always been a law unto himself. He's gone off on his own in the past, he just usually lets me know where he's going first.'

'Can't we use our . . . you know,' Deborah wiggled a hand in front of her forehead, 'our telepathic link to contact him?'

Mike shook his head. 'As I'm sure you've discovered yourself, it only works when you're in close proximity. It's no different for me, my girl. I wouldn't be too concerned just yet though. I haven't yet known a scrape that Aristo couldn't wriggle out of. Give him a few more days, then we'll start to worry.'

* * *

A few more days and he did. At Deborah's insistence they set out to look for the AWOL cat. Leaving the frenetic building site behind they drove up into the surrounding hills, Deborah arguing that since Aristo had set off to do a bit of hunting, it was as good a place as any to start looking. But they went more out of hope than any real conviction. After several hours of fruitless searching, along a bewildering maze of narrow forest tracks, they abandoned the car and struck off into the dense undergrowth on foot.

'This is hopeless,' declared Deborah as they arrived at a small clearing below a rocky outcrop, 'we're not likely to just bump into him in an out of the way spot like this. We've got to do this systematically.'

Mike was equally concerned. 'I fear you're right my dear. We have to apply some sort of logic to this problem. Perhaps we should drive down to the village, see if Hywell has heard anything about a geriatric stray cat with a bad attitude?'

As Mike started talking, a funny sensation overcame Deborah. She felt herself weaken suddenly, drift eerily out of the conversation. Clumsily, she sat down on the mossy grass to take a breather. The craggy outcrop that she'd noticed as they first came into the clearing had inexplicably started to bug her. She kept looking up at it, studying it intently, and her eyes kept noticing a patch of blackness beneath its rocky summit.

Mike knelt down beside her, laid a hand on her shoulder. 'Are you all right, dear?'

Deborah pointed vaguely at the crag, still a bit dizzy but her mind now beginning to clear again. 'Mike? Do you see that cave up there? Does it seem . . . odd to you?'

Mike followed her gaze. 'Not especially, my dear. The hills are riddled with them round these parts.'

Deborah frowned. 'I don't know. I feel funny. It . . .

bothers me. There's something not quite right about all this. And . . . have you noticed that smell?'

Mike sniffed the still air. 'Now you come to mention it there is quite a pong isn't there. Almost sulphuric . . .'

Suddenly Deborah was up and drawing her jacket tightly around her. 'I don't like this place Mike, it gives me the creeps. Let's get back to the car, please. *Now.*'

Mike was about to agree wholeheartedly when he was interrupted by a fearful crashing and breaking of branches from the undergrowth behind them – something big moving towards them through the woods at high speed.

Guttlehog and Rubicante, who had spent a very frustrating morning searching the barren hillsides and secluded valleys for a certain individual themselves, blundered back into the forest clearing that was serving as their temporary base. And they were in a foul mood.

'That's the last time I follow your suggestions,' muttered Rubicante, as he leaned his massive head to one side and tapped it with a taloned paw. 'That swamp water has got everywhere. None of my ears are going to be the same again.'

Guttlehog was about to counter that it had been Rubicante's idea to check the marshy areas 'in case Nostrus is hiding in there' when he clapped eyes on their visitors.

Meanwhile the humans' moods were going through an equally extreme polarity shift. 'Oh my goodness!' exclaimed Mike, with an entirely genuine look of horror on his face. Deborah just gazed on in a stupor, her usual pragmatism drunk and disorderly in the face of reality.

First to react were the demons. 'That's him!' declared Rubicante excitedly, 'I'd recognize that ugly pink face anywhere. Let's get him Gutts.'

Guttlehog was slowed down by the extent of his initial enthusiasm. His hind legs rubbed together so fast they threatened to start a fire amongst the bracken.

'Yaaaaaaaarg!', he yelled from amongst a cloud of smoke as he began his charge.

But the lumbering Boar Demon only managed to get one cloven hoof down in front of the other before he was stopped dead in his tracks. From out of the undergrowth beside him he was hit by a ginger and white blur that streaked all over him in a frenzy of fur and claw. The biological cluster-bomblet wrestled the giant demon to the floor with heroic ferocity.

Aristotle had been trailing the demons on their morning hike, just as he had done since watching them gatecrash Crystal's informal coven. His had been a subtle plan of patient intelligence gathering and observation. Today, he felt confident enough about the idiotic demons' motives to think about reporting back to his human assistant – but now that same human assistant had blundered in on the act, complicating things as usual. Aristotle resolved to give Mike a severe dressing down for compromising the artistic beauty of his achievement up to that point, but it would have to wait until later. Not for the first time in their acquaintance he scampered to Mike's rescue.

With Guttlehog down and thoroughly confused by the pace of events, Aristotle turned his attention to the Fire Demon. One swift swipe of his claws to the demon's delicate insectoid nether regions had the desired effect. Within seconds Rubicante was writhing on the floor in agony next to his bewildered accomplice, sickly green fluid squirting into the air from his numerous lacerations.

Aristotle kept greetings to his friends as brief as possible. *Follow me quickly and don't argue. They won't be down for long.*

'We've got the car,' Deborah said breathlessly.

Aristotle flicked his tail. *I'd gathered that. You were hardly out for a quiet stroll from the village, were you.*

Mike and Deborah raced after him, past the thrashing demons. They had no time to marvel at the timing of

Aristotle's reappearance, they were too glad just to be leaving the nightmarish scene behind them.

As they reached the car, the three of them piled in through any convenient orifice, Deborah landing at the steering wheel.

'Where to Mike – the house?'

The Professor had gone deathly pale. 'No. It's . . . it's not secure yet. We've got to put as much distance as possible between us and those things. Just drive, we'll work out the details later.' Deborah engaged the clutch and they rocketed off amidst a shower of gravel.

When they'd all calmed down as much as they were likely to under the circumstances, Mike turned to the cat. 'And where the hell have you been? We've been out of our minds with worry. The least you can do is warn me if you're going to disappear for the best part of a week.'

Aristotle's brow furrowed ominously. *'Where the hell have I been,' you ask? Well, today I've been saving your ungrateful hide from a pair of crack assassination demons, that is where I've been. Before that, I was trailing said demons in a completely successful attempt to ascertain their mission.*

Mike gave Aristo a long look then said through gritted teeth, 'If you hadn't disappeared, we wouldn't have tried to find you, we wouldn't have been ambushed and you wouldn't have had to be a hero.'

Deborah took Mike's arm, patted it gently. 'Mike, he saved our lives. I think you're being a little hard.'

There was silence for a moment then Mike let out a long breath. 'I know, I know. I'm sorry, old friend. I spoke out of turn . . . but I was just so worried.'

Aristotle gave him a disdainful sniff. *Unlike you, o calm one in extreme situations. You should have seen your face when they came after you. You aged another 500 years in a second, you wrinkly old prune.*

'All right, don't push it.' Mike chuckled. 'You were going to tell us about their mission.'

Those demons were looking for you, and doing a very bad job of it until you presented yourselves to them on a plate. The only accessory you were missing was an apple stuffed in your mouth. If I hadn't been there to save you I don't know what would have happened.

'I do,' said Deborah with a shudder. 'Where the hell were they from Mike?'

They're demons Deborah, Aristo butted in. *Where the hell do you think they're from?*

The colour drained from Deborah's face, but this time there was no protest against the obvious. 'So what do we do now?' she said eventually, in a very small voice.

'We lie low until the farm's defences are complete. Back to London my dear, and step on it,' Mike proclaimed, reverting suddenly to type, speaking, in fact, as though nothing extraordinary had just happened, had ever happened, in his long and uneventful life.

Karma-On-Down

If Karma could be thought of as a cosmic bank balance then Bill Winslow was currently running a massive overdraft. If he died right now he'd be lucky to come back as a member of the Top Of The Pops audience. The *Daily Trumpet*'s Editor in Chief had been writing some very large spiritual cheques lately and was in grave danger of being called in by the Great Bank Manager in the Sky to discuss his credit terms. But then, in this job you had to be ruthless to survive.

'Have you gone completely bonkers, MacArthur?' the big Australian blustered. 'If you think for one minute you can pass this pot of piss off as a story you're dumber than a delirious dingo. You've been hitting the grog again haven't you?'

Adam held his ground manfully as all the while his stomach did somersaults halfway up his throat. He'd seen

Winslow like this too many times to remember but it was still like standing too close to a jumbo jet at take-off – you always got burned, and you never got used to it.

'Boss, if you'll just take a look at this stuff, you'll see what I mean. Have you ever known me to come to you with anything less than the best? Read it – it's dynamite.'

Adam was sitting in Winslow's dirty cluttered office looking across his dirty cluttered desk at his dirty cluttered boss. And the current centrepiece of disorganization in Winslow's room was a pile of stained and crumpled papers – the evidence. Adam had spent the past two days removing bits of food and assorted debris from the sheets, but somehow the mound managed to retain its fruity odour.

Winslow barely paused for breath. 'The least I can do, as you put it, is turn you over to Environmental Health you festering freak. You're a disgrace to our honourable profession of journos, and ya reek like a roo with a ruptured bowel.'

Adam was in no way deflated. Persistence, cheek and full body armour were required to get your point across to Winslow. Adam only had the first two, but then he liked to live dangerously. 'What we've discovered could be the story of the Millennium. The biggest story, in fact, since some Roman DIY fan nailed up that Palestinian carpenter's apprentice on the first Easter Bank Holiday instead of some shelves.'[1]

Was Adam imagining it or did Winslow finally show a spark of interest? Bravely he pressed on. 'This Nostrus guy somehow knew about the Pyramid theft before it happened – these letters prove it. Either that or it's the biggest coincidence since Noah's missis got her washing

---

1 Not many people know it, but the correct sequence for chocolate manufacturers' favourite holiday runs: Good Friday, Easter Sunday, DIY Monday.

in "just to be on the safe side". These letters are dated last week, look Boss.' Adam thrust a spotted sheet under Winslow's nose.

The bloated sweaty mountain that was Bill Winslow stared at the printed page with faint disgust. He had to admit that any new angle on the Great Pyramid Heist was worth a look. The frenetic newsroom beyond his door was occupied with covering little else. One rival paper had even gone so far as to claim the monuments were stolen by aliens – now that really was ridiculous . . .

'He knew about last week's fish fall too – that's how we first tracked him down.'

Winslow held the sheet and studied it intently. It was clearly a first draft but despite the scribbled alterations the message was clear. The letter was from some Professor to Kestrel Alliance Insurance, claiming the dividend on a policy covering the Pyramids. He now had to admit this could be more than just an angle. The word 'conspiracy' was always worming around Winslow's frontal lobes. Now it had burrowed its way into his eyes and was there for all to see.

'Have you talked to him yet?' Winslow demanded.

'He hasn't been at home for the past two days. From what we've been able to gather he's sodded off house hunting in North Wales.' Adam said the words as though he could barely get them out of his mouth, such was his utter incomprehension: *North Wales?* 'God knows why – but some of the letters are addressed to estate agents up there. And the story gets even better. We've found more sheets ready typed with other predictions coming up. They're addressed to bookmakers and loss assessors!'

Winslow looked from the young reporter to the heavily soiled desk before him surveying the accumulating evidence, and an almost angelic expression broke out on his round face. Adam knew this was too good to last, and suddenly his boss crashed back down to earth like a meteor late for a meeting.

'Well, arsehole – what are ya waiting for? Get out there and reel this baby in!'

Take Me, I'm Yours

At that very moment, two hundred million miles above Bill Winslow's head, a huge dark shape slid silently through the black cosmic void. The cargo hold of this massive star transporter currently held six-and-a-half million tons of carefully masoned sandstone, a small cloud that had been unfortunate enough to be floating overhead at the time, a large chunk of the Sahara Desert, and one very startled camel called Trevor.

So the five-thousand-year lease on the Saharan Desert site was up. However, the Dolman Corporation had not become the galaxy's foremost marketing managers and real estate speculators by failing to cover their multifaceted rear ends. The contract that the long-dead Pharaoh Khufu had signed with the not-quite-so-dead Q'almn had included some very fine print. So fine in fact that the ancient Egyptians were unlikely to have developed the sophisticated image intensifying equipment needed to read it. And the gold-plated tablets that held the 999 verses of untranslatable quasi-religious poetry which made up the contract were buried under three hundred metres of inhospitable desert – on Mars. This minute text, etched with the finest calligraphy lasers, stipulated that should the Dolman Corporation fail to be informed otherwise the site in question would revert to them on termination of the lease – for The Rest Of Time, or until 6:30 p.m. Friday 14th March 2001AD, whichever came first.

Since those heady days in the early Bronze Age when planet Earth was a major tourist attraction, trade had slackened considerably. Once you'd seen one nitrogen/oxygen-dependent planet with carbon-based life-forms and atrocious weather, you'd seen them all. Altair gave a slightly prettier sunrise, Tau Ceti Gamma had more entertaining wildlife (the herbivores were armour plated to protect them from the plants). Many races had concluded that any planet where the surface temperature dipped below 300°C was simply dull, dull, dull.

Despite the drop in interest, the Dolman Corporation maintained a small office on the planet's single, rather sad moon.[1] This complex was hidden round the back, permanently facing away from Earth thanks to very powerful ion-displacement engines and ingenious use of lime jelly.[2] The base was considered a distant outpost, where failed alien ad executives and discredited accountants whiled away the tail end of their careers monitoring countless broadcasts of *Celebrity Squares* and kidnapping the odd hill farmer now and then, just to keep their tentacles in.

There had been a brief upsurge in interest forty planetary cycles ago, when for a while it looked like Earth's two major power blocks might put on a firework display that the more voyeuristic visitor might enjoy. Sadly for the tourist business, if not for the human race, the little altercation over Cuba had singularly failed to live up to its potential. But now things were picking up again. It was hard for an outsider to comprehend, but down there something was bubbling, and this cosmic home brew would

---

1 No match for the hilarious Juggling Moons of Jakaara-Beta VI.

2 Everybody knows about the many Apollo space missions that orbited the moon in the '60s and '70s. Very few people know that, along with their crew of American astronauts, these capsules carried surprising quantities of lime jelly in their overcrowded cargo lockers, smuggled aboard at the last minute by alien deep cover agents working within NASA. This luminous green comestible was, of course, of no earthly origin, being in fact a powerful psychedelic drug fed to the crew to make them forget what they saw. It has long been noted that many astronauts on these missions reported them to be strangely spiritual experiences, often returning to Earth changed men.

give the locals more than just a screaming headache and a desire to consume the entire contents of their fridge in one mouthful.

It all had to do with the strange hairless bipeds who inhabited the planet, their customs which were stranger still, and the one very powerful innate ability that set mankind apart from the run of the intergalactic mill.

Imagine

Not many people, not even Mike, knew that all gods exist. Of course, it rather depends what you mean by 'exist' and 'gods', but taking for the moment the usual definitions this statement stands as valid. Atheists, agnostics and Church of England vicars fail to credit the creative powers of the human subconscious. If enough people believe only slightly in Cello-Flame, Lord of Masking Tape, then somewhere nearby 'The Great Sticky One' will spring into existence.

There's nothing mystical about it. It was all explained long ago in a galaxy far, far away, by a nameless, warlike and philosophical race. This rather unfortunate species were the first to record what has since become known as the Second Law of Thermotheology. Simply put, this states that the Multiverse is awash with faithons, the smallest measurable particle of belief. When enough sentient beings concentrate these sub-belief particles into one particular form the new god appears in a flash of fidelity and in full accordance with the Laws of Conservation of Conviction. With dawning dread the Nameless-ones realized that when enough entities accepted the Second Law as fact, the Second Law would itself spring into existence in a hail of faithons. This horrible discovery led to numerous letters to the editor of the planet's favourite magazine,[1] seven

1 *Angst-Ridden Warrior-Philosopher Today* – Brought to you by Far-Future Publishing Ltd, 30 Monumental Street, Aqua-Sullis.

bloody global wars, and so much navel gazing that the entire race disappeared up their own primary rectums.

Millions of years later, when the first Dolman Corporation scout ships passed through that part of the galaxy, they found only a hasty inscription carved on the inside of a toilet door as a mark of that once-great-race's passing. When it was at last translated the awestruck aliens discovered that it read:

WHATEVER YOU DO,
TRY NOT TO THINK ABOUT IT . . .

For countless aeons this simple philosophy had stood the universe in good stead. But now, sadly, someone, somewhere was crapping in the bidet of spiritual peace.

Despite its many failings, such as a complete inability to live happily with itself, humankind has one thing going for it – imagination. The sheer weight of this dynamic driving force had in the past five thousand years propelled human technology like a turbo-charged cheetah running for the last night bus home. In this tiny speck of comparative time, humanity had gone from a squatting-in-a-cave-rubbing-two-sticks-together primitive existence to the highest pinnacle of civilization: neutron bombs and microwavable chicken tikka massala. It had taken the Nameless-ones twice as long just to develop underarm deodorant.

Sadly, innate creativity has inevitable drawbacks. Apart from the million new ways it found to kill itself, humankind became afflicted by that most horrendous of vices – non-fact-based belief systems. Nowhere amongst the uncountable stars do so many gods gather as around Earth's crackling aether. Human theology became a cosmic soap opera jam-packed with rape, incest, mindless violence and countless acts of all round unbridled debauchery. Over the past few months the Dolman Corporation's monitoring teams on Lunar had watched in fascination as the human psyche began to put on a show that made the average supernova look like a wet Sunday afternoon around Casiopea. With all haste they reported back to their superiors that an apocalyptic conclusion was nigh. As slime-green amorphous marketing mangers pulsated in baths of bubbling cryogenic fluid back at head office, the commercial angles of human theology were not lost on them.

Of course with these deranged gods and goddesses came their equally obnoxious sidekicks. Two of which were currently planning a very special surprise party in Professor Nostrus's darkened front room.

Leave A Light On For Me

Two very bruised and battered servants of hell spent the entire afternoon licking their wounds in the small forest glade where they had surprised Mike and Deborah. Rubicante and Guttlehog were not known for their convivial frames of mind, and seeing the target they had spent so much time and effort tracking slip through their talons had not done much for their tempers. With revenge as well as what little professional pride they had left burning in all their eyes, they had resumed their search.

Their second piece of stunning good luck that day was to stumble upon Mike's new home as dusk fell on Noddegamra. Despite Rubicante's initial relief he was disappointed to find their victim wasn't there. Guttlehog's disappointment was not entirely genuine however – he had no desire to continue his acquaintance with the Professor's fearsome familiar.

The builders had left for the night, leaving the farm in a frightfully insecure state. Cement mixers and bulldozers stood next to packing crates, amongst great reels of deadly barbed wire. Oddly shaped packages lay beneath tarpaulins like surreal sculptures in the dark and still garden. Once inside, Guttlehog and Rubicante set about waiting with some apprehension for their prey to return.

'Do you think they'll be back tonight?' mumbled Guttlehog, trying unsuccessfully not to think about that afternoon's events, and the pair's first painful brush with Aristotle.

'Who's to say?' hissed Rubicante bitterly. He had developed a pronounced limp and he wasn't happy about it. 'You never know with these humies. Here one minute, gone the next. Unreliable sods, the lot of them. And since you messed things up today, they might have been scared off. Though with that little bodyguard of his I don't know what he's got to be scared of.'

'Sssssshhhh!' spluttered Guttlehog, an exclamation particularly suited to his dental setup. 'I thought I heard someone!'

The two demons froze. Not literally, though Rubicante had colleagues who could do just that. They crouched in the darkness straining all their senses to the faint sound that came from outside the window. Between them they had detection equipment the CIA would have killed for, but whatever had made the noise was staying very still.

'Quick,' whispered Rubicante. 'Into position – this time we nail him!'

I Don't Want To Set The World On Fire

'Get down!' hissed Gwylym, Commander in Chief of The Gwynedd People's Liberation Army (Noddegamra Front). He and his elite shock troops of the Celtic Revolution – Ivan – were currently lying face down on the gravel path beneath Mike's living-room window. As usual, the Colonel was in complete control of the situation. 'Stay put,' he growled, 'I thought I saw something move in there!'

'But you said they left this afternoon?' Ivan protested.

'Watched 'em drive off in that old banger of his.'

The combat-jacketed young man was not above burning houses in pursuit of a Free Welsh Homeland but he drew the line at torching people – even if they were only English. Adding to his general unease, Ivan had the nasty suspicion one of the petrol cans was leaking over his nice new camouflage trousers.

'Silence in the ranks! How can I listen with you yapping away like an 'Ampstead arsehole?'

The freedom fighters lay still, straining their ears for the slightest sound. When it became apparent all was quiet once again Gwylym rose slowly to his knees and peered into the dark house. Assured that the room was empty, he motioned for his accomplice to get up from the flowerbed.

'You sure 'bout this?' Ivan asked nervously – second thoughts were second nature to him. 'Doesn't look like any normal holiday home to me. What 'bout all 'em boxes?'

As well as having the humility of Hitler, Gwylym had the patience too. 'I dun'ow do I? Probably British Military Intelligence opening a branch office – cracking down on us no doubt. Yeah! . . . This is a secret MI5 Command Centre to suppress the Welsh language and culture! Grab the gasoline 'n lets torch the scum before they let rip.'

Gwylym took a crowbar from his well-stocked webbing and jemmied the back door. Shortly, the pair stood nervously in the dark kitchen, looking for all the world like two small boys who'd snuck into school at midnight with enough flammable material to take out most of Britain's secondary education system.

Gwylym broke the uneasy silence. 'Right then, reconnaissance before attack!' With that he rushed off through a dim doorway leaving a trembling Ivan floundering in his wake. Once Ivan had pulled himself together, he followed suit. But as he arrived at the foot of the stairs, alone and in the dark, Ivan felt the hairs on the back of his neck rise up in alarm.

'Let's get on with it Gwylym,' he called faintly. 'I got a bad feeling 'bout this one. I want out of 'ere.'

'What are you,' called his commander from the gloom above him, 'man or sheep? 'Aint no one 'ere but us – though there might be some sensitive military documents lying about.'

'But –'

'Ivan, we can't pass up a chance like this. Stay put till I get back and don't start the operation without me.'

With that Gwylym disappeared from view, leaving Ivan with nothing but his primeval dread to keep him warm. Pretty soon he went from warm to hot. He'd never liked the dark and the blackness around him seemed filled with shadows. In an attempt to allay his fears he struck a match and peered about him.

The house was sparsely furnished, the dark shapes he'd mistaken for SAS troopers lying in ambush were nothing but unpacked furniture. It all looked new, as if the owner was still in the process of moving in. Silly sod, Ivan told himself with a relieved grin, the only danger in this place was from breaking an ankle on the bottomless shag-pile rug.

Ivan gave a small yelp when his match burned down, fanning his fingers like a demented morris dancer. Cursing his clumsiness he fumbled for a new light. As he did this, he became aware of a dark shape gliding up to his shoulder. Sighing with relief at a return of human companionship, even if it was only Gwylym, he relaxed.

'My last match just went out, you got us a light?'

Generally speaking this is not a wise thing to say to a Fire Demon, especially when you're wearing petrol soaked trousers, standing in a deserted house at midnight and two hundred miles from the nearest burns unit.

Rubicante was somewhat taken aback by this breathtaking overfamiliarity on the part of a mere mortal. Reflecting sadly that manners were not what they used to be, he struck his inbuilt thumb-light, creating a fizzing ball of orange flame.

'Allow me, human dog,' he said with a rictus smile.

For one second man and demon locked vision sensor to bulging eyeball. What Rubicante saw was an open-mouthed young male with a shoe-polished face, holding two sloshing petrol cans and shaking like a malaria victim. This not-so-innocent bystander was clearly not the demon's designated target, but he was ripe for becoming the butt of a particularly hellish joke.

What Ivan saw was an eight-foot scarlet grasshopper with the lower body of a grizzly bear, enough hind legs for a five-a-side football team and a blow torch for a thumb. As if that wasn't enough, another hulking shadow had glided up behind the first. Ivan was not exactly up to speed at judging insectoid emotions, but the creature before him seemed to be grinning through two sets of mandibles. Ivan's eyes saw all this but, by this stage, his brain was mercifully out to lunch, an extremely long lunch – with prawn cocktail starters, rare beef-on-the-bone steaks, Black Forest Gâteau, coffee to follow and plenty of wafer thin mints. In the great tradition of countless horror films he chose the only option available . . .

'Aaaarrrrrhhhhhh!' he said and leapt from Rubicante's side like an exploding oil rig. A split second later this image became ever more fitting; any fast-moving, even vaguely flammable, body in the presence of a Fire Demon has an unfortunate tendency to spontaneously combust. Ivan rocketed towards the front door, crashing from wall to wall like a fiery pinball. Each collision left greasy soot stains on the brand new plaster. By the time he reached the exit his trousers were fully ablaze. Adjacent to the stout oak door were two full-length decorative windows. Despite his rather preoccupied state of mind Ivan correctly chose the quickest route to freedom, departing the hallway in a shower of glass.

From the bedroom above, Gwylym felt before he heard his comrade's combustion and subsequent exit. He rushed to a window just in time to see Ivan powering down the drive like a human dragster. Reasoning that they'd been rumbled, Free Wales's gallant leader scrambled out the window and down an ivy-covered drainpipe. Reaching the ground with a thud, he called:

'Wait for me, coward – I'm not getting nicked on my own!' But catching him wouldn't be easy. The last glimpse Gwylym got of him, Ivan was still accelerating towards a distant lake.

Five minutes later the demons stood on the front steps of Caer-Mathonwy Farm, watching the stars and reflecting philosophically on the vagaries of man. 'So, who were those two then?' asked Guttlehog, plucking an irritating parasite from his lower left armpit.

'Dunno,' replied Rubicante, voice dripping with disappointment. 'They didn't seem to want to stay and chat.'

SEVEN

> In those days witches and demons shall roam abroad,
> Though not in Ibiza.
> From the West a dark star shall fall from heaven,
> A wholly unholy holy-man.
> *Quatrain VII.13 The Lost Centuries of Nostradamus*

Salisbury Hill

Under what had once been a set of strangely shaped earthworks, near Britain's oldest spa town, a group of very famous individuals stirred. Slowly they woke from an extremely long sleep – the sort of slumber that made Snow White and Rumpelstiltskin look like coffee-guzzling insomniacs.

The fact that fifteen years earlier a local authority planning guru had decided to build a bypass clean across the ancient site had no bearing on this sudden animation. The eternal alarm clock in each man's armour-plated head was ringing for a different reason – a reason that threatened to make bypasses, nuclear power stations and all other manner of man's creations a thing of the past. But these boys did not fear mere death, they were to courage and valour what Adam MacArthur was to effortlessly written garbage. Besides, if they'd wanted to avoid trouble they would have done well to stay where they were.

All around the roughly hewn cavern the sleepers woke groggily from their trance. In the centre of the hall, atop an imposing granite altar, the room's chief occupant muttered incomprehensibly to himself as he shrugged off fifteen centuries of sleep. Over the last hundred years he'd developed a nasty crick in his neck and it was going to take rather more than the usual vigorous rub down with goose fat followed by a quick plunge in a cold mountain stream to shake this one loose. The rest of his battle-scarred body was in no better shape. All things considered, like countless overstressed man-managers before him, Arthur Pendragon was none too happy at having to get up and go to work.

Slowly he began to move. Some indecipherable signal had been passed to stir the world's champions to return, and this fellow was always at the front of the queue when a fight was brewing. Now it was almost time. The last grains of sand in the Cosmic Eggtimer had run away, signalling that planet Earth was done to a turn and the final confrontation between the diametrically opposed forces that lurked in the shadows of mankind's subconscious could begin. When it did, the Forces of Light's most steadfast hero would be ready, sword in hand and cliché on lip.

The apparently middle-aged men who'd shared Arthur's enchanted dreams were moving too. Their rest had been, by and large, peaceful. Some time during the twelfth century Sir Gawain, who had always been a light sleeper, had tossed restlessly and fallen off his granite bed. The sound of a fully armoured man hitting a stone floor would have wakened a mogadoned mastodon, but not these weary knights, they had slept on. Several minor earthquakes had rocked the cave over the years, littering the floor with debris and a few very shocked earthworms. No one had batted an eyelid. Even when, just fifty feet above their heads, the JCBs had destroyed one of the nation's beauty spots, none had stirred.

The years had seen changes to the sleepers themselves. Sir Bedwyr now clutched his sword like some steel teddy bear, sucking an armour-clad thumb through the visor of his dusty helm. Sometime before decimal coinage a small spider had made its home in Sir Bors's huge left nostril – living a happy life eking out a meagre existence sustained largely by the meatiness of the huge man's steady breath.

But now life was speeding up. Several of the knights were sitting up on their stone beds, shaking great armour-clad heads to throw off the grogginess of centuries. Even Arthur, recumbent on his stone dias, left his dreams of battle and creaked open one rheum-filled eye.

Sheep (Reprise)

'Aye, there's been lots of funny goings on round 'ere lately and no mistake.'

Emmyr was a farmer and, like country dwellers the world over, an expert at the art of understatement. He leaned on the gate of his top field, passing the time of day with Dick Richards his neighbour from down the valley. Nearby, the Noddegamra road shimmered silently in the hot sun. If they'd been wearing floppy hats or sucking on bits of straw Emmyr and Dick would have been a cliché. And proud of it.

Emmyr lazily swatted a fly from his nose. 'Purity Roberts swears blind Crystal's been summoning demons.'

Dick nodded thoughtfully. 'Lucky we never found that meeting place then – don't think I'd want to meet one.'

Emmyr grimaced at the memory. He still bore the scars from that night's uncoordinated ramble. 'Crystal might be horny but she can't summon demons, Dick. Whole bloody thing's just an excuse to strip off and prance about. They must'a got spooked when Purity showed up, that's all. Enough to scare anyone, that is.'

Dick shook his head in agreement. ''S not the end of the matter, though. I been talking to Old Mad Megan. She saw young Ivan running down from the Big 'Ouse with 'is trousers on fire, last night. That thug Gwylym was with 'im – lots of strange coloured lights in the sky too. She reckons that's where these demons're coming from. That new bloke's been calling 'em from the Pit of Foulest Acheron.'

Emmyr chuckled disbelievingly. 'Oh aye? Where's that when it's at 'ome then?'

Dick looked mystified, the natural set of his face. 'Down Bala way ain't it?'

There was a moment's silence before their geographical speculations were interrupted by a distant explosion. Emmyr glanced apathetically over his shoulder to the source of the detonation – a clump of trees down in the valley. 'That'll be another one gone,' he said stoically. 'Nothing I can do 'bout it – tried everything, I have. Still, the insurance'll cover 'em.'

Dick looked up. 'Your policy covers exploding sheep, do it?'

'Don't know for sure,' admitted Emmyr, 'but I'd like to see some suited young ponce from down the city try tell me otherwise.'

The farmers gazed down over Emmyr's best lambing field to where the remains of his flock drank at a tumbling mountain stream. Their number had depleted by half in little short of a week, and those still in one piece had a haunted, distant look in their eyes. All that marked the passing of their unfortunate brethren was a series of small craters dotted around the lush pasture.

'One minute there's a healthy young sheep. The next . . .' Emmyr made an expansive gesture with his hands, '. . . just four steaming hooves and a faint whiff of ba-ba-cued mutton. At me wits' end I is. Called in Vet Price from down Dollgellau. You know the one – he's a bit overfond of the ewes.'

'I know the one.'

'Well, he lost three fingers when Flossy went supernova on 'im during an internal inspection.'

'Serves him right, then. You got to keep emotional involvement out of it, especially when doing the internals.'

'Granted, but what did *I* do to deserve this?'

Dick tutted sympathetically – the whole affair was beyond even his skills of animal husbandry.

'Maybe you said something nasty to one when you was a child and you've since blocked it out . . .'

Emmyr surveyed his friend quizzically. 'You what?'

'They remember, sheep do. Maybe, as a species, they're getting their revenge.'

Before Emmyr could reflect on the Swiss-cheese-like quality of Dick's intelligence, the farmers were interrupted by a white sports car screeching to a halt beside them. A narrow-eyed young man glared out from the driver's side window and spoke very slowly.

'You there . . . um . . . country squires,' said Adam. 'Could you be so good – as to direct me – to the home of Michael Nostrus? He much important bigwig.'

Blank looks all round.

'Old, white hair, hasn't shaved in a while, bit of your sad professor type . . .'

Ditto.

Adam paused a second. 'Um, how about . . . 'e's not from round 'ere.'

'Wuurrrrrrrrguh' Dick bellowed involuntarily and started to dribble, a Pavlovian reaction to the phrase. It set in train a strange transformation deep inside his murky, confused subconscious. He was overcome with the condition that descends on country folk whenever asked directions by city dwellers. His accent put on seven league boots and strode off in the general direction of Somerset in a parallel universe where there are too many vowels and not enough consonants. 'Aaaaaaarpens ay doooooooooooooo . . . and aaaaarpens I don'.'

Then there was silence. Adam looked from one man to the other. There was enough material here for a whole series of articles . . .

'Well, could you possibly *'apen* to bloody well hurry up,

then? I'd like to get there before you catch up with the rest of the human race. Not all of us have time for sheep worrying and casual incest, which in your case must be pretty much the same thing.'

From somewhere beyond time and space a piece of straw appeared in Dick's mouth. 'Well 'at depends dow'n it . . . on whether you wants to take the quick route . . . or the slow route?'

Emmyr had seen enough. He gave his friend a hard, open-handed slap. You had to nip this sort of thing in the bud, otherwise the victim would spend every night for the rest of time drinking cider until he couldn't walk, tying his trouser legs with bits of string and talking endlessly about crop rotation. Dick looked startled and spat the piece of straw out in disgust.

Straightening his shoulders, and raising himself to his Welsh Standard 5′ 7″, Emmyr said: 'If you think you can talk to us like that, you've got another thing coming townie.'

'At least it was in English, Worzel. I'm surprised you understood me.'

'Who the 'ell do you think you are anyways? Driving up 'ere in your I've-got-a-two-inch-erection sports car and frightening my sheep. *Don't you know what they're going through?*'

Adam's lip curled menacingly. Emmyr had struck Adam's single raw nerve at the mention of his car. 'If you must know,' Adam said stiffly, 'I'm from Her Majesty's Press, investigating the story of the century. And I've got a cheque book to prove it.'

Emmyr's eyes lit up, and the second character transformation of the day was under way.

'Goin' to be in the papers then are we?' He wasn't about to let this snot-faced suit know, but he'd had a soft spot for Britain's elite corps of newshounds ever since receiving favourable reviews for his Jersey Milkers at the Royal Welsh Show.

'Might be,' Adam said coyly. 'Depends how helpful you are.'

Emmyr licked his lips, wrestled briefly with his self-respect, then lost by two falls and a submission. 'Some city outsider just moved into Caer-Mathonwy Farm – might be the one you're after. You want to be careful up there though, place is crawling with workmen by day and spooks by night. Some say the new-un's a wizard. I reckon he's the one exploding me sheep. He probably does it for the fun of it . . . Barstard.'

For a second it looked like a tear might form in the eyes of the less stupid of the two farmers. Adam stepped in before unruly sentiment got the better of his informer. 'Your sheep, I know – it happens. But this is national security, and I need directions. Like now –' Adam was interrupted by a faint explosion from the valley below, the origins of which he wisely chose not to pursue. It unnerved him slightly to see the two farmers ignore the detonation completely, as if such things were commonplace. In a faltering voice, Emmyr told him the way to 'the Big 'Ouse'. It wasn't far at all. Even if you got completely lost and had to go via Swansea it wasn't far, he was told.

'And if you want to 'ear 'bout me sheep,' he added, trying in vain to spark Adam's interest, 'you can usually find us in The Sword, down Noddegamra. Can't miss it.'

Adam nodded. He wouldn't miss anything round here – sooner he was back in London the better.

He crunched his car into gear and left the yokels for dust.

The two farmers stood quietly and watched the city ponce disappear with his advanced vehicle in a plume of dust. Shortly, there was no sound but the birds twittering in the trees and the soothing gurgle of the brook at the bottom of the field. Then a deep bleat and two explosions in quick succession shattered the tranquillity.

This time Emmyr winced. 'That's Snowflake gone. Thought with 'is constitution he might last out.'

Dick spat into the dust. 'They never do,' he said, shaking his head. 'Never do.'

I Like Driving In My Car

Unfortunately for Adam, Mike wasn't currently at home. Since returning to London the previous afternoon the Professor had been kept busy obtaining last-minute provisions and generally putting his affairs in order. At that precise moment, as Aristotle guarded their flat from possible rampaging demons, Mike and Deborah were returning from such an errand – sitting in a traffic jam on the M25 glorying at that wonder of modern technology which made it all possible.

'Aaaaaaaarrrrgh! I think I'm going slowly mad. I've been through a fair deal in my lifetime: I sat calmly in the Bastille for two years until the Revolution got me free, hardly batted an eyelid when I missed the boat and spent the best part of the 1840s in Tahiti, I didn't even blink when bad timing and the Waffen SS trapped me in Switzerland for so long I still shudder whenever I hear a cuckoo-clock – but I swear, if this traffic doesn't start moving soon I'll kill the next person that picks their nose and flicks it out of the window!'

Deborah was taking events in a rather calmer frame of mind. Cars had a strange effect on the brain. Put a normally sane person behind a wheel and all rationality deserted them. Things that seem like a good idea while in the driving seat had a slippery way of careering out of control. 'That gap looks big enough,' or 'The central reservation's looking pretty clear' or 'It's a bank holiday, lets go to the beach!' being cases in point. Norwegian lemmings couldn't outdo such spontaneous suicidal impulses. But Deborah didn't consider now a good time to share her theory.

Mike went on. 'It's almost as if there's some unseen force preventing us from getting home.'

Then, all too suddenly, the cause of the monumental snarl-up became clear. Running up the hard shoulder, and between the lines of stationary vehicles, came an intimidating file of smartly suited young men. Each wore a pair of mirrored Ray Bans and carried a wedge of brightly printed leaflets. Twenty yards behind, an outnumbered squad of exasperated police officers did their best to give chase. It was a losing battle. No sooner did an officer succeed in tackling one of the athletic young men than his accomplices would round on him and give him a severe going over. So cocky were these thugs that they had time to stop and hand out flyers to each of the bemused motorists who watched their steady progress.

'Good grief,' muttered Mike from between clenched teeth. 'It's those tiresome Trundellites again. Why can't they keep their loopy, unsubstantiated beliefs to themselves?'

Deborah looked aghast. 'This is madness. They've caused this traffic jam just to hand out some bloody leaflets? Why can't the authorities do something?'

'I'm rather afraid that Trundell has friends in very high places. He's tolerated because he gives the masses what they want: communion bread and circuses. These are his clowns.'

'They're not very funny.' Deborah watched as a Trundellite stepped over a prostrate policeman giving him a heel on the back of the neck just for good measure. 'Maybe we need an Armageddon.'

When one of them made a bee-line for their car, Deborah took events into her own hands. You could watch and tut from a safe distance or you could do something about it. She knew on which side of the lace curtain she stood. As the tall, earnest young man approached, Deborah shoved her door into his path, catching him with the wing mirror in a spot uniquely calculated to halt any man's progress, even a man of God's. He collapsed to the ground, wheezing pathetically. Deborah coolly stepped out and accepted one of his pamphlets.

'Thank you so much,' she said brightly.

She beckoned over one of the haunted-looking police officers, who seemed only too glad to accept help from whatever quarter they could. 'I think you'll find he's causing an obstruction,' she said, before calmly climbing back into the car.

Mike gave her an appraising look as she handed him the leaflet. 'Well, I suppose that's one less jaywalker for the Met to worry about.'

'Always honoured to do my civic duty,' Deborah said with a satisfied smile.

Mike gazed at the gaudy brochure for a moment, as if it were a recipe for mustard gas, then thrust it back at her. 'If you think this stunt is madness just wait and see what they've got planned for tonight. Read it, my girl. Just don't expect it to make any sense. Organized religion stopped making sense to me just about the same times as I hit puberty.'

'I didn't know you had . . .'

Jesus Wants Me For An Electromagnetic Wavefront

Later that evening, just a short executive helicopter ride from Mike's flat, forty thousand pining souls packed Wembley Arena to hear God's disciple on earth proclaim the gospel according to Trundell. He was in full flood, both verbally and perspirationally. Preaching to the converted he may been but 'Ten-Ton Ted'[1] didn't let that hold him back.

---

1 'Every sermon:
Ten tons of sinners saved,
ten tons of money made.'

The louder he ranted the more he sweated, the more he sweated the more he became agitated. It was a dangerous positive-feedback situation that threatened to cause major flooding throughout the North London area.

'Ayyyyyyyyyyyyy-men brothers and sisters!' he screamed, standing beneath a seventy-foot TV image of his own immaculately sculpted head.

'AYYYYYYYYYYYYYYYY-MEEEN!' came the answer from the slowly swaying throng. Even the most frenzied of the faithful couldn't fail to keep up with the lyrics, thanks to the banks of monitors suspended high above the arena. This first gig had been carefully planned – only selected members of affiliated local denominations were present so a red-hot reception had been guaranteed. Still, the Church's battalion of travelling warm-up men had handed over the marks in fine mood, thought Ted as he adjusted the gain on his radio microphone.

'Now, now . . . ladies and gentlemen.' Ted held up a beautifully manicured hand for silence. It was a long time in coming. In their near trance-like state the audience's wailing and moaning went on for an eternity. In the aisles several of the worst affected twitched maniacally, mouths foaming. When the security guards, in their dark glasses and Italian suits, had carried them away, Ted continued.

'Please brothers and sisters, be at peace. There'll be plenty of time for a-hootin 'n' a-hollerin later. First, I have some great news to shar with yo'all.'

A hush fell over the stadium as the lights dimmed to a single spotlight on the lone figure on the stage. Behind Ted, images of stars and planets faded in and out of the blackness. He crouched down low.

'We live in great times, brothers and sisters.' He almost whispered the words, and later many of those present would claim Ted had spoken directly to them. 'We're privileged to live at a time foretold long ago in prophecy. But don't think we're granted this boon lightly . . . Oh no. Just like any privilege this one entails responsibility. The greater the privilege, the greater the responsibility – and this one's a real humdinger.'

Ted rose to his feet as behind him great galaxies swirled and formed on the giant screen. 'Yes, my fellow travellers, we're lucky to be living in The Last Days. Those alive on Earth and safe in God's love will live to see the Final Judgement, and the Paradise on Earth that comes hereafter. It's not long now, I can feel it, we can aaaall feel it, coming like a great freight train thunderin' across the prairie.' From the immense sound system came a barely audible *toot-toot*. An awed moan rose from the audience. 'But fear not, my children, you here tonight are all set to move in the right direction on that great day. For move we must, every last one of us – pink, black, yellow, brown, red, white and blue . . . Yes, even the Eskimos must stand up and be counted when the Final Trumpet sounds. And you know, of course, there are only two directions you can travel. Up or . . .'

The single spotlight on Ted turned from a brilliant white through a sickly yellow, to the sort of red they used to paint hospital operating theatres back in the days when penicillin was something you scraped off your sandwiches. Forty-foot flames leaped and crackled on the screens around him.

'. . . DOWN! My children, all the fornicators, faggots, felons, fakirs, flesh-pots, philanderers, false witnesses, false prophets, pansies, pagans, papists, pacifists, pantomimes, pantheists and pan-worshippers will be cast down into the pit from whence they crawled – to burn for all eternity!'

Not entirely spontaneously (there was ample prompting from the giant speakers either side of the stage) the audience broke into an ear-splitting cheer. Ted rode it like the old pro he was.

'Rights and responsibilities. Reward – or retribution . . . Yes, the Lord God he may be all-powerful, he may be the Rocky Bilboa of this particular ring, the undisputed heavyweight champeeen of this here universe, but this is one event where he needs our aid. Before the chosen hear his heavenly call there remains the small matter of smiting his ancient enemy once and for all! And this won't be some allegorical fight behind the scenes, it'll happen right here on Earth, with both sides manifest in all their heavenly and hellish splendour. The good news is that we lucky few get to carry the Lord's banner into battle against the forces of evil arrayed against him.'

More cheering from the crowd, if a little subdued this time.

'Even though we're assured of victory, the Big Fella wants to lift as many of our wayward brethren up to heaven as possible. In the few weeks left, make it your mission to save a lost soul. Reach out to your friends, neighbours and families, tell them the good news of God's everlasting abundance. And what better way to do that ladies and gentlemen, than to bring 'em along to our brand new all-round-fountain-of-family-fun, The Wings Over Creation Theme Park and Shopping Mall Experience. Conveniently situated just off Junction 12 of your M1 Interstate Expressway, this facility offers everything you and your family could wish for on the perfect day out. Why, even the most stubborn unbeliever couldn't help but be swayed by the wide selection of high-quality, low-cost goods, services and entertainments on offer at this site. So bring 'em along folks, and sign 'em up for the fight of their lives. I, myself, hereby pledge to find and rescue the most wayward souls on earth, and if I can do it, you sure as heaven can. After all, I'm just a small-town country boy, out of his depth in this big, big city.'

Ted gave 'em his best winsome look. It had the desired effect. Soon the whole building was rocking to the steady beat of stamping feet and frantic hymn singing. The tune was familiar but some bright boy in the Church of the

Eloquent Announcement's Psychological Warfare Division had been playing around with the lyrics. They flashed up on the giant screens in bright neo-gothic letters . . .

Onward Trundell's Children,
Marching as to war,
With the sword of Jesus,
Crushing all before.

Make no peace with sinners,
God is on our side,
We will be the winners,
When we turn the tide.

Oooohh!

Forward Ted's brave army,
Slaying all in sight
Cut them up in pieces
'Til they see the light . . .

And so it went on. It wasn't likely to win any music industry awards – its creator would never stand before an overfed, dinner-jacketed audience, accepting a deformed statuette from a scantily clad hostess made top-heavy by a surfeit of teeth and silicon implants. But it did the required job.

Despite the air of euphoria around him, Ted was not a happy man. As he came off stage he was met by his long-suffering Personal Assistant, Casper P. Addleflower.

'Not good enough Casp! We're not getting through to these Engle-lish people. I want a big improvement starting yesterday.'

'But sir, your reception was second to none. I haven't seen a crowd stirred like that since Atlanta '97 when they had to call out the Guard to stop our people torching that mosque.'

Ted waved a dismissive hand back towards the arena where the info-screens were telling the leaving multitudes how Paradise on Earth would affect their tax situation beneficially. 'Oh, I don't mean these folks. They're hotter than a coyote's callus on a Death Valley black top – but they was already half-ways round to our line of thinking. I mean the Engle-lish folks in general. Why, out front of this pissant tin shack they call a national stadium, I only saw one outside broadcast truck from a national network! Back home we'd get them all killing for position at a gig like this.'

Casper cleared his throat uncomfortably. 'They only have four and a half networks here, sir.'

Ted looked like he'd just heard his grandmother was having triplets. 'Well I'll be the simpleminded son of a five-bit whore! I thought these folks was meant to be civilized . . . It's still no excuse Casp. Who's our top PR guy here?'

Casper rifled though the sheets on his clipboard. 'There's no name on my list, sir.'

'Sack him. If he can't even look after his own name, how can he be doing his job properly. There's no room in God's great work for name-losers. You take over that side of things yourself Casp – I need someone who can spell results with their eyes closed. Everyone in this piss-poor country gotta know we're out here, ready to save souls and smite the devil wherever he shows his scaly little hide.'

Casper smiled as wide as he could. 'Mr Trundell, I'll get on it right away. We do have a number of new initiatives in the pipeline. Would you like me to run with them?'

'Let's hear 'em first. Seems I ain't been givin' this side of things enough attention, lately.'

Casper shifted nervously. 'Well, we've got activists picketing twenty abortion clinics up and down the country. The British po-lice brought out the water cannons last night – made great TV.'

'Been done before. What else? It better be good or I'll knock twenty stars off your Salvation Rating.'

Casper was about to ask why he was taking the blame when he'd only been in the job two minutes, then wisely thought better of it. Trundell was not a man you talked back to if you wanted to collect your pension. 'There's the sponsorship deal with Songs of Praise sir – that's a local religious TV show. We've got the presenter to wear our logo on her frock.'

Ted smiled happily. 'I know all about that Casp. That show has been run by one of our deep cover agents since before you were out of diapers. Glad to see she can finally come out of the closet.'

Casper breathed easier. Despite his years of experience he'd never got used to Ted's sudden mood shifts. Now, the great man was smiling, the put-upon PA felt confident enough to make a suggestion all his own. 'Something you said on stage sir, it got me to thinking.'

'Good Casp. That's what you're paid for.'

'Something about you personally saving the most wayward soul on Earth. Don't think it was in the script . . . but . . .'

Ted's temper flared like a supernova. 'So I ad lib a little? The Lord can come to us at any time!'

'Sir, I wasn't criticizing. It's just I think we could hang something on that – maybe tie it in with the theme park's opening ceremony.'

Ted's face took on a far away look. 'Like it Casp. Earth's most holy man saves Earth's most horrendous sinner. Got a nice ring to it, don't you think?'

Casper's brow furrowed, perhaps indicating the first dreadful realization of the monumental hole he was fast digging for himself. 'Of course sir, now all we have to do is *find* the most hopeless lost soul on the planet. The most depraved and malevolent sinner ever to walk God's bountiful earth. The most hopeless Devil-worshipping warlock abroad in the land today.'

'Knew I could count on you, Casp.' Trundell patted his

man heartily on the back. 'Have him brought to HQ by the end of the week. It might take a while to make him see the light.'

Casper sighed. After all this time with the man, he really should have known better.

Brothers In Harm

Adam slumped against the bar of the quiet country pub. He was having a bad day and travelling all this way for zilch wasn't helping. The place might have been called The Screaming Sword but in its current incarnation it was quieter than Beirut Airport's arrivals lounge on a wet and windy Tuesday night.

'Yes sir – what can I get you?' An attractive, if rather unearthly looking, barmaid approached him.

Adam instantly perked up. He couldn't help noticing her black nail varnish and the slightly manic glint in her indigo eyes, but she was the first bit of half-decent crumpet he'd seen all day. 'Pint of lager please,' he said, picking for her his best smile, the one that wrapped round his face and joined up at the back. 'And whatever you're having gorgeous.'

'That's very kind of sir. I'll have an orange juice thank you very much.'

The way she said 'orange juice' . . . Adam, who spent much of his life studying humans who were not-men, suspected she was the least-male creature he'd ever clapped eyes on – a suspicion which occurred to him almost every day of his life, and with almost every woman he came across, admittedly, but still . . . she really was something else. He set about dedicating much of his conscious mind to admiring this fact.

'Odd name for a pub,' he said conversationally, leaning over the bar to get a better look at her bum.

'Isn't it just,' replied Crystal brightly, as she glided down the bar with their drinks. 'My husband came up with it. Thought the old one was just too depressing. You might have seen him out the back. He's the brick privy of a man cutting firewood with his chainsaw.'

Adam's smile didn't waver for a second. 'How rustic. Got a *cutting* sense of humour, has he?'

'Only when the customers get a bit free with their hands.' Crystal shot him a look that would have mangled a monk's manhood. 'The name comes from local legend. Apparently this valley was the site of an ancient battle. Some folks say on a quiet night you can still hear the screams from the froth-corrupted lungs of the dying.'

'How nice,' Adam said on autopilot, dreaming of licking spilt orange juice from Crystals thighs. 'That must be really lovely.'

Crystal gave him a queer look. Just what sort of a weirdo was she dealing with here? 'So what brings you to these parts, young man?' she asked.

'Why am I here? Oh, I'm just looking for someone or other.'

Crystal's eyes narrowed in suspicion. 'If it's someone, I might be able to help. I know most everyone round here. If it's other, I know a few people might help you with your problem.' *With a pair of pliers*, she added to herself.

'Oh, it's definitely someone, someone very important, but I doubt you'll know him. Goes by the name of Nostrus. Just bought Caer-Mathonwy Farm –'

The look on Crystal's face froze him in his tracks. All colour drained from her face. 'Caer-Mathonwy? What business do you have up at the Big House?'

Before Adam could answer, his conscious mind was hijacked by an outside force. What was worse, this new voice seemed prepared to give her a truthful answer.

'Well, hey, baby black lips we're from the Pre –'

'PARAS!' Adam screamed, momentarily gaining control of his mouth. 'We're ex-members of the Parachute

Regiment and I needed to contact good old Nostro for a reunion.'

Adam thought best on his feet. Actually, he thought best naked on his back, one hand holding a bottle of Johnson's baby oil, the other . . . but that didn't exactly seem applicable at this moment. He'd seen Crystal's expression countless times on members of the public before – then as now he doubted honesty was ever the best policy.

Crystal was now looking very uneasily at him. 'You don't look like an army type to me. In fact, you look to me like you're a bit –'

'I know, I know,' Adam interrupted trying desperately to keep her onside. 'It was a long time ago – the Falklands. That's why I suddenly go out of character sometimes,' he added, tapping his head. 'Took a piece of the Argy shrapnel in the brain. Don't know whether you know much about frontal lobes but –'

Adam was just beginning to get on a roll, his bullshit generator synchromeshing from fourth to fifth without use of a clutch when he abruptly realized the sympathy for wounded veteran approach wasn't going to cut the mustard with this cool cucumber.

Crystal said coldly: 'We don't need your custom round 'ere. When you've finished your drink, you can bugger off and don't come back.'

With that she turned on her heels and stormed from the bar.

Adam's journo nose twitched excitedly. Like Billingsgate on a hot summer afternoon there was something fishy going on here, and you didn't have to be Sherlock Holmes to catch its odour. But he had an even more pressing story to deal with. His own story. Like what the hell had come over him back there?

He suddenly felt weak and in need of a seat. He slunk over to a quiet corner booth to collect his thoughts. Schizophrenia? Embarrassing, but at least you always had someone to talk to. Shame it wasn't a woman – could have led to some very interesting possibilities . . .

Adam silently mulled over his next move. Before he could come up with an idea that didn't involve KY Jelly, two new patrons entered the bar. They moved furtively between the tables, as if not wanting to be seen. So complete was their preoccupation with stealth that they failed to observe the silent reporter. With a stunning display of ineptitude the pair chose the booth directly behind him.

At first Adam tried to ignore them, content to sup his pint and take a well-earned breather, but they were talking in such loud whispers that even if he'd put ear plugs in and driven half way back to London, he'd still have heard them.

'Last time I go on a mission with you, Gwylym – high-value target or not. Second degree burns the doctor said. I'm lucky to be walking.'

'In war, there are always casualties, Ivan. If you can't stand the heat, stay out of the colonial oppressor's kitchen. You botched a battalion-level tactical operation and left three gallons of paraffin up at the Big House. You've probably put the Revolution back years. *I'm* the one should be complaining.'

At this point Adam's ears pricked up. He had a fair idea of the sort of people he was dealing with, but details like that weren't his concern. All that mattered was the connection with Nostrus, however tenuous. With a deep breath the reporter got to his feet and confronted them.

First impressions were not good on either side. Adam saw a pair of shady young men dressed in combat jackets and filthy jeans. One seemed to be bandaged from the waist down. Gwylym saw a casually dressed guy with a look of manic zeal burning in his grey eyes – probably an SAS agent been trailing them for months. Ivan would have jumped out of his skin, if he'd had enough left to leave behind.

Gwylym grasped the initiative manfully. 'DON'T SHOOT!

DON'T SHOOT!' he screamed. 'We surrender. Names, places, people – got 'em all. You can have them. I don't want to die. I'm not bad really, just a product of my environment.'

Adam didn't care if this idiot was a product of ICI. A little confused at the reaction he'd set off, he held up a calming hand.

'Mate, mate. I'm not gonna shoot you. All I want is to sit down and have a nice little chat. Do you mind?'

'Depends,' said Gwylym reclaiming his arrogance with alarming speed, 'who the 'ell you are.'

Adam took a chance and showed him his card. He opted for the forged NUJ one he'd got done in Thailand a few years ago.

Gwylym flipped it over. 'Press then, are we? Least you're affiliated. If we're going to be subjected to invaders, might as well be union invaders.' He lifted his dull eyes to Adam's and the journalist knew he'd made the necessary connection. 'Believe in journalistic confidentiality do you?'

'You bet.' Adam put his hand where he thought his heart might be. 'Discretion is my middle name.[1] Adam Discretion MacArthur at your service, *Daily Trumpet*. First with the big story, first with the fat cheque.'

Gwylym perked up at the c-word as Adam knew he would.

He might have been a narrow-minded terrorist but Gwylym knew the value of publicity. And he might have been a virulent anti-capitalist, but he knew the value of money. All world authorities on guerrilla warfare agreed on the subject. At his bedside, next to his collection of *Big Guns Monthly*, rested a selection of treatises by Mao, Che Guevara and Max Boyce.

'Sit down MacArthur,' he said cordially, 'we've obviously got things to discuss.'

---

1 Actually it was Lesley, but he didn't like to spread it around.

After a few minutes, the three of them were getting on like a holiday home on fire. Adam's initial suspicions concerning the pair's nocturnal visit to Caer-Mathonwy Farm seemed to be justified. Ivan wasn't in a talkative mood – he just sat and fiddled with his bandages – but Gwylym more than made up for his comrade's reticence.

'. . . So you see, we're desperate men, freedom fighters for a Celtic homeland. Point by point, and I think you might want to take this down, our strategic aims include: a) to . . .'

'That's all very brave and visionary,' Adam interrupted, 'but for the moment could we concentrate on events last night at the farm. I'm investigating the new owner, and I can tell you now he's not the sort you want living on your doorstep. Nostrus is one of London's top property developers, and I have information that he's planning on turning this valley into a massive caravan park for OAP English settlers.'

'Barstard,' Gwylym hissed. ''E can't do that.'

'He can – and you know what he's gonna call this valley? . . .The Vale of Bournemouth.'

'That's just . . . that's just *evil.*'

'He's an evil man. But I'm doing everything in my power to stop him. So – are you going to shed any light on the skeletons in his many cupboards?'

Gwylym looked at his fellow-in-arms, who shifted nervously and gave off a faint whiff of Germolene. 'You gonna tell him or am I?'

But Ivan was in no state to answer. Adam watched as the boy began to vibrate from head to toe like a pneumatic drill.

Adam proceeded cautiously. 'If you help us we'd give your organization the sort of publicity you've always dreamed of and a few quid to go towards your printing costs. All those pamphlets . . .'

Gwylym gave Ivan the sort of look hungry lions gave

juicy Christians about 1500 years ago. Ivan's common sense finally won the battle over abject terror.

'It was huge,' he began, 'covered in tentacles and dripping slime everywhere. When I asked it for a light, the thing nearly blew me balls off . . .'

The notebook came out. The story was on. Adam scribbled furiously.

The Story Breaks

That night, Adam raced back to London. Next morning Britain's favourite daily paper ran the following front page splash:

WHACKO WIZARD PINCHES PYRAMIDS
Another groundbreaking exclusive from Adam MacArthur

Your favourite paper can at last exclusively expose the man behind the GREAT PYRAMID HEIST and much of the other STRANGE PHENOMENA sweeping the nation. Sinister student corrupter, Professor Michael D. Nostrus, 62, of no fixed abode, is the man at the centre of a tangled web of lies, corruption, WITCHCRAFT and multi-million pound insurance FRAUD.

Some of THE TRUMPET's findings may seem INCREDIBLE, some of our FACTS may seem hard to believe, but this newspaper has uncovered HARD EVIDENCE that this man is a powerful practitioner in BLACK MAGIC who plans to enslave YOU, the British people, to his dark ways.

FACT! – Nostrus took out an insurance policy for £500,000 on the Pyramids TWO WEEKS BEFORE they disappeared.

FACT! – Nostrus has bet over £60,000 predicting otherworldy events over the past month, including THE LONDON FISH FALL.

FACT – Nostrus has recently purchased a LUXURY HOME in a quiet corner of North Wales. Locals are alarmed at the strange lights and noises coming from the residence. EYE WITNESSES insist DEMONS roam the property!

FACT – When THE TRUMPET attempted to interview Nostrus, our reporters were bustled off the premises by BURLY WORKMEN busy FORTIFYING the site. The estate is surrounded by THREE twelve-foot-high ELECTRIC FENCES and defended by what appears to be a stockpile of HI-TECH WEAPONRY. Our security experts have told us that the construction on top of the roof is an ADVANCED AIR RADAR of the type used to control ANTI-AIRCRAFT MISSILES! Why Nostrus needs his arsenal is not clear, but terrorism cannot be ruled out.

The Professor is a man shrouded in MYSTERY. Even his age cannot be precisely determined. For the past fifteen years he's worked as a HISTORY Professor in the department of LIBERAL STUDIES at London Borough University. No evidence is yet apparent, but it would hardly be a surprise if Nostrus received TAXPAYERS' HARD-EARNED CASH in council grants to promote his MINORITY INTERESTS.

THE TRUMPET will not rest until this MEDDLING MANIAC is brought to justice. And when he is, be assured we'll be the first to bring you an EXCLUSIVE!

Spirits In The Material World

'The message said to stay put and await further orders.' Guttlehog was anxious, his primary antennae banging together at a frequency designed to shatter dogs and make glass howl. 'Don't make things worse by wandering off.'

'Make things worse? We're in shit up to our armpits. Why do you think He wants to see us?' Rubicante twitched hysterically at the mouth of the small cave as he peered down over Noddegamra Valley. The pair had been lying low since their little meeting with the revolutionaries.

'I don't know,' mumbled the Lord of Boars, foam flying from between his great curved tusks, 'perhaps he knows where Nostrus is. Perhaps he's got some friendly advice.'

Rubicante groaned in frustration. 'The only friendly advice he's going to give us is "Don't pick the scabs when the Operational Efficiency boys have finished with you." We're going to sent to the Seventh Circle of Hell,[1] Guts. We're done for.'

As if to confirm his predictions of impending doom, a faint buzzing started to emanate from the corner of the cave. it was a sound like a million not-at-all-happy bees swarming over a nearby hill – and heading straight for you. The air shimmered, as if someone had taken a slice of reality and was shaking it like a Christmas snowscene diorama. Then a bright flash and sharp crack heralded their superior's arrival.

Their boss seemed momentarily disoriented. He looked quite different from when they'd last seen him. The hooves and tail had gone, and he was wearing a short-sleeved cherry-striped shirt. On top of his carefully combed hair rested a small cardboard hat. As well as the faint whiff of brimstone that usually accompanied the Prince of Hell, Guttlehog was sure he could smell popcorn. Despite these wholesale changes, the baleful red eyes remained constant. Nick turned them on the demons, cutting the darkness like twin laser beams. 'Well, hello boys,' he said. 'How may I help you?'

Guttlehog and Rubicante stared down at their cosmopolitan collection of feet.

Nick had expected such a reaction. These two were so

---

1 Where the inane and futile must beat themselves with wet chrysanthemums, and force each other to watch sub-titled b/w Swedish films.

damned predictable. 'I think it's only fair to warn you that I was having a whale of a time until I was rudely dragged away by Head Office. I do so love my *rare* evenings at the cinema, you know.'

'Sir?' Rubicante looked up enquiringly, and instantly regretted it.'

'Yes, the cin-e-ma. You don't think those hot dogs are the work of man, surely?'

The two demons stood very still, trying hard to think themselves into non-existence. And failing. Nick strolled round them, casually gazing off into the middle-distance and smiling blandly.

'It's truly amazing what humans will put into their mouths if the lights are dim and you plaster your wares with enough mustard. I'm not at liberty to divulge what ingredients make up the recipe but believe me, you two could soon become intimately involved in their production. But I digress.'

Nick frowned, and outside a sparrow crashed into a tree. 'I am very . . . disappointed with your performance. I'm not too young to remember the good old days when demons were demons and humans were rightly terrified. This mission wouldn't have taken a stormy evening to complete. Bumping off a son of man was something we did in our sleep – or their sleep, whichever came easier. Sigh . . .sigh . . .sigh'

As he circled, he started to tap a small battery-powered torch in one meticulously manicured hand. His expression shifted from frown to severely crestfallen and a yawning crack appeared in Tasmania's largest dam. 'The Final Battle is coming. It is urgent that your current target is dispatched with all due haste. He knows too much and constitutes a security risk. The *opposition* were relying on us to remove him from the scene. It has been a little embarrassing explaining your failures to Mr Sanctimonious All-Bloody-Mighty upstairs.'

Now Nick tightened his path, getting closer and closer until he was almost in their faces. 'Despite all that has happened, you have one last chance. Maybe it's my generally sunny disposition, or my unswerving faith in demon-nature, maybe it was seeing *The Sound of Music* last night – an artist does so love to be reminded of his greatest work – maybe it's because I have absolutely no choice at the moment. Whatever, you are reprieved. So, show me what you can do boys – please?'

Guttlehog almost fainted in relief. 'Thank you great master, we will not fail you.'

'No, you won't – because from now on you'll have someone to hold your hand.'

On cue the air in the corner of the cave broke into light once again. 'I think you both know Alastor, Chief Executioner of Hell and First Architect of Daytime TV?'

The figure before them would have frightened a house-brick. Alastor was big even for a demon. His size was only accentuated by the billowing scarlet cloak which surged unnervingly even though the air in the cave was still. Slowly, Alastor turned his visored helmet toward Rubicante and Guttlehog, his only visible feature, a single oscillating eye. One massive gauntleted hand held Soul Stealer, the great black Rune Sword forged by the Deep Dwarves at the dawn of time from the bones of petulant Frost Giants. Some people said the Hell Blade drank the very life-force from its victims as it tore through their delicate innards and those some people tended to be right.

'Aaarrrrrgghhhh,' said Alastor by way of greeting.

'Nice day for it,' chirped in Soul Stealer with a voice that sounded like George Formby after ingesting a helium balloon.

Guttlehog and Rubicante froze like statues – statues created by a sculptor too fond of heavy meals close to bedtime perhaps, but statues nonetheless.

Nick smiled radiantly. 'I can see you're all going to get on famously. Reports on return boys, and I want the word 'success' clearly written in the victim's blood at the top of every page.'

Then, with a snap of his talons, he was gone – leaving the four new friends to plan their next move in the increasingly complex assassination of Professor Nostrus.

Head Over Heels

This was it. This was the moment.

Adam tensed at his steering wheel as he watched a dilapidated old banger pulling up outside the mansion block. He'd been parked outside the old git's flat ever since the story had broken and he ached all over. Finally it was time for a stretch.

As Mike slipped out of the car and up the steps to the foyer, Adam went into forced interview mode – speedy but quiet approach to target, microphone at waist level ready for the draw and, most importantly, the well-practised 'You think I'm going to buy that' sneer already curling into his lips.

Mike was oblivious to the fast approaching menace. After another tough day shopping, he'd taken Deborah to her lodgings to pick up the rest of her stuff. Now, all Mike wanted was a stiff drink and a hot bath. He reached the entrance and paused as Aristotle slalomed a greeting between his legs.

He turned to watch Deborah parking the old rustbucket and caught rapid movement at the edge of his vision.

Adam hurdled a garden wall like an out of practice athlete. 'Professor Nostrus.'

Mike looked up, keys in hand, surprise creasing his weather-beaten face. 'Who wants to know?'

Adam skidded to a halt, fumbling with a camera as he did so. 'Give us a front page smile, Mikey.'

Mike threw up his hands. 'No photos . . . I said *no photos!*'

Adam took advantage of the geriatric's momentary confusion to thrust the microphone in his face. 'Could you answer a few questions for our readers Professor Nostrus? They're anxious to hear about your demon-summoning skills – and what do you know about vanishing Pyramids?'

All trace of colour drained from Mike's face. He looked like he'd just been told he had six weeks to live – along with the rest of humanity. 'The Pyramids? How –?'

'And last week's fish fall? You won a small fortune on that bet didn't you?'

'No comment.'

'Professor Nostrus, exactly what pleasure do you derive from detonating innocent sheep?'

Mike's mouth worked for several seconds before anything came out. '. . . Sheep? I can assure you I know nothing about exploding sheep.'

Adam's smirk could have out-smugged a parachute sales rep on a wingless 747. Backing Mike up against the wall with his thrusting mic, Adam pressed home. 'Come now, Professor Nostrus, we know what you've been up to. Why not level with us? We'll pay you handsomely.'

To a man who presently had no more need for extra cash than a snake had for hand-stitched Gucci loafers, it was an opportunity to regain the initiative.

'If I'm so rich, why would I want your grubby bribes?'

Adam shrugged. 'Standard line. Works on most people.'

'Well in that case how much do you want to forget you ever saw?'

Adam had no time to protest his journalistic integrity because the conversation was interrupted by the feet-first, horizontal, fairly violent arrival of Deborah. All Adam remembered about the next half second was that one minute he was about to crack his man, the next he was lying on his back with a strange numbness spreading through his legs. Any cartoon artist charged with recording Deborah's arrival would have employed a gigantic speech bubble containing a word such as 'Whammooooo'. There was none passing at that particular moment so the exact grammar will forever remain a mystery. The same hypothetical cartoonist might then have drawn a circling carousel of birds, stars and planets revolving above Adam's throbbing head, added an exaggerated red bump rising through his hair and finished off with a tongue lolling out of his mouth at a ridiculous angle. Then he might have stopped, taken a step back to survey the work and decided: not worth the effort, scribbled him out, and started all over again with a more rewarding character.

Aristotle wanted in on the act too. He attached himself to Adam's exposed ankle via claws and mouse-breaking teeth and didn't let go. It was a testament to the tidal wave of pain Adam was experiencing that this minor puddle of discomfort entirely passed him by.

Deborah grabbed Mike by the arm and pulled him back down the steps to the car, bundling him unceremoniously into the passenger seat. Reluctantly, Aristotle followed. Before Mike had time to belt in, he was binned back into his seat as they accelerated away. Several heart-jolting minutes later, Deborah finally checked their headlong flight in a quiet side street.

Mike turned to his companion, his face tinged with alarm and what just might have been a new respect.

'Where did you learn to do all that?' he asked.

'Self Defence Initiative. New class at college. Only been to a few and we haven't even done reverse jump-kicks yet.'

'God help humanity if you do.'

'He was only a journalist. He doesn't count.'

I think he does, actually, Aristo said. *He seems to know an awful lot about you, Mike.*

The old man rubbed his eyes. 'Our security has certainly been compromised. He even knew about the demons – which means he followed us to Wales.'

There was silence for a while as the implications of that fact seemed to hang in the air around them.

'So what now?' asked Deborah eventually.

'We find a tobacconist's.'

Deborah was going to ask why, but instead, shaking her head to herself, she just put her foot down and drove. It was easier that way.

Ten minutes later things were looking worse than Quasimodo's plump older sister – the one in the family who'd got the brains and the 'nice personality'. Deborah emerged from a corner shop clutching a tabloid as though it was a soiled nappy.

'You want the good news or the bad?' she said through a forced smile.

Mike slumped despondently in his seat without offering a reply.

'Nice front page pic of our secret hideaway.' She flipped the paper in front of his face. FISH AND TIPS, the headline read – *We track down Prophet Prof: the man behind the missing Pyramids*.

'Seven pages on it inside.'

Mike groaned, his head sinking into his hands. 'So what's the good news?'

Deborah's lips curled up at the corners. 'At least they spelt your name right.'

Love At First Fight

'Did you see that? Like Bruce Lee in a dress she was. Incredible.'

Adam was still on his back outside Mike's flat, staring dreamily up at clouds stroking the sky. For a moment he didn't register that someone else had said what he was thinking – he was too busy contemplating a strange new sensation in his heart and wondering whether there was a word for it (could it be love?). But when the voice said: 'We just got beaten up by a girl,' and sniggered in an all too familiar way, Adam could ignore it no longer and he swivelled his eyes towards its source.

An oddly dressed middle-aged man was standing over him, shaking his head in disbelief. He had over-large sideburns and greying hair and the collar of his bright orange shirt was slightly too wide as were the flares on his beige safari-suit trousers. He looked for all the world like the male lead from one of the faintly smutty '70s Britcoms which Adam had wasted his formative years watching. But the oddness was more than just bad dress sense. The man had a misty, surreal quality about him. Adam felt sure he could see the sky though his hazy form. And that *voice* . . .

With a yelp Adam suddenly realized where he'd heard it before. Once, alone in his car, more recently at that bloody pub. It was a tribute to the quality of Adam's upbringing that he could maintain his manners at this moment of intense personal stress.

'Who the fuck are you?'

'I'm part of the team,' the stranger said, tapping the side of his head. 'Nothing to worry about.'

'Is that meant to be an answer?'

'You want me to be more specific?'

Adam nodded, his mind clearing momentarily before flopping back into a semi-conscious daze.

The man chuckled, throaty and lascivious. 'I'm you,' he said.

Adam decided this was a weird, but rather interesting dream.

'I'm no dream, mate. I'm your mate. I'm real.'

Who cared? The nice bit of the dream was that feeling in his heart – caused by the woman who had rebuilt it with a single act of unselfish violence. He tried to concentrate on that, but the man with the sideburns wouldn't let him.

Suddenly, Adam felt himself being lifted into a sitting position and the geezer's face was right there in his own, all tobacco-mixed-with-peppermints breath. 'You like her, eh?'

From far away Adam heard his own voice say: 'She's the most amazing thing I've ever seen.'

'Wouldn't mind slipping her a crippler myself,' the geezer chuckled.

Adam went with the flow of the dream – why fight it? 'That's not what I meant, though.'

'Oh yeah.' That doubting, knowing chuckle again.

'Really, my whole life just shifted into focus. Now I know why I was put on this earth.'

Adam's worse half looked at him strangely. 'You've had one too many bumps on the head, mate. Want to watch it when you talk about a bird like that. Here, I'll give you a hand up.'

But Adam waved him away. The strange bloke would disappear into the ether, but she . . . he knew she was real. So he said: 'I think I'll just lie here a bit longer if it's all the same with you. I'll get up in my own time.'

He didn't want to move from the spot where he'd got his first look at her. He wanted to savour the image, just as he was savouring the faint hint of perfume that still hung on the air like cordite over a battlefield. He remembered everything about her, the way her golden tresses streamed behind her as she accelerated across the lawn, the way her lips had pulled back into a delightful snarl, the way she'd driven her delicate fist into his solar plexus like God's own battering ram.

Like a high-diving midget, Adam was in way too deep.

EIGHT

And when they have finished their witnessing, the beast that ascends out of the abyss will make war with them.
Revelations 11:7

00 – The Number Of The Feast

Despite Adam's startling revelations in the *Daily Trumpet*, not to mention vanishing pyramids, melting money and the ongoing catalogue of bizarre events that kept unfolding like some hellish route-map, humanity's butterfly-like attention span was focused elsewhere in the early hours of the next fateful day.

For years sweating ranks of crumpled computer programmers had warned of what might happen when their carefully crafted computer systems encountered the big '00'. All manner of apocalyptic disasters were forecast, from global financial chaos to out-of-control express trains. Judging by recent events most people could have been excused for thinking: 'So what?' But the programmers pressed their point regardless. Of course it went without saying there was only one way of saving the world economy's humped and furry back from this potentially fatal final straw.

'We want triple overtime and as much pizza as we can eat,' the programmers mumbled from around vast mouthfuls of grub. Some were heard to mutter other things darkly – 'Make sure there's extra olives on mine' most often, or 'This is all the operating system manufacturer's fault.[1].' But none were heard to admit who'd caused this entire mess in the first place. None could bring themselves to point out it was their own sloppiness which had caused this shambles to develop. It was very hard to talk when your mouth was so stuffed with pepperoni and cheese.

After months of frantic planning, often dragging on long into the night when most respectable pizzerias were closed, the representatives of the hack-masters passed their judgement. The problems were solvable. But what they really needed was to be able to test their code before the big day itself. What they needed was a dry run to see if the systems would integrate smoothly. If only one day could be set aside before the Millennium to put the date forward temporarily, much heartache and extra pizza could be saved later. If things didn't go smoothly there'd be plenty of time to put things right before the big day of no turning back. The date chosen for this momentous test was October 28,1999 – the midnight after Adam and Deborah's fateful meeting.

With hushed voices and as much reverence as they could muster the world's software engineers slouched back from their keyboards and waited with barely suppressed awe as the digital clocks approached midnight. As they did so all was quiet, the electrons themselves seemed to take on an air of quiet expectancy. All over the planet, for perhaps the first time in months, the world's business parks were empty of the sounds of delivery boys' scooters.

Five minutes in and things were looking pretty stable. Okay, so the Russian Federation's Missile Launch Computers had crashed again but then that was nothing out of the ordinary. Then, less than an hour into the great day of test, things began to go badly wrong.

The first cracks appeared in Britain. As the banks and

---

1 A favourite programmers' joke of the period ran:

Q. How many Nanosoft ® employees does it take to change a light bulb?

A. None, they just defined darkness as standard.

building societies' master systems woke up to the new date they calmly cancelled a significant percentage of mortgages. As frantic technicians scrambled for an answer it was coolly printed out before them: those living in sin shall be cast out into the snow. The programmers barely had time to wonder what that meant before they were hit by the second whammy. All personal loans and credit cards were cancelled. When the diagnostic checks were run the reply came back smugly: never a borrower or a lender be. Next to go were state schools' and university records. Down the workhouse with the lot of them was the only reply that could be coaxed from the software.

It seemed that almost as one the world's computer systems had reverted to a state of good old-fashioned Victorian morality. In their haste to prepare their silicon children for the turn of the century the coders had neglected to tell them which century that was. Whether this was down to further sloppiness, deliberate sabotage in the hope of yet more overtime, or one too many special 'herb' pizzas, we shall never know.

Next to go were the airlines' booking systems. All flight reservations were cancelled and all air traffic control computers shut down. If the good Lord had intended man to fly he wouldn't have bothered with birds, declared the machines, as those unfortunate enough to be in the air at the time were soon to find out.

Far out on the bleak plains of cyberspace British computers were busily digging their own graves. After demanding special treatment over internet access rights due to their status as servants of the greatest nation on earth, any server with a UK mail address was very quickly on the receiving end of a virtual mugging. African and Asian systems seemed to be performing this task with considerable relish.

But all this was very small potatoes compared to what was developing in the former Soviet Union. At 0600 hours

Russia's main defence computer, the one that controlled its extensive arsenal of intercontinental nuclear missiles, sprang to life and began to ask awkward questions of the federal government in Moscow. Top of its list, and repeatedly delivered in an increasingly agitated tone, was 'What have you done with the Tsar?'

As all over the world programmers scrambled over empty pizza boxes to reset clocks, the Russian President was frantically rushed to the capital's premiere fancy dress store. Meanwhile, for some at least, that morning brought an entirely different set of concerns. If ignorance truly was bliss then that might explain why the head of the Church of the Eloquent Announcement was always grinning.

One Man's Religion Is Another Man's Belly Laugh

Ted Trundell had no time for doubt, just as he had no time for spotty curates in open-toed sandals, playing tambourines and acoustic guitars while singing rousing renditions of Kum-Bye-Yaah M'lud. His God was a strange being. The object of his adoration was omnipotent, omniscient and omnibus, which meant that if you missed him in the week you could catch up with a double dose on a Sunday afternoon. Ted believed the meek would inherit the earth, but only in six-by-four-foot plots. So perhaps it was hardly surprising that he was capable of believing what he now saw before him was God's idea of architectural progress.

'Just magnificent Casp! I sure do like what y'all've done with the stained glass. Gives those shoe shops that Notre Dame feel.'

Casp took it modestly, 'Our Psycho-Sales Design boys did a fine job – every feature optimized to maintain a sense of religious fervour, while maximizing profits of a more earthly nature. I just supervised the finishing touches, minor details is'all.'

'Good Casp, wouldn't want you fretting over the little

things, coz this place gotta be open in three days' time. And we both know you've got other irons in the fire – warming nicely to be rammed up the unbelieving assholes of Lucifer's sacrilegious servants.'

In truth Casper could have been forgiven for letting his workload get the better of him. What with overseeing the completion of the giant theme park and conducting the search for Ted's guest of dishonour at the opening ceremony, he had plenty to keep him busy.

The pair stood at the head of a small delegation of high-ranking Church officials – Ted's Chief Lieutenant conducting a guided tour of the new 'Manna From Heaven' Shopping Complex. This vast edifice, which did for understatement what Henry VIII did for marriage guidance, stood slapbang in the middle of the theme park – first step in Ted Trundell's plan for the conquest of Western Europe. All about them workmen were putting the finishing touches to this great shrine to free market capitalism, cheap consumer durables and Silky Soft Hairspray™.

Casper led them through airy marble-lined atriums, along wide walkways and finally to a cavernous hallway glazed far above with stained-glass renditions of well-known Bible stories and dramatized scenes from Ted's early life. It was all there, from the great man's infamous 'loaves and chargrilled chicken' revival tour, to the day he opened the first Eloquent Announcement financial services department. The overworked PA beamed proudly as he addressed his boss.

'Here we have the Central Arena Mr Trundell, sir – room for ten thousand faithful to let their feelings show. One day soon it'll be packed to the rafters as you address the congregation, with millions more receiving the Word through God's optimum medium – TV. The floor below is made of twelve-foot-thick reinforced concrete, strong enough to withstand even the most frenzied of stamping. Perhaps the Reverend Harvey Banger, our Head of

Security, would like to point out some of its other useful functions.'

All members of the party were smartly dressed but the tall, granite-jawed young man who stepped forward made them look like tramps. The lines of his crisp new suit were broken only by an ominous bulge above his left hip. The dark glasses wrapped round his crew-cut head were presumably to shield him from the glare coming off his shoes. When he spoke it was like John Wayne auditioning for the lead role in *Elvis: The Movie*.

'That's a big positive on the flooring situation Mr Trundell. It could take a direct nuclear hit of up to ten kilotonnes. Underneath it is our emergency Command Bunker. If push comes to shove ain't no one gonna be telling us which way to jump.'

As Ted nodded approvingly Casper added: 'The offices y'all can see around the top level will comprise our organization's command and control post here in Englelandshire. We're just waiting for the contractors to finish installing the Earth to Heaven Communications Suite[1] then we'll be ready to move in.'

''Bout time too,' said Ted gazing up at the ring of plush offices, 'I'm getting almighty pissed off working from those portacabins.'

Casper decided to move them on. It wasn't wise to let Trundell mull over a grievance, however minor. 'If y'all just follow me I'll show ya to one of the stores nearing completion. It's a novelty religious gift shop – 'Blessings-R-We'. Everything you could ever need for a wedding, christening, or simply that special day when a holy benefaction will lift the hearts of your family.

Casper halted outside a garishly decorated shopfront nestling between 'Life Everlasting Assurance Inc.' and

---

1 Comprising a ring of satellites that would have produced a bulge in a media tycoon's trousers.

'Unleaven-Bread-U-Like'. The store's interior was a hive of activity, workmen busily laying thick carpets and finishing off decorations. In one corner a team of electricians wired an elaborate lighting system behind a life-size diorama of Jesus blessing a group of doe-eyed young children. One section of glass showcases was already complete: inside, cuddly Old Testament prophets fought for position with inflatable Moses dolls but both were swamped by a vast sea of plastic Dying Orphan figurines. SOON TO BE SAFE IN GOD'S EMBRACE read a banner just above them.

Ted and his entourage surveyed the scene happily. Casper gave a quiet sigh of relief. It looked like his boss was going to leave without criticism, always a cause for celebration. Trundell was grinning with a manic intensity that outshone even the Road to Damascus Reading Lamps.

'Well Casp, I can tell you now I'm mighty proud of what we've achieved here. I never thought these slack-faced, no-brained, Limey workmen could be so . . .'

Like the Red Sea before the Israelites, Ted cut off in mid-flow. Casper stared at his boss's face as his stomach sank like a lead-lined lifeboat. Ted was glaring off into one corner and looking like he might rupture at any moment. With terrifying ferocity one sapphire eye began to convulse. They all followed their leader's gaze to whatever monstrous evil had created such ire. Sitting on a saw-horse, oblivious to the activity around him, a workman was drinking a cup of tea, reading a paper and eating what looked like a cheese and pickle sandwich. Ted Trundell stormed off like a hurricane looking for a church roof.

'What in the name of howdy-doody du yu think yure doin'! There's work to be done, no time for lolly-gaggin! Where the hell you from boy anyways?'

The workman, who hadn't been called boy since his last day at Streatham Secondary Modern, looked up nonplussed. 'Sarf London – and if it's any business of yours

I'm waiting for me glue to dry. No sense rushing in and botching the job now is there, John.'

Ted bulged. 'No wonder this piss-poor country's going downhill like the Red Coats at Valley Forge!' he roared. 'You ask why the Krauts and Nipps have got you beat?'

'Nah.' The workman shook his head, a faintly amused expression on his face. 'Didn't.'

Ted continued oblivious, 'I'll tell you why – unholy indolence! Where I come from, when you finish a job you look round for another, you don't sit on your ass like a two-bit whore waiting for work to come your way!'

The workman regarded Ted calmly. 'Listen mate, I'm a professional. Don't tell me my job and I won't tell you yours, John.'

'Communists everywhere! Union slackers! You're all fired. Get out, before I set mah dogs on you. AND STOP CALLING ME JOHN!'

All those in earshot regarded each other, downed tools and filed out stoically. They were used to such interruptions: if it wasn't the wrong sort of cola in the canteen (the church was heavily sponsored by one brand), it was unholy floor panelling that needed tearing up. As far as they were concerned the more enforced tea breaks, the better.

Casper drew a bloodless hand across his tired brow. 'Do you think that was a good idea, sir? I mean, sacking that entire work crew. There was only one slacking and we are on a very tight schedule.'

Ted shook his head. 'No way, Casp. That union shit spreads like wildfire. When one of 'em starts blowing hot, you gotta douse the whole cell. Henry Ford – now he had the right idea, and that Muscleeni too, even if he was a Wop. Hell, this is how that damned Bol-shevik Revolution started!'

Casper shifted uncomfortably, but he wasn't going to argue. Ted put a fatherly arm around his PA's shoulders and led him away from the church bigwigs.

'You remember that little chat we had at the show the other night, 'bout finding me a sinner? Well, what you got for me? A serial childkiller? Crooked politician? Hit me Casp.'

For one terrible moment the image that rose unbidden in Casper's overloaded mind was of beating his boss round the head with the remains of the idle workman's cheese sandwich. Abject terror had thrown his brain into a state of dire confusion. Slowly the clouds of bewilderment parted, to leave . . . a huge black void. The simple fact was, Casper hadn't had time to set things up. There was so much else to do. Finding Ted a lost soul to save had been bottom of his list and he'd just plain forgot. Like an exam candidate who's just realized he's read all the wrong books Casper's mind raced in terrifying circles. Tell Ted the truth? Not likely. Casper subscribed to his own Eleventh Commandment: *preserve thyself – even if the truth goes out the stained-glass window*. To Trundell, mistakes were the work of Satan.

But Casper hadn't lasted this long in Ted's service without becoming a born-again survivor. As on countless occasions in the past when put on the spot in this way, Casper improvised. They say the Lord works in mysterious ways, but if this was his doing Jehovah must have been skateboarding round his office while wearing a false moustache and swinging a kipper above his freshly shaven head. Looking down, Casper saw the front page spread of the workman's newspaper. 'Wacko Wizard Pinches Pyramids' screamed the headline.

'Ha . . . ha . . . ha . . . him!' was all Casper could say as his boss followed his gaze in bewilderment.

'Waddayasayin' Casp? You've got me Himmler? Dead German guys are out. Anyway, being misunderstood by Liberal historians ain't such a crime is it? I want a *sinner* with a capital triple X.'

Before Ted became stuck in his legendary far away look from which no man or deity could shift him, Casper grabbed for the paper and waved it in his face. 'Him! Him! Getting you him.'

'You okay Casp? Sound like you've got a hungry horntoad in your shorts.' Ted finally took a closer look. 'Michael . . . Nose-truss? Great, Casp! He sounds like the spawn of Satan we're after. Bring him to my office tomorrow morning. I'm gonna rip a strip off the sonofabitch.'

With that Ted marched off to join his other subordinates, who were mulling around a point of sale display for Holy Hermit Hairshirts. Casper was left slumped and shell-shocked, shaking faintly in the great man's wake. With considerable trepidation he looked down at the tabloid clutched between his white-knuckled hands. Whoever this Nostrus guy was, Casper needed to track him down – and fast. At least he had something to go on, the paper said the man worked at a London university.

Half an hour later Casper sat in his chaotic temporary office, a telephone receiver gripped between shoulder and ear. He'd just dialled a very special number, a number known only to a select few high up in the Church organization. It put him through to a morally dubious and very greedy computer operator at a secret British Government facility somewhere in southern England.

'Hi. Casper here. I need the usual – address, occupation, bank details, anything you can give me. Kinda unusual this one, shouldn't be too much trouble to track down. Guy by the name of Michael Nostrus.'

Incommunicado

'You know, I don't think they're coming back.' Mike stood at the front window of his flat, peering through the blinds at the half-lit empty street. 'Perhaps your little martial arts demo convinced them it was unwise.'

In a nearby tree a half-awake sparrow coughed, spat out a huge glob of green phlegm then croakingly spluttered into song. Deborah and the Professor had spent an uneasy night waiting tensely for the dawn to arrive, along with the hordes of pressmen they both expected. The previous evening they'd debated at length what their next move should be, without coming to a satisfactory conclusion. Eventually Mike had drifted off to bed, only to while away the twilight hours staring at the ceiling and dozing fitfully. He had even tried counting sheep, but the furry imbeciles had shown an infuriating tendency to combust just before jumping over his imaginary fence. Finally giving in, he had got up to make breakfast. Learning that his top secret plan to escape from Armageddon had been the page one lead on yesterday's *Daily Trumpet* had scuttled even his powers of relaxation. Now Mike was paying the price. He stifled a large yawn and took another sip of black coffee.

Aristotle lay sleeping in his favourite position on top of the silent TV, oblivious to human worries. The only thing distinguishing him from a large furry ornament was the slight twitching of his limbs as he chased imaginary newspaper photographers through the shrubbery of his dreams. The cat's contribution to the previous night's discussion had been typically cryptic – *One swallow does not a summer make, but it does do for a tasty snack.*

Deborah had been less philosophic about their predicament. Before the day's first glimmer had spread across the eastern sky she'd slipped out the back door, darted down to the local convenience store and bought all the morning papers. She now sat at Mike's desk wading through the great mass of newsprint, a bemused expression on her young face.

'Nothing there either. Whoever tracked us down has done a pretty good job of protecting their exclusive. Still, I wouldn't bet on it staying quiet for long. I'm sure there are plenty of people that'd like to get a piece of this story.'

'How can they know so much? How did they find out about the insurance policy – and the bet?'

Deborah shook her head. 'However they did it, they're onto us now. Why don't we get away from London – the house in Noddegamra is almost complete, and that joker's bound to return here sooner or later.'

The Professor nodded sadly. 'True enough, my dear. But he knows about Caer-Mathonwy too. There's a photo of the farm. If we run, he'll just follow us down there. We need to finish him off once and for all. Lose him right here in the city.'

'You're not suggesting we bump him off? Thought you were the morally upstanding one?'

'This has nothing to do with morals – it's about survival. But it shouldn't come to that, anyway. We might be able to salvage something from this mess, if we play it right. I'm sure that reporter doesn't really believe I'm responsible for demon summoning and vanishing pyramids. He just wants a good story to give to his boss who just wants to sell papers. Am I right?'

'So . . .' said Deborah. 'What are you getting at?'

'Well, this sort of story feeds off publicity. After a while it'll burn itself out. If we're secretive it'll be read as confirmation of their suspicions and we'll be hounded 'til we drop. But if we give our man the very story he wants right now . . .'

'Make a deal with them? I'm sorry Mike but I didn't risk life and limb kicking that oily git off you yesterday just so you could waltz down to Wapping and sing "I'm the one that you want."'

'It won't be like that. We'll be in control. With the right setting and costumes to match we can make them believe whatever we want. In this case . . . that we're a couple of cranks who just happened to get lucky. Trust me, I know what I'm doing.'

Deborah snorted. 'There's been little evidence of it so far,' she said, but no more than that and Mike knew she'd go along with whatever he had planned, however embarrassing, morally bankrupting or just plain stupid it turned out to be. Very little of what she'd been through since meeting him made any sense, so why argue now? A little extra piece of lunacy wouldn't make a blind bit of difference. It would be rather like the Chief Architect at Stonehenge saying in his Wiltshire twang as his army of sweating savages dragged the last sarsen the final yards from the Cambrian Hills: 'Well, if truth be told I'm having second thoughts 'bout stone cladding for the finish. What we want is a nice bit of marble.'

'So is that a "Yes, Professor, I bow to your great wisdom," then?' Mike said with a smile.

'Actually, it's an "Okay, but it's a hell of a risk and don't say I didn't warn you,"' Deborah replied with a scowl.

Mike grinned wide and rubbed his hands together. 'Now,' he said, 'where did I put that Egyptian Priest's ceremonial head-dress?'

Comfortably Numb

'She did *what*?' Bill Winslow looked like he'd just heard the Martians had crash landed, and they needed his gonads to repair their space-ship. He may not have been able to spell incredulity but he was exuding it by the bucketful. Adam stared dreamily off into space.

'It's true. I had Nostrus cornered, then they hit us from all sides.'

'They?' Winslow said suspiciously. 'I thought you said there was only one of them? And a sheila at that!'

For a second, Adam was troubled by the menace in Winslow's reaction then it didn't matter, and his troubles disappeared into the ether. He explained breezily: 'Well, there was this cat as well . . .'

Winslow degenerated into gales of laughter, his belly quivering like a half-set trifle. 'You mean to tell me that you were beaten up by a bit of totty and a flea-bitten moggy? Oh that's good that is, now that is a story. Jim, come and get a load of this.' Several of the office staff, who'd been circling like vultures, closed in for the kill, grins at the ready.

But Adam, who was finding it hard to concentrate on any one thing for more than a few seconds, was oblivious to the situation. Since meeting Deborah he'd been on a natural Prozac. He'd spent last night restless in bed, tossing and turning – but mainly tossing. Occasionally, his brain had to remind the rest of him to breathe.

'She wasn't a bit of totty,' he whispered. His voice hardened defensively. 'And you shouldn't talk about her like that. She was a goddess in human form – sent to Earth to save me.'

But no one heard him, they were too busy cracking up.

Winslow finally wiped away his tears of mirth and dragged himself back to the issue at hand. 'Look son, you've entertained us so much I'm prepared to forgive you this once.' He paused as a fresh bout of giggling swept his gang. 'Get back round there, get me an interview and none of us will mention this again – without pissing ourselves laughing.'

Adam looked up suddenly. 'You want me to go back? Where *she* is?'

'You got the hots for her? That's more like it,' encouraged Winslow, 'a bit of go get 'em. A photo of the female bodyguard, muscles flexing, legs akimbo, big gun throbbing. You won't even have to write anything. The only thing that sells copy faster than sex'n'violence is sex'n'violence at the same time.' The other journalists stood and gave a rowdy ovation as a suddenly regenerated Adam sprang to his feet.

'Watch out for tiddles,' sneered a Junior Sub, clearly hoping to gain approval from his peers, '–might pee in your lap.'

'Oh, I will,' said Adam, swiftly lifting a cold cup of tea from his desk and pouring it between the spotty boy's legs, 'because it looks like he's already got you.'

Don't Look Now

Over the next ten minutes Adam turned the busy West End streets into a fair approximation of downtown Monte Carlo on Grand Prix day.

He had good reason to be driving like a madman. The old geezer was back and sitting by him in the front seat.

And he was still faintly transparent.

This time Adam knew he wasn't suffering from concussion. And no matter how he looked at it, he couldn't dismiss the man's existence as a trick of the light, or an imaginary figment, or some other cock-and-bull explanation. The man beside him was very real. He just wasn't quite all there.

The ten minutes in question had started uncalmly enough and degenerated into chaos as the man repeatedly tried to get Adam to see him for what he really was. 'If you are ying, then I'm your yang, heh, heh,' he'd explained. Which meant nothing to Adam who just repeatedly kept banging his head against the windscreen hoping this seedy apparition would disappear back to wherever it was he'd been loitering before. So the man had tried for a bit more detail: 'When your emotions are running high, I can take on physical form. You're in a spot of bother? Then your mate's by yer side ready to lend an 'and before you can say "Lordy, what the effing eff am I going to do?"'

Now, weaving insanely around Hyde Park Corner, Adam had latched on to the only rational explanation available.

'When did they release you?' he said.

'Don't catch yer drift, Adam. *You* released me.'

'Care in the community job, aren't you?'

The man shrugged. 'If you say so. Don't know what you mean though.'

'I mean, you're ga-ga, loony-tunes, an oopsy-daisy-my-brain's-fallen-out-of-my-head-and-I've-just-trodden-on-it mad bastard.'

The man shook his head. 'You really are stressed, aren't you? I can do massage, yer know. Normally reserve it for the birds but –'

Adam rounded on him. 'I don't want a massage – I want my head back. And I want you, whoever you are, out of my car now.'

The man sighed. 'Didn't think I'd ave to do this but,' and he vanished. Just for a second he wasn't there at all, leaving behind him only the impression in the seat where he'd been sitting and a crackle of static in the air. From deep inside him, a primeval moan came rumbling up Adam's throat, threatening to become a full-on wail. But as it reached his lips, the man, just as impossibly, was back, this time with a friendly smile.

Which turned rapidly into a grimace of terror.

'Watch out mate! You nearly hit that little old lady!'

'What little old lady?'

'The one in front of that huge lorry!'

'What huge lorry?'

'Aaaaaaaarrrrrrgh!' Adam's companion's entire existence flashed before his bulging eyes, an experience almost as depressing as being intimately involved in a high-speed collision. A few seconds later, the old man's state was further shaken by the car abruptly skidding to a halt outside Mike's flat.

'Keep yer eyes on the road, mate, why don't you?' he said shakily after peeling himself off the dashboard and wiping a crusty sleeve over his sweaty brow.

This was too much for Adam. 'How can I keep my eyes on the road if you just disappear in front of me?'

The man considered the question for a moment then

nodded and held up his hands. 'Point taken mate. It was reckless, but you *were* being a bit stubborn. I had to give you proof.'

Adam leant back in his seat, put his palms to his eyes and rubbed them down his face. Then he shook his head, breathing out heavily and letting his shoulders drop. The actions of a man marking a line between what had gone on before in his life and what was going to happen next. Between what he thought he had known, and what he now knew to be true.

Adam inhaled deeply. 'Okay,' he said, as much to himself as to his passenger. The world was turning upside down everywhere else. Now, the madness had just come a bit closer to home. That was all. He was Adam MacArthur, journo extraordinaire. He could deal with it. A smile crept onto his face. Would make a decent story too.

Besides, he was in love. And that was much more important. He felt the glow of anticipation return to him at the very thought of her. Adam turned his smile to the man. 'Stay in the car,' he told him. 'I have some serious business to attend to.'

'Too right you 'ave,' the man said, underlining his words with a suggestive laugh.

But Adam was out of the car and bounding up the steps to the Professor's apartment. Before pressing the intercom, Adam composed himself.

It's truly incredible how the average human male can delude himself. Adam's preparations consisted of straightening his tie and running a hand through his dishevelled hair. Over the course of human history this procedure has been used as a general panacea to help men face all ills. It has been used by desperate politicians in a misguided attempt to prevent wars; it has been employed by countless job applicants who seem to be under the impression that a slightly straighter tie is just what the Personnel Manager's been looking for; but most of all it has been used by men of all ages to make themselves more attractive to the opposite sex. On the cosmic Richter Scale of effectiveness this process has to rank alongside pouring the little sachet of sauce onto a pot noodle, or shaking one last time after visiting a pub toilet. But still, all men do it at one time or another, no matter how hairless/gormless/tieless/hopeless/ugly they happen to be.

Once Adam was adjusted to his satisfaction he pressed the buzzer. After a few seconds he was rewarded with Mike's cultured tones.

'Hello, who's there?'

'Professor Nostrus, this is Adam MacArthur of the *Daily Trumpet*. I'm waiting outside until you give me an interview. Our readers deserve to know the truth and none of your bully-boy tactics can protect you now. Why don't you do yourself a favour and open up.'

'Okay.'

'Excuse me?'

'I said Okay.'

'I know what you said, but –'

'Shall I explain it to you?'

'No, of course not.'

But Mike went on regardless. 'It means: righty-o, affirmative, absolutely, amen to that, thumbs up, confirmed, endorsed, your request is ratified, you have my assent, and if you wanted a visa to enter the country known as positive, I, in person, would rubber stamp it with a big tick . . . yes, in other words, come on up.'

There was a loud buzz and the door swung open a few inches.

Adam hesitated. This wasn't how it was meant to happen. There should be argument, cold hours on the steps, cupping your hands around a luke-warm mug of thermos coffee that tasted like plastic – a good old will-he-won't-he-break journalistic war of attrition. 'Yes', however long it took the old git to get there, was not the way things were done. But hey . . . Adam had never been one to punch a gift horse in the mouth.

A day ago, Adam would have been mighty suspicious at this turn of events, at the ease with which he was gaining entry, but that was a day ago. The world was different then. It was 'World Without Woman'. Now it was 'World With Woman' and in such a world, anything was possible.

Besides, she was probably up there right now. Waiting for him . . .

Nostrus broke his train of thought. 'Are you coming up some time today? It's flat 1B. Wipe your feet and close the door behind you. But I warn you, the slightest hint of trouble and I won't be responsible for your safety. Understood?'

Adam gulped as he set his jaw. 'Understood. Best behaviour.'

There Must Be An Angel Playing With My Head

Adam sat alone in Mike's dark living-room drinking tea and trying not to fidget. He was about to meet, face-to-face rather than foot-to-chest, the only girl whom he would ever truly love. After ushering him in, the Professor had disappeared into another room, muttering something about putting the sacrificial camel to bed. The tripod of incense burning in one dim corner looked genuine but he was sure ceremonial daggers should not have MADE IN TAIWAN stamped on the blade. All a bit suspicious, but he was prepared to run with it. The ultimate prize would be worth it.

With a loud crash the bedroom door flew open revealing Mike posing theatrically in full regalia. He was wearing a white floor-length robe and a black velvet headband. On his forehead shimmered a bright golden disc.

'So, Professor Nostrus,' Adam said calmly, ignoring the dramatic entrance, 'how was it you knew about the Pyramids? Care to share that information with us?'

Mike strode regally to his couch and sat down. He made a great show of clearing his throat then started in a self-important tone. 'I was told of the Great Pyramids' dematerialization by none other than Crom-Akradath, last of the God Kings of ancient Atlantis. He called to me across the countless ages from his sapphire-encrusted throne, saying he would steal them as a sign.'

'Of what?' Adam looked up from his notebook.

'Er . . . a sign that he wanted his Pyramids back.' The reporter's prompt arrival had caught Mike and Deborah in the middle of preparations. The Professor hadn't had time to put the finishing touches to his story so was going to have to improvise in places. He wasn't sure how his guest was taking it, but if Adam's frantic scribbling was anything to go by, he was lapping it up.

'And the fish fall? Did Crom-what's-is-face tell you about that too?'

Mike looked confused for a moment. 'Oh no. That would have been Bel Yarkoth, last but one of the Priest Wizards of slumbering Lemuria. He spoke to me from his cursèd tomb saying – "Beware ye traveller of a week next Thursday. If ye go out, make sure to wear a hard hat, or be prepared to suffer the wrath of Oannes, the vengeful fish god of Chaldea."'

'I suppose his wrath is a response to the way man unthinkingly overfishes his peaceful oceans, and lets Captain Birdseye turn his little children into fishy-fingers?'

'I wouldn't be at all surprised.'

'I also have evidence you knew about last week's stock market crash. Who tipped you off on that one? The Sorcerer-Accountants of Lost Guildford?'

Mike played his last remaining trump card. Rising to his feet his voice boomed around the flat like thunder. 'Great god Anker! Great god Anker! Bring me the colon of a merchant banker!'

At this prearranged signal the kitchen door swung open

and Deborah entered the room. She wasn't so much wearing the costume as supporting its various strips of sequinned material with strategic parts of her anatomy. She stood framed in the doorway, back lighting from the kitchen giving her a golden halo. It looked like Michelangelo, Rodin and a group of repressed fifteen-year-old schoolboys had got together, taken all the best bits from Aphrodite, Florence Nightingale and Helen of Troy, finished them off to perfection, then rearranged them for optimal effect.

Adam looked on open-mouthed. She was standing right before him, looking hornier than a thorn bush full of rhinos. They say love is blind, but at that precise moment it was deaf, dumb and immobile as well. The reporter tried hard to articulate his tender feelings for the girl.

'Arg blmmmn grg hrt?' he said suavely. Somewhere along the complex journey between crotch, brain and mouth his stunningly eloquent opening line had become encoded beyond even the cracking powers of Enigma.

Deborah looked at him worriedly, giving the poor idiot she saw before her a faint smile. Then the earth-bound goddess spoke, her voice like soft rain on a spring morning. 'Hello everybody. Anyone like another cup of tea?'

Only Mike seemed capable of coherent speech. 'Not for me my dear. Why don't you come and meet our guest. I believe you're due a formal introduction.'

Somehow, Adam managed to sit still as Deborah glided towards him. The only part of Adam that seemed to be moving was his heart, which was making a fortunately unsuccessful attempt to burst through his chest. The woman's smile filled the room.

'Hello sir, pleased to meet you, though I think we've met before . . .' She gave him a slow wink. 'I'm Deborah – Vestal Virgin First Class. I must apologize for my behaviour yesterday afternoon. I'm afraid I rather got the wrong idea when I saw you questioning Lord Michael.'

Still Adam couldn't speak, the main reason being that

there was an out of control nuclear reactor in his pants which was nearing terminal meltdown. Unless the fire brigade arrived soon there might be a spillage that would make Chernobyl look like an overturned milk float. After an embarrassingly lengthy silence, he managed to shake himself back to life, recapturing some of his usual bravado in the process.

'Hi, I'm Adam. They call me that 'cause I'm everyone's number one man.'

Oh my God, thought Deborah, he's one of those.[1] She took to him instantly like a sheep takes to water polo.

Adam ignored her look of faint distaste. He'd try the professional approach first, win her over with a good, hard question. 'So tell me Deborah, why the sudden need for cash? What use has a small spiritual cult like yours got for money?'

Deborah put on her best evangelical voice. 'Our organization does not intend to stay small for long. With the money we get from the information entrusted to us by the Great Old Ones we intend to reach many more people. That's why we're talking to you.'

Adam took it all down in his notebook but his eyes stayed firmly fixed on Deborah. Seeing her still looking at him oddly he decided to switch to the direct approach.

'Forgive me for staring, but you're the most beautiful person I've ever seen.'

Deborah looked taken aback. 'This physical body is merely a shell, brother. True beauty comes from within.'

Adam sighed. 'I'm sure you have very pretty intestines. Shakespeare could have written sonnets about your pancreas.' He wasn't sure what she meant by the word 'brother' but it sounded vaguely kinky.

So next he pursued the kinky approach, asking all manner of personal questions, but despite his best efforts

---

1 A tosser.

the talk always turned back to fundraising activities. It quickly became clear that Adam was getting very little new information out of either of the interviewees. Both simply spouted a lot of meaningless pseudo-mythological rubbish in reply to any sensible question. They refused categorically to have photos taken, saying it was against their beliefs to allow their image to be recorded other than in the minds and memories of man and creature. And although it would have been a simple matter to whip his camera out and take some anyway, getting to the hospital afterwards might not be.

Adam could see he wasn't going to make any headway, professionally or personally – at least today – and he didn't want to wreck what little progress he'd made by outstaying his welcome. Far better to retire gracefully and engineer a meeting with Deborah at a later date. Preferably one without Charles Manson's personal vicar getting in the way.

'Right, that's about all I need for now,' he said, rising to his feet. 'Do we have an agreement? The *Trumpet* won't reveal your true identities or your whereabouts, we'll bung you this four hundred quid, and you won't talk to any other papers?'

'That's right.' Mike nodded and reached for the plain brown envelope. Adam had left on the table. 'If Great Marduk – High King of Interior Decorating – gets in touch again you'll be the first to know.'

As Deborah showed him to the door, Adam couldn't help but make one final attempt to impress her. 'Tell me darlin,' he said with a wolfish grin, 'what qualifications do you need to become a vestal virgin? Some sort of medical certificate perhaps?'

The expression on Adam's face told Deborah full well he was willing to cure her of the condition right away. Going all doe-eyed she put on her best yokel accent. 'Well – it 'aint much of a test I'll grant you but each May Day Eve the girls in me local village 'ave a runnin' race. Twice round the church and first back from the May Pole. Whoever wins is crowned Chief Vestal Virgin and sprinkled with apple blossom. It ain't foolproof but it's the best test we got.'

Adam looked at her for a long while, unsure if she was being serious or yanking his plonker like there was no tomorrow. Still undecided he gave a half-smile. 'So, does your cult have any vacancies at the moment? Maybe you could show me the erotic secrets of ancient Atlantis. See if we can sink this continent too.'

Deborah looked delighted. 'We're always on the lookout for new recruits, aren't we Lord Michael?' She shot the Professor a glance.

'Indeed, we are.'

'Only the other day, Lord Michael was lamenting our lack of a chief eunuch in the ranks.'

'It's a simple procedure, you know,' Mike said, slipping a friendly arm around Adam's shoulders. 'We have the equipment on premises. We can do it while you wait, if you want.'

Adam squirmed out of his grasp and made rapidly for the door.

'I take it that means you'd like to think it over?' Mike called to his back as Adam stumbled into the hall and hurled himself down the stairs.

Once outside in the fresh air Adam regained some of his usual colour. And when he climbed into his car's amazing uncomfortable High-G IMPREGNATOR™ seat he also regained his unearthly companion, who it seemed had been with him all along.

'I 'ope you didn't believe any of that crap in there . . .'

Adam stared up at Mike's window and sighed. 'The Professor's a scheming con-artist, for sure. But Deborah could never tell a lie. An untruth could never knowingly get past her perfect lips. Maybe she's been duped by him.'

The old man looked disgusted. 'You'd better watch it,

mate. You shouldn't risk your nest egg for the sake of some bird. This is the biggest break of your life.'

Adam had spent his whole life being sure about things – it was his job, his nature. Going with hunches, getting to the heart of seedy affairs, or better, being a part of seedy affairs. But now he was experiencing horribly conflicting emotions. On the one hand he was sure that those two were keeping something from him and all his professional instincts told him to ruthlessly pursue the story. On the other hand he couldn't ignore his increasing . . . *tenderness* . . . towards another human being. The last thing he wanted was to set Deborah against him by pushing things too far, too fast. Not that he was perturbed by her initial frosty reaction to his advances. Adam found that most women behaved like that when he first met them; it was just their way of letting him know they wanted to be chased.

Before he could take heart from this reassuring conclusion, Adam's thoughts were interrupted by a piercing screech of brakes all around him as three huge black limousines skidded round the corner and pulled up in front of the building.

Black Lines, Black Magic

'Okay boys, this is a nice simple job.' Casper surveyed each one of his troops in the back of the limo. 'We go in, we apprehend the evil spawn, we get him into the car and off to Church Headquarters. Got the picture?' Despite his free use of 'we', Casper had no intention of taking an active part in the mission. He was needed in a command and control role here in the main vehicle.

He was addressing six of his finest men, wearing the Church's regulation suits. They looked like they'd just stepped out of bible college and into a six week course of advanced combat training. Their shiny new teeth reflecting in their shiny new shoes were outshone only by the light of religious zeal shining in their bright but vacant eyes. Their leader was the Reverend Harvey Banger, Trundell's head of security and top Stormtrooper for Christ.

'We have a unanimous Yo! response on that, Mr Addleflower, sir. We've located and locked on to our primary target. Task Force Zachariah ready to roll!'

Harvey had been shipped over together with his platoon of shock troops to form the cutting edge of the Church's evangelical campaign. To date, Alpha Company – 1st Faith Marines had notched up battle honours including some heavy duty menacing at an abortion clinic and a stint of highly professional intimidation down at the local Humanist bookshop – an operation which proved just how well books burn when you've got the wind of theological certainty blowing a gale behind you. But today was something special. It wasn't every day an ambitious young security operative for the forces of truth and justice got to apprehend a dark wizard, guilty of acts of foul necromancy. With military precision the athletic young men exited the limousine and drew up in a rank on the roadside. Harvey clambered after them and surveyed his troops.

'Men, you've all been briefed. You've trained with the best. Now we put it into practice. Today, we face a CSS/43 situation. 'Compulsory Soul Saving Abduction For Publicity Purposes'. I want it done by the Book. Straighten that tie Kowlaski! Who do you think we are, Mormons?'

When Christ's elite commandos were smartened up to his satisfaction, Harvey led them at a trot up the front steps. The intercom security system was no match for a righteous crowbar and in no time at all Harvey had led his avenging angels to Mike's front door. He hammered at it impatiently with his fist. 'Emergency plumber! Open up!'

When the door opened, he was confronted by an attractive blonde hastily tying a bathrobe round her slim figure.

'We didn't call for a pluh –' she said as Harvey barged past her into the flat.

'No, but the Lord did. We're here to cap the stopcock of filth your master has spewed into Heaven's clear waters. Where's Nostrus? I've got God's monkey wrench – and I'm gonna tighten his nuts.'

In a daze, Deborah surveyed the room. It seemed to be filling with Raybanned Jehovah's Witnesses. They took up defensive positions – against the walls, behind sofas, one under the coffee table – and put hands to the ominous bulges in their jacket pockets. Deborah suffered a second of indecision, then began to slowly back away from them, marking the position of each intruder in her mind. Mike chose that moment to come through the bedroom door, still wearing his high-priest outfit.

'What the . . . Who?'

'Grab him!' bellowed Harvey. Two of his men lunged at Mike. Instinctively, Deborah sprang to his defence. She was halted by the shining barrel of Harvey's 9mm automatic appearing two inches from her temple. 'I wouldn't do that if I were you, Miss. The Lord allows me special dispensation to use extreme violence. Perk of the job.'

Despite her violent success the day before, Deborah was by nature a realist. She had no idea if this rather earnest young American would actually use his gun. She also had no intention of finding out. Her suspicion was that any attempt to free Mike would give her a life expectancy shorter than a minor character in an episode of *Casualty*.

'Don't do anything silly,' Mike said calmly.

Deborah glared at Harvey with open contempt. 'If you harm so much as one hair on his head, you're dead.'

'Do as we say, Miss, and no one gets harmed. We're here for your own good – looks like we rescued you just in time.'

But Deborah wasn't listening. Out of the corner of

her eye she'd seen Aristotle slink silently beneath an easy chair.

'Rescue her!' Mike shouted. 'On whose authority do you invade my privacy? This is a free country, or do you apes know something we don't?'

Harvey eyed Mike's costume with disgust. 'Apparently too free from the looks of things. We've come to Engle-land to change all that.' Turning to his men, he said: 'Seems we was just in time, evi-dentally interrupted one of their satanic rites. Search the flat for goats and chickens.'

His troops set about ransacking the place. Helpless, Mike could only watch as they pulled his flat apart. 'You do this in the name of your God? This is an outrage.'

'You'll thank us soon enough,' Harvey said, stony-faced and then he motioned them to the door. 'Pull out, pull out, he bellowed. As they left the building, Deborah tried to spot Aristotle, but he was nowhere to be seen. Mike said nothing further, calmly allowing two of the Marines to lead him.

With a brisk glance up and down the street, Harvey bundled them into the waiting limousines. Deborah did her best not to make it too obvious she was looking for Aristotle. The three troopers wedged in with her on the back seat watched her every move. In fact, for men who had supposedly renounced all worldly pleasures, they seemed to pay an inordinate amount of attention to her cleavage. She'd just about given up hope when from nearby the cat's voice came clearly into her head.

There's enough space under this seat for a tiger.

Aristo? How did you get in here?

How do you think, woman? The door was open. It seemed rude not to join you.

Reporter To The Rescue

Adam had seen it all. He'd seen the convoy pulling up and armed men rushing inside, then watched with mounting horror as Nostrus and Deborah were led away – clearly against their will.

He may not have known her long, but he couldn't fail to recognize the look of stubborn determination in Deborah's eyes. Her 'I-want' line was clearly visible across her brow. Adam strongly suspected it had been saying, 'I want to get away from these cretins and I might just snog anyone who helps me do it.'

He couldn't pass on a chance like that. So when the limos had started to pull away, Adam had keyed his underpowered engine to life and followed them, muttering a determined: 'Hold on Deborah, I'll get you out of this yet.'

With a cackle that was fast becoming a trademark, his shadowy companion echoed: '"Hold on Deborah, I'll get into you yet."' He sat lecherously in the passenger seat like a Viagraed pensioner ready for his annual outing. Adam briefly considered pushing him out of the door, but there was no time and anyway, like herpes, he'd just keep coming back.

Now they'd been driving for two hours and the convoy showed no signs of slowing down. After leaving the motorway, they'd passed along a bewildering array of winding lanes deep into the countryside. Dusk was settling all around like a vast marmalade quilt. Adam didn't know what he was getting into but the love-of-his-life had been carried away by what looked like the local branch of Accountants For God, and he was determined to audit their books.

Sid, as Adam had christened his passenger, was decidedly less enthusiastic about the whole venture.

'How come you get so worked up about a bit of fluff? You walk into any pub in the country, you could have your pick from types like her.'

Adam shot him a glance filled with menace. 'If you refer to Deborah as "a bit of fluff" again, I'll smash your face in.'

'You couldn't hit me.'

'Don't bet on it.'

'No, I mean it's not possible, mate. I'd just disappear.'

'I wish you bloody would.'

Sid looked hurt. 'Oh very constructive, I don't think. Here's me trying to look out for our survival, and you're wanting rid of your only friend.'

'You're not a friend. I don't even know you,' Adam retorted.

'Yes, you do. You know me like you know yourself. If you know what I mean.'

'Not that again, please.'

'Want me to prove it?'

'No.'

'Does Hartley's strawberry jam under your duvet mean anything to you?'

'Stop it.'

'Does to me. I keep a full jar ready under my bedside table in case the urge takes me.'

'Leave me alone!'

'Novel form of lubrication admittedly, but it seems to do the trick.'

'JUST SHUT UP WILL YOU!'

A pause when the only sound was the drone of tyres on tarmac, then: 'Now you know why I want you to call me Adam,' Sid said.

Adam winced. Nobody, but nobody knew about him and Hartley's. He looked at Sid. Is this what he would become? An oily old man with an irritating laugh. Was he like that now – just minus the wrinkles? Adam grimaced at the thought then blanked it. Some truths were just too unpalatable for the conscious mind to take on.

They drove on a couple of miles in silence. Sid broke it first.

'The thing is Adam, do you know what you're getting us into here? I don't think those lads ahead of us are afraid of a friendly bit of GBH. Looks to me like we're dealing with a heavy duty organization.'

Adam nodded vaguely, then, with a start, realized he could no longer see the convoy's last vehicle. He'd been keeping back to avoid detection but now the limos were out of sight. Cursing, he drove on a few hundred yards until he saw the entrance to a small, gravelly driveway that disappeared under an arched avenue of mature poplars. Leading up to it was a substantial moss-covered wall along the road verge which ended at an imposing gatehouse. Opposite the gatehouse rose a gentle hill dotted here and there with thorn and briar that could only just be made out in the gloom.

Adam stopped before reaching the turning. They could only have gone this way. The road ahead was straight for half a mile. He would still be able to see them. With a dawning smile of relief he realized that this just might be their destination. The avenue shielded them from what looked like a large country estate. Then he heard dogs barking, and quickly saw, in succession, surveillance cameras and barbed wire along the length of the wall.

He sat tapping the steering wheel thoughtfully. He doubted driving up and politely asking for an audience with the Lord of the Manor would be met with a friendly reaction. The owner was obviously someone who took their privacy very seriously. With a determined frown he made his decision.

'I'm going to climb the hill. See if I can get a better look at what's in there. You're welcome to sulk in the car and tend to your arthritis.'

Sid couldn't be put off that easily. 'Not bloody likely mate. Someone's got to keep us out of trouble.

Ten minutes later the sight that met their eyes could truly be described as unbelievable. It looked like Walt Disney, Donald Trump and the Pope had got together and decided to throw a party. Huge cranes towered above a partially completed amusement park, their running lights turning the evening dusk into bright day. Work continued as great masses of stainless steel glinted under the glare of a bank of floodlights. It seemed the construction was going on around the clock. Not even the forces of nature could stop the man behind this development.

Adam went pale. 'Oh no,' he mumbled. 'Oh no. This is all beginning to make some sort of horrible sense. We've got to get her out now. It's all my fault she's in there in the first place.'

'Don't be daft,' Sid said. 'You were only doing your job, exposing two dangerous loonies. Anyway, what's it got to do with them being kidnapped?'

'You don't know what this is, do you?'

Sid shook his head defensively. 'I don't know everything you know – just your innermost thoughts.'

On a horizon blurred by searchlights, a giant roller coaster loomed. The last piece of track was being slotted into place around a garishly painted cathedral.

'We're looking at Supreme Bishop Ted Trundell's opening bid for the lost soul of Great Britain. A theme park designed by heaven that'll be hell on earth to visit.' Adam gulped. 'He wouldn't have stolen my Deborah if I hadn't exposed them in the *Trumpet*. I just about accused her of being a witch. I'm responsible.'

Sid took hold of his partner, arms on shoulders and stared him in the eye. 'Listen very carefully. We are not responsible. Someone else would have broken the story, even if you hadn't. The man is a psycho – he'd have got a hold of them anyway. He's dangerous, Adam. Which is why we're leaving.'

Adam shrugged him off. He wasn't listening. He just looked down at the distant building site with its insect workmen scurrying between Tonka toy cranes. Inside his head the first glimmers of a plan were taking shape. Finally Adam had the courage to ask the one question they were both trying very hard to avoid.

'Please tell me,' the young reporter said, fighting hard to maintain a level tone, 'that you can't see a two-hundred-foot polystyrene statue of John the Baptist over there.'

Bonfire Of The Insanities

While Adam was speeding west after Mike and Deborah, another party were approaching from the east. But while Adam intended rescue and prolonged mouth-to-mouth resuscitation, this other group had far from honourable intentions. This second group was comprised of two demons, one Duke of Hell and his dark rune-sword with a very silly voice.

'Can't you make this crate go any faster?' squeaked Soul Stealer, the malevolent hell-blade wielded during the Creation Wars by the Vowless God King of Ra'Leih.

'I've got my hoof flat to the board!' Guttlehog snapped. He'd had enough of the caustic comments from Alastor's sidekick. 'If you think you can do any better why don't you take the wheel!'

Soul Stealer managed to look peevish. 'All right, all right . . . I was only asking. I mean, it's just a question isn't it? Isn't it? What's wrong with a question?' He received no reply. As the sword rested in his master's armour-plated lap Alastor stared out from the juggernaut's cabin at the monotonous motorway ahead. The Chief Executioner of Hell's breath was like the escape of fetid air from a newly opened crypt. Rubicante sat next to him, trying hard not to notice the green haze that condensed on the windscreen each time Alastor exhaled. It was making him rather nervous.

The juggernaut thundered on through the night carrying its deadly cargo. It was a huge eighteen-wheeler carrying a large cylindrical chemical container with a glowing green label on its side which read: DANGEROUS LOAD: FIRE HAZARD.

Soul Stealer was still not satisfied. 'Why didn't we get

an Aeroene powered vehicle?[1] We'd be there by now. Oh why why why why why whywhywhywhy?'

'It washn't neshesshery,' spluttered the Boar Demon. 'We've got a shtrong fixss on Noshhhtrushhh's new position. He'ssh not going anywhere. We can get there in plenty of time by road.'[2]

'That's right,' said Rubicante, regaining some of his old gung-ho attitude, 'there'll be no slip ups this time. We'll be in position to hit them tomorrow night. Nostrus has seen his last sunrise – well, his last-but-one sunrise anyway.'

'Oh very dramatic,' squeaked Soul Stealer and drew a big breath. He was about to indulge in another sarcastic monologue when Alastor sheathed him firmly and finally at his side.

Even The Chief Executioner of Hell had his limits.

---

1 Aeroene is a little-known high energy fuel used extensively by the Forces of Darkness whenever they venture topside. It's made by gathering together thousands of small imps and minor devils, for whom no better purpose can be found, then squashing them in vast presses designed specially for the purpose. The vitriolic green fluid that results is imbued with all the latent theological energy (anti-faithons) stored in the tiny bodies. It has the useful ability to give any vehicle the gift of flight so long as the passengers believe in it. Aeroene is a very expensive commodity, due to its labour intensive manufacture, and as a result is always in short supply. Guttlehog had a long-running feud with the Chief Logistics Imp over a practical joke involving two hundred yards of piano wire, a small donkey and a very large cheese-grater. Needless to say he stood little chance of laying a hoof on any of the stuff.

2 Your Satansoft Translatomatic ™ software has crashed. Please insert disc 12 and reboot this book. Thanking you in anticipation of your co-operation.

NINE

Accursed is he who quotes the Bible out of context. And that includes you, Aristo.
The Count of St Germain, 1676–

You can always spot a moral victor. He's the one bleeding on the ground.
Anon.

No Freedom, No Cry

When Mike and Deborah were finally escorted from the limousines night had fallen completely, but that only accentuated the scene that met their eyes. The theme park was a sight that few who saw it would ever forget – though the prisoners were not given long to admire the view. They soon found themselves in a luxurious hotel complex, differing from other five star accommodation only by the giant neon sign blinking above the foyer:

Why sleep in a stable when there's room at the
BETHLEHEM CARLTON ASTORIA
Double rooms only available with proof of holy wedlock

Deborah and Mike were split up and each taken to a lavishly appointed suite, there to spend a long night of frustrating solitude and fruitless calls to their captors. The Professor wasn't surprised to find his door locked. For the moment it seemed they were to be well-treated guests, but guests who wouldn't be allowed to understay their welcome. Muttering ancient Hindu curses under his breath, Mike made the most of his comfortable prison cell.

It wasn't hard to settle in. Despite his worrying predicament Mike got a good night's sleep. He had long learnt that there was no point worrying about things you had no control over. So, when the dawn came he sat down facing the door, to await whatever fate had in store with a brave face and the sort of cheerfully resilient frame of mind that had seen him through more spells of incarceration than Australia's first boatload of colonists. He waited that way for most of the day. At lunchtime a well-stocked tray was brought in, but the stony-faced guard hovering by the door proved impervious to Mike's charm. Mike used the time to speculate on the motives behind his abduction. He couldn't tell for sure what these people wanted but he was beginning to make an educated guess.

Mike had heard all about Ted Trundell and his Church of the Eloquent Announcement. When you'd lived through what he had, you made a point of staying abreast of local customs concerning religious tolerance – and those who sought to change them. Throughout history men like Ted had used men like Mike, often as firelighters, but also as pawns in their political games. Once more, Fate had put on her running shoes, grabbed Mike by the testicles and taken him jogging. The Professor wasn't by nature a fatalist – he believed in free will as much as anyone in his profession could – but sometimes you just had to go with the flow. For the time being at least he was a passenger on the cosmic roller-coaster – and he might as well sit back and enjoy the ride.

So, becalmed and ready for whatever was in store for him, Mike didn't bat an eyelid when late that afternoon the door to his suit flew open with a loud crash, revealing the broad shoulders of the Reverend Harvey T. Banger.

'You there, Satan's Scoutmaster! Your hour of judgement is at hand. Grab your ass by the butt-ocks and haul it over here right now. Supreme Bishop Trundell wants to see you, and believe me he's not a man you wanna keep waiting.'

As he got up the sweet smile never left Mike's lips. 'How nice. A bigot a day, keeps boredom at bay.'

The Expected Un-Spanish Inquisition

Over the course of Mike's long and eventful life his many paths had crossed those of old-style foaming-at-the-mouth religious nutters on more than one occasion. Anyone capable of visualizing the twisting turning, crazy-paved walkways of Mike's wanderings would have been amazed by the melée of Scientologists, Moonies, Seventh-Day Adventists, Branch-Davidians and Agnostic Fundamentalists fighting for a piece of his time. It was almost as if misguided individuals were drawn to him by some cruelly inhuman force. Mike was always the one who caught the eye of the ubiquitous tube loony. To this day he couldn't look at a map of the Northern Line without hearing *Deuteronomy* 1:7 blared out at full volume in his left ear. When he walked down a crowded high street any clipboard-wielding, satchel-wearing, bobble-hatted loon with an armload of pamphlets so crass they'd even be an insult to the art of arsewiping, invariably made a beeline for him. Great masses of shoppers had been known to part like corn in the wind as these losers advanced on Mike. At one stage it got so bad he had kept a boxload of prepared statements by his door for the benefit of convert-seeking callers.[1] But in all his years nothing had come anywhere near topping the unforgettably unpleasant and totally unexpected fortnight Mike had spent in the company of Torquemada, Chief Sergeant at Arms and Witch Smeller Pursuivant of The Spanish Inquisition. But then every

---

1 His current favourite being: 'No I don't have time to accept the little baby Jesus into my life, as I am currently conducting a black mass. You wouldn't happen to be a virgin and/or blood donor, by any chance?'

record was bound to be broken sooner or later. Maybe today was the day?

As Mike was led from the sumptuous hotel, the sky seemed to darken before his eyes. His captive hours had passed far quicker than he'd realized, and now, like some great black beast, night was rolling in from the east. The first stars had begun to twinkle coyly, almost as if they knew better and would rather have stayed indoors. For those on the ground, however, there was no escape.

Mike was frogmarched to a waiting line of armour-plated jeeps. Shortly, the convoy set off down a wide boulevard at enema-inducing pace before pulling up at a dingy collection of prefab buildings, the sort that spring up on building sites the world over like psilocybin around a cowpat. Waiting outside the largest portacabin on the wide expanse of gravel forecourt stood Deborah, looking slender and out of place surrounded by her gun-toting captors. And also angry.

'Get your hands off me you neanderthal thug! Touch me again, you'll be carrying your gonads to heaven in a paper bag!' On spotting Mike her mood didn't improve. 'Oh, glad you could make it. Tell me Mike, how can one wizened old man piss off almost the entire universe?'

Mike could only shake his head. 'Maybe some people just take offence rather too easily.'

Then Harvey entered the conversation by cocking his pistol and aiming at Mike's face. 'That's enough of the chit-chat Satan Spawn. My boss wants to make your acquaintance, so in you go.'

An hour later Mike and Deborah sat tied back-to-back on a pair of cheap plastic chairs. The Professor was by nature a patient man. If he ever got into a patience-testing competition with a saint, in which the loser had to swallow a smouldering stick of dynamite, they'd be scraping ecumenical intestines off the walls for a fortnight to come. When combined with one of his mellower moods Mike's gift gave him a very high irritation threshold – a threshold that this evening Ted Trundell was doing his Bible-bashing best to break down.

At first, Trundell had been civil enough – that's if it's possible to be civil to guests you've just had trussed up like the Marquis de Sade's special friend. Trundell had made it clear that if Mike was prepared to play along they could come to a mutually beneficial arrangement – an arrangement, in fact, that began with a large sum being deposited in a Swiss bank account and didn't end in four broken legs. Mike had been rendered momentarily speechless by the temerity of this offer, but was helped out by Deborah who suggested that Ted should take his cash, fold it until it was all spiky corners and shove it into a place where even he was unlikely to ever get a suntan. Upon which Mike helpfully pointed out that this spot was probably inaccessible.

Since then the mood had darkened considerably. The captives refused to budge an inch while Ted got more and more frustrated. Mike was quite prepared to sit around all evening answering silly questions. Ted on the other hand had a fine collection of ulcers and a prize-winning set of bulging veins. He was currently working his way to major coronary, topped off with a severe nervous breakdown. Years in a viscious stressful job had given his arteries a lived-in look, and now not even the finest doctors could have turned back his biological clock. As he wiped the sweat from his fat red face Ted launched himself wholeheartedly into yet another assault.

'I'll ask you again Professor Nose-truss – do you renounce the foul works of Satan and agree to follow the path of righteousness, or is it time for Harvey and his boys to fetch the baseball bats and rubber hose?'

Mike looked pained. 'For the last time, Trundell it's Nostrus. At no time in my life has my proboscis required artificial support. If it ever does, you'll be the first to know.

Why don't you stop beating around the burning bush and get to the point?'

Ted reddened with fury. 'If you don't watch your lip grandpaw your nose'll need all the artificial support it can get.' Ted's normally immaculate hair hung down in a damp fringe as he ranted on. 'Now answer me this . . . Do you freely accept into your life the Lord Jesus Christ, who was sent to Earth to save your soul from Hades' damnation, or do you want to settle for earthly damnation right now?'

To be perfectly honest, as he sat in the poky windowless room along with Deborah, Ted and a pair of twitchy security personnel, metaphysical speculation was the furthest thing from Mike's mind. The sort of speculation that hit just a little nearer the mark went something along the lines of – 'Where is Aristotle and what is he doing to facilitate our escape?' – not to mention that old favourite – 'How are we going to get out of this mess without throwing in our lot with a man who makes Prince Ludwig of Saxony look like a guitar strumming vicar.' So instead, when Trundell gave them an ultimatum – which amounted to the not very original conversion/death dilemma – Mike looked thoughtful for a moment before answering, 'Can we get back to you on that one?'

That was when Ted Trundell finally lost it. If he could have exploded, he would have. 'Fell Wizard!' he screamed with a Vesuvian eruption of saliva that hung in the air like a fine mist, 'You dare mock me?! I try to save your immortal soul – that's if it ain't already sold to Lucifer – and all you do is . . . you just keep on taking the shit!'

'Piss,' Mike offered.

At this Ted moved in on Mike, until he was so close Mike could smell his rank breath. Ted's cheeks started to twitch, above his eye a vein pulsed to a manic disco beat. In a grating, slow, determined voice, he said: 'I don't care if it's running down your leg, you're staying put 'til I get a civil answer!'

Mike suppressed a smile. He did so love to find an enemy's weak spot. Once you knew where to prod you could keep them off balance indefinitely. This ranting baboon was blown up with self-importance. No doubt he was surrounded by the sort of sycophantic yes-men who did nothing but bolster his illusions. Ted Trundell didn't like it when people failed to take him as seriously as he took himself. Mike reckoned he had to be all bluster and no bullets.

So he struck back. 'My immortal soul was doing quite nicely by itself thank you very much. The last thing I expected was to be apprehended in my own home by your overdressed monkeys and carted off to this grotesque waste of concrete, which was once no doubt a pretty nice field. In this country – which I might add still holds nominally to the principles of free speech – a man's home is considered his castle. What do you think this is Trundell, the bloody Dark Ages?

'An honest citzen has the right not to be kidnapped in broad daylight and interrogated to within an inch of his sanity by the sort of scumbag who should have died out along with dark Satanic mills and child slavery. Why don't you pack your bags Trundell and bugger off back to the land where the buffalo used to roam and the deer and the antelope pray. We don't want you here.'

During Mike's monologue Ted passed beyond speechlessness, transcending territory known only to screaming drill sergeants. Trundell's face got redder and redder until the radiation it emitted slipped off the visible spectrum and began to interfere with short-wave radio transmissions. Overhead, the panic-stricken pilot of a jumbo jet dived five thousand feet on seeing a huge blip on his radar screen heading straight for him. With a monumental effort of will Ted took a deep, deep breath and got a grip on his stampeding emotions. For once his voice was quiet, trembling with repressed aggression as he towered over Mike. 'Like all of your master's agents you sure do talk mighty prutty baw. We'll see just how prutty you talk when you're tied to a stake with the flames tickling your toes.'

Mike scoffed. 'Oh come now Trundell, let's not get melodramatic. We both know you wouldn't do something like that – you might be mad but you're not stupid.'

Ted's piggy eyes glinted. 'Perhaps not Professor, but this facility does boast a lavishly equipped Medicentre. Amongst other things, we do a bit of research into proving the holy truth behind stigmatism and the miraculous effects of faith healing. I'm sure my loyal staff would be only too pleased to knock up a little cocktail just for you. The sort crammed full of high powered drugs which would have you singing my tune in no time!'

'Like Elvis, Mr Trundell?' Deborah asked chirpily.

'Don't you take the Lord's name in vain foul Whore of Babylon!'

'Actually I've never been to Babylon, though I did spend a summer holiday with an aunt in Basildon. Does that count?'

'Fallen Woman!' Ted bellowed and struck her hard across the face with the back of his hand. Deborah's head jerked back under the severity of the blow. When she slowly pulled herself upright again, one cheek held an ugly red welt.

She gave him a long look. Something in her eyes made Ted pause. He got the unmistakable impression he'd just made a very grave error – an error that might just cost him his life. For a brief instant he knew exactly what went through JFK's mind a split second after the bullet, or how Charles I might have felt when he mounted the scaffold to receive his final short-back-and-sides. It was the feeling all sentient creatures get when they know they could meet their doom if they weren't careful.

At the sound of Deborah being struck the gravity of their situation crashed home to Mike. He couldn't believe it had just happened. He'd overestimated Trundell. He'd credited the man with some vestige of civility. Now he realized how wrong he'd got it. Trundell had the resources to get what he wanted, he had the lackeys to do his bidding and had no regard for any law other than his own. Mike could almost hear the wheels turning behind the dead eyes as Ted calmed himself and changed tack. Halting his pacing, he rested a highly polished cowboy boot on the chair between Mike's legs. Trundell leant on his up-thrust knee and stared at the old man nose-to-nose.

'So tell me Professor, what system of belief do you subscribe to. Fire worship? Paganism? Or are you just an atheistic commie? Come on, lay it on the line mister "I snigger at others' beliefs", let's hear what tenets you hold true.'

Mike smiled. 'You're right of course Trundell, it is very easy to ridicule most religions – but I promise to stop the day I discover a religion that I don't find inherently ridiculous. In answer to your question though, I was brought up in a Jewish home. I'd be happy to prove it, but there is a lady present after all.'

Deborah mumbled, 'Don't mind me, boys,' and stifled a snigger.

'I'm on pretty firm ground here,' Mike continued. 'After all, I take after most of the cast of the Bible in that respect so I'm in good company.'

'You say you were brought up a Jewboy. Maybe that ain't as bad as some say, but what pits of unbridled debauchery have you slithered into since, eh? Judas was a Jew. Herod was a Jew.'

'And Jesus was a Jew,' muttered Mike, under his breath. With a sigh he resigned himself to lying to make the whole process easier on everyone involved. 'Actually, if you must know, I'm currently a Druid. Any objections to that?'

Ted's eyes lit up. 'Oh, a Druid are we? Aren't you the guys who offer up human sacrifices to your suspiciously horned master, then dance round till dawn calling for him to do unspeakable things to lumberjacks? We all know who your 'Lord of the Dance' is – Beelzebub in a floppy-eared rabbit outfit, that's who!'

Mike paused for a second to admire Ted's baffling twists of reason. The man certainly knew how to conjure up a horrific image. Only after a deep breath did Mike feel able to go on. 'It's not like that at all. We Druids of the Eternal Wood wouldn't stoop so low. We'd run out of followers for one thing. Nothing thins the congregation quite like random ceremonial murder – a lesson your lot were quick to learn. As a matter of fact we shun dogma, adhering to a simple canon. Our only rule is that we must constantly touch a piece of wood, maintaining our bond with the Earth Mother at all times.'

Ted looked pleased. 'Wood eh? *The Devil's material.* I don't see you touching no wood now baw! Maybe that's why you've lost your demonic powers.' Turning to his two security men he said without even a hint of irony, 'Nobody gives this man a match!'

'Actually,' Mike continued meekly, 'I don't mean to throw a spanner in your theological engine or anything, but I am maintaining our rigid stricture as we speak.'

Ted looked confused, then alarmed. 'Where's the wood, old man? I don't see none. And you're sitting on plastic. I'd mighty like to see you maintain your links with some bulging-breasted soil-slut through that!'

Mike looked smug. 'If you must know it's our custom to wear wooden underwear at all times. The splinters are a problem at first but it gives one a sense of security.'

Ted's scream of rage almost woke the neighbours.[1]

Knocking On Heaven's Non-wooden Door

'Watch the bloody roof, you'll put a dent in it!' Adam

1 Mr and Mrs Arthur J. Smith, of 37 Hawthorne Road, Harlington – a small village three miles due south as the bat flies.

hissed as he sat astride the high stone wall. He'd found a narrow break in the barbed wire and was trying desperately not to move backwards or forwards.

Nearby, a towering oak tree shielded his car from prying eyes. All around, the shadows of autumn twilight stretched into the primaeval wood like the fingers of some monstrous wicker man. With a grimace Adam reached down to give an increasingly substantial Sid a hand-up from his crumpled car roof. Sid did his best to scramble up, grabbing low-hanging branches in the process.

Thwack!

As Sid clambered into position he let go of a sizeable branch. Briefly, Adam knew how the guest of honour at one of Robin Hood's infamous Launch-a-Squirrel Contests must have felt when its flight path was terminated by a bark-clad barrier. Only when he'd plucked the last of the acorns from between his teeth and his vision had congealed into a single unblurred image, did he feel able to speak.

'Thanks. Think you can make it down the other side without felling a forest?'

'What about some respect for your elders?' Sid wheezed.

'When you earn it,' Adam replied.

They'd spent a night and a day hidden in Adam's car, concealed in a small wood half a mile back up the road. Regular reconnaissance sorties to the top of the low hill visited the previous evening had provided useful information. Most areas of the vast building site were complete and stood empty of workmen – no doubt waiting for the gates to be thrown open to hordes of eager first day pilgrims. A few zones were still hives of activity, with busloads of contractors being ferried in at regular intervals to get the job finished in time.

Adam had hoped the initial phase of the rescue would be the easy bit – simply sneak up to a part of the wall close to a completed section and slip in unobserved. That was until he'd spotted the patrols. These regular convoys sped round the park in armoured jeeps. So he'd decided to delay penetration until the gathering dusk afforded some measure of protection.

The section of wall he now sat upon stretched through an area of dense woodland that lined one side of the park. There didn't seem to be any surveillance cameras nearby, and those further along the perimeter were shielded by trees.

'We'll proceed on bearing two-seven-zero to the wood's inner edge then perform a visual reconnaissance of the ground ahead. Affirmative?'

'You what?'

Adam sighed. 'We'll slide on in, check how the land is lying. That's if it's okay by you.'

Sid looked more worried than Jack the Ripper's PR man. 'If you get us both killed, I'll never forgive you.'

'Where's your sense of adventure?' Adam said and jumped down onto the carpet of dry leaves below. Reluctantly, and ungracefully, Sid followed suit.

As the avenging angels for the forces of truth and justice blundered off into the woodland, they didn't see the squirrel nestled half-way up a tree. They didn't see its head swivel round on tiny bearings, or hear the gentle hum of its miniature electric motor. They didn't notice the delicate eyelids sliding back to reveal the wide-angle lens beneath.

The 'T' Plan Excercise Program

It was obvious what Mike was trying to do, Deborah thought. Keep Ted tied up with irrelevancies – it might not set them free, but it was the best they could do until an opportunity to escape presented itself. Remembering that attack was often the best form of defence, with the possible exceptions of nuclear confrontation and trench warfare, she thought it about time she made a contribution to the debate. Nostrus was always holding centre stage anyway.

'Trundell,' she said in a loud clear voice, 'why have you kidnapped us? You can't really want us on your side. Your boss upstairs wouldn't be too impressed. We've been honest with you, how about giving some back?'

At this point, Ted experienced a very strange sensation. It was that same feeling that inevitably descends upon villains at the end of TV cop shows – the incomprehensible urge to justify one's motives.

'It's quite simple, harlot. Our grand opening is just two days away. We're having a mass revival meeting – you know, curing cripples, laying on of hands, the usual thing. And it'll all be broadcast to two hundred nations by GOD TV.

'The high point of this extravaganza will star your friend and mine, Professor Michael D. Nose-truss. In front of a worldwide audience I'll publicly exorcise the infamous embezzler and con man of the wild devils that rule his soul. The children of the world will sleep safe in their beds knowing the Purloiner-of-Pyramids is no longer in business. And it'll all be down to li'lle-ole-me.'

'But I have never summoned demons! They stink to low hell, apart from anything else.'

'Ah-ha!' Ted was finally triumphant. 'Finally, you admit your associations!'

If he hadn't been tied up, Mike would have kicked himself. It was a stupid mistake to make just when he was getting the man rattled.

Deborah, realizing, quickly tried to change the subject. 'Trundell, there's just a small flaw in your plan. You need a willing co-star for a performance like that. Mike wouldn't do it in a million years.'

A nasty grin spread across Ted's face like four-star across a fjord. 'Well, my little Jezebel, the Lord he works in mysterious ways. We didn't reckon on you being at Nose-truss's flat. But you have to admit you offer the perfect incentive for your evil master to play ball. It'd be such a shame if anything happened to your devil-given good looks. Wouldn't you agree Nose-truss?'

Mike looked at Trundell in disgust. 'You know something, even for a Christian Fundamentalist, you're a real git.'

American Pies

'This place is huge,' said Adam. 'We'll never find them at this rate. At least not if we keep playing hide and seek with the US Marine Corps Chaplaincy Division.'

They sat huddled under a table in the vast dining hall of the Loaves and Fishes Eatery, just across the theme park's main concourse from the Manna From Heaven Shopping Mall Experience. The hall was currently dark and empty, all set for the big opening just forty-eight hours away. They'd slunk inside after almost falling foul of a security patrol and were now huddled in fear of their lives, performing a strange sort of yoga around the table's single plastic leg whenever a searchlight cut through the hall's murky depths.

The patrols seemed a bit much to protect a building site from some light-fingered local who could do with just one more bag of cement to finish off his garage. The deeper he dug into this story, the more convinced Adam became that he was onto something big here. Just what part his Deborah played in all this escaped him, but he was going to risk all to find out – once he'd overcome his fear of machine guns and searchlights. Maybe Trundell was, one by one, bumping off the competition. First Nostrus's cult – eliminate the small fry before building up to take on the C of E. With luck, Deborah would be more than grateful for Adam's crusade for religious freedom.

As if reading his thoughts Sid said: 'This isn't going to help you get inside her knickerbox you know.'

'Shut it slimeball – before I force feed you pâté de foie gras made from your own liver.' Adam extracted himself from the streamlined plastic table and clambered to his feet. Sid shuffled after him.

Time to check the immediate surroundings. On the face of it the cavernous hallway looked like any other fast food establishment. The airport-check-in-esque serving area, the impersonal operating theatre lighting, the horrendous seating – designed to be uncomfortable to prevent customers taking the time to notice the crap they've just paid £5.99 for – and, of course, the obligatory potted plants. The only thing that set this place apart from McDonkeys and BurgerTurds the world over were the twenty-foot statues of well-known biblical figures spaced evenly around the walls. Adam had never seen Moses portrayed carrying a huge, pictorial fast-food menu before, but he had to admit the image was quite imposing.

Adam's voice held far more authority than he currently felt. 'Spread out. We're looking for a map, a noticeboard, anything that might show us where to go.'

'Good to know that a day and night of reconnaisance is paying dividends,' Sid muttered.

Adam looked back at the menu. Myrrh Burgers™ seemed very good value at only £4.75, especially if, as claimed, they 'Bring you closer to the Kingdom of Heaven through a pure 100% beef-and-soya-base taste experience'. Other delicacies included the 'Salvation Salad' and the 'Madonna Milkshake' coming in sixteen different flavours, served in a choice of small, medium or God's Omnipotent Love sizes. 'Just ask for a GOL', the sign said. Adam gawped at it all. There was only so much of this place you could take without beginning to question your sanity. He half-expected the Osmond family to come crashing out of the lush shrubbery at any moment and break into a rendition of 'Silent Night'. Absorbed in this horrific thought, Adam nearly jumped out of his skin as a soft voice broke the dark stillness. It wasn't little Jimmy. It was only Sid.

''Ere mate, take a look at this.'

Adam peered up at another display held in the kindly hands of a giant King David. The great ruler's hands were the only kindly thing about him though. The huge plastic figure was fully decked out for a spot of heavy duty Canaanite bashing. Adam couldn't remember them having hand grenades in those days. He'd done time at Sunday School but they never taught him this bit of the scriptures: 'And the enemies of the Lord did tremble in their great multitude, saying unto one another, "Run like Michael Johnson, he's got an Uzi!" But before they could depart, Jehovah spoketh unto the Children of Israel, saying, "Look now unto your grenade-launchers and your 5.56mm miniguns, for they are great damagers when fired on full-automatic."'

Jordan: The Comeback

As a matter of fact Ted Trundell's interior designers had hit nearer the mark than even the most combat-crazed Vietnam Vet-turned-RE teacher could have guessed.

When the Lord God, Leader of Hosts and Stealer of Other People's Countries said unto the Children of Israel, 'Go forth and take the land of Canaan,' the land of Canaan was not actually empty. It wasn't as if the elders of the Ten Tribes turned up one day at the banks of the River Jordan, like a gang of ancient New Age Travellers, and said: 'Bugger me this looks like a nice spot, no one around neither. Let's form a commune.' However, one similarity does stand the test of rigorous historical investigation. When the Israelites arrived in Canaan the locals were none too pleased to see them.

As battle raged all around, a talkative Canaanite called

to the ferocious Israelite he faced. 'What gives you the right to come and steal my country, Israelite dog? The world's one big empty place, so why not piss off and discover America?'

The ferocious Israelite peered out from under his low-brimmed helmet thoughtfully, then replied. 'A big old guy in a white frock with a long grey beard spake from the sky and said we could, Canaanite scum. His word is law, so don't get his back up or he'll smite your first-born sons. Honestly, we've just been through this once. I can put you in touch with some folks in Egypt if you don't believe me.'

'Ha-bloody-ha!' the Canaanite laughed. 'I've heard it all now. Very existential, I don't think. That's even better than the story of how the universe got sneezed out of the nostril of Hankyless Three Nosed Dragon. Or, for that matter, the one about the . . . Hrrnnnn!' At that, the Israelite indulged in a spot of Old Testament ethnic cleansing.

Despite their legendary ferocity, the Children of Israel faced an uphill struggle. They were few against many, and their spiritual Big Brother's use of thunderbolts as tactical air strikes was of limited value. The Lord God – who had been around a bit and knew when things were more severely buggered than the City of Sodom's only male hairdresser – said unto them: 'Don't worry boys, here's some nice new toys for you to play with. You may have some trouble begetting any more 9mm caseless armour-piercing rounds in ancient Palestine, so go easy on the ammo. And for my sake be careful with the flamethrower . . . it has a tendency to explode like a flatulent camel left out in the sun all day.'

The West Bank Show

With this new tactical edge, the Children of Israel swept all before them. Their army was unbeatable, the opposition in despair – and it was all down to the Big Guy upstairs.

The famous incident involving the young King David (not a king then of course, just a Lieutenant Colonel with the 1st Judea Tank Battalion) and Goliath the Philistine, has over the years been edited slightly for dramatic effect. A more honest rendition might read something like this.

'And God did say unto the Israelites, "Go forth and smite the uncouth Philistines, for they are uncultured and know not the works of Melvyn Bragg."'

And after the elders of the tribes had sat around for forty days and forty nights arguing over what he meant, they came to the conclusion that The Supreme Being, Lord of Heaven and Earth and creator of All Creatures Great And Small[1] could say just about whatever he bloody well liked, and they better jump to it or he might get pissed off with them. So the next day the armoured columns did roll.

At a vital river crossing, the barbarous Philistines made their stand. Their commanders pushed to the fore a huge man by the name of Goliath, saying unto him, 'See if you can't bite the tracks off their tanks as they drive over your head oh mighty Goliath, for then we will be most pleased.'

And Goliath did say, 'Bleh?' for he possessed more palm hair than brain cells, having been dropped on his head as a child.

As the huge man stood at the river bank, waving his copper sword and chanting his ancient Philistine war hymn, the young Lt Colonel David did unhatch his Armoured Command Vehicle and bring forth his 'Sling' anti-tank missile. Muttering grave thanks to the Lord as he did so, Israel's brave Lion then proceeded to disassemble Goliath's head into its component molecules with one shot from the mighty weapon.

Young David then jumped onto the roof of his tank in

---

1 But not the bits where James Herriot sticks his hand up a cow's arse.

triumph, his bandanna resplendent in the sun. Shouting for all the multitude to hear he cried: 'Yo verily – don't push me!'

Cover Me

'Sid, tell me they didn't have digital watches in those days.'

'Nah, that's artistic license, that is.'

Adam studied the large schematic map in front of him. One of King David's fingerless-gloved hands pointed to a central complex with the words, 'Yea are here' written up his bulging forearm.

'Okay, this is a bit more like it. Everything seems to be marked. There's the River Jordan Water Wonderworld we came past, and the Garden of Eden Retirement Home.' His eyes lit up enthusiastically. 'Here it is! The Temporary Administration Complex. Should be easy to find too, right next to the Tower of Babel Bungee Jump Centre –'

He was interrupted by an ominous double click.

Adam and his not-so-alter ego turned around very slowly. Arrayed behind him was enough firepower to, if not actually start a war, then at least keep it going long enough for the Italians to change sides. At the handle-end of this plethora of weaponry crouched a small army of highly excited young men in recently dry-cleaned suits. From behind a row of lush potted plants on one flank rose the right reverend Harvey T. Banger. He glared at the shaking intruder then said something completely unnecessary.

'Freeze punks, we got you covered!'

Route 666

Despite widespread public opinion, when demons travel long distances in the UK they rarely use the privatized railways. When you've got a spot of chartered haunting to do, an edition of *Celebrity Squares*, or even your standard supermarket opening, clapped out rolling stock trundling along broken bits of metal overseen by random signal boxes is not the best guarantee of getting there on time, if at all. It's not just due to the wrong sort of ectoplasm on the line, either. For many years the former British Rail had been a subsidiary of Forces of Darkness (Transport Division) Plc – a shady holding company run on behalf of the hosts of Hell. For this reason the organization was monstrously inefficient and no self-respecting demon would use it given half a choice. When a dark field agent needs to move quickly, the motorway network offers a far more attractive proposition.

Anyone who has ever made regular use of motorway service stations will be aware of this fact. Dark forces manifest themselves in their very architecture. If you enter these Temples of Hell and take a given series of turnings in the Stygian complex of corridors, taking that same series of turnings later will never leave you in exactly the same place. This is because all motorway service stations are set out in the form of one of the twelve uncopyable runes found on the sarcophagus of King Yrrsss XXXIV, last of the Philosopher-Princes of The Sunken Land – a realm so nefarious that even visiting gods carried mace. These dark runes fail to obey the normal rules of spacetime. In addition to the standard dimensions they possess the subsidiary vectors of Amusement Arcade, Self-Service Restaurant and Gift Shop. This fact goes some way to explain the phenomena of service station cafés. No one has ever seen food delivered to such an establishment. Wherever it comes from it's certainly not on this Astral Plane. And it also explains why video games found in service stations can be found nowhere else in the known universe.

And the Gift Shop? Her name tag may read JULIE,

she may smile and say 'How may I help you?', but rest assured she is in fact a Gatemaster for unholy Acheron sent to Earth to spill havoc in her wake. Whatever twitches beneath her pinafore certainly shouldn't be there. These vile succubi are vessels of purest evil, waiting to prey upon the unsuspecting lone traveller and suck out their vital life force in the deepest hours of the unending night. It is the job of Gatemasters to provide sustenance for demonic travellers, fresh information from their superiors and news of road works ahead.

One such sickeningly petite creature currently sat at the gift shop check-out of a large and unspeakably evil service station on the M1. It was past midnight and the she-demon's hellish lair had been empty for several hours. Not since 10:30 p.m., when a weary sales rep had stumbled in to buy a chicken salad sandwich, had she been able to ply her true trade. The unknowing traveller had left with far more than an overpriced comestible however. The small 'cuddly toy' he purchased for some unfortunate infant had twitched excitedly as Julie forced it into its bag, but the customer had been too sleepy to notice. Now, another potential victim stood above her.

'Hello, my name is Julie! How may I help you?' the she-thing chirped with an avalanche of sincerity that would have made Bob Monkhouse retch.

The customer looked down through heavy, dark glasses, though outside it was blackest night. He was a huge, smartly dressed man who walked with a strange rolling gait. This was because he wasn't used to having his current number of legs. 'The swimming salmon are plentiful for this time of year,' he zithered mechanically.

Julie's large brown eyes glazed over. 'My Aunt Beryl has a teaset with only one cup . . .'

The customer leaned forward expectantly.

'. . . And it is half full of treacle,' she finished.

Demonic identities established, the customer relaxed

both sets of massive shoulders. 'I am Rubicante,' he hissed, not quite managing to break his usual speech patterns. 'I am on a vital mission of assassination. What news? And make it quick for I can't maintain this illusion long.'

The impette looked impressed. 'I have heard rumours of your mission Fell Master, and this human known as Nostrus. You have an important task indeed.'

Even through his latex face mask Rubicante looked sick to his oversized back teeth. 'Enough subservience. Information. Now, before I melt.'

'Apologies master. I will be brief.' The huge brown eyes took on a far away look as the creature known as Julie downloaded travel info from the sub-aether infernitynet. When the data had been located, sorted and processed, her brown eyes cleared.

'There are severe roadworks on the approaches to junction thirteen, master. Highway Destruction have been a little over-zealous lately. I've heard tell of thousands of Cone Imps partying the night away down there. In addition there is a major accident just past Northampton. I fear your journey will be greatly impeded.'

Rubicante looked distraught. 'We can't afford any more delays, Alastor will be furious. Do you have a supply of Aeroene here? This is an emergency.'

'Aeroene, master? That is only for the direst need! Standing Order 237/B states so.

'This *is* dire need,' fumed Rubicante. 'My career's at stake. Now do you have some or not?'

Julie looked cagey. 'At the rear of the complex great master, in the tank marked 'Non-Specific-Orange-Based-Drink'. Be careful with it though, the stuff can go through concrete like oatcakes through a puppy.'

Shortly the demonic death squad were speeding down the motorway, gaining velocity all the while. As the needle touched eighty the massive wheels began to lift off the ground. By the time the speedometer reached three figures the huge juggernaut was sailing majestically into deepest night.

In The Air Tonight

Back at Trundell Towers, things were beginning to hot up. A certain clairvoyant cat was just getting into position to begin his long-awaited, single-pawed rescue bid.

Since slipping out of the limo the night before, Aristotle had spent a long day dodging patrols, sneaking in where he wasn't noticed and generally having a good snoop around. Curiosity might have killed his brethren, but when you'd lived through the Great Fire of London with not so much as a singed whisker, survived Napoleon's retreat from Moscow by curling up and pretending to be a Cossack's hat and tipped yourself over Niagara Falls in a suitcase (twice), you developed a certain nose for danger. The information he'd gathered had left him in mixed spirits. True enough, Trundell's followers were armed to the teeth. But in the brains department they were no sharper than the average human rabble. And to Aristotle's nose they had a major hole in their defence. They smelt overconfident.

Even so, there were other factors to consider. This madhouse sprawled across such a vast area that navigation during the egress phase of their escape might be a problem. On the other paw, the site contained plenty of promising hiding places. These modern ideas on religious architecture had the cat baffled. At least you knew where you were with a nice cathedral. Nothing that human beings did surprised him any more, but this place took the tuna-and-chicken-flavoured Kitty-Kake. Organized religion was such an alien concept that it defied even Aristotle's monumental intellectual powers. Still, if this was how these poor inahabitants of an evolutionary backwater chose to spend their leisure time, who was he to argue?

It had been a simple matter to locate the command

centre, positioned as it was at the park's hub. His field skills had not been tested to any great degree in making his approach. He'd found a warren of black spaces beneath the largest of the temporary buildings. In one of them was an open heating vent which had provided his means of entry. It hadn't been hard to track down Trundell and his unwilling house guests – Aristotle had simply followed the howls of rage. Now, after thirty minutes of careful crawling, he was finally in position.

Deborah – don't look up. I'm in the air-conditioning duct above your head.

She froze in response, which wasn't hard seeing as her hands were tied to the chair behind her back. In the dark hours since their abduction, she'd almost given up on him. She'd noticed the small grille just below the ceiling line when they'd first come in. It was one of the few features that punctuated the bland room. Now it took all her willpower not to repeatedly glance up at the opening.

Crouched just inside the rectangular conduit, Aristotle could peer down into the small room below – if he didn't mind extending his neck as far as it would go, and a bit more besides.

That was the easy part over. Things were going to get a tad tricky from here on in. One cat, unarmed, was bound to encounter a few problems. Like:

(i) Distracting a small army of highly motivated and heavily armed guards.

(ii) Disabling the three enemies in the room.

Then . . .

(iii) Untying the prisoners and leading them to safety over unfamiliar terrain in the dead of night.

Aristotle entertained no illusions over his chances of success in this venture. Just as he was commiserating himself with a quick mental count to see just how many of his nine lives remained, his thoughts were interrupted by a commotion from the hallway beyond.

Rescue Me

He'd been talking on and on and on, ever since they discovered him.

'What the hell do you think you're doing?' Adam bleated. 'I've got rights you know – I'm a founder member of S.P.A.N.E.R.[1] They won't let you get away with this.'

Harvey pushed his prisoners through a rickety wooden doorway. Outside in the compound the best part of a platoon of Faith Marines kept their weapons trained on their every move.

'Where are you takng us? I demand the return of my civil liberties. Just you wait 'til I get my hands on my notepad.

'Shut it, bed-wetter!' Just to let him know he meant what he said, Harvey repeatedly banged Adam's head against the wall. For the first time since capture the reporter's constant stream of complaint subsided. For his part, Adam quietly gave thanks for the declining standards in the building industry, as the soft plaster wall gave way beneath his forehead.

The damage to fixtures and fittings didn't go unnoticed. 'If there's any more wan-ton damage to Church property we'll sue your ass off until your buttcheeks bleed! Now get *MOVING!*'

For one surreal moment Adam could think of nothing but bowls of aromatic Chinese soup causing severe structural damage to places of worship up and down the country. Just before he'd worked out what the American had really meant, Adam passed out.

* * *

---

1 The Society of Press And Newspaper Enlightened Reporters.

When he came to, Adam looked up groggily and suddenly his mind and vision cleared. To an operatic crescendo of hallelujahs his heart leapt with joy. Tied to a chair, bound and bemused but still radiantly beautiful, sat Deborah. Back-to-back with her was the geriatric psychopath who'd started all this – Professor Michael D. Nostrus. Across the room in a big leather chair Adam recognized the fat-flushed form of Ted Trundell – the man famous the world over for singlehandedly putting the fund$ back into fundamentalism.

'So you see Professor Nose-truss,' Ted smirked with all the charm of a gecko on steroids, 'the rescue bid of your scheming minions has failed utterly.'

'Trundell, I have no idea what these *idiots* are doing here. He's a reporter from a tabloid newspaper. I met him for the first time minutes before your lot turned up. Apart from that, I have no connection whatsoever with him – and I'd be very grateful if it remained that way. As for the older one, I've never seen him in my life, though he looks familiar. Perhaps they're related? Dad's on day release from the special hospital? I don't know.'

Ted smiled incredulously. 'Oh come now Nose-truss. We find them snooping round our li'l-old-spread just after we take you into protective custody. You admit you know him – what kinda idiot you take me for?'

Several choice answers came to mind but wisely he declined to share them with Ted. If he got his way there'd be plenty of time for that later.

Meanwhile, from beneath the heel of Harvey's snakeskin cowboy boot, Adam looked up wide-eyed, almost breaking his neck in his attempt to catch a look at Deborah.

'Have they hurt you sweetikins? If they have I'll . . . I'll – gggggrrgh!' Harvey slowly applied more pressure.

Deborah rolled her eyes in disbelief. 'You'll do what? Chat them up? Ask them out on a date and try to stick your tongue down their throat? Not even these bastards deserve a fate that gruesome. Pleeeease – have mercy on them, they know not what they do.'

Losing patience, Ted snapped his fingers in Harvey's direction. 'That'll be all for now son. We've shown Hell's Handyman here that he can't expect rescue from any quarter. Leave him with me for the time being. And as for that piece of trailer-park trash,' he said, gesturing at Adam and Sid, 'take 'em off to the Medical Centre. We'll see if the Chemo-Boys can pick their brains for useful military intelligence.'

Deborah reckoned they'd be picking a long time for any type of intelligence but Adam, turning absolute white with panic, was inclined to disagree: 'Not our brain,' Sid pleaded, 'it's our second favourite organ!'

Harvey dragged him to his feet. 'When we've finished with you, you'll love all your organs equally, just as the good Lord intended.'

Actually, the future of Sid's and Adam's internal organs, and everyone else's in the room, was about to be chaotically thrown into doubt.

TEN

And they have over them a King, the Angel of the Abyss.
His name is Abaddon.
Revelations 9:11

Old Red Eye Is Back

Private Elroy Kowlaski was bored. Standing guard outside Ted Trundell's temporary command post did not rank highly on his list of all-time interesting activities. It didn't come close to the day he'd shaken Billy Graham by the hand, or compare with the time he'd taken holy orders to the most arse-kickingest church militant in all of the good Lord's creation. Since that great day, when he'd stood on stage before the massed ranks of the faithful and received Supreme Bishop Trundell's blessing, things had rather tailed off for Elroy. It was a cold and lonely life in Alpha Company 1st Faith Marines – at least it was when you weren't bullying die-hard dykes at the local motorcycle maintenance workshop. The only thing keeping him awake at present was a pleasant daydream concerning Dolly Parton, a pair of piping-hot blueberry muffins and a gallon tin of maple syrup.

As he shivered under the clear autumn stars, he had plenty of time to reflect on life's little unfairnesses. Hadn't he performed efficiently on yesterday's abduction mission? Hadn't he been a vital part of the crack team that whisked away that Devil's imp for reprogramming? And hadn't he been the one in line for Harvey's promotion? Of course he had, but that brown-nosed slimeball had his tongue so far up Trundell's backside he could probably smell the holy halitosis itself. And what had been Kowlaski's reward? Standing guard on the graveyard shift in the middle of an empty building site. He'd even missed out on the minor excitement of capturing the two prowlers earlier that evening. Nothing went right for him. Nobody appreciated his contribution to the movement.

So it was a tired and frustrated Kowlaski who paced the gravel car park that night, his automatic rifle hanging forlornly over his shoulder. The trouble with this organization, he reckoned, was it had favourites. Harvey was already well on his way to becoming a Deputy Deacon. The playing field of life just wasn't level. Though he didn't know it, for Private Kowlaski at least, the playing field was about to get very bumpy indeed. In fact, it was going to get carpet bombed.

The Marine halted mid-step as a strange sound broke the still night air, faint but growing stronger. At first, Kowlaski thought an inattentive workman might have left a pneumatic air-compressor running, but the sound had subtly biological undertones. It was a hoarse cyclical wheezing, almost like something breathing.

When Kowlaski was a kid, he'd seen *Star Wars*. About a hundred times. So what came to mind now was an image of Darth Vader, who, suffering from a bad case of bronchitis, had just swallowed half a bag of Fisherman's Friends then decided to make an obscene phone call.

There was no escaping it now. And as it grew louder and closer, there was no doubting where it was coming from: behind the nearest portacabin. He looked closer. There seemed to be an unearthly red glow spreading through the cracks beneath the structure. Silently, warily, he unslung his rifle, thumbed the selector to full automatic, and advanced.

He turned the dark corner with considerable caution

but, as it turned out, with not nearly enough. All his advanced training and sophisticated indoctrination failed in any way to prepare him for the sight that met his eyes.

Alastor, Chief Executioner of Hell and Lord of Daytime TV stared down at Kowlaski in all his hellish splendour. In one massive, gauntleted hand he held Soul Stealer which muttered to itself in some long-forgotten tongue that hurt the ears of any human unfortunate enough to hear it. Alastor's voice creaked like a tomb door at midnight. 'Nossstruuusss, bring meee Nossstruuusss.'

Kowlaski's trembling hands raised his gun to his shaking shoulder. Training it on Alastor's single oscillating red eye he asked the world's most pointless question.[1] 'F-f-f-f-friend or foe?

Soul Stealer's contralto pierced the still night air. 'Why *friend* of course! We represent Hades Life Assurance Inc. Is your cover sufficient for today's dangerous Multiverse? If not ring this toll-free number now!' The sword quivered, and suddenly in the air beside it hung three neon sixes fizzing and blinking against the night sky. 'Think you can remember that?'

Kowlaski's reply would never be known. Before it got past his lips, Soul Stealer, with a little help from Alastor, got considerably further – though unfortunately from the opposite direction. The last thing that passed through Kowlaski's exploding mind, apart from Alastor's hammering fist, was 'I must tell Auntie Beryl about the eels.' Who Auntie Beryl was and what she needed to know about eels will forever remain a mystery. It was, however, a sad fact that Kowlaski's ghost was destined to spend the next three centuries haunting various seaside piers up and down the east coast, until one day it was exorcised by passing members of the Lincolnshire Vicars Deep Sea Angling Society.

---

1 At least since Neville Chamberlain asked, 'Now, you are going to be nice after this agreement aren't you, Adolf?'

Back in the present, the right and left halves of Kowlaski suffered a moment of indecision, then took the only option open to them, going their own separate ways in an unceremonious parting. The cause of the divorce was, as always, a third party – in this case a sword with a crap voice.

As Alastor stepped over the crumpled remains, Soul Stealer savoured another nourishing life-force.

'Hmmmm,' he squeaked, 'a bit bland. These fundamentalists, they've just got no taste.'

Attack Of The S.T.E.A.L.T.H. Demons

While Alastor and Soul Stealer dispatched Kowlaski with ruthless efficiency, Guttlehog and Rubicante's assault was going less smoothly. The demons' targets were the other two guards circling the compound. Accompanying them on their mission was a very nasty Weapons Imp called Boris.

Weapons Imps are handy creatures to have around – if you can find, and stay on, their good side and happen to have the morals of an international terrorist. Actually, they don't have a good side, just a permanent bad attitude with enough spite to boil a kettle. Their moods hover between petulant and antagonistic, dipping, if prompted, into psychopathic malevolence now and then – a lack of social skills only partly mitigated by an ability to transform into any weapon in the known universe. Thankfully for the authors of the Geneva Convention, The Nuclear Non-Proliferation Treaty and the Marquis of Queensbury Rules, Weapons Imps are not generally for sale on Earth.

And Boris was the best: undisputed champion of Satan's infernal arsenal and winner of the coveted Golden Flamethrower Cup an unprecedented three centuries running. Unfortunately, he was being handled by the worst.

'There's one! Next to those oxygen tanks!' Rubicante

hissed excitedly, pointing out a blissfully ignorant sentry. 'Get 'im next time he comes round!'

Boris, who was cradled against Guttlehog's monstrous shoulder, felt duty bound to speak. With a deft flick of a tiny tonsil the Weapons Imp temporarily unchambered the 40mm grenade from his throat and croaked in a husky baritone.

'Noble colleagues, I must point out that my grenade-launcher function is not suitable for this attack profile. The collateral damage indicator on my carnageometer is going off scale. I suggest we retire a safe distance before engaging target.'

But Guttlehog wasn't listening. To him collateral damage meant holding a machine gun in each paw while firing in two directions at once. In a picture of demonic concentration, great globules of sulphurous sweat trickled down his forehead as his tongue played over callused lips. One huge red eye was wedged shut as he sighted along the imp's backbone. Getting Boris to play with was better than Hallowe'en, a major civil war and The Young Conservatives' Annual Val d'Isère Ski Beano all rolled into one. Ignoring the imp's protests, the Boar Demon squeezed a small catch behind the fleshy part of Boris's left knee and with a loud whoooosh forty millimetres of high explosive shot from the imp's open mouth.

Guttlehog's aim was just a touch too high.

In the ensuing inferno, three tanks of oxyacetylene detonated simultaneously, sending chunks of molten metal in all directions through the sound barrier. Even Rubicante, who was well used to bright lights and intense heat, had to admit that the maelstrom engulfing the car park was quite impressive. The explosions just rolled on and on in a seemingly inexhaustible supply of fiery destruction. When things eventually quietened down a bit the giant locust sat up on his rear set of haunches and peered out from cover.

'I think we got'em,' he said.

Guttlehog, whose organs were just a little less desensitized to such things, was having considerable difficulty reorienting himself. 'Whaa? Why are these lobsters landing on my face?'

Rubicante threw a cursory glance down at his dazed colleague, who was doing his best to stuff all his hoofs into his jaws in panic. Figures were appearing from smouldering doorways on all sides. Every one of them seemed to be armed and hellbent on adding to the destruction all around. From all sides the crack of gunfire split the thick night air.

Never one to be outdone by mere humans, Rubicante grabbed Boris by his still rigid thighs and set about joining the fast developing mêlée. His eerie insectoid voice shrieked over the scattered gunfire: 'Big Gun mode, Boris. Let's Rocccccccck!'

The Sound Of Violence

'What in the carpentry-capable-name-of-Christ was that!' Ted looked up as what seemed to be the whole world started to shake outside.

Nearby, ostensibly from surprise but in reality from sadism pure and true, Harvey dropped Adam and Sid once more. In the centre of the room, still tied to the chairs, Deborah looked up startled as yet another unexpected development threatened to overtake them all. Mike, on the other hand, seemed unperturbed. He whistled tunelessly to himself as the world went mad around him. Hidden in the air-conditioning duct, Aristotle drew back, his ears flat to his head and his hackles higher than a stoned seagull.

Harvey was the first to react. He reached inside his jacket and pulled out an unfeasibly large gun, turning back to Ted as he did so. 'Don't worry sir! Allow me to make a prelimininiminary reconnaissance of the auto-mobile park area!'

'It's "preliminary",' Mike whispered.

Harvey hefted the gun in Mike's direction. 'What was that you said?'

'Nothing, nothing.' Mike started whistling again then added, as though it was an afterthought, 'Better hurry up, though. By the sound of things there won't be a car park when you get out.' He turned his attention to Trundell. 'What's the matter Supreme One, your flock finally flipped?' As if to punctuate his words the flimsy cabin was rocked as the compression wave from yet another explosion struck it broadside.

As Harvey bounded to the door, Ted turned on Mike, his face ablaze with anger. 'Don't think I'll fall for none of your cheap tricks! More of your followers attempting to spring you from justice? Ain't got a chance – no ways they'll get past my people. They're trained for just this sort of eventu-ality.'

Mike looked blank. 'I don't care if your people have trained since birth for the Freestyle Combat events in the Theologian Olympics. Your thugs seem at this very moment to be using their colleagues for target practice. I put it down to pent-up urges, denied them by your moral crusade.'

Ted gave a frustrated snort of disgust and stormed after Harvey's massive frame.

Alongside Sid, Adam lay groggily on the floor, seemingly undaunted by developments, almost as if he had a subtle plan tucked up the sleeve of his crumpled Italian shirt. Anyone who knew Adam could have pointed out that subtle plans were as much a part of his repertoire as Rio de Janeiro was a part of West Yorkshire. Adam's schemes were more likely to involve hidden video cameras, copious amounts of warm mayonnaise and high-ranking members of the Church of England. As he took stock of the new situation a dangerous thought crashed around Adam's love-sick cranium.

Since Harvey and Ted had left the room, just two guards remained to oversee the captives and as far as Adam could tell they were more interested in watching the fireworks outside than their four charges. One of them shifted nervously near the back wall, fingering his rifle. The other was at the entrance, straining to see down the corridor and through the doorway beyond.

It was really quite simple: all he had to do was distract the guard at the back of the room, deal with his jumpy colleague with a swift foot to the groin, get his weapon and fill the first guard so full of lead that you could use him to lay a church roof. The fact that Adam had never fired a gun in his life, dealt someone a swift foot to the groin, or purposefully caused a distraction for that matter, failed to register. If it had, the reporter might have realized that the chances of him doing all three in quick succession were worse than non-existent. But Adam had now entered Suicide-Action-Film-Mode, a mental condition that the US police know all about. (When stopped by traffic cops it's this condition that causes fourteen-year-old gang members to reach for their bulging inside pockets and dive for cover, screaming the local equivalent of: '*You won't take me alive copper!*' When their bullet-riddled bodies are finally searched all that's found is a slowly steaming chocolate bar. This affliction has been around for a long time – it's the frame of mind that made General Custer shout to the massed ranks of the Seventh Cavalry – 'Indian hordes? What Indian hordes?' And it's what makes thousands of lemmings throw themselves off Norway each year.[1] In short, SAFM stands for completely unwarranted belief

---

1 There's nothing very strange about this. For any inhabitant of Norway, of whatever species, suicide is always an option.

in eternal invincibility – it just uses different words – and Adam currently had a very bad case of it indeed.)

With a glint in his eye that would have made Rasputin nervous, Adam got slowly to his feet and turned to face the first guard.

SAFM does nothing for its victims' creative abilities. 'What's that behind you?' gasped Adam, a look of feigned horror on his face. 'God, it's revolting. I think I'm going to be sick!'

'Lord, give me *strength*,' muttered Deborah between clenched teeth.

The sentry chuckled. 'Yeah, yeah. You think I was born this morning, drainface?'

Before Adam could ponder the abject failure of his gambit, fate hijacked proceedings faster than a 747's cargo bay full of terrorists decked out in the very latest in full-body high-explosive evening wear.

Unbeknownst to them all, perhaps the greatest distraction in world history was beginning to unfold just three feet behind the chuckling guard. The first the room's startled occupants knew of it was the sound of tearing plaster accompanied by a high-pitched screaming that made their teeth ache. But this cacophony was like a maiden's song on a summer morn compared to the voice that was soon to follow.

'HI FOLKS, IT'S PARTY TIME!!!!!' shrieked Soul Stealer, as he ripped through the portacabin's flimsy wall and split the guard with laser speed, top to bottom. Every head, except the sentry's, turned in horror. Moments later the entire rear wall was torn asunder as Alastor made his entrance.

'Noooostruuuussss! I smell his presencccccce!' he boomed like a badly tuned church organ.

Now Mike was alarmed. For all his belief in taking things as they come, this was clearly time to consider mindless panic. Try as he might the Professor couldn't prevent the words 'frying-pan' and 'fire' spinning to a halt before each eye like some monstrously inappropriate fruit machine.

Adam stood rooted to the spot, all thoughts of Milk Tray advertisement rescues flung from his mind like dwarfs from a dwarf-tossing machine.

First to react was the unsplit guard at the doorway. While not exactly taking events in his stride, at least he wasn't tangled up in his own entrails. In a state ratchets up from vertiginous terror he reached into his suit and produced a cylindrical metal container. After spending what he felt sure were his last seconds on Earth fumbling with a ring at one end, he threw the object at the approaching demon and dived for cover.

Alastor caught the small device deftly in one huge hand and examined it curiously. In all fairness, the Demon Prince hadn't kept abreast of human military technology. The last time he'd been involved in a stand-up fight the nastiest thing mankind could throw at him had been a crossbow bolt laced with double-distilled holy water. Since then, apart from his Daytime TV duties, he'd spent the entire 500 years at Decapitation of Innocent Bystanders Class perfecting his backhand swordswipe in readiness for his moment of glory come the end of the world. Nobody had told him about hand-grenades which might go some way to mitigate his appalling lapse in professionalism.

'Noooostruuusss?' asked the demon, staring down at the smooth metal cylinder. 'Not smeeell right.'

'No master!' screamed Soul Stealer. 'He's the one tied to the chair! For Hell's sake, *drop it*!'

At that precise moment, Adam snapped out of his trance, and dived for Deborah, knocking her and Nostrus to the floor. In the confused tangle of bruised limbs, cheap furniture and nylon string, the reporter clambered over them both. Adam placed his hands over Deborah's ears and bade her do the same for Mike. She looked at him stupidly then realized her hands had come free in the fall.

A split second later an ear-shattering detonation shook the room. Sid, who was heroically attempting to dig through the carpet to safety using his bare teeth, was too preoccupied to notice. The force of the blast lifted Alastor's massive armour-plated frame clear off the floor, and blew him back through the demolished rear wall. Just as suddenly, a cloud of tear gas filled the breach obliterating the demon from view.

There was a moment of total silence, broken only by the quiet crunching of Sid running up a massive dental bill. Cautiously, almost as if performing self-circumcision with a rusty chainsaw, the remaining security guard climbed from beneath Ted's desk and surveyed the room. It was not a pretty sight. The back wall was a smoking ruin, contrasting starkly with the freshly applied, bloodstained decor of the other three. In one corner the ceiling sagged ominously, and from all sides a deep groaning suggested the place might give way at any second.

Considering what he'd just been through, it is perhaps understandable that the guard ignored his captives and advanced cautiously towards Alastor. Although the demon which had just ripped his colleague limb from limb was nowhere to be seen, the unearthly red glow emanating from the wall's wreckage suggested all was not as it should be. Knuckles white around his gun, the guard flicked the safety and peered into the gloom at Alastor's recumbent form. In light of his initial success, which had surprised him almost as much as it had the demon, the sentry now felt well prepared to deal with archdukes of Hell coming at him with sentient rune-swords. What he was less prepared for was a belligerent tomcat leaping from an air-conditioning duct onto his succulent shoulder blades.

Aristotle had picked his moment carefully, adapting his plans to the developing situation far quicker than his human counterparts. When the distracted sentry presented an unguarded back to the mouth of the air vent Aristotle knew his only chance to free the hostages had arrived. With a wiggle of his rear-end Aristotle launched himself through the air like a miniature rocket-propelled tiger. The cat hit the guard like an uncontrolled explosion. The guard crumpled to the floor, almost as if he half expected some supernatural fate worse than death and was glad to get it over and done with.

In the centre of the room, Deborah was busily fighting off Adam's continued amorous advances. 'Haven't you got *any* sense of proportion?' she screamed at him. 'We're in the middle of a war zone and all you can think of is that chipolata between your legs!'

The reporter just grinned back inanely. His limbs were operating purely on automatic, his hands instinctively seeking out Deborah's soft spots all by themselves. The reason for his sudden lack of motor control was quite simple. When the deafening grenade blast reverberated around the room Adam had been the only one without his ears covered. At the moment his brain could do nothing but idle in neutral.

Aristotle untangled himself from the prone guard who, not without some justification, seemed to have fainted from shock. Then the quivering bundle of blood and fur spoke to Deborah in his own peculiar way.

If you two have quite finished your pathetically human attempts at copulation, do you think we could decamp sometime close to . . . now?

Mike, sprawled on the floor and still bound, beamed with relief. 'Aristotle – you can sharpen your claws on my leg any time. You're a genius.'

Within seconds Deborah had stumbled over to Mike and made short work of freeing him. She helped him to his feet and pulled him towards the hole in the wall. But Mike resisted for a second and turned round.

'What about those two?'

Deborah gave Adam a swift kick as he pawed at her ankles. 'What about them?'

'They came to rescue us. Whatever their motive, we can't leave them here.'

Deborah just shrugged. 'Well, I'm not touching either of them. He, I am certain,' – she pointed at Adam – 'is littered with contagious diseases.'

So it was Mike alone who had to pull them upright. 'No milk for me today Mister Postman,' Adam spluttered as he was manhandled onto his feet. Sid followed suit in a daze.

Arm in arm, they stumbled across the rubble towards the exploding night beyond, giving the slowly convulsing Alastor a wide berth. He might have been dead to the world, but Soul Stealer had recovered enough to scream from the safety of one armour-plated fist: 'You won't get far, humie dogs. Nowhere's safe from us. When we've finished with you, you'll look like you've been through a mincing machine.'

'Eat rubble, you overgrown tin-opener,' Deborah said, kicking a mound of debris over his hilt.

Then they were out into the crisp night air. Mike turned to Aristotle with new hope in his eyes. 'All right old son, lead us out of this hell-hole.'

Sniper At The Gates Of Dawn

'How many?' Ted Trundell crouched behind the upturned husk of a steaming limo as tracer fire laced the air above him. His theme park was fast turning into a smouldering wasteland in all directions and yet he was watching it all with an odd sense of detachment. It was just too unbelievable to take in rationally.

'We're not sure mister Trundell sir,' Harvey spluttered. 'Lieutenant-Vicar McLean reports we're being attacked by a battalion of Russian Air-Mobile-Commandos. Curate-Major Anderson swears it's a brigade of Iranian Revolutionary Guards.' Another burst of machine-gun fire sent them sprawling for the dirt once more.

'Jeeee-sus!' Ted blasphemed. 'That came from the Ten Plagues MediCentre! I thought we still controlled that sector?'

Harvey blanched. 'We are . . . were . . . I'll check it out on the comms-net.'

Ted just growled. 'I'll have your ass for this, son – if it ain't shot off before I get to it.' Ted chanced a look around the side of the bonnet but it did nothing to clarify the situation. The night was lit up by a cat's-cradle of gunshots as groups on all sides engaged in withering crossfire. Every so often a fresh explosion temporarily illuminated a scene of hundreds of milling figures all firing wildly at anything that moved.

'Doesn't anyone know what they're shooting at? This is crazier than a hog in a whorehouse!' Putting his faith in a divine right to life, and the inaccuracy of his berserk followers, Ted clambered to his feet and screamed: 'Hold fire! This is a direct order from Supreme Bishop Trundell! Next man I see shooting gets double pew-cleaning duty!'

Between professional football and bible college, Harvey had been a Green Beret with US Special Forces: that's how he recognized the eerie whistling sound that was fast drowning out Ted's impassioned plea. The young man had seen first hand what an anti-personnel mortar-bomb could do and it wasn't pleasant. Harvey hit Trundell with the full force of his beefy shoulders, dragging his employer to the relative safety of the gravel-strewn ground.

While doing all this he had the presence of mind to yell at the top of his lungs, 'Incominggggggggg!'

I'm On Fire

'Rubicante! My gun's jammed. We've gotta find Alastor and get out of here! Rubicante!'

But the Fire Demon was having way too much fun. All around him the corpses of ex-cultists formed a barricade of death as he wielded Boris like some monstrous hosepipe. All things considered, giving a Fire Demon a Weapons Imp in flamethrower mode was a bit like handing a partially recovered alcoholic the keys to the Jack Daniels distillery and telling him to take it easy for a while.

'Burn humie dogs, burn!' the frenzied locust cried. He was a fiery tornado – a whirlwind of legs, mandibles, twitching antennae and napalm, spraying 360° death and destruction and loving it.

After weighing up the relative dangers involved in keeping Alastor waiting, or tackling his partner, Guttlehog quickly plumped for the latter. With a surprisingly deft piece of hoofwork the Boar Demon closed in and wrapped hairy arms around Rubicante's midriff, screaming:

'It – is – time – to – *go!*'

Rubicante heard only an oddly familiar voice somewhere off in the far distance telling him to retreat. Coward's talk – the battle was almost won. He burst from Guttlehog's grasp and resumed his pyromaniacal progress, rebounding across the smouldering wasteland like a blazing pinball. Whatever he touched went up like a hay-barn in high summer. Dancing up to one startled fundamentalist he rammed Boris's muzzle down his disbelieving enemy's open mouth, crying, '*Drink my steaming jism!*' as he let rip with the napalm.

It ended the only way it could have – when Boris finally coughed out his last gobbet of petroleum jelly and croaked hoarsely, 'Pardon me comrade, but I think I need a glass of water.'

Born To Run

They crept from shadow to shadow, the sounds of the ongoing battle fading into the distant night. Aristotle had done his homework, leading them from one hiding place to the next, sniffing out the route to safety. The area they passed through looked like the sight of a major air disaster, with twisted metal and smouldering debris littering their path. Off in the distance sporadic bursts of gunfire signified that, for some at least, the night was still young.

Sid's frayed nerves were getting the better of him. He grabbed Adam by the collar and whispered hoarsely into his ear: 'They're slowing us down. We should scarper. No bird is worth this, mate.'

'Keep your voice down,' Deborah hissed, ignoring the insult, 'they're everywhere.'

Indeed, the twisted wasteland was roamed by bands of suicide squads looking for nothing more than an evil enemy of God to blast into oblivion. Whenever they caught sight of a dark shape moving through the rubble they would unleash a terrifying volley of lead on the off-chance it represented a legitimate target.

Thirty yards ahead of them, Aristotle froze, linking minds instantaneously with Mike and Deborah. *Group of twelve gunmen approaching. They haven't seen you yet but they're heading your way.*

Mike signalled a halt. Adam went careering into his back. 'What's up now Nostrus? We leaving this mad-house or do you and Miss Mayhem want to play paintball all night?'

Mike was losing patience faster than Simon D'Smirtov, the short-sighted surgeon of sixteenth-century Seville. He grasped Adam by the collar and hurled him into the cover of a nearby bush.

'Listen sonny boy! In my day I'd have been more grateful if someone I'd vilified in public, splashed all over the front pages and generally given a damned hard time, took the trouble to save my worthless life from certain death. I'm not asking for gratitude, or even common courtesy, just for you to can the whinging and to do as I say until we're out of danger! Now put a sock in it and get under this bush.'

'I'm in it already,' came a muffled reply.

'Well stay there and shut up.'

Deborah soon followed, keeping a safe distance from any of Adam's limbs, and after a moment's hesitation during which he considered intrepidly striking out for freedom on his own, so too did Sid. Someway off, Aristotle hid up a tree. From his vantage point he could observe the patrolling guards and warn if they passed too close to the twitching shrubbery.

Eventually the cat called: *It's safe, they've gone. Nevertheless I suggest in future you desist from performing the Lambada if you want to avoid detection.*

As they untangled themselves from the foliage Adam gave Deborah a winning smile. 'Did the undergrowth move for you darling?'

Without warning, Deborah caught him with the sort of right hook that would have left Mohammed Ali twitching like a wired-up corpse. When most of the bleeding had stopped, Mike helped the dazed reporter to his feet. 'You deserved that son. Now, can we go?'

Another hour's stealthy advance through a realm of desolation brought them into the comparatively normal surroundings of an undamaged bit of theme park. Next to Great Tabernacle of Solomon (£9.99 per pew – hymn books extra) they found a car park big enough to land a jumbo jet in. Lines of parking spaces stretched as far as the eye could see. Haphazardly sprawled across this space were numerous vehicles, many with their engines still ticking as they cooled in the still night air.

One in particular caught their attention. It stood nearby will all its doors open. A large black limousine, beautifully polished and ready to go.

'I don't like this,' muttered Adam. 'It's too easy – must be a trap.'

'A trap?' spluttered Mike. 'It's synchronicity. We leave in the style we came. Trundell's men have no idea where we are. They're too busy practising friendly fire manoeuvres.'

He made his way over to the limo and peered inside. 'They even left the keys in the ignition for us. All aboard!'

Mike settled himself along the voluminous back row seat, as the others clambered in. 'There's a great advantage to stealing a limo,' he said fiddling with the clasp on a walnut veneer cabinet beside him. 'It's fast, it's bullet-proofed and, aaah! There we go. You can always rely on Fundamentalist Christians to leave a minibar unpillaged. Anyone for a Scotch?'

Last to the car, Deborah looked quizzically through the open window. 'So I'm driving am I? I don't remember volunteering for that particular honour.'

As Mike poured himself a drink that would have done Ernest Hemingway proud, any debate about who was to do the driving was cut short by the original occupant's overdue return.

From out of a thicket of nearby bushes, an anxious looking church member came running. In fact, it would be more accurate to say he came hopping. Unsure of which task to perform first – whether to bend down and pull up his flapping trousers, or to stop and aim his rifle – he performed an obscure sort of folk dance before collapsing in a heap on the tarmac.

Deborah lost no time in diving into the driver's seat and gunning the engine.

'Just a minor point Mike,' she said, turning to the communication hatch, 'where exactly are we meant to be going?'

'I always wanted to say this,' said the Professor from the other side of a huge ice-filled tumbler. 'Driver, take us home – *hic*.'

Warriors Of The Wasteland

Dawn creaked over the rim of the world like a rickety silver-haired old lady as Ted and Harvey stood assessing the damage. It would have been quicker to assess the still intact. Even the damage had been destroyed – then burned, blasted, cut up into little pieces and trodden on. The practice walls at the Walls of Jericho Rock Climbing Club were unclimbable – there was nothing left unless you found a horizontal stroll challenging. Across the park The Tower of Babel Bungee Jump Centre was looking more like the Leaning Tower of Pisa Multiple Amputation Centre, as the charred and blackened remains of so many of Ted's followers decorated it like some grizzly Christmas tree. Wherever they looked, all Ted and Harvey could see, smouldering in the half-light, were the shattered remnants of the ecumenical entertainment complex they had so lovingly created.

Ted forlornly shook his head. 'So Harv, what happened to the armies of attackers? If your men did half as much damage to them as they did to the park the enemy must be crucified by now. Shall we ring round the local hospitals to find out if five hundred Ruskie paratroops have been admitted since last night? Why is it I don't think we'll find us none?'

Harvey, who was well used to Ted flying off the handle at the slightest provocation, didn't know what to make of his boss's new quiet mood. Surely it wasn't resignation? If anything it scared him even more.

Ted calmly trod on the remains of a badly singed Cuddly Jesus doll. 'I want some answers, Harv. I want to know who sprang him. I want to know where he's gone. And I want you to find out the most painful cause of death known to mankind.'

Keep On Running

As October 22nd, 1999 dawned, the British Army unveiled an emergency recruiting drive based around the slogan, 'It's a Man's Life in The British Army'. Meanwhile, halfway round the world, it was fast becoming a South Korean's life in the North Korean Army, as wave after wave of short, green-clad comrades streamed across the border to liberate their less fortunate cousins. In high streets and shopping malls the planet over, the price of consumer electrical goods tripled overnight triggering massive panic buying of personal stereos and toasters. The resultant increased demand on the national grids of much of the developed world as customers tested their new purchases all at the same time caused severe blackouts in several major cities. To make good the shortfall, in the control rooms of nuclear power stations around the globe, the men in white coats grinned madly to themselves and cranked up the gain another notch.

Speeding through the early morning mist, Mike's party left the slowly smouldering theme park to its slowly smouldering creator. They'd encountered little resistance on the way out – all the security personnel were too busy hiding under the rubble or lying around bleeding to put up a meaningful fight.

In the back of the car, Adam was ready to make another gentle play for his one true love. He stuck his head through the communication hatch and grinned wide at Deborah. 'So tell me darlin'. Where you taking me – and do they have a beach?'

Deborah broke hard going into a sharp bend, jamming Adam's neck tight against the glass and temporarily cutting off his windpipe.

'One: I'm nobody's darlin'. Two: least of all yours. Three: I'm not taking you anywhere. You happen to be coming with us because Mike's a soft old pensioner at heart. We're going to his house in North Wales, if you must know. You remember, it's the one you splashed across the front page of that budgie-cage-lining of a newspaper you work for.'

'Why Wales?'

'Security,' Mike burped.

'Just looked like any other luxury mansion to me.'

'That's probably because, genetically, you're an idiot. You can't help it.' Mike took another sip from his huge tumbler. 'Actually, I've taken the precaution of installing a few defensive measures up at the farm. Nothing too elaborate you understand; just enough to allow a chap to live quietly in these troubled times.'

'You reckon they'll follow us, then?' Adam took out his notepad. 'What have you done, pissed in their font?'

Mike looked thoughtful for a moment. This horrible creature beside him was already in it up to his eyeballs. What the hell . . . The truth couldn't hurt him or anyone else now. Adam couldn't get back in time to break the story, because by then it would already have broken. And his weird old coot of a tagalong snoring away beside him, Sid wasn't it? He had to be harmless, surely? Besides, Scotch always tasted better when you had one hell of a story to tell. So he said to Adam: 'It's a little more complex than that. Thanks to your paper, Ted Trundell seems to think I'm a dark wizard hell bent on subjugating humanity to my evil whim.'

Adam chuckled. 'And you're not I suppose? All that stuff back at your flat with the ceremonial daggers and sequinned bikinis was just for my benefit, right?'

Mike looked pained. 'We thought that if we gave you the story you wanted you'd leave us alone. But the damage was already done. Trundell must have read your report from the previous day and got it into his tiny mind that I'm the Antichrist's best friend. As soon as you finished the interview they nabbed us. It's not that I'm criticizing journalistic free speech you understand, I'm as much in favour of a vibrant press as the next man –'

'Yeah, yeah, the next man being Joseph Stalin presumably. You liberals spout all this bullshit about freedom of information, so long as it doesn't intrude on your hashish hideaways. You're all for it when we expose government ministers' dodgy financial dealings, but when we blow the whistle on incompetent leftist councils sending disabled Bolivian refugee muggers on lesbian windsurfing sessions to the Seychelles you're up in arms! It's a double-edged sword mate, you can't have it both ways.'

'I can see you've thought about this long and hard Adam, and come up with a rational analysis of the various groups different to you that inhabit this planet . . . Listen son, politics isn't my thing. As far as I'm concerned there are only two types of people: those that want to control others and those that don't. I'm a member of the latter group and have always thought that the former should be rounded up, put in a field, and have bombs dropped on them from a safe height.'

'So you're an anarchist then?'

Mike sighed. 'Not unless you count failing to rewind rented video cassettes when you take them back to the shop. If you insist on pigeon-holing me I'd describe myself as a radical free-thinking libertarian.'

Adam sat up straight in his seat and developed a troubled frown. 'Okay, fair enough. So who was . . . you know . . . that other guy? The one with the billowing red cloak. Surely you can't blame him on us?'

Mike scratched his chin thoughtfully. 'That was Alastor, Chief Executioner of Hell and his screaming rune-sword Soul Stealer. They're the Forces of Darkness' top assassination team, sent only on missions of the utmost importance. I'm almost flattered they think I'm worth it.'

Adam scribbled away in his notebook like his career depended on it. 'So you are involved in the supernatural, after all. Why do these "Forces of Darkness", as you call them, want you out of the way?'

Mike took another gulp of the Scotch, this time direct from the bottle. 'Back in my younger days I dabbled in the astrology business. In the course of my studies I obtained information that certain entities would rather I didn't possess. This information relates specifically to mankind's future on this planet and the rough ride we can all expect before the year is through.'

'The Millennium.'

Mike nodded. 'Unfortunately, these entities' chosen method of gagging me seems to involve gruesome torture resulting in death. Rather extreme, really. They'd've got much further with reasoned debate and half a crate of this excellent mouthwash, especially seeing as I had no intention of making my findings public in the first place. Sure you won't take a shot?'

Adam was beginning to feel just a little bit out of his depth. This mad professor's revelations were all a bit much to take in, but in the light of recent events they didn't seem beyond the realms of possibility. 'Think I'd better,' he said.

Mike continued unabashed. 'We've had two highly inept demons dogging our steps all through this fun-filled trip. Back at the park they finally caught up with us, along with what I only can assume were some heavyweight reinforcements. Trundell and his crew just got caught up in the crossfire – a fact I find very hard to feel guilt over. His insurance claim should make interesting reading.' Mike chuckled to himself. 'Delete as appropriate. Was property damaged by a) fire, b) flood c) Act of Satan. If c) please give details . . . homicidal servants of hell seeking immortal prophet with doomsday fixation.'

Adam gazed at Mike with the first dawnings of a new respect. 'This astrology lark you were involved in – it wasn't like Russell Grant was it?'

'Not quite,' said Mike. 'My work was generally . . . how can I put this without sounding conceited . . . a little more apocalyptic in scope.'

'So, out of all this shit you reckon is gonna happen, what exactly have you got right so far?'

Mike examined his fingernails modestly. 'Well, more or less everything, really.'

In The Clouds

The sky above the motorway did not look healthy. In fact it looked like it had been out all night on the town, had just slunk in at five a.m. and was now doing its level best not to kick the milk bottles and wake the neighbours. The clouds were black. Not a normal, everyday, wholesome black. They were black in the way that only witches' cats and graveyard shadows can be – not simply lacking brightness but looking like a bottomless pit that light from surrounding space falls into screaming. In the limousine, racing to Wales under this lowering sky, the four fugitives and cat peered through the car's bullet-proof smoked-glass windows, and an uneasy foreboding descended upon them.

'Where's everyone gone?' Adam asked, staring out at lane upon lane of deserted highway. 'It's past nine and not a car in sight. Something's not right here at all.'

Far in the distance the motorway stretched like a great concrete ribbon, gift-wrapping the land like some greedy property developer's Christmas toy. No sales reps pretended to talk into mobile phones; no lorry drivers played chicken with suicidal minicabs which refused on pain of death to give way; no buses full of grim holiday-makers crawled along hard shoulders on their way to spend fortnights sunning themselves in airport departure lounges; and no workmen grinned down cheerily as they sprawled casually across their rusting equipment. There were, however, millions upon million of red and white plastic cones. Apart from these minor servants of Hell, Mike's group had the road all to themselves.

The Professor chose that moment to chip in with a level of equanimity not really suited to the circumstances. 'I strongly suspect most of the population are either queuing at the supermarket in a desperate attempt to stock up on baked beans or cowering in their basements as Radio Four tells them how to avoid the worst effects of radiation sickness. Ahh –' sighed Mike nostalgically, taking another swig from the bottle, 'those were the days. The twin threat of cold baked beans straight out of the tin and the BBC Home Service did more to avert global meltdown than all the free chocolate-guzzling trips to the Geneva Arms Control Talks ever did.'

'What on earth are you wittering on about now?' asked Adam, with a petulance borne of too much to take in on too little sleep.

Mike smiled ruefully. 'I take it you haven't been keeping abreast of the current international situation?'

Adam looked perplexed. 'I've been too busy chasing after you. Anyway, the Ed doesn't go in for that sort of thing. Foreign affairs is only news to the man in the street if one of our European friends has just elected an ex-porn queen to what passes for their parliament, or when the Yanks get their fingers burnt in some jungle hell-hole populated by a bunch of pyjama-wearing dog-eaters. Unless "Our Brave Boys" are involved it's strictly small column on page thirteen material.'

Indeed, the readers of Adam's paper could easily tell you what colour Y-fronts the current President of the USA was wearing – thanks to the miracles of judicial interrogation and eight-hour video recordings – or twenty things you never knew about beetroot. But ask them to explain the coming conflicts in the Middle East and the closest they'd come would be the latest scores in the Syrian Football League. 'Wars is depressing:[1] they want boobs, bingo and bonking bishops!' as Bill Winslow was so fond of saying. So it wasn't really surprising that Adam was a bit behind on the global news front. Mike felt duty bound to fill him in.

---

1 Unless we're winning.

'Put simply, it looks like things are heating up in the Middle East. All the Gulf States hate the Saudis because they've got all the money. The Iraqis hate the Iranians, no one knows why. Maybe they've been getting each other's mail. The Syrians hate the Egyptians because they made peace with the Israelis, and everyone hates the Israelis because the Israelis hate everyone else. This sort of thing has been simmering on low for years. The difference now is that they all think they've got the muscle to get what they want. It's not just the Big Five that have got the bomb now – every tinpot dictator under the sun is just itching for an excuse to press that shiny button. Well, recently those excuses have been piling up . . .'

On this upbeat note Mike drained his glass, sighed contentedly and settled down to join Sid for a well-deserved snooze, leaving Adam to ponder briefly the fate of humanity and at length how he was going to get into the driver's knickers, until he too succumbed to the somnolent drone of the limousine's engine and drifted into a fitful sleep.

Thunder Road

Deborah was making excellent time. All was going perfectly – clear roads, a purring engine, the kids in the back asleep – until the peace was shattered by an ear-splitting crash on the roof.

'What was that!' screamed Sid, almost jumping out of his crumpled safari suit, a nasty portion of his dream – the slavering demon with single glowing eye – still lingering in his mind's eye.

Deborah called through the communications hatch. 'Look at the sky! Just look at it! It's falling everywhere.' The 'it' in question seemed to be fist-sized chunks of glistening black rock that hurtled to earth as if fired from a gun.

'Is . . . is that coal? Should it be doing . . . *that?*' asked Adam.

'I don't know.' Deborah shuddered. 'How should coal

fall from the sky? Parascend down singing "The Yellow Rose of Texas"? I wasn't aware there was a precedent.'

Sid opted for extreme hysteria. 'This is too much. I want to get off this crazy planet now! It's your fault, Adam. I'm holding you personally responsible!'

'*Me*! You gatecrashed the party, mate.'

'What, and you're guest of honour, I suppose,' said Deborah, joining the fray.

'*Some bloody party!*' Sid screamed.

Hmm . . . We all get a bag of coal as a going home present. It's novel. Aristotle thrummed his tail against the gear stick. Deborah started to giggle.

'Children, children!' Mike shouted above the din. 'Calm down.' He had an explanation, as usual. 'It's all part of the plan. Before the powers-that-be can rearrange things to their liking they have to fulfil certain prophecies. It's almost as if they have a contractual agreement to supply the right sort of omen. That way, those in the know can take cover in good time. The trouble is, being ineffable beings, they do tend to be a bit obtuse. Not many folks can recognize the signs for what they are – even Noah needed a tip-off that first time round.'[1]

'Except you, I presume!' Adam almost screamed. In the absence of a well-defined enemy on which to vent his anger, Adam went for the nearest target at hand. Grabbing Mike by his lapels he shouted in his face. 'What the bloody hell is going on? Do something, you freak – *do something!*'

What Mike did was slap the reporter hard across the mouth.

---

1 In the celebrated case of the famous shipbuilder, the first signs sent to warn him that it was time to start visiting local pet shops in a very baggy raincoat consisted of:

(i) His eldest son Shem developing a small pimple behind his left ear.

(ii) A three-headed talking sheep appearing at the edge of his lands to offer a free year's subscription to *Exploding Intestines Quarterly*.

The world's first yachtsman-to-be needed rather more direct instruction later on.

Adam stared wide-eyed for one second, then crumpled into a sobbing heap. Meanwhile, Deborah was having to follow an ever more meandering course. As she swerved to avoid what was rapidly building up into a whole coal-face, she half-turned and said in an overly cheerful voice. 'Look on the bright side boys, at least this solves the world's energy crisis.'

It's The End Of The World As We Blow It

As Deborah celebrated the end of one energy crisis, another was fast getting off the ground not a hundred miles from where she sat. Although British industry was not in good shape, having for the past thirty years been going down hill as fast as Franz Klammer, there was one business where Britain led the world. It wasn't an old industry – there had been no need for it before 1945 – but it was just the sort of hi-tech, twenty-first-century venture that the government wanted to promote. And the good news was that Britain had a virtual monopoly in this rapidly expanding market. Not even the Japanese could, or would, touch this job. So what was this salvation for the state of Sterling, this messiah for the monetarist dream? Well, it certainly didn't involve silicon chips or some sort of service sector invisible earnings fiddle. This was very much a hands-on industry. As the stolen limousine swerved up the motorway back to North Wales, things were getting a tad dicey down at Britain's largest nuclear reprocessing facility.

The general manager of the Avonmouth WEASEL-9000 Fast Breeder Nuclear Reactor was on his third packet of cigarettes. Until that morning he'd never taken a drag in his life. The plant's chief engineer, however, had been a hardened smoker since birth and was currently on his second lighter of the day. But trying to smoke in peace with the claxons squawking all around you was just like a terminal Viagra addict – very hard indeed.

There was considerable justification for this nicotine

blitz, not only on this fateful morning but over the course of both professional lives. Each man had a nasty stressful job, the sort where they were constantly watched by dark-uniformed men in dark glasses who sat in darkened rooms watching dark video screens noting their every move for the first signs of stress. The very fact that they knew this was going on was, of course, the most stress-inducing part of the job. Taking this into account it is perhaps surprising that these two living chimneys hadn't had their tar-covered lungs confiscated by the Ministry of Transport years ago, for use in building the Nuneaton bypass.

The plant where they worked turned normal everyday common-or-garden nuclear waste into highly enriched non-common-or-garden nuclear waste. Since there now existed in the world many more nuclear reactors than just a decade ago, there was far more nuclear waste to go round. When an old clapped-out reactor came to the end of its useful life it wasn't simply a case of finding a breaker's yard, dumping it at night and running off before being nabbed by the security man. Spent nuclear fuel rods tended to be rather conspicuous, no matter how many old prams or rusty bikes were piled on top – mainly due to their unfortunate tendency to glow in the dark. Help was at hand, however. Blighty was more than happy to take whatever the lead-gloved hands of the world's nuclear powers could hurl at it – for the right price of course.

This willingness to act as the planet's radioactive rubbish tip did have its drawbacks of course. Even a people as famously stoic as the British were going to complain if they found their island home had been hollowed out like a canoe and packed so full of the stuff you could see the glow from the Moon. But, as with most problems, solutions were at hand. 1) Don't tell anybody. Great if you lived in a totalitarian regime, but a bit of a problem if the streets swarmed with investigative journalists eager to make the big time. So . . . 2) Refine the garbage, reduce it and compact it until you were left with . . . an even deadlier garbage – but one that occupied less space. This even deadlier garbage, which was called plutonium, could then be unsafely shut away with a huge flashing DO NOT DISTURB sign stuck on it for fifty thousand years.

To be fair, plutonium did have its uses. This everlasting Play-Doh of the gods could be used to make a fiendishly clever device called a neutron bomb – a weapon so smart it made other smart-bombs look like members of the Royal Family. Over and above the common bomb ability to go 'BANG!' and scare you shitless, it could leave buildings standing while conveniently disposing of all the people – thus reducing those pesky rebuilding costs after Armageddon. The last thing the tail-end of humanity wanted when it crawled out of the bunkers was a load of jobbing builders knocking round saying: 'That wall, see – gonna 'ave to come down. Who built this shocker for ya then? Bunch of bloody cowboys!'

Not that anyone made bombs with British plutonium of course. That would have been immoral. What the newly privatized British Nuclear Export Plc did was sell the material on to friendly states for use in purely peaceful scientific research. It was a sure way of generating foreign currency in a competitive world – and the owners of BNE who, conveniently enough, happened to be Britain's biggest electricity generating company, wanted all the cash they could get.

Mohammed 'Mad Dog' McClinchy, a man who took a deep interest in theoretical physics when he wasn't busy running one of the Middle East's smallest and nastiest dictatorships, was one of their best customers. When 'The Haggis of the Desert' earned another two Glowing Green Stars – free with every ten tonnes of Happy Hydro-B™ – he'd have enough to collect a tasteful cut-glass decanter next time his emissaries visited the DTI in London. This half-Scottish, half-human ex-oil-engineer had come to power after a chaotic *coup-d'etat* in which he'd proved to be the most resilient and least moral of the country's technical elite. The regime he set up was based on a strange mixture of fundamentalist Islam and a psychopathic hatred for all things English. It was his avowed intent to gain revenge for the battle of Culloden, the 1978 World Cup (relations with Peru were delicate) and the way Sassenach sports presenters referred to Scottish football teams as 'British', but only when they won. He ruled his pet kingdom, and those around about it, not so much with a rod of iron as with a rod of throbbing fissile material that threatened to wipe out most of the region on a whim. The fact that this cudgel of Caledonia had the words MADE IN ENGLAND running through it like a stick of rock bothered him not a jot.

But 'Mad Dog' would have to wait a while for delivery of his next consignment. At present it was looking like the Avonmouth plant, and all those working there, would shortly be joining the CFCs, spiralling satellites and voyeuristic aliens in the Earth's overcrowded upper atmosphere. The morning's excitement was all down to an inattentive technician who, after falling asleep at his post the night before, had dropped his lit cigarette into a wastepaper bin full of discarded safety memos. The fire that had raged throughout the purified highly oxygenated corridors of the complex was completely out of control and now eagerly licking at the reactor core. Minutes ago, the heat exchange system had ruptured, releasing ten thousand cubic metres of radioactive steam into the central hall. As the plant's general manager and chief engineer sat down to a tense breakfast of nicotine and tranquillizers (both inhaled) they began to accept that the situation was beyond critical. Their only option to avert major catastrophe was to open the seals on the reinforced concrete bunker that housed the reactor and vent the superheated gases gathered there. If the reactor wasn't allowed to cool down soon the results didn't bear thinking about. The panic-stricken controllers were stuck between a rock and a radioactive hard place. With a heavy heart, the general manager gave the order to open the seals and release the gases into the peaceful autumn morning.

As the MD of ElectroGen UK – 'Britain's Brightest Spark' – sat down to his breakfast in the luxury Sussex mansion he shared with his lovely Filipino wife, he was blissfully unaware of the chaos unfolding at his newest plant. He put his ear to his bowl of breakfast cereal, just as he'd done so many times with nanny all those years before, and was reassured by the familiar snap, crackle and pop. The beautiful irony of the situation was lost in the great empty space above his head where so many conversations he was involved in ended up. For at that precise moment that exact same sound was being made by his stricken reactor. Only, about 1,000,000 times louder.

Ask A Question . . .

Deborah might have been unaware of the fun developing at Avonmouth but she'd hear plenty about it over the next couple of days. Death and destruction in Britain won out over death and destruction abroad every time in the strictly prioritized minds of television news editors.

There was, however, plenty enough to worry her much closer to home.

'What does it all mean?' moaned Sid. 'Falls of fish, vanishing pyramids, demons wandering around like they own the bloody place.'

'It's quite clear really,' said Mike levelly. 'These are The Last Days.'

'The last days of what, though?' Adam gripped the front of Mike's jacket as hope drained from his eyes like blood from a bathtub.

Mike looked him straight in the eye. 'Simply . . . The Last Days.'

ELEVEN

And the armies shall gather at the appointed place,
bringing much fury as well as ammunition.
Where it shall be remains a mystery,
though hopefully somewhere nice and sunny.
Quatrain VII.14 The Lost Centuries of Nostradamus

Riders On The Storm

The mood in the limo that sped along the Noddegamra Valley Road was as sombre and black as the vehicle's paintwork. Overhead, the redness of the morning sky hinted that any shepherds nearby would be well advised to take their full quota of warning. Deborah drove in silence as Aristotle slept peacefully by her side. On the back seat Mike continued to down whisky and sodas like there was no tomorrow, which seemed like a pretty safe bet. Adam and Sid appeared to be in a semi-daze. Simply staring out of the armoured windows as the eerily silent countryside sped by in a blur.

By the time the weary travellers pulled up to the twisting driveway of Caer-Mathonwy Farm it was way past dawn. Their progress was halted by a high iron gate set between two stout stone pillars. On arrival Mike reached into his jacket pocket and produced an oddly shaped keyring bearing a small red button. When he pressed it the massive gates swung silently open, allowing the limo to continue on through the trees. Before they had gone fifty yards Mike tapped Deborah on the shoulder.

'Remember my dear, be sure to stop at the white line. This is no time for silly mistakes.'

Deborah nodded and brought the car to a gentle halt. The farm building looked like any normal luxury mansion, apart perhaps from the flashing orange hazard lights positioned under the roof eaves. From the trees on all sides a recorded female voice reverberated around the car.

'Be advised you are now approaching an actively defended property. Trespassers will be evicted with extreme prejudice. Defensive options include anti-tank guided missiles, anti-personnel cluster bombs, needle lasers and napalm-mines. Rest assured, we also have first-rate liability insurance. You have ten seconds to give the appropriate response or leave the premises. Have a nice day. Counting . . . One . . . Two . . .'

At this point Mike hurriedly re-produced his keyring and pointed it at an unusually shaped tree. After he'd given three short and one long clicks the counting stopped. Adam hadn't realized it but he had been holding his breath. When Mike was certain the warning lights had stopped flashing he gave Deborah the word to drive on. She took them into the gaping hole left by a large steel door that had just swung open, then down to the underground garage.

Once inside, Mike let out a huge sigh of relief. 'Safe at last. I'm glad to say all systems seem to be set up to specifications. The last contractor must have trod very carefully on his way out. By the gods it's good to be home!'

Shortly the five escapees had exited the basement via a flight of blastproof stairs and were gathered in the plush hallway of the farmhouse proper.

Mike coughed self-consciously as he addressed his new guests. 'As you might have noticed the estate is surrounded by a ten-foot razor-wired electric fence. Highly illegal of course, but then planning permission is about to become one of Gwynedd County Council's least concerns. The fence itself lies just beyond the tree line. A safety fence lies twenty feet further out to prevent casual electrocutions.'

'Very humane,' Adam muttered groggily.

'There's a little more to it than that,' said Mike, rather resenting the young man's lack of enthusiasm. 'Do not under any circumstances stray into the area between the two fences. The zone contains an assortment of anti-personnel devices that are designed to incapacitate rather than kill. I have to warn you though, the manufacturers err on the side of caution in this respect.

'And while I'm at it the small room at the top of the stairs may look like an airing cupboard, but I wouldn't advise you to go looking for clean towels in there. It houses the magazine for the roof-mounted surface-to-air missile-launcher. It's perfectly safe as long as you don't go fiddling with it or hover a helicopter gunship menacingly over the building.'

Mike looked levelly at his two dead-on-their-feet guests. 'Right, that's the basics covered. I suggest you get some sleep. Lots to do in the morning before Trundell and his followers show up.'

As they all trudged wearily upstairs to their quarters, the Professor couldn't shake off a nagging feeling. It wasn't anything specific, just that trusty sixth sense that in the past had always warned him of danger. He knew Trundell would soon track him down, but that wasn't it. This was something deeper, more fundamental, some tiny detail he was certain he'd forgotten.

There was an angle that he wasn't seeing yet. Something about the timing of events. Not just the disasters that were sweeping the planet, Mike had expected them – but the way they seemed to be peaking too soon. If it was like this at the tail end of October what was it going to be like come December thirty-first? Maybe, he pondered blackly as he slowly got undressed for a dearly needed sleep, the Millennium wouldn't be so survivable after all.

As the occupants of Caer-Mathonwy Farm settled in, a battered line of cars, trucks and coaches snaked its way up the motorway towards them. After a frantic morning spent cannibalizing parts from damaged vehicles to patch up the few that were worth repair, what was left of The Church of the Eloquent Announcement set off after Nostrus. They were a rag-tag convoy, and badly shaken, but they were heavily armed. Mike might have had other ideas, but many of the Church members were intent on rather more than a quiet tête-à-tête with the shy old Professor. Foremost amongst these was their holy leader himself.

Onboard his bullet-riddled mobile-command-post sat the weary figure of Ted Trundell. Fatigue was etched on his face as he rode at the head of the column clutching a two-way radio like a loaded gun.

'Breaker breaker one-five, this is Steel Hedgehog calling Iron Butterfly – talk to me buddy. If there's an ambush out front we gotta know.'

'Er – that's a big negative Mr Trundell sir.'

'Steel Hedgehog.'

'Steel Hedgehog, sir!'

Then Harvey was cut off by a crackle of radio static. Ted banged the offending instrument repeatedly in the palm of his hand. It did little good. It seemed that on this accursed morning even inanimate objects were developing lives of their own, packing their bags and heading for the hills in droves. This was a worrying thought for Ted's Head of Security, because at the moment he hovered two miles ahead of the advancing column in the Church's single remaining scout helicopter. It had been a struggle to get just one chopper back in the air, but Ted Trundell had been most insistent, making it clear that he wasn't about to go charging after Nostrus without thorough aerial reconnaissance.

After a prolonged period of fiddling, in which Ted

briefly tuned into an Argentinean Police frequency and discovered more than he ever wanted to know about their problems with 'Llama attacks', he finally got the haywire device back on track. From far ahead his subordinate's voice crackled through the loudspeaker.

'... I say again Steel Hedgehog, that's a big negative on the ambush situation. Though there does seem to be a whole lotta' coal blocking the freeway.'

Ted's eyelid twitched madly for a second. The image of a huge, short-sighted burrowing animal armed with a rocket launcher formed in his mind. Ted didn't quite sound his usual confident self. 'Did you say mole Harvey?'

'That's another big negative sir. I said coal – C for Christ, O for octopus, A for Armageddon and L for Lucifer. Plenty of it too. Should take the best part of a day to clear the road. You got all that – over?'

Ted's twitch got progressively worse. 'What's that you say, baw! Lucifer, Christ and an octopus? I think you're right about the Armageddon part, though I can't remember many tentacles in the Book of Revelations. Are you sure it ain't a seven-headed dragon ridden by the Whore of Babylon? And what about this giant mole, is he still there too?'

By this stage Ted was on his feet, a small cloud of vaporized saliva condensing in the air around him. Nearby, his everpresent aid, Casper, looked at his boss with some concern. 'Take it easy sir,' he cooed. 'Everything's gonna be fine, you just wait an see if it ain't.'

Ted's convulsions subsided. 'Will it Casp? Will it? Please tell me so. Tell me we'll bring Nostrus to justice, tell me we'll rebuild our shattered dream, but most of all tell me these lobsters will stop landing on my face!'

Casper gave his boss a long look. They'd been through a lot lately and something had to give. But he'd never seen Ted like this before. Now was definitely not the time to start losing it.

'I can assure you Mr Trundell,' said Casper with all the

dignity he could muster, 'that no lobsters will ever land on your face again.'

True to form, Casper's promise would turn out to be one hundred per cent incorrect.

A Town Like Malice

Events around the world that fateful morning weren't just an endless catalogue of large-scale international crises – there was a wide selection of minor domestic crises as well. Because these smaller stains on the planetary duvet affected people on a local scale, they failed to make the all-too-frequent news flashes that were playing havoc with daytime TV schedules around the globe.

While the Californian earthquakes or the Himalayan volcanic eruptions might have been considered a particularly impressive pizza stain, or the result of a prolonged evening of frenzied rutting, it was the sum total of minor dribbles, splashes and oozings that meant there would very shortly have to be a major trip to the laundrette. In one such rural puddle, not a million miles from Mike's present location, the inhabitants were quite understandably getting rather hot under the collar.

'Never mind yours, Mr Chairman, what're you gonna do about *my* sheep? Your lot have only gone and infected mine, and now I'm 'aving to offer my little lambs ready-bloody-cooked.' Dick Richards was in no mood for compromise at Noddegamra's hastily convened town meeting. He spoke from the crowded floor to a low stage where several uneasy individuals sat fiddling with bits of paper and generally looking out of their depth. In the chair, playing his part as town father and all round decent bloke sat Emmyr, Dick's neighbour and partner in adversity. The small Methodist meeting hall was packed to the rafters with concerned villagers, all eager to know what the Town Council planned to do about the present state of emergency.

'It's the knock-on effects we have to consider too,' Dick continued. 'What about sheepdog unemployment? What about the costs of unusable ewe disposal?'

Meanwhile, from another part of the hall, Wales's greatest freedom fighter chose that moment to make his bid to spark the long-awaited Celtic revolution. Gwylym signalled to Ivan with a swift kick and jumped to his feet brandishing a fistful of badly photocopied pamphlets.

'It's a plot, this is,' he screamed, waving his arms to signify the state of the world in general. 'This is MI5's way of disrupting economic life in rural communities, specially Welsh ones. It's all in our press release. Mark my words –'

'And mine,' Ivan butted in. 'There's some of mine in there too.'

Gwylym thought about hitting him, but he'd lose the momentum then. He cleared his throat. 'You mark mine – and his – words. First our sheep, next our children. This is how Nazi Germany started! Our only 'ope is to rise up and cast off the shackles of English oppression like the degrading chains they are. Now are you with me?'

'No, we're against you, dick'ed,' said a deep political thinker from the other side of the room.

Perhaps not hearing this Ivan clambered to his feet and gave his leader a rousing round of applause. For one confusing moment it wasn't clear whether he was applauding Gwylym's speech or the comment that followed. The GPLA's second-in-command then broke into an off key rendition of *Land of Our Fathers*, which musically borrowed heavily on *How Much is that Doggy in the Window?*, only to falter when he realized no one else was joining in. In fact the whole hall was staring at him as if he were a turd bobbing in a paddling pool. As Ivan's half-hearted singing came to an abrupt end he coughed self-consciously and delivered his carefully rehearsed monologue.

'Rise up! Rise up sons of Cymru and drive the foetid

English dogs from our land! Do not rest until every one of the evil oppressors is mashed to smiling jeans!'

Gwylym's face appeared close to Ivan's left ear. 'It's "smashed to smithereens" pin-brain. Get it right or you're court-martialled!'

'It's not my fault,' Ivan retorted. 'Couldn't read your scrawl, that's all! If you want to lead a revolution you is really gonna 'ave to do somethin' bout your joined-up writing Gwylym! That's all I gotta say on the matter.'

Gwylym again considered hitting Ivan, but he didn't consider for long. This time he plumped for instinct and proceeded to beat Ivan about the head with the stack of flyers calling for the forcible repatriation of the English back across the Severn.

Atop the wooden stage Emmyr saw a chance to reinstate his flaky authority. The old farmer banged his gavel and called for order at the top of his lungs. 'Does anyone want to make a sensible contribution? Yes, you at the side there? The chair recognizes Hywell Jones.'

Noddegamra's sole publican got tentatively to his feet and cleared his throat. 'What I wants to know is what's this mess going to do to me business? You can't run a quiet country pub when all the out-of-town trade is too scared to set foot outside their front doors. It was bad enough just getting 'ere with great bucket loads of coal flying round the place. My profit margins is narrow enough without ten tons of anthracite clogging me car park.'

The other members of the village's small yet vocal Chamber of Commerce greeted Hywell's stand with a hearty ovation. Denzil 'The Batter' Edwards, proprietor of the local chip shop, had a suggestion.

'Maybe we could rig up a system of netting, make Noddegamra a coal-free zone? That would certainly pull in the visitors. We could 'ave the only meteorologically protected shopping facility in south-central Gwynedd. Show those buggers down Bala a thing or two!'

Denzil's suggestion received widespread applause, though one frustrated physics student rather put a dampener on proceedings by calling for the valley to be declared a nuclear-free zone too – though whether to protect against the radioactive cloud spewing from the stricken reactor further south or against any North Korean surprise attacks on major shopping centres in the south-central Gwynedd region was not specified. Even Denzil had to admit that this unilateral measure was unlikely to be an adequate safeguard.

'I can't believe what's going on 'ere,' Emmyr cried desperately from the stage. 'We're in the middle of an international emergency and all you lot can think about is shopping! If we don't have some sensible measures from the floor I'm goin' to adjourn this meeting and bugger off down the pub!'

At this revelation the mood in the hall turned nasty, with scattered shouts of 'Shame' and 'Do something'. Finally Emmyr could stand it no longer. Banging his gavel so hard the head flew off into Purity Roberts' floral-print lap, he pleaded for peace. 'Look, there is absolutely nothing, repeat *nothing*, we can do about exploding sheep, world revolution, imminent nuclear destruction, falling coal, or the Guatemalan price of fish for God's sake. Can we please agree to limit this discussion to things we can actually do something about? That way we might make some progress.'

'What about the Pyramids?' said a small voice from the back. 'Maybe we could form a co-op to make pharaoh key-rings. Cash in on the current interest.'

'Just watch it!' Emmyr shouted. 'I've 'ad just about as much as I can take for one day! As far as I'm aware this great land of ours is not renowned for its pyramids – vanishing or otherwise! 'Ave I made me point?' A silence descended on the crowd like a pregnant pigeon. Emmyr continued. 'Now, why don't we just all take it easy and hear a report from the village's Civil Defence Officer?'

Everyone seemed to agree this was an eminently sensible suggestion and there might be hope with good solid men like Emmyr in charge. When the Civil Defence Officer failed to materialize this hopeful mood was replaced by a nervous silence. Everyone seemed to be casting sidelong glances at their neighbours as they waited for the aforementioned public servant to step forward. Finally Dick broke the embarrassed lull.

'Errr, Mr Chairman-sir-your-'onour-worshipful, just who exactly is our Civil Defence Officer? I can't remember us ever needing one in the past.'

Emmyr hurriedly leafed through the substantial pile of notes before him. When he found what he was looking for, a wry smile crept across his sly old face. 'Seems it's you, Dick. Says 'ere you got voted in unopposed back in '73. Says you had unlimited access to the hall pushbike plus spotlight in respect of your standing within the community.' Dick turned a not altogether healthy shade of purple as Emmyr continued. 'I move that our first priority should be to do something about this Nostrus fellow. I know some of you are concerned that since he moved up to Caer-Mathonwy there's been lots of funny goin's on. And I'm sure we've all read the reports in the nationals – exaggerations maybe, but whatever's going on in the world at large I'm sure we'd all feel safer with this outsider back where he belongs. Are you with me?'

Amongst the shouts of affirmation there were scattered cheers. Somewhere at the back someone started to clap. On the crest of this wave of righteous indignation Purity Roberts got to her feet in the middle of the crowded hall and began to speak.

'I'm sure I can speak for the whole village,' she started as she had done so many times in the past, 'when I say that this Nostrus is an utter disgrace.' For the first time in her life Noddegamra's moral minority had the populace firmly behind her. Revelling in her new-found support Purity continued. 'If half what I've heard is true he's a foul demon summoner, sheep disemboweller and pyramid thief. He's most likely responsible for the Leicestershire cholera outbreak too. I say we run him out of town before he enslaves us on behalf of his dark master.'

Her speech was met with the most rousing of many rousing ovations that day. The small mauve-haired lady was not used to such public acclaim. She went quite red as a result, creating a ghastly colour clash that threatened to spoil the mood.

'All right, all right!' shouted Emmyr from the stage. The meeting was slipping away from him again. 'We can't go running around taking the law into our own hands. I suggest we send our CDO up to the farm to talk to Nostrus and find out just what is going on. I know for a fact he's back there 'cause I saw 'im drive in this morning. Does the resolution have a mover?'

'Moved!' someone called.

'Seconded!' shouted another.

'Carried!' yelled Emmyr, getting rather over-excited at his motion being passed.

Now, at least, they'd done something positive and could all return home in bright spirits. For his part, Dick sat and magnanimously accepted all the pats on the back and shouts of 'Well done' that were offered in his direction. Despite his rapid elevation to hero status, Noddegamra's CDO couldn't help feel rather perturbed. It was all very well deciding some brave soul should go and sort Nostrus out but when that someone happened to be you the situation took on a whole new perspective.

As the crowd thinned a strange figure clad in camouflage-fatigues and swathed in bandages from the waist down approached the new hero. Ivan limped to a halt and grinned maniacally into Dick's worried face. 'Just a bit of advice Dick me old mate,' he said with an evil glint in his eyes, 'Don't ask the big one with the antennae for a light.'

Like A Bat Into Hell

Guttlehog and Rubicante sat nervously in the cab of the huge flying juggernaut as it cruised majestically above the windswept arctic ice. It was the early morning of October 31st, not that time had much meaning here at the roof of the world where the six-month winter night was well under way. Inside the cabin the Boar Demon gnawed anxiously at one massive hoof, trying hard not to think of the fate that awaited them. At the wheel, Rubicante drummed three sets of stalk-like fingers on the black plastic as his mandibles chattered incessantly. The two demons had good reason to feel insecure. Shortly after take-off from the grounds of Ted's destroyed theme park they had been instructed by sub-theology radio to break off their chase and set a new course for GATE A. It seemed they would soon have to justify yet another failure to their boss.

At least the trip up had been largely uneventful. Alastor and Soul Stealer had retired to the lorry's vast articulated chemical tank for a spot of much needed recuperation. Then after giving Manchester air traffic control a very worrying few minutes, and causing more than one pilot to contemplate voluntary retirement, this strange aircraft had made its way to the agreed rendezvous – GATE A or, as its more commonly referred to, The North Pole.

Though no longer a widely held fact, the Earth is, of course, hollow. GATE A represents one of the few physical connections between the upper world and that nether region that is often referred to but not really believed in anymore, except perhaps by devouter collectors of Judas Priest LPs. Demons usually pass between the two realms using the favoured puff-of-smoke method, mainly since it gets them to their destination instantaneously, convenience being a prime concern for Hell's lazier field agents. However, when there are large numbers of demonic bodies to be moved this method is far too wasteful of psychic energy. It's much easier to use the front door, or its counterpart, GATE B, at the other end.

When the first two Viking explorers chanced upon this hundred-metre-wide chasm and peered down the eight-thousand-mile drop, one turned to the other and said in a voice thick with the fluid falsetto of the fjords: 'Flørdy blørdy førker høle,' which roughly translates as, 'That's one fuck of a big hole.'

His companion turned to him and replied with all the emotion he could muster; 'Yes, it is isn't it. I wonder how many dried herrings you could fit down there?'

But before the explorers could speculate further they were ripped limb from limb by Frost Giants who guarded the gate. In later days it was a simple matter to confuse and badger the frost-bitten survey parties sent to map the region. Nothing's guaranteed to convince a cold and tired Geography postgraduate it's time to call it a day quite like a close encounter with an angry Frost Giant.

Currently, Rubicante was piloting the demons' unconventional craft in a holding pattern above the entrance. Through the darkness and snow, he could just make out the stygian chasm, encased in a sleeve of ice, reaching down below the level of the sea-bed to where the first galleries opened off into the Earth's crust. It may have been his imagination but when they passed directly overhead the Fire Demon felt sure he could just make out a tiny speck of light at the shaft's other end. Any doubts he may have entertained as to just what this pin-prick of light represented were dispelled as a tiny fluffy black body came hurtling through the hole at bewildering speed. Rubicante's eyesight might not have been up to much but he was a great fan of David Attenborough, and that's how he recognized it as an Emperor Penguin – a species he knew to be exclusive to southern latitudes. The unfortunate creature continued upwards in a graceful arc, before decelerating to hang in mid-air for one confused second. It then resumed its cyclic journey in the opposite direction, a look of stunned disbelief fixed between its wide glassy eyes.

All told the gate made an impressive sight, all the more so for the vast army that was assembling within its infernal depths. They were all there, Caco Demons, Fire Ogres and Pit Zombies. Off in one corner a yammering elder-thing breakfasted on the massed ranks of a regiment of Night Goblins, as at his iron-shod feet a platoon of Cave Trolls squabbled over the leftovers.

'So the rumours were true,' Rubicante muttered forlornly to no one in particular. 'The biggest stand-up-fight in the history of creation and we're going to miss it. Termination will be such a bore.'

Guttlehog seemed too worried to reply. The consequences of yet another failure didn't bear thinking about. Shortly, the only sound to be heard above the rush of air came from the cabin's glove compartment, where Boris petulantly fired off another airgun pellet to signify his continued foul mood.

Rubicante finally broke the silence. 'I don't think I can stand much more of this. If The Boss is going to lynch us he can bloody well get it over and done with! The suspense is killing me.'

Guttlehog placed a reassuring hand on his friend's scaly shoulder. 'Be careful what you wish for. The message said to hang round the gate and wait for further orders. Maybe he'll be in a good mood, what with all the excitement.'

Rubicante gave the Boar Demon his best withering look, the one he saved for shrivelling cornfields and turning cows barren. They both knew their boss no more had good moods than Rupert Bear had drunken sex orgies. Boris chose that moment to perk up with a level of cheerfulness not altogether fitting with the cab's sombre mood. He had had an almost smug grin on his face as he opened the glove compartment and sneered out.

'You're really up ectoplasm-creek without a medium. But you're not draggin me under with you. I'm a three centuries' champion. Who d'you think they'll side with?'

Before their half-formed replies were past their lips, the demons were cut short by a noise like two thousand dung-beetles stamping their feet in time with a Barry Manilow classic, soon followed by a now all-too-familiar shimmering in the air above the cab's unoccupied seat. With a wet pop, Young Nick sprang into existence on the cushion next to his trembling servants.

Despite their abject terror, the demons couldn't help but notice their youthful master sported a strange new disguise. He wore a purple crushed-velvet tuxedo and a ridiculously frilled satin shirt with collars that could have powered a small yacht. On his lap sat a bad likeness of a luminous green duck wearing a comically large nappy. The duck-thing fixed them with two button eyes as Nick's voice cut the atmosphere like a scalpel.

'Well hello boys. Anything new to report?'

Rubicante gulped.

Guttlehog whimpered.

Nick grinned his hellish grin.

When he spoke it was like being stabbed with a silk-bladed stiletto. 'Allow me to introduce our much respected colleague, Trainee-Demon Orville. We've been having lots of fun on prime-time TV haven't we Orville?'

The duck's green fluffy head rotated mechanically. 'They think I am a ventriloquist's dummy,' it rasped incredulously, 'Ha, ha, ha, haaaaaaaaa!'

Nick looked at Guttlehog, then Rubicante, then back to Guttlehog. 'Well now . . .' he said, and left it hanging in the air.

Floundering under Nick's inscrutable gaze, Guttlehog

attempted to justify their failure yet again. 'We . . . I . . . I mean we couldn't . . .'

Nick held up a talon for silence, then pointed it at Rubicante. 'You, tell me what happened and make it quick before I make you dead.'

'Once more we have failed Fell Lord,' Rubicante whimpered simply, bowing both his heads.

'It wasn't my fault oh Great Master,' blurted Boris from the glove compartment. 'They botched the entire operation. I told them not to use me in grenade-launcher mode, but would they listen? Would they bollocks. Consign them to The Pit for all eternity, that's my advice, but rest assured that your faithful servant Boris Winchester Maxim Gattling did his duty.'

'Silence worm!' Nick's thunderous command was accompanied by a stare that wouldn't so much have soured milk as turned it into peach-melba low-fat yoghurt. Boris shut up quickly and did his best to hide behind a London A-to-Z. Guttlehog and Rubicante had settled for the old ploy of shutting their eyes tight ostrich fashion and hoping for the best. But suddenly, Nick broke into a smile and said: 'Oh well, can't be helped.'

Rubicante and Guttlehog froze in mid cower. They had heard rumours of Nick's habit of easing the terror before driving in the knife, but this seemed genuine. Their boss continued candidly. 'I was going to have you ground asunder by a pack of wild rhinos, but something rather important has come up at the last minute. You know how it is, boys.'

The two demons nodded vigorously. Whatever Nick had in store for them, it seemed it was more important than their impending executions. 'I hope both your diaries are free for the coming weekend, because it's show time.' Nick finished with a flourish that sent Trainee-Demon Orville's fluffy little wings all a-flapping.

With that faint hint of annoyance that even the most

patient person wears when speaking to imbeciles, Nick explained further. 'The Big One. Armageddon. Even two gormless prats like you are needed in the infernal scheme of things. Though I sometimes wonder if you wouldn't do more damage if we decked you out with harps, and got you to fight for the other side.'

In a rare moment of insight Guttlehog caught Nick's eye, instantly regretting it. 'But I thought that was still two months away?'

The Prince of Lies looked shifty. 'After high-level discussions with the opposition we've decided to bring it forward. It seems some of our accountancy personnel were a little too free with the advertising budget. Horrendous expense-account lunches, too many grandiose overpriced omens. The cash ran out. But at least it means we get to win all the sooner.'

Rubicante's face lit up with new hope. It hardly seemed possible but they were getting another reprieve, plus a chance to redeem themselves in the Mother, Father and Great Aunt of all battles. 'A million thanks Great Master! We will not let you down.'

Nick just grinned at such inanity. 'I've got to leave you now lads. Tell that slacker Alastor that I was considerably vexed by his poor showing on this mission. If he wants to get back in my good books I'll expect plenty of trophies after the coming scrap. As for you two, your new orders are to proceed to the chosen place where Alastor himself will lead you into the glorious fray.'

Nick turned to go, then seemed to remember something else. 'Just one more thing. We've got a bit of a transport problem at present. Thousands of demons, imps and minor devils to move and not so much as a Student Railcard between us. All vehicles are to be filled to capacity, so I hope you don't mind having a few hitchhikers on the way down.' It was a statement, not a question.

'Who, pray tell Dread Lord?' asked Rubicante.

'A platoon of our finest demonic infantry: The Masticating Monks of Montpellier?'

Rubicante came out in a heat rash.

Guttlehog fainted.

The Masticating Monks Of Montpellier

Half an hour later the demons sat jammed into the cramped cabin as the juggernaut sped south through the frigid Arctic air. It was like a sardine tin, although anyone opening it could have been forgiven for asking for a refund on the grounds that sardines were not meant to wear habits – not even those caught in the Irish Sea. Alastor, Soul Stealer and Boris accompanied them glumly, but the bulk of the cab was taken up by assorted monks in a selection of physical orientations that would have made a contortionist wince. They were everywhere. One of them even seemed to be clinging to the outside of the cabin door, though Rubicante didn't like to look too closely. Above the rush of the icy air the monk's feeble moanings could be clearly heard.

Earlier the Fire Demon had watched as they all trooped aboard. Each wore a collection of rat-gnawed rags held together by mud, sweat and an assortment of stains that Rubicante chose not to study too closely, though his keen nostrils caught a distinct whiff of Chicken Chasseur. Each brother carried a wide range of cooking utensils tied to a rope belt and held a large metal spike in his callused, fire-blackened hands. Just when he'd thought the horror was over, Rubicante had been introduced to their leader: a short, black-cowled individual with blazing red eyes and breath that would have startled a horse.

'Alloo,' he had said with a strong accent, 'my name is Jean-Paul. I am ze Black Abbot of ze Masticating Monks of Montpellier. We chew a lot and we are vary vary Franch. We make best soufflé zis side of Toulouse.'

The monks' *modus operandi* was feared and respected throughout the demonic world. To start with they would cook their target the best French meal on this or any other astral plane. When the unknowing victim sat down to feast the Monks would creep up behind them, take out their long metal spikes and stab the unfortunate individual repeatedly until the twitching eventually subsided. What it lacked in finesse this plan more than made up for in its subtle juxtaposition of taste, texture and gratuitous violence. Despite their widely known method of attack, the monks had proved very effective over the centuries, the offer of a well-cooked French meal being too much for most. Such is their renown, even to this day it's not uncommon to see an individual who is *au-fait* with the occult and has reason to fear for their life check behind the curtains before sitting down to a plate of *Moules Marinières*.

When Tomorrow Comes

Everything was about to be made clear.

In the past, his dreams had been hazy symbolic things, requiring painstaking analysis before any meaning could be gleaned. But not this time – it was like putting on new glasses after years of assuming the world was faintly blurred.

With a sudden jolt, Mike recognized where he was: at the bottom of Noddegamra Valley, just up from the village and not too far from his own home. Off to his left the main Bala road skirted the hill then dipped into town.

But this was not the valley he knew. The lush greenery was all gone. A few blackened stumps were all that remained of the woodland that once surrounded Noddegamra. The village itself was a slowly smoking ruin, the buildings blasted out of all recognition. The communal lake, fed by the bubbling mountain stream, was a stinking sulphurous pool. The only movement in this shattered landscape came from huge black crows which seemed to be congregating around the many twisted dark forms that lay sprawled on the broken earth.

He turned away – and started with fright. He was no longer alone. It was surprising Mike hadn't noticed this newcomer sooner since he cut quite an imposing figure. The stranger was fully seven feet tall, robed in white and bore a striking resemblance to an overly intelligent German Shepherd. An unearthly golden light flickered around his fur-covered ears. Mike wasn't certain but he thought he could just make out one of the scorched hillsides through the dog's billowing robes.

After a moment's silence Mike felt a call to speak. 'Well,' he said gesturing to the scene of desolation before them, 'is this what we can expect?'

The dog licked his lips, panted for a while, then said, 'Yup, mighty fine ain't it par'ner. All put to the sword. Could'na planned it better if I'd writ the script myself – which, between you and me,' he said tapping the side of his muzzle with a large paw, 'I did in places. Though I gotta tell you I had one hell'ova editor. Made me cut all my best scenes she did. Next time, she gets it too – know what I mean.'

At this candid revelation the creature gave a terrible grin that was all teeth and spittle. Mike briefly knew how Little Red Riding Hood must have felt when she turned up at the old-people's home and found her granny in desperate need of a shave.

'Pardon my ignorance, but who exactly are you?'

The dog, as well as he could, given his limited range of facial expressions, looked incredulous. 'Oh come on! A smart guy like you must have figured it out long ago. D-O-G, G-O-D – pretty *big clue* wouldn't you say? Don't you think the Creator of the Universe would rig it so he could lick his own balls given half a chance?' As if to prove the point the creature was soon down on all fours with one leg stuck jauntily in the air.

Mike shuddered. Even for one of his dreams this encounter had reached a plateau of surrealism that made Salvador Dali look like a gritty-nosed realist. There was nothing for it when this sort of thing happened but to unlatch your brain from its insanity cut-off and tear along for the ride. 'But what's the point?' he asked. 'If your followers have to inherit a clapped-out wreck of a planet wouldn't it be better to let your enemies alone? Scratching out your existence in this wasteland is no way to live.'

The dog looked up at Mike as if he were a country cousin just stepped off the bus into the big city. 'Oh my, but it isn't all this way. Whatever gave ya that rootin-tootin idea. The rest of the world's an idyllic paradise with compulsory hymn singing thrice daily and everyone growing to look like Cliff Richard as they get older. This is it pal, Heaven on Earth.'

Mike looked confused. 'But then why does my valley have to be turned into downtown Nagasaki? I'm all for making sacrifices for the common good but . . .'

The dog looked genuinely disappointed. It seemed he'd expected better from Mike. 'You honestly mean to say you don't know? This is rich, 'specially seeing as what you once did for a livin' an'all. Wait till a tell the boys at the Social – we all thought you'd moved here to get a better view of the fireworks!'

Mike had to force the words past his gritted teeth. 'Just what are telling me?'

'This here valley, my blind little soothsayer, is the site of the Final Battle.'

Very slowly at first, but with ever increasing force, Mike began to slam the palm of his hand into his forehead, but it didn't do his predicament any good. All it left him with was a sore hand and the beginnings of a nasty headache. It was some time before he could bring himself to speak again. 'You mean to tell me, that come January the first . . .' Mike's words trailed off. His canine companion was slowly shaking his shaggy head.

'Oh dear, oh dear. Not having a very good day are we. Whoever said anything about January first? Listen son, let me put you straight on a few small points.'

Panic

Mike woke bathed in sweat. With the same feeling that an honest hard-working, dependable student, who's never forgotten his mother's birthday or taken a library book in late, knows when their alarm-radio wakes them half an hour into their final exam. Sudden realization hit him like an express train to Hell. Mike had an infinite amount to do and a negative amount of time in which to do it.

After precisely 1.67 seconds sat wide-eyed and half out of bed, which seemed to last longer than the seventeenth and eighteenth centuries combined, Mike's brain finally snapped into gear and he dived from beneath the covers. Moments later he was sprawled on Deborah's bed. '*Wake up, wake up! We must leave right now. Do you hear me? Now!*'

Deborah's unkempt head peeped out from under the duvet. 'Wha-ya say? Too early Mike; lea-me-lone.'

'Deborah, this is an emergency! Snap to it!'

To her credit, she came round quickly once she realized he was serious. 'What's up? You look like you've seen a coachload of ghosts.'

'I just have, and they were all ours. Now get up and get dressed.'

'Sure. But what's the rush?'

'No time to explain. Get the others. I'm off to check the surveillance cameras. Meet me on the landing in two minutes – no later!' With that he was gone, leaving Deborah wondering if she hadn't imagined the entire episode, but the sound of Mike taking the stairs a flight at a time told her not. With sudden fear she sprang out of bed.

Minutes later, they were all gathered at the top of the stairs, sleepy and confused. Mike seemed even more agitated. He hadn't seen anything conclusive on the command-bunker's wall of close-circuit TVs but then that in itself didn't prove anything. There was plenty of time for the day to go downhill. When Deborah enquired again about the sudden rush, Mike had to pause to get his fury under control.

'For some reason the powers that be have seen fit to choose this corner of Earth as the site of The Final Battle. I can't think why, though warped celestial humour is always a possibility.'

'You mean it's not going to be the in the Middle East like everyone thought?' Deborah asked in disbelief. 'We don't want to be round come January.'

Momentarily Mike was too angry to speak. When he'd removed his fist from between his teeth he went on. 'How could I have been so stupid? The signs were here all along.'

'What do you mean?'

Mike looked like he was about to cry. 'Deborah, we currently stand in one of Europe's most ancient nations – a Celtic country. The Old People used a different calendar.'

Adam looked confused, which made a change from looking at Deborah's flimsy nightdress. 'What have a bunch of druids got to do with the end of the world? If that's what's really happening, which I'm not saying it is.'

It was Sid who made the connection. 'The Celtic New Year . . .' he said, his voice beginning to falter, 'isn't in January. It's . . . it's . . .'

'OCTOBER THE BLOODY THIRTY-FIRST!' completed Mike, almost exploding with rage.

Suddenly, like tuning in a TV and finding Des O'Connor

beaming back, the whole picture became horribly clear. Deborah felt blank, a terrible numbness sweeping her body as she fought to speak. 'But that's today! Mike?'

Ever the optimist, the Professor refused to admit defeat. 'Perhaps not. What's the exact time?'

'Six-thirty-three a.m.'

'Right. Fill up the car with petrol, then pack – nothing fancy, necessities only for a few days' fast travelling.' Deborah was gone before he'd finished speaking.

Mike's next concern was Aristotle. The cat had a nasty habit of sleeping through all the worst crises, and this was no time to be caught napping. The bumpedy-bump of four stout paws pounding up the stairs told him he needn't have worried. Aristotle had been monitoring proceedings from afar.

Well Old Man? Some prophet. I wouldn't be surprised if the Union revoked your membership after this fiasco.

Now was not the time to argue it out with his oldest friend. Turning to Adam and Sid he said, 'Get down to the basement and see if you're capable of helping Deborah. We've got to be out of this valley before the Shadow of Death turns up and starts forcing us to walk through it. Now let's get moving!'

Watchers In The Skies

As dawn broke over the western hemisphere a group of VIPs, cunningly disguised as a large cloud, slipped silently out of hyperspace and into low orbit. They had journeyed far to witness what the travel brochures described as 'A once in an artificially enhanced lifetime's opportunity to watch first-limb this charming local custom, vibrant with ethnic colour and flair.' Which was odd as most of them had come hoping to see a really good scrap.

They weren't so much Very Important People as Very Intergalactic Polymorphs, and their mission was one of pleasure. The aliens weren't here to take sides. They were merely interested spectators willing to pay a small fortune to watch this long-awaited bloodfest from pole position. If some half-crazed radio ham had possessed a receiver powerful enough to penetrate the spacecraft's EM shielding, plus one of the new Dolman Communication Corps' Multi-tongue-Translato-Units™ and the static interference from his plastic anorak wasn't too bad that day, this is what he might have heard . . .

'Good evening ladies and gentlebeings. This is your chief steward Kwarmph-IV speaking. On behalf of the entertainment staff may I welcome you to the viewing lounge of the Dolman Leisure Enterprise's Starcruiser *Globular Beach*. I hope your re-entry from hyperspace wasn't too nauseating. In keeping with traditions of our locale, our carbon-based friends will find brown paper bags to deal with any little accidents, while creatures with standard metabolisms are requested to make use of the lead-lined buckets provided.

'I'm pleased to announce that we are now on station above the planet known locally as Earth, hovering at a height of some five thousand metres above sea level. We will shortly be descending to a lower altitude to get a better look at the amazing phenomena we've all come so far to see. We're lucky indeed to be here to witness one of the galaxy's most remarkable manifestations of collective belief. Never before has so much raw creative energy been channelled into one titanic confrontation between the two major subconscious elements of a race's psyche. I think I can safely say that after today, things will never quite be the same for good'ole *Homo sapiens*.'

[Gratuitous recorded laughter]

'And remember folks, this once-in-a-lifetime opportunity to witness what is sure to be a spectacular display of primitive theology in action is brought to you in association with Honest Sandyfan's Secondhand Star Yacht Emporium, your local dealer with all the best buys in the executive star dinghy market. Why not pop in and check out some of the truly remarkable offers next time you're passing Wolf351. You'll find us just off junction 38 by the big asteroid with the flashing nav-beacon, orbiting the third moon on the left.

'Well I'm sure we'll all bear that in mind next time we're looking for a new set of wings – I know I will. Now, before the fun starts, let's get some background info from our very own recently civilized native. Please, put your forelimbs together for the sole surviving member of our abductee breeding experiment. He's small, he's pink, he's got less hair than you might think. Let's hear it for . . . Andy!'

[Polite applause, cordial squelching and a gut-churning low frequency hum]

Despite having had most of his bodily fluids sucked out from various tender parts of his anatomy over the past few weeks, Deborah's former suitor retained all his charm and sophistication. 'Yah, hi there. I'd just like to say that this "Final Battle" gig, when you get right down to it, is just all about sex.'

Kwarmph looked confused in a carefully rehearsed manner. 'Sorry, but how does shutting yourself away in an ice-cave for two months with nothing but a Yertagian genital-orchid and one of your maternal grandmother's egg-sacs explain what we're about to see? Just my little species-specific joke there ladies and gents.'

Unlike his xeno-morphic virginity, Andy hadn't lost his attractive sneer. 'Sorry Kwarmph, you're a really great guy and everything, an absolutely top chap, but you don't know the first thing about human reproduction. Us bipeds really know how to party, know what I mean?'

'No, I'm glad to say I don't. But what's that got to do with the big fight?'

'Simple. If a human male can't shag it, he'll kill it. Do you think our gods are any better?'

'Apparently not, thank you son for that most biological

of explanations. I'm sure it'll help us in understanding what we're about to witness. But before we all sit back to enjoy the fireworks, just two things you should remember. First, on a linguistic note, despite their famed imagination, mankind has not been able to come up with a more original title for their home planet than *Earth*. Thus, it seems, conforming to the almost universal lack of creativity in this important field. Compare, if you will, this title with the Ossla-Raxxla name for their home planet – *Soil*, and the Verangian linguistic label for theirs – *Ground*. So needn't worry, perhaps humanity's not so clever after all. We can all sleep safer in our low-grav cots for knowing that this master-race won't conquer the universe when we're not looking!'

[More gratuitous recorded laughter]

'Secondly, on a more serious note, some of the scenes we can expect may be of a highly distressing nature to our more sensitive guests. Mankind is one of the galaxy's most savage races, prone to acts of reckless barbarity that would make even the infamous iron-plated Scorpion-people of Antares VI rust in disgust. If you're a member of a species with high empathy capability, or lack the required death-by-shock life-insurance cover, or you're the sort that generally wouldn't say boo to a Gargamemnan Mega-goose, then please make use of the visual-stimuli overload-goggles provided.

'Enough of the unpleasantness. Time now to settle back and wait for the fun to start. This has been your chief steward Kwarmph-IV speaking. Please note that the duty free shop will be open shortly after we begin our return journey, selling a wide selection of otherwise illegal and dangerous beverages, drugs and body deodorizers. Thank you for your attention and just thank whatever gods you pray to that they don't expect you to go through this sort of thing back home.

'Enoy the show . . .'

TWELVE

Jesus saves, Allah protects, Great Cthulhu thinks you'd make a nice sandwich.
Abd Al-Hazred 730 AD

Uninvited Guests

By the time Mike had bundled Adam and Sid down to the basement it was almost 7.45 a.m. Deborah had meanwhile topped up their limousine and disappeared upstairs to fetch her few belongings. Aristotle had offered to venture out on a preliminary reconnaissance but Mike had been quite insistent – there was no way he was letting them get separated now. It was a rather sullen cat that sat on the limo's back seat with firm instructions to keep their guests under control. For their part Adam and Sid were not about to argue. The story of the century might have been unfolding beyond the grounds of Mike's heavily defended estate, but in the light of recent events both had decided discretion was definitely the better part of suicide.

As Mike was about to dive down the concrete steps to the basement for the last time, a startled scream from the hallway spun him round. After a moment's panic, in which his long life raced before him like the trailer to a surprisingly good film, the Professor stumbled in to find Deborah ashen-faced at the window. Before he could ask what was the matter the words slipped from his lips like a wet whisky bottle from a drunk's hand. Arrayed along the Noddegamra Valley road, straddling the very route they had intended to take and resplendent in the slanting morning sun, stood the massed ranks of the combined armies of hell. This vision of doom didn't so much take their breath away as rip it from their bone-dry throats, fling it in a muddy puddle and jump up and down on it until it stopped trying to escape. Far off Mike could have sworn he heard the manic laughter of some idiot god, who didn't so much play dice with the universe as cheat outrageously at Scrabble.

Deborah was the first to get her trembling tongue under control. 'We're too late.'

Below them on the valley floor, the first battalions of goblin skirmishers were dancing their way through the trees. Close behind came wave upon wave of minor imps, all tooled-up with the very latest in fifteenth-century military hardware. Behind these came the crack regiments of Flame Demons, lashing out with their fire-whips whenever an unfortunate imp began to fall behind. Above this teeming throng swooped the airborne Household Cavalry of Hell, mounted on the sort of creatures you expected to see with a bikini-clad Rachel Welch dangling between their claws. To the rear of this awesome vanguard strode the Heroes of Hades themselves; stout Caco Demons topped off with plumed helms, and brave Chaos Knights cutting dashing figures in their obsidian armour as they strode through the swirling mist. Somewhere at the centre of this slowly advancing horde, surrounded by his personal bodyguard of elite and scantily clad succubi, Young Nick lounged aboard his blood-red open-topped Cadillac, poring over infernal battle plans and cackling to himself in nefarious glee.

The Professor turned to Deborah with all the equanimity he could muster. 'Unpack the car, my dear. We're not going anywhere today.'

Terminator III – Armageddon Day

The Chief Executioner of Hell was not a good loser. In fact he hated to fail. Not much of a distinction perhaps, as Alastor hated the universe and all that resided in it – personal failure merely sharpened and focused this anger until it threatened to tear the very fabric of time and space. There exist as of yet undiscovered deep-sea fish that Alastor hated. There was a certain type of small purple, alpine flower that he loathed with every ounce of his bile-filled black heart. The contempt he felt for game show hosts could only be guessed at. As for silky kittens, wide-eyed baby deer and girls called 'Wendy', baths of sulphuric acid were considered only a starter.

Alastor may have been an equal-opportunity loather but there was one thing that had him more wound up than usual today: a certain Professor Michael D. Nostrus. Mike was still walking, talking and doing all the other hateful things associated with a living being. In a nutshell he was undead. Not undead in the sense of wandering around a Caribbean sugar plantation in an old movie with a glazed expression and the dress sense of Man at C&A (though from Alastor's point of view this would have at least have been a start), but undead in the sense of being alive. This state of affairs was a blow from which Alastor's monumental pride would not recover until the situation had been rectified.

The Fell Horde's stoutest champion currently stood like a colossus just outside Noddegamra in the small, tree-lined field that had become Assembly Area 34b/MadMonk(ATTACK). Next to him, embedded in throbbing earth, twitched Soul Stealer, who prided himself on his qualifications for his unique job: a first in nastiness, a PhD in spite, an 'O' Level in awkwardness and a voice like a gelded choirboy. None of these fearsome qualities were evident now however. He slept fitfully, dreaming like some great black cat of the souls it would feast upon that day. The sleep before the slaughter.

All around Alastor's feet the monks scurried like demented

gargoyles as they prepared for the coming battle. This mainly consisted of sautéing great mounds of onions, chopping huge baskets of herbs with evil looking cleavers and gently sweating several hundredweight of garlic in vast open pans. Off in a corner of the field Rubicante and Guttlehog sat in the shade of the platoon's massive transporter and stuffed their mouths with a late breakfast. Earlier that morning, in a regrettable 'friendly fire' incident, a crack Romanian Vampire Battalion had been decimated when they were mistakenly mustered two fields downwind from the monk's position.

But Alastor was unconcerned with black-on-black casualties now. As he quietly fumed beneath the swirling scarlet sky that heralded the approach of Armageddon his ancient neck creaked as he sniffed the warm breeze. Through some ineffable twist of fate Nostrus was near. Alastor couldn't understand why this should be, but he could taste the man-thing's presence on the crackling, supercharged air. It was an affront to his dignity to be so close to a former target and let him live. Never one to look a gift-horseman-of-the-Apocalypse in the mouth, Alastor resolved to do something about it. Surely The Dark Army's most feared field officer wouldn't be missed for five minutes?

I Want To Ride My Bicycle (Very Fast Indeed)

Dick pushed his rusty old bike up the hill to Caer-Mathonwy Farm. He couldn't help but feel something wasn't quite right. Maybe it was the scarlet clouds swirling overhead that roused his brain momentarily into life, or the way the sparrows looked at him as if they knew something he didn't. Or was it the strange atmospheric effects far above that seemed to be producing fair likenesses of well-known Bible figures? And those crows sitting along the cracking blue telegraph wires – Dick blinked – they almost looked like vultures.

Over his shoulder Dick carried a scruffy satchel containing his spotlight, a handful of 'Protect and Survive' leaflets and a tightly packed bundle of chicken sandwiches. On his head he wore a battered dark blue helmet with the letters 'C' and 'D' stencilled onto the front. Between these stern characters some local wit had painted an 'N' in typewriter correction fluid. It was with such resolute kit that the typical British Civil Defence Officer was expected to meet and face down the snarling, ravenous beast that was global thermonuclear war.

Special kit or no, he wasn't taking any chances though. He'd wrapped his sandwiches very tightly in double-strength clingfilm to shield them from those pesky gamma rays. He wasn't sure what sort of foul multi-limbed radioactive creature chicken sandwiches might mutate into, so it was best to play safe. At the moment, however, the cell structure of his lunch, mutated or otherwise, was the least of the farmer's worries.

Dick stopped in the middle of the tree-lined country lane and tutted to himself. Some irresponsible individual had parked a huge articulated chemical tanker haphazardly on the grass verge by the side of the road. A party of schoolchildren passing this way on a nature field trip would have to risk the main body of the highway in an attempt to bypass the obstruction. Dick might have been new to the job but he knew a hazard to passing schoolchildren when he saw one. This was just the sort of careless disregard for others that had led to the world's current state of affairs. When he got his hands on the men responsible Dick resolved to give them a very serious talking to indeed. Just because Armageddon was around the corner was no reason to go flouting the Highway Code.

As he approached the juggernaut Dick's mind returned inexorably to the subject of food. From a field to his right wafted the unmistakable aroma of frying onions. The bewildered farmer didn't get a chance to stay bewildered for long. Suddenly, with much rustling of undergrowth and a smell like the Devil's very own jockstrap, a dishevelled head appeared from the hedgerow.

Dick spent a confused second taking in the new arrival's appearance – then shuddered. The individual wore what looked like a tattered brown sack and held a wooden cookery spoon in his blackened hand. This long distance lorry-driver-cum-barbecue-chef must have been extremely sensitive to onions Dick thought, as his eyes were very red indeed. In fact they almost seemed to be glowing with an internal light of their own. Dick tutted again. Additives everywhere.

The unkempt cook broke into a rotten-toothed grin.

'Greetings Monsieur,' he said with a flurry, producing an immaculate napkin from under his habit. 'We are just about to eat. You join us for lunch, no?'

All thoughts of Highway Codes, children's safety and the end of the world evaporated from Dick's head. Even the mission he'd been sent on, 'To sort out Nostrus' became a distant memory. When it came to offers of free food, Dick had a one-track mind.

'Oh, all right then,' he said after putting up a manful struggle.

Shortly the peckish farmer was seated on the damp grass, a wooden serving bowl resting on his knees, a large serviette tucked in the front of his shirt, and a steady trickle of saliva cascading down his receding chin. The hospitable monk had disappeared behind a nearby bush, to engage in much banging and clanking of pots. It smelled just divine.

Suddenly Rubicante came bursting through the bush, seemingly still holding a conversation with someone on the other side. 'Okay, okay! I get the picture. Give him the meal and keep him distracted until the guy with the spike turns up.'

Dick froze, his mouth half-open, his brain halfway to insanity. He had been about to compliment the monk on his generosity amidst so much conflict, but all that came out now was a strangled scream. His consciousness took a second to confirm that his eyes were still interacting with reality, and that he was indeed staring at the face of a seven-foot talking grasshopper. Then three things happened all at once. Firstly Dick's feet began to interact very quickly with the ground, then his breakfast began to interact very quickly with his trousers. Finally, what was left of his sanity dribbled out of his ears and down his shoulders, leaving a wafting vapour trail in the crackling air behind him.

The road ran downhill all the way to town, so Dick had gravity as well as panic on his side. Over the next few seconds he was to discover just how fast his rusty old bicycle could travel. The answer, as far as he was concerned, was not nearly fast enough.

There's A Thing At The Bottom Of My Garden, And His Name Is Bel-Astroth-Slannesh, Lord Of The Worms

As Deborah stood at the front window of Caer-Mathonwy Farm, hope drained from her face and formed a desolate puddle on the plush carpet. Beside her Mike was in no better mood. The high-powered binoculars he held were not really necessary to monitor the advancing horde in the valley below, but they at least gave him something to do rather than just gaze on in despair. From behind them came a distraught whimper – the sort of sound an orphaned puppy, who'd just hurt its paw, might make on Christmas Eve as it was locked out in the snow. All things considered Sid was not doing much for their flagging morale.

'Game over!' he wailed. 'When that lot get here we're gonna be mincemeat. Ain't none of your fancy plans gonna save us now you old git.'

Mike snorted in disgust. When he'd broken the news of their fast-approaching house guests Aristotle and the others had raced upstairs to see for themselves. Their reactions had been depressingly inevitable. Deborah on the other hand looked troubled, but not in the *oh-my-God-I-think-I'm-going-to-die* way. Her expression was more quizzical, almost detached. With a thoughtful frown she jogged off towards the kitchen, which gave commanding views of the hillside behind the house.

Mike gazed back at the approaching horde and sighed. So this was it – his long and troubled life would end here, squashed beneath a stampede of cloven hooves. 'Any ideas old friend?' he asked dejectedly. 'I can't begin to tell you how sorry I am I've got you into this. It rather looks like we're done for.'

Aristotle fixed him with two huge amber eyes. *What sort of attitude do you call that? We've come through stickier patches in the past and lived to fight again. Let's just see what pans out.*

'Maybe.' Mike put on his best optimistic smile, the one he saved for dying old ladies and reformed gamblers who said bingo didn't count. Just when his expression was beginning to look strained Deborah's startled voice echoed from upstairs.

'Mike – come quickly! I think you'd better see this.'

Deborah didn't say a word, but simply pointed up to the jagged ridge-line that cut across the forested hillside behind the house. Above this idyllic scene the sky was in turmoil, hazy shapes forming and reforming in a mesmerizing whirl.

Even for Mike, who had seen some pretty incredible things in his time, the view was amazing. Along the hillcrest stood row upon row of man-like figures glowing with an unearthly golden light. If Mike had brought his binoculars with him in the rush to see, he might have recognized some familiar faces. A large proportion of the unearthly ensemble was made up of individuals who, five hundred years before, had been fellow sufferers at the hands of the Inquisition. Rooted to the spot next to a mighty oak stood Saint Cuthbert the Unswervable. Some way down the line bobbed Abbot Wilfred the Worrisome, wringing his hands in his usual way. Next to him bounced Saint Horatio the Unipedal, the heroic cleric who'd gnawed his own leg off rather than renounce his faith.

But under the circumstances it was perhaps understandable that Mike failed to recognize his one-time partners in pain. Behind the line of Lesser Known Saints, hovering in mid-air and glowering with self-righteous glee, fluttered five hundred radiant figures. The airborne contingent didn't so much steal the show as mug it off a frail old granny, smuggle it out of the country in a Tesco carrier bag, transport it by overland caravan to a Moroccan flea market, then flog it off in the back room of a Casablanca carpet shop.

They had the faces and bodies of beautiful young men but the wings, halos and belligerent expressions of what could only be an Angelic War Host. And they looked like they meant business, the sort of business conducted by shadowy figures who claimed to be in 'Import/Export'. The angels' long slender hands held an assortment of archaic weaponry – swords, spears, maces and things that looked unnervingly like twelve-gauge pump-action shotguns.

'Assault Angels,' whispered Mike hoarsely. 'How could I have been so blind?'

'*Aaaaaaaaaaaaaaargh! What in the name of God is that?*'

For a split second Mike and Deborah exchanged slightly more than bewildered glances, then took off to join their guests. They arrived to find Sid, who seemed to be experiencing total sensory overload, pointing out the window towards what had once been the front lawn. Mike and Deborah followed his petrified gaze to the scene of desolation beyond. Out in the garden the farm's carefully manicured lawn would never be quite the same again. Amongst a large pile of excavated earth, half sitting in a round hole, throbbed Bel-Astroth-Slannesh, Lord of the Worms.

He may have been Bel-Astroth-Slannesh, Lord of the Worms and general all-round lowlife, but BAS (as he was known to his few close friends) looked far more like a giant translucent maggot topped off by a tiny humanoid head. In fact his official title was 'High Lord of Wriggling Things You'd Rather Not Find Staring Up At You From Half An Apple', but as it didn't trip off the tongue so nicely at cocktail parties he stuck to the shorter form.

Whatever his title, BAS was a gut-heaving sight. His bulbous yellow body pulsated to the rhythm of mysterious internal organs, his translucent skin revealing their multicoloured throbbings. Every so often strange bulges would appear in one meaty flank, as if some unfortunate being were trying to escape his monstrous stomach. From his rear-end stretched a repellent yellow secretion. At the thing's front-end hung a humanoid face whose eyes nose and mouth all seemed to be sucked towards a central hole.

'Greetings humie pigs! I am Bel-Astroth-Slannesh, Lord of the Worms and acting Field-Marshal in the Subterranean Self Defence Force. I have come to commandeer this building in the name of Hell. Prepare to meet your maker – that jumped up Jehovah in most cases, or something with a rather better sense of humour if there are any Belgians present.'

The maggot continued with an air of pompous officialdom. 'You have two options. One, you come out and die quickly with some vestige of pathetic humie dignity. Two, you remain inside in a misguided hope that those four walls offer any sort of protection from my advancing hordes – in which case my smaller brethren will hatch inside each of you and gnaw at your innards for all eternity.' BAS's piggy little face grinned slyly. 'You have thirty seconds to decide then we're coming in.'

Deborah looked at Mike and Mike looked at the thirty foot incontinent invertebrate sitting in what had once been his front garden. The awkward silence was punctuated by the dull thud of Sid's senseless body hitting the floor. In his place Adam staggered groggily to his feet and rubbed his red eyes, as if spotting the aberration against God and nature squatting amongst the begonias for the first time. Half incensed he turned on Deborah.

'Don't think for one minute you're dragging me down into whatever pit of madness you two call home. I want out of this crazy outfit *right now!*'

With a snarl Deborah grabbed Adam by his lapels and slammed him against the wall. 'Look loverboy, you better just start handling this or you'll have me to deal with. You can bet your silk-gusseted posing-pouch that I'm a far greater threat than any creature from another dimension, astral plane or cosmic helicopter for that matter. So unless you've got any constructive suggestions, shut it!'

But Adam was too far gone to stop. 'What have you people done to the inside of my head? You're the fruitiest pair of nutcakes since Nero and Caligula teamed up and decided to play lick the leper! You must have slipped something in my drink when I wasn't looking – it's the only explanation. This just cannot be happening, it cannot be happening.'

Deborah punched Adam in the face. It went against her core principle of non-violence. but extreme circumstances demand extreme measures and besides, it made her feel a whole lot better. Looking very much like she wanted something else to hit, she advanced towards the window with fury in her eyes and an apocalyptic snarl upon her lips. Mike gave her plenty of room.

Outside BAS was giving a remarkably good impression of someone passing the time by casually inspecting their nails – remarkably good considering he possessed neither nails nor fingers, nor even a trace of an arm. Yanking open the window Deborah let rip with both lungs.

'We choose neither, you festering mountain of fish food! Take your infernal children and piss off out of our garden.'

BAS raised casual eyes and smiled sweetly. 'Your attitude is most unfortunate my pretty one. I will feast upon your innards myself. Pray to whatever gods you find comforting, for you will soon wipe your feet upon their welcome mat.'

Regaining consciousness momentarily, Adam looked up from the floor. 'Oh very clever. We've not only got a thirty-foot maggot intent on our destruction outside, we've got one that you've just pissed off. Someone call me a cab!'

Before Deborah could redirect her rage Mike stepped between them and took hold of her. It seemed the Professor had rediscovered his resolve, grim determination furrowing his brow. 'In case it's escaped your notice we really don't have time for this. We have to barricade ourselves inside the command bunker – it's our only chance.'

His words seemed to have the desired effect. As Deborah regained a vestige of her self-control Mike dragged Sid to his feet. 'Move it Deborah. Bring that snivelling slimeball with you – and make sure Aristotle doesn't go walkabout, that's the last thing we need right now.'

Since the Demon Lord's arrival the cat had done nothing but stare transfixed at the monstrous abomination, his thick coat on end as if charged by some massive electrical field. Deborah could only call out for him as she hauled Adam across the floor. Reaching the hallway she began to unceremoniously drag the reporter down the stairs a flight at a time. At the basement entrance she discovered Mike beside the huge blast doors, fumbling furiously with the complex locking system and swearing under his breath. To her intense relief Aristotle snapped out of his daze and followed. He wasn't the only creature who seemed intent on joining them. A dull rumbling marked BAS's lumbering advance.

'Hurry Mike!' Deborah felt the first pangs of panic rise.

Beads of sweat had broken out on Mike's furrowed brow. 'Nearly there . . . just one more digit – nearly there . . .'

CLICK!

With barely a nudge the vast steel doors swung open on silent hinges. Four panic-stricken humans fell over themselves in their haste to get inside, soon to be followed by one slightly more dignified cat.

Garden Party

Outside, BAS paid scant heed to his prey's flight. They always did this – vainly run away in some dim hope of escape. Predictably futile. Present one of the ugly bald apes with a brick wall and nine times out of ten they'd find some way to bang their heads against it. Still, the adrenaline rush made them all the more tasty. With a shrug he began to bounce towards the house.

But before he'd taken two flops his legless progress was halted by an explosion from the trees to his left. Another bang was accompanied by a blinding phosphorus flash. Burning foliage obscured the view but it seemed a safe bet something substantial was approaching through the wood. Peeved at this unwanted interruption BAS halted and scowled into the smoky gloom.

BAS's hearing was not good at the best of times. A twenty-foot stomach left little space for ears. BAS's gut gurgled constantly like Hell's very own central-heating system after being left on all night. If the Lord of Worms had eaten something particularly spicy that day, like say the odd Indian restaurant, then the effects were all the more apparent. All he was used to hearing was his lunch, so BAS had to strain pretty hard to make out the new arrival over the din. What he could have sworn he heard was the stomping of armour-clad feet accompanied by a high-pitched nasal singing.

'Ten anti-personnel mines, lying on the ground! Ten anti-personnel mines, lying on the ground! And if one anti-personnel mine, should accidentally detonate killing innocent bystanders instantly! There'd be five billion, 3-6-5 million, 4-8-2-thousand, one hundred and thirty-three left for little old me.'

Or was he imagining it? BAS was far too close to his still percolating breakfast to be sure. In the absence of evidence to the contrary The Lord of Worms was about to resume his lumbering advance when movement caught his eye. Through the swirling mists towered a hulking silhouette with two curling horns jutting from a baroque obsidian helm. In one hand it carried a long black shape that seemed to drink the very light from the sky. To BAS's strained ears it sounded like this dark shape was the source of the voice.

At that moment Alastor came blundering through the smog. Behind him Mike's carefully laid minefield had just become a slowly smoking ex-minefield. The Duke of Hell may have been behind in military techniques. But he learnt from his mistakes. With the debacle at the theme park still strong in his mind, he'd pulled rank and acquired one of the new full metal jacket packs of Titanium-Francium alloy. This time he came through the explosions looking like he'd just been polished. A few bits of ancient rusted armour hung loosely from their straps but that was the extent of the damage. The light of malicious intent shone in his single burning red eye, and in one huge hand Soul Stealer sang merrily to itself of the life-forces it would soon consume.

For an instant of blinding intensity the Demon Lords locked eyes across the shrubbery. They were old acquaintances, and thanks to a misunderstanding over the disembowelling rights to a group of thirteenth-century choirboys, also deadly enemies. Theirs was a love-hate relationship – minus the love. If one had found himself entrapped by a deadly gang of guitar-playing sandal-wearing born-again Christians, the other would have just sat back and laughed. Now it seemed their final showdown was at hand.

Alastor glared at BAS, BAS glared back. If looks could kill they would have sterilized the air between them.

'What are you doing here?' demanded the King of Worms, grinding his decaying teeth with rage. 'This sector has been allotted to me. Bugger off before I butcher your heaving entrails and serve them up for tea!'

Alastor simply pointed to the house, his voice like a seized-up shotgun. 'Nostruuuusssss, innn therrrre. Miiiiiine!'

BAS looked fit to burst, never a far-off possibility. 'I don't care who's inside, it's no business of yours! My regiment's got orders to seize this building as a forward post. This is tactics, so don't meddle in things you don't understand!'

Soul Stealer wasn't going to let his master be talked to like this. The blade was well aware Alastor was under-endowed in the conversation department, so he was used to assuming the role of spokes-sword. 'Watch it you limbless little shit! No one speaks to us like that. Step aside if you value your purulent hide!'

'Don't tell me what to do you overblown pen-knife!' BAS bounced on the spot in fury. '*And what are you looking at?*' he screamed at the staring Alastor.

Soul Stealer stuck his hilt-guard haughtily in the air. 'Thirty foot of juvenile blue-bottle perhaps? When you finally grow up there won't be a pile of shit big enough for you to sit upon.'

With a bellow of rage BAS charged at Alastor. At least, he attempted to charge. What he in fact managed was a bouncing waddle that propelled him at all of two feet per second. Having seen the gauntlet thrown down in no uncertain fashion Alastor gave a howl of pure hatred and began his own advance. It was just as well, had he waited for BAS he would have waited all day. Not before time the demons collided with a wet thwack! Even for a contest between two diabolical elder-statesthings it was not a pretty fight. On his side Alastor had arms, legs, and Soul Stealer, while BAS had size, strength and great folds of bulbous flesh that rippled like pus-flavoured blancmange. The fight quickly degenerated into a desperate wrestling match, a limbless foetid blob against a spiky black crustacean. The Duke of Hell's limbs were soon wrapped in the maggot's pliant body and it became a terrible race – could Alastor bring Soul Stealer to bear before BAS's overwhelming strength crushed him like a tin can?

Waiting For The Worms

In the command bunker the battle was watched with grim fascination and more than a little dread. The wall of closed-circuit TVs gave off an eerie light, oddly in keeping with the scene they portrayed. The dim room's silent occupants had to face the fact, whoever won the ferocious fight would get first shot at them. There were no cheers for either side. Mike broke them from their trance.

'Quick Deborah – to the control console, you know what to do. This might be our only chance!'

Deborah assumed position. Thankful for the time she'd spent under Mike's instruction familiarizing herself with the controls, she sent her fingers dancing across the switches. Short seconds later a glowing red cross-hairs appeared on the central screen. Adam and Sid watched in awe as an ominous line of text was printed out letter by letter beneath:

MISSILE LAUNCHER [ROOF] ACTIVATED

Outside, the deadly duel continued. Alastor had somehow manoeuvred himself to the top of the squirming maggot, but one arm and sentient sword were still pinned beneath the worm. Making the best of the situation he furiously pummelled his opponent with his free fist. This tactic had little effect, his over sized gauntlet merely disappeared into the folds of gangrenous blubber. Relayed through loudspeakers BAS could clearly be heard to chuckle.

'Not so clever now are you rust-rectum. Chew on this!' And the Lord of Worms begun to frantically nibble at Alastor's exposed knee.

With a loud clank one iron-shod lower leg fell to the turf.

At the computer terminal Deborah had hit a snag. Panic rose in her voice as she pushed every button in sight. 'It's no good – I can't get a lock-on! They're not giving off a strong enough heat source. We're going to have to find another way!'

Mike dived under the desk for the weapon system's voluminous instruction manual. In a near frenzy he leafed through the pages with an expression of mounting alarm. 'Would you bloody believe it! It's in Russian.'

A furry shape clambering beneath Deborah's forearm signalled Aristotle's arrival on the scene. All eyes fell on the cat as he gazed down over the convoluted Cyrillic script.

It's really quite straightforward. You simply have to switch the Status Indicator to un-arm, then turn the Acquisition Mode Selector to manual. That's the big red switch, in case you hadn't noticed.

Deborah lunged for the button.

To a seemingly operatic crescendo, an unspeakably phallic joystick rose slowly from a hidden slot on the console. The thing was covered with thumb-switches, coolie-hats and triggers. It had more knobs than the House of Lords Formation Adultery Team. Adam was reminded of certain mechanical devices available only from specialist magazines in the UK, and local supermarkets throughout Scandinavia.

Mike grabbed for it like it were a rope thrown to a drowning man. With sweat breaking out on his brow he wrestled with it until the glowing cross-hairs were brought to bear on the struggling demons. '*Now!*' he yelled at the top of his lungs.

Deborah hit the fire button.

The missile went whoosh!

The demons disappeared in a blaze of light.

The monitors went a bright shade of orange and stayed that way for what seemed like eternity. Even deep underground, behind twelve feet of reinforced concrete, the blast knocked Mike and the reporters to the floor. Deborah sat braced in her command chair. Aristotle, goggle-eyed and ears-flat, dug his claws into her lap.

Mike was the first to his feet. As he worriedly peered at the TV, Deborah broke the deathly silence. 'The blast must have damaged the video link,' she said, tapping the screen repeatedly. 'We're getting bad interference.'

Mike leaned over her shoulder to get a better look. The signal did seem to be breaking up severely. All over the smoky image a strange yellow snow was falling steadily. The first trace of a smile slowly crept over the Professor's dry lips. 'I don't think that's interference my dear.'

As if to illustrate his point a lump of smouldering metal fell suddenly across the screen. Then another plummeted to the ground, then another. Mike grinned. 'Two down, infinity to go.'

Stairway To Heaven

The lead coach screeched to a halt on the winding mountain road. Ted Trundell jumped down from the cabin and wiped his tired brow. It was only 10 a.m. but it had already been the sort of day where the only thing to go right was his impatience-ometer, which had gone right offscale shortly after dawn. The column of battered vehicles had been beset by problems throughout the night. After a bright start spending the previous day shovelling coal, the journey had rapidly worsened. Gale force winds had whipped at their faces, to be followed by horizontally falling hailstones that had almost looked scared. It seemed the very forces of nature were rushing away from some terrible doom – one that Ted and his followers were heading straight into. At least the weather had cleared since entering the hills, though the morning sky did look an unhealthy shade of puce. But the self-proclaimed New Messiah currently had problems of a more mundane nature. Geriatric jaywalkers at least made a change from falling coal or vehicles which had lost the will to live.

Speaking of the will to live the figure before Ted didn't seem overly imbued with this suddenly scarce commodity. She wasn't so much jay walking as jay-sitting-in-the-middle-of-the-road-hunched-over-a-bowl-of-muddy-water-muttering-something-about-sheep. In light of his recent encounters with the supernatural Ted approached the heavily shawled figure cautiously.

'Shift your scrawny ass old woman!' He poked her with an immaculately polished cowboy boot. 'Ain't you heard the Good News? Me and my men are on a mission from God – and we're gonna save your immortal soul whether you like it or not.'

The frail figure looked up with a cheeky glint in her piercing eyes. 'That's strange, I don't recall your boss telling you to go chasing after Michael Nostrus. They may not have seen eye-to-eye over the years but Nostrus is basically a decent chap, and certainly not one of the enemy you'll soon have to face.'

'What in the name of howdy-doody do you know about Nostrus? You one of his cronies are ya?'

The small old lady gave a gap-toothed grin.

'Listen little boy, hubble-bubble-toil-and-trouble never was quite my scene – can't stand the smell of burnt bat's wing for starters. I may go round in a gang of three but that don't mean I'm some refugee from Central Casting's Crone'U'Like.'

Not surprisingly Ted looked bewildered. 'Well in that case would you mind telling me who you are, what you're prattling about, and why you're blocking my way?'

A far away look came over the old woman's eyes, a manoeuvre she had practised for hours in private and was now very good at. With a theatrical flourish she began to sway back and forth, humming under her breath in a minor key. 'In answer to your question I've borne many names over the years, though the one I'm known by round these parts is Old Mad Megan. As regards Michael Nostrus, just how extensive an answer do you require? A life that long deserves the full treatment.'

Ted looked suspicious but this mad old biddy did seem to have her ear to the ground. Perhaps she could be squeezed for useful information. 'All I want to know,' said Ted hunkering down to face her, 'is if that son-of-a-gun Nostrus is holed up in that there valley? If he is, just leave the rest to us. I'm gonna have me a good-ole'fashioned lynchin!'

The ancient hag cackled merrily for a moment, sounding rather like a mortuary's rustiest door-hinge on the stroke of midnight. Almost despite herself Megan began to feel her persona conforming to Ted's expectations. With gay abandon she resolved to ham it up to the best of her considerable abilities.

'Aye, if truth be told Nostrus is hiding down there at The Place Of Reckoning. Though he's only just realized what he's let himself in for. But by the looks of things you ain't even done that yet. Take Old Mad Megan's advice and turn back now before ye meets yer maker in more ways than one. Ain't nothing down in Noddegamra Valley this day but death and destruction for all who enter! Turn baaaack, turn baaaack!'

Anger flared across Ted's face. 'Listen up witch. The only death and destruction today will be dealt by us – and Nostrus is first in a long queue. So as regards your bonny butt – move it or lose it bitch, before I have you burnt alive for hindering an agent of heaven as he goes about his lawful business.'

'Very well,' said Megan with a philosophic display of her aged parchment palms, suddenly seeming far less the stereo-typed crone. 'I would have been failing in my duty if I hadn't warned you of the dangers. But as long as you proceed of your own free will I'm absolved of blame. Now, if you'd be so kind as to proceed towards the shrubbery behind me the Commander in Chief of your team will give you your final briefing. I'd say good luck but I wouldn't mean it – so piss off and I hope you die in pain.'

Ted was about to respond in like manner when the words slipped from his lips like yesterday's calimari down the U-bend. From behind a small thorn bush (which showed no signs whatsoever of bursting into flame) stepped a figure straight out of Ted's tortured, hormone-drenched adolescence. Zombie-like the big man took an involuntary step towards this new arrival. 'Oh my God!' he gasped, falling to his knees in awe.

'Well gee Yogi, I'm glad you recognize me,' said the glowing likeness of Boo Boo bear, standing just three feet before the trembling preacher. He proceeded to pick a startled grasshopper from one fluffy little ear and began to munch on it happily.

For a blinding instant Ted was transported twenty years and half a world away to Dwayne's living-room couch. His mouth moved but no sound came out.

'Don't get yourself all worked up on my account,' said Boo Boo, straightening his small green bow tie. 'Yogi old pal, there's something I'd very much like you to do for me.'

With some difficulty Ted managed to get his struggling voice box into gear. 'Tell me Lord . . . thy will be done. I am your humble slave.'

From the doorway of the front coach Casper looked on with some concern as his boss continued to converse with an empty bush. Shortly the Reverend Harvey Banger appeared at his shoulder.

'Who's he speaking to now? Maybe we should cut our losses and leave him to it.'

Disgust flashed in the PA's eyes. 'That's treasonous talk boy! Watch your mouth or it'll be latrine duty for you. Just remember what that great man's done for us. Get back on board and check your weapons, you'll need them soon enough.'

Back at the roadside Boo Boo sighed heavily, as was his habit, and began to inspect the claws of his left forepaw. After absentmindedly cleaning out a cocktail of soil, grass and small wriggling things the bear fixed Ted in the eye and continued in his dull monotone. 'I need your help Yogi old friend. Down in the valley the Forces of Darkness are gathering under the command of the foulest heathen ever to walk my clean Earth.'

Ted rose to his feet, the fanatical pride shining from his face threatening to eclipse the hazy scarlet sun. 'I'm already on my way Lord. We'll kick some holy ass for you this day!'

THIRTEEN

> And the Kings of Earth and the top-ranking ones hid themselves in caves and the rock masses of mountains.
> *Revelations 6:15*

Two Tribes

Despite Ted Trundell's headlong dash to get there on time, Armageddon had the temerity to start without him. The niceties of social etiquette were not generally respected by those taking part. Blabberghast, the crimson-horned cutlass carrier of the ancient Nemorian nether-gods was not known for his good manners. Lip service to the social graces were paid by none, not even Lip-Lap Limpoom the last of the floppy-lipped Leprechaun Kings of perpetually licked Lemuria – and he had plenty to spare. On the heavenly side things were no better. The only creature a self respecting Assault Angel hated more than a Demon Prince was any sort of human being. Discovering they had to follow one into battle had gone down about as well as a rusty scalpel at a ceremonial circumcision. To put it as bluntly as this hypothetical blade, the angels were more than a little pissed off.

There was no time for dissension in the ranks, however. As the two great armies drew themselves up across the narrow valley they glowered at each other with unconcealed contempt. On both sides strange supernatural bodies jostled for position in the coming charge. But before it could begin there was one custom which had to be observed.

Towards the middle of the large field that separated the quivering hordes strode two very different figures. In fact one ambled disjointedly, seemingly engaged in the latest round of an ongoing personal battle with his limbs, while the other fluttered gracefully, his gold spray-painted combat boots a good six inches from the turf.

Field-Marshal Archangel Gabriel and Brigadier-General Beelzebub (Lord of the Flies) came face to face with a low growl and a frenzied insectoid clicking.

'Are you ready for kick-off?' asked Gabriel sternly, his camouflaged face contorted into a grimace of spite.

'My master relishes the fray,' Beelzebub spat back, chambering a 40mm round into his garishly painted grenade-launcher.

'Errrr . . . good,' countered Gabriel, unsure for a second of what was meant to be said next. 'Because even if you weren't, in five minutes me and my boys are gonna come from over that there hill and kick your satanic arses back to Hell. When we've finished with you the worms won't even have to chew!'

'Haaaaa!' cackled Beelzebub. 'That's rich, because in two minutes me and my demon horde are going to come steaming up *that* hill to ram your self-righteous rectums so far up themselves you'll be able to taste your own moralizing shit. We'll be eating angel cake till the end of time – about half-past four by my best estimate.'

Gabriel seemed ready to respond but, perhaps realizing there'd be time for personal vendettas later, held himself in check with monumental restraint. With a look in his eyes as if to say, 'You may have just spilt my pint, which under normal circumstances brings instant death, but this time it simply means I'll be waiting outside with my mate Damage', Gabriel turned and fluttered away.

Beelzebub chuckled to himself merrily at this minor victory, but quickly shut up as the first sniper rounds began to impact around him. With his scorpion tail clutched between his multi-jointed legs, the Duke of Hell scuttled back to his own lines.

Now they were ready to begin. From behind Heaven's hill a vast disembodied voice, which bore surprisingly little relation to that of Boo Boo bear, boomed out, 'Do you agree to abide by this decision?'

On a broad ridge cutting across Satan's army, a bright red Cadillac had drawn up. Go-faster flames were stencilled on the sides and two enormous speakers hung from the bonnet. Nick's voice echoed metallically in ear-splitting stereo. 'You bet old timer! When I've got your job, I think I'll move upstairs.'

'Pride comes before complete humiliation boy, but we'll soon see. Let battle commence.'

'With bloody bells on!' screamed the speakers amid a deafening whine of feedback.

That was all it took. Amongst a heroic blaring of trumpets on the one side and an infernal banging of Percussion Imps on the other the two armies charged, shortly to collide with a sickening splat.

Despite the plethora of advanced weaponry on show it began as a hand-to-hand affair. Generally speaking, sitting in a foxhole pressing a small red button marked PRESS TO KILL is not half as satisfying as ramming a .45 down your enemy's throat and screaming '*Die Satanist scum.*'

They were all there, just about every loopy deity ever consciously conceived by man, and quite a few that weren't. Thus the heavenly ranks were swelled by such ferocious fighters as the Tax-Free Tooth Fairy and the Sexual Guilt Pixie. Next to them lumbered none other than the Forgotten Birthday Phantom. In addition to these worthy warriors, from the right flank of the Forces of Light, strode the Asgard gods. The previous day a pristine convoy of Volvos had marked their arrival at Ragnarok. Odin and the boys were taking a well-earned break from their hectic schedule of specialist video shooting and threw themselves into the fray with reckless abandon. Any mortal who'd ever seen the seminal classic *Byørn ønd Benny a Bøng Bøng* would know that what set Thor apart from mortal men wasn't just the size of his hammer.

Meanwhile, from the opposite direction, rushed, dribbled and bounced a multiplicity of demons of all shapes and sizes. Dagon Shamroth, Lord of Dragons led his host to battle tearing great swathes through the heavenly throng. Gryth Jrff-Lymon, King of the Pancake People, flopped his way into the fray absorbing enemies like giant sultanas into his infernal batter mix.

From Hell's opposite flank thundered six fearsome riders. Out of their dark-hooded cowls, bone-white skulls leered. The light of piercing red eyes was reflected in the well-polished blades of scythes wielded high in scrawny wrists. These figures rode strange supernatural steeds which, while looking like they should have been recycled into kebabs aeons ago, nevertheless managed to spit green fire from every orifice. Bernard(PLAGUE), Gary(PESTILENCE), Frank(FAMINE) and Dave(WAR) were the four old hands and held well-established briefs. Trevor, a junior member, was less well versed. He wore a pin-stripped suit and carried a circa 1987 mobile phone in place of the normally *de rigueur* farmyard utensil. From his saddlehorn hung a worn briefcase. Across it, in burning red letters six inches high, smouldered the words SELF-ASSESSMENT FORMS.

In the thick of things the Lesser-Known Saints were already taking a pasting. A special crack troop of Motorway Service Personnel had set about them with fury and were quickly reassembling the canonized cannon-fodder into fluffy key pendants. The screams of, amongst others, Saint Dolby the Overfiltered were lost amidst the deafening clamour of steel on breaking bone. Within minutes the saints had ceased to be an effective fighting force – if indeed they ever were.

Watching impassively on top of Hell's hill stood Young Nick. Against the advice of his generals the Prince of Darkness had disembarked from his Command APC to survey the battle through a pair of thermal-imaging goggles. His chief lieutenants crowded about him, each hanging on his every word for some sign that they might be allowed to descend into the fray.

Suddenly Nick perked up, perhaps spotting something that sparked his fancy. 'Go on, my son!' he cheered. In the distance Baron von Smallsword led his elite Teutonic Titans through the remnants of a regiment of bewildered Anabaptists. Though it was still early days, the battle was clearly going Nick's way. After some intimidatory prompting from their CO the group of dour demons round about him broke into song. A diverse array of supernatural voices sprang haltingly into the air, quickly rising in confidence as they realized today might be their day after all. The group jabbed their talons in the air in time to the words, gesturing arrogantly in the general direction of the dismayed Heaven HQ.

'Iiiit's all gone quiet over there! (Over there). Yes, it's all gone quiet over there . . .'

Hell's Kitchen

Meanwhile, off in a quiet meadow well away from the main battle, a fiendish ambush was currently in preparation. But any military tactician who happened to be passing could have been forgiven for failing to recognize the situation for the foul trap that it was. In fact this ambush looked far more like a sophisticated French restaurant than it did a cunning tactical ploy – just without the walls and ceilings that establishments of this nature usually possessed. But what it lacked in architectural trappings this gallic gastrodome more than made up for in its reverence to the al fresco ideal.

In the middle of the peaceful field stood a long antique dining table holding place settings for twelve guests. A huge candelabra made up the centrepiece of the display, the candle flames unnervingly still despite the brisk breeze. Along the table's length crystal vases holding rare jungle orchids glinted beneath the scarlet sky. In what would have been a corner had this set-up been indoors, a potted plant twitched in a suspicious manner. The only other clue that all was not as it should be were the spikes protruding from several bushes around the meadow. Even so, the trap was a good one. It would have taken an eagle-eyed observer with the brain of Hercule Poirot and the occult knowledge of Dennis Wheatley's nanny's cat to recognize the situation for what it was.

Standing by the side of the table, an immaculately dinner-jacketed figure straightened a spotless white serviette over his hooked forearm. The waiter's upper lip held an obviously pencilled-in curly moustache, just as his black shoes held the highest shine since Aladdin's teapot shortly after he'd used up his last wish. The *maitre d'* stood perfectly still, not even tapping his feet to the sounds of the Strasbourg Philharmonic playing the hits of Jean-Michel Jarre over the restaurant's non-existent stereo. This low-key muzak seemed to seep up from the very grass beneath his feet.

Shortly, the peaceful Arcadian scene was shattered by the thundering of horses hooves. With a tremendous clatter of steel-on-steel and more naying than the House of Commons debating an MPs' pay freeze, Arthur and his Knights of the Rotund Table arrived from over the hill.

'Sire,' called Sir Gwalchafad eagerly, 'a strange feast is lain before us!'

'I have eyes,' the king snapped, struggling to put away his sword and pull out his copy of *The Good Food Guide AD407*.

The word 'feast' has a strange Pavlovian effect on any heavily armoured knights who happen to hear it. Throughout history doughty feudal warriors have only had to see a stuffed pig for their jowls to open and their defences to come down faster than a maiden's knickers. Arthur's knights were no exception.

Having seen this sort of thing all too often Arthur sighed wearily and bowed to the inevitable. Now he came to think of it he was more than a little peckish himself. Nothing quite gave you an appetite like lying on a cold stone slab for fifteen centuries, he thought to himself, as he thumbed through the guide's Welsh entry. But try as he might the great king couldn't seem to find anything about this strange outdoor eatery. Must be a new establishment, he reasoned with all the naïveté of a turkey making out a Christmas list.

With more than a dash of relish, not to mention a blob of mayonnaise and a generous helping of tartar sauce, Arthur raised his enchanted Diners' Card and gave his famous battle cry. 'Okay boys, let's get stuck in.'

Despite the all too apparent temptations, Sir Gwalchafad looked a trifle alarmed. 'Sire, I council caution in this matter. Our orders were to perform an armed reconnaissance of this sector, not to unhorse and consume a three-course meal. I fear this to be a foul trap set by the Forces of Darkness!'

But his concerns were to no avail. No sooner had Gwal finished his warning than Arthur was down from his horse and tucking a peach-coloured napkin into his armoured breastplate. 'For God's sake don't be such a wet blanket man!' the king reprimanded. 'Get off that horse and have something to eat. We won't be missed for ten minutes, will we?'

But despite express orders the young knight stayed put. Gwalchafad's horse pranced back and forth nervously as its master eyed the trees around the clearing with suspicion.

Meanwhile, Arthur and the others sauntered towards their seats to be greeted by their affable host.

'Good day to you, Messieurs,' said the waiter with a low bow and a dainty flourish. 'May I welcome you to our 'umble abode. My name iz Jean-Paul and I will be disposing of you today. A table for twelve I thinks, non?'

'Eleven actually,' corrected Arthur, eyeing the still-mounted Gwalchafad with disgust. 'There is just one small point. I don't want to be a pain or anything . . . but . . .'

'Go on Monsieur, your whiz iz my command.'

'You don't have anything . . . slightly rounder do you? I wouldn't normally ask, but it's tradition, you know?'

Jean-Paul looked apologetic as he gave a genuine gallic shrug. 'I am zo zorry zir, but az you can zee we are very busy today.' With a white-gloved hand their host motioned to the field before them.

'Er – right you are,' said Arthur, looking out across nothing but mist-shrouded grass yet not wanting to seem foolish in front of a foreigner. 'I suppose it'll have to do then, won't it. Could I possibly see the wine list?'

At this point their host disappeared behind a nearby bush which rustled busily for several seconds. In the meantime all eleven ravenous knights seated themselves round the plush table, with gluttony in their hearts and greed in their bulging eyes. Serviettes were tucked into armoured collars and cutlery grasped eagerly in gauntleted hands. Just when they were on the point of banging their armoured fists on the table with impatience, Jean-Paul reappeared with the menus and began to pass them round.

'Excuse me garçon!' Sir Bedwyr called with all the urbanity of a Sea Lion. 'I don't understand these prices. They all seem to be marked with little skulls and daggers?'

'Oooh Monsieur, do not be worrying yourself about ze bill. Such honoured guests az yourselves will not be paying zem pricez! I am sure we can be coming to some ozer arrange-mon.'

'I must say, that's very kind of you,' said Sir Cai. 'I had heard that you Frenchies were the sort of chaps more likely to shit in a blind beggar's cap than give him a shiny new farthing. Ummm . . . I'll have the smoked salmon mousse.'

Five minutes later the armoured diners were heartily tucking into a sumptuous feast. An armada of small hunch-backed waiters had appeared from nowhere and produced the orders one by one. The gnome-like figures would disappear behind the large bush that seemed to double as a kitchen, then return with a dish of daintily crafted delight. Each guest agreed it was the finest food they'd ever tasted. Palates more used to roast-boar soup followed by roast-boar joint with roast-boar trifle to finish were exposed to the higher reaches of culinary creativity.

The wine flowed just as freely, and pretty soon the 'Thomas-à-Beckett'[1] of armoured men were well on their way to a state of inebriation, far past the town of tipsiness and too far gone along the boulevard of blowing your guts up over your own shoes to care. As with all gatherings of this sort, one closet opera lover decided a little live music might be in order. Sir Bors tottered to his feet to lead the singing. 'Ooooow! Fooooour and twenty virgins came down from Caerleon-on-Usk . . .'

But the mood of light-hearted frivolity was not to last. Sir Gawain was the catalyst for the inevitable. 'Waiter, waiter! There appears to be something moving in my soubei. Fetch the manager at once!' But before there was time to react the old warrior had more to worry about than an overactive pudding. From beneath the folds of the billowing tablecloth between his legs, three feet of carbon steel appeared gripped by two grubby hands. Sir

---

1 Diligent scholastic research has revealed this to be the correct collective noun for a group of heavily armed and heavily drunk knights of the realm.

Gawain's next comment was cut short, as a yard of specially sharpened spike was thrust upwards through his exposed crotch-hinge, pinning him to his chair in the process.

Sir Bors, who had just broken into a rendition of *My Way* which, had he heard it, would have prompted Frank Sinatra to send round some of his Sicilian mates, looked down at his colleague in disbelief. Opening his great beard-framed mouth the huge knight cried, 'What the . . . Errrrgggg!' As yet another deadly weapon found its mark.

Thus began the later infamous Unexpectedly Pointy Steel Enema Party. None had noticed the cowled figures that crept out of the surrounding undergrowth, nor seen the potted plant hop towards its intended victim. All around the table monks went about their work with speed and efficiency. Where armour-plate intervened, a cunningly wielded can-opener did the trick. They worked in teams, delicate flesh exposed by one section as the other stood by spike at the ready. Within seconds the monks had achieved what the combined armies of the Anglo-Saxon SS had failed to do. Arthur's heroic knights were systematically cut to pieces.

But as so often in the past, the king himself proved trickier to deal with. The monk assigned to knocking off Britain's finest champion made one crucial mistake. Pausing momentarily to admire his own handiwork on Arthur's plate, he bent over to rearrange a crooked asparagus spear. This fraction of a second delay was all his prey needed. With a roar of pure rage the old war-horse jumped to his feet and plunged headfirst into the fray. Almost of its own accord Excalibur sprang from its scabbard, going about its grim duty with cat-like grace.

Arthur's erstwhile assassin had stuffed his last mush-room.

Before he had time to rally his men, Arthur realized with dismay that he had no men. This did nothing but spur him on to new levels of fury. The king proceeded to lay about himself with unbridled ferocity. Arthur had heard it said that an ability to inflict wanton slaughter was just like riding a bike – once you'd learnt, you never forgot. Evidently, after fifteen centuries this still held true. As he hacked and chopped, stabbed and slashed, Arthur felt like he'd never been away. Steadily he worked his way through a seething mound of semi-human flesh.

But in the long run the king's position was hopeless. The sheer weight of monks throwing themselves at his steel-clad body threatened to take the great man down. Just when it looked like he'd felled his last opponent, salvation appeared from an unexpected quarter. Suddenly, a great thundering of hooves cut across the wet *thunk* and *splat* of battle.

Sir Gwalchafad charged from the trees, flashing sword in hand. The young knight had watched as his companions went down one by one. He himself had been set upon by the monks' foraging unit – a handful of novice cooks armed with roast potatoes and specially sharpened courgettes. Having fought them off with little difficulty, Sir Gwal now came rushing to his liege's aid. As he came flying past, he unceremoniously scooped the king up and onto his trusty steed.

'Ten good men down, Sir Gwal. But my, that asparagus was good,' King Arthur sighed as they rode out of trouble.

The Tide Turns

Back at the main battle things were not going entirely Hell's way. To start with a pair of Major Flame Fiends, who had been limbering up for the final push, had exploded when their swollen belly sacks flopped down too close to a sparking-up Lightning Lord. The detonation that ensued had been quite extensive, showering a cocktail of armoured body parts over vast swathes of the Hades' legion. But so numerous were the Dark Forces that even these terrible losses could have been sustained if, at that very moment, a half-mile wide chasm hadn't opened up beneath their cloven feet. The sheer weight of the advance now worked against them. Rank upon rank of infantry ploughed headlong into the hole, unable to stop due to the swollen surge of their brethren behind them. When some semblance of order had been regained by Nick's fuming generals the causes behind this disaster became clear. It seemed that, bereft of leadership, BAS's subterranean worm-warriors had dug in completely the wrong direction.

Then, just when it seemed Beelzebub's forces might rescue the situation, the hammer blow had fallen. To the half-heard sound of a US cavalry bugle Ted Trundell and his Church of the Eloquent Announcement came storming over the hill.

What they lacked in numbers Ted's men more than made up for in gut belief. They were determined to prove that the mayhem at the theme park had been caused by extreme elements of surprise. This time they were going to let their professionalism shine. Hours of squad training and tiring weapons drill in the barren Texas wilderness now paid off in the only fight that mattered. Where their commander told them to go, they went. When he told them to charge, they charged. But most of all Ted Trundell screamed at them to lay down a withering suppressive fire with their battery of lavish guns.

It wasn't so much that Ted's equipment was that much better than the rest of the heavenly arsenal. His troops just knew exactly what their equipment could do – and they did it again, and again, and again, until the muzzles of their rifles glowed as red as the eyes of the demons they downed. A squadron of Giant Bat Bombers, who had harried the Forces of Light all day, were made short work of with shoulder-launched surface-to-air missiles. Everywhere he happened to look, Ted's men were making breakthroughs into enemy lines.

Not wanting to be outdone by mere mortals, General Gabriel and his crack guard of Assault Angels changed tactics. Until now, Heaven's elitest unit had relied on traditional weaponry – swords, maces, and flintlocks and the like, with arrogance and a sense of tradition winning out over kill-efficiency. But fear of being left behind in the carnage stakes prompted the Archangel to grudgingly give the order to cut loose. Almost as one a veritable armoury of anti-tank mines and flame-throwers were pulled from beneath fluttering robes.

As if this wasn't enough Young Nick's men had yet another revitalized enemy with which to contend. Through the rear of their ranks two armoured figures charged on a single horse, spreading panic and confusion in their wake. After escaping the ambush and mopping up the remaining monks, Arthur and Gwalchafad had set about avenging their fallen comrades with their usual boyish glee. Over the din of battle the king could be clearly heard to cry, 'For God and Albion. Fillet a demon todaaaaay!'

Floating In The Air

Young Nick's long fingers tightened menacingly around the panicking Messenger Imp's scrawny neck, causing beads of acidic sweat to break out on its ashen brow. As the unfortunate creature fought for breath in the Cadillac's stale air, the Prince of Hell rasped through ground-down fangs, 'Make it quick or I'll promote you to my second in command – which if we lose this fight won't make you too popular with the other side. Catch my drift?'

The imp forced a gulp past Nick's knuckles and stammered. 'I'm afraid it's bad news Your Highness. Our forces give ground on every side; whole units desert by the second. If this goes on much longer we're . . . we're . . .'

Nick looked sore, and not merely due to the rough ride

they were getting as the vehicle traversed the cratered ground. 'Do not analyse. Do not elaborate. Just tell me the facts.'

The imp's eyes bulged sickeningly. Unfortunately, the creature's very nature inevitably worked against it. Messenger Imps were notorious blabbermouths, never using one word when a party political broadcast would do. And like the rest of his kin, this one didn't seem to know when to stop.

'But Dread Lord, if we were to be defeat . . . forced to tactically withdraw, what would become of us? If we let *them* win we're as good as dead!'

A sly look slipped over Nick's satanic face. 'Never fear my little one. There'll be no tactical withdrawals from this battle. The only withdrawal I'll be making will be my enemy's beating heart from his shattered chest. We've one last chance, for I have a plan.'

'A plan!' gasped the imp hopefully. 'Pray tell Great Master, what does it involve?'

Nick looked supremely pleased with himself. 'Being the skilful strategist that I am . . .' he glared at the imp until it had the sense to nod vigorously, '. . . I took it upon myself to maintain a tactical reserve. An ace up the sleeve like you'd never believe. In the boot of this car I have stashed a small nuclear device of the sort the man-things have lately been so fond of producing. All it needs is about four tonnes of extra ballast to make it aerodynamically stable when we fire it through the air. It may not help us win but it'll sure as hell guarantee we don't lose alone. And because that's classified information, I'm afraid I'm now going to have to kill you.'

Nick drew back his scaly fist ready to puree his loud-mouthed lieutenant. But the punch never landed. Just before the moment of impact, the vehicle lurched heavily to the right sending Nick and his target sprawling to the floor.

Momentarily forgotten, the imp crawled into a corner and concentrated on looking very small indeed. Meanwhile, Nick clambered out of his car and found his bemused driver peering down at the wide trench that had completely swallowed the vehicle's right wheel.

Nick gazed gingerly into its stygian depths. From the sandbags and ammunition boxes scattered around it seemed to be some sort of fox-hole. A movement caught his eye. Then a feeble whining caught his ear. A pitiful voice rose from the chasm.

'Please don't kill us, we both surrender! Don't we Ruby?'

A second voice, insectoid in intonation, buzzed up from the opposite corner. 'What do you mean "surrender"? I'll have you know I've always been a God-fearing churchgoer!'

If Nick had been mad before now he was as ballistic as his missile. 'I DO NOT BELIEVE THIS! You pair manage to get in the way while hiding in a hole! Even the most incompetent ignoramuses can be successful cowards – but not you! Get out before I come in and get you.'

Shortly Nick was joined by the two downcast demons. Guttlehog was the first to speak. 'I'm sorry master. When the shooting started we just wanted to get out of the way. Please be merciful.'

'Mercy?' he bellowed. 'I don't know how to spell the word. I've had just about as much as I can take of you two. You're a disgrace to demonkind!'

As one might swat a fly, Nick extended a talon to consign them both to oblivion. But then suddenly his smouldering eyes ignited. 'Wait a minute. Why kill two birds with one stone when you can wipe out an entire flock? I've just found myself some volunteers!'

Short minutes later Guttlehog and Rubicante sat strapped to a small thermo-nuclear warhead whilst sitting in the vast launch bucket of Hell's sole remaining long-range catapult. Next to it stood Young Nick, his taloned hand wrapped around the firing lever and his gleeful eyes cast upon his newly press-ganged warhead.

'Take it easy lads. You have my personal assurance that neither of you will ever hit the ground. My word of honour on that point – no questions asked.'

Rubicante looked up hopefully. 'You mean it? We're to be saved!'

Nick smirked. 'No. You won't hit the ground because I've set the bomb's automatic detonation height to one hundred feet. The blast will obliterate you long before any impact has a say in the matter.'

The Prince of Hell barely paused as the captive's faces sank once more. 'And remember boys, it's a far, far better thing you do today than you've probably ever done before. Something to console yourselves with as you face your zero hour. Are you ready?'

Guttlehog was blinking furiously. 'Now you mention it I do seem to have a small speck of dust in my eye. If you could just . . .'

Nick smiled. 'Chocks away!'

Twang.

As they tumbled through the sky Guttlehog clung frantically to his comrade's carapace. The Boar Demon had to shout to be heard above the whistling air. 'Well, this is it old chum. Not even time to say goodbye.'

Rubicante had to fight back the tears as he looked over his spiny shoulder. 'I've always meant to tell you, how much I really do lu . . .' Overcome with emotion he turned his giant insectoid head and tightly shut his many eyes.

As so often at moments of high stress, one minor detail assumed immense proportions in the mouldy bag of banana-flavoured blancmange that passed for Guttlehog's brain. There was a notice printed on the bomb about two inches from the Boar Demon's snout. If only to pass the time, he started to read:

Thank you for purchasing another quality product from the **WEAPONS4U** Summer range. If you're not entirely satisfied with the performance of this bomb, please return it for a full refund to the address below.

WEAPONS4U Plc.
PO BOX 666
ROCKALL

For our latest catalogue please include $US1, or alternatively your firstborn sons for the next seven generations (who will make a valuable contribution to our extensive research programme). This guarantee in no way affects your statutory rights.

Instructions and suggestions for the operation of your FIRE CRACKER232 Low-Yield Thermonuclear Device:

* Place in a well-ventilated upright position.

* Light the blue touch paper and retire briskly to a safe distance.

* Duck.

* If for any reason the device fails to detonate, do not under any circumstances approach the warhead. Stay put or go and do something else. It will go off in its own good time.

* As ignition commences, astonish your friends and confound your enemies. Sure to liven up even the dullest party. NB: This model is not suitable for milkbottle launch.

* No need to hang around for those lengthy decontamination periods! This bomb's ultra-low radiation discharge ensures you'll be safely dancing in the crater before you can say: 'Mutually Assured Destruction.'

Guttlehog looked away from the sign, and noticed that the ground was above his head. He thought now might be a good time to faint.

At Heaven HQ, the missile was spotted too late. A brief spluttering of woefully inaccurate ack-ack was all they could muster. Most of Heaven's top brass looked on in horror as their doom fell towards them, flailing its arms and sobbing uncontrollably as it did so.

At the predetermined altitude there was a blinding flash, a shockwave of heat, and then utter, utter stillness.

Market Square Heroes

The village of Noddegamra lay in smoking ruins. Steam rose from a sad collection of foetid pools that were all that was left of the duck pond. Nearby, a sad collection of charred beaks were all that was left of the ducks.

Nothing moved, apart from a lonely tumbleweed that blew dejectedly across the main street's blistered asphalt. The confused piece of vegetation bumped forlornly into a concertina post-box, perhaps wondering what it was doing in an atomized Welsh village and not happily bouncing across the prairie in front of Clint Eastwood's horse.

At first sight, it looked like there was no one left. But in the dingy, well-stocked cellar of The Screaming Sword the best part of the town's population cowered in confusion and fear. To tell the truth, the cellar was no longer as well stocked as it had been that morning, and for the most part the townsfolk didn't so much cower as loll dejectedly.

'The thing ish,' spluttered Emmyr, prodding at Dick Richards' heroically stained shirt, 'life – what'sh it . . . for? You tell me that. End of the world? My arse! Not when Hywell's still got some Gut Rot left it ain't.'

Through eyes like two piss-holes in the snow, Dick peered at his old friend and steadied himself in his chair. For one potential-filled moment the old farmer seemed ready to speak, then began to snore loudly instead.

Emmyr merely took this as confirmation that his point had been a good one and well made. He settled back in his seat contentedly. Now that he came to think about it, he could do with a little rest himself. It *had* been a strenuous day.

Since Dick's disastrous trip up to Caer-Mathonwy that morning, in his capacity as Noddegamra's Civil Defence Officer, things had gone catastrophically wrong.

At first, Dick's insane babblings had been met with scorn. None had time for the prophet of doom as he'd raced from door to door feverishly telling of what he'd seen. His stories of ferocious demons roaming the hillsides and illegally parked juggernauts driven by French New Age Travellers had seemed a bit crap even by Dick's standards. But when the first units of goblin skirmishers had come charging down the main road wielding their swords and screaming at the tops of their infernal voices, even Noddegamra's most sceptical inhabitants had had to admit Dick might be on to something.

As the first shells began to fly, a hastily convened town meeting had decided the basement of Hywell's pub afforded the best means of protection. It had been quite a squeeze, but under the circumstances there were few complaints. Especially after they had found solace from the one source of comfort that was readily to hand.

It certainly did the trick, taking their collective minds off their homes being reduced to rubble not twenty feet above their heads. In no time at all the steel-nerved villagers had passed through all the usual stages, starting with a bout of cheery singing to raise their spirits, followed by a period where everyone argued in loud voices about what 'the authorities' should do to remedy the situation. Those not already passed out were sitting around morosely pondering their and humanity's fate.

All except for Gwylym. 'Can't you see, this just proves my point!' he hissed, waving a half-eaten tin of corned beef wildly in the air. 'They just want us to think it's the Apocalypse – it's all part of the master plan to con us out of our racial inheritance. Ethnic cleansing . . . It's how it started in Bosnia.'

Hywell removed a stray chunk of corned beef from his immense beard and looked doubtful. The pub's landlord was less inebriated than many of his neighbours, mainly since he had no desire to drink away yet more of his profits, but also because he had a sneaking suspicion a clear head might yet be required.

'Just who exactly do you mean by "they"?' he asked, giving Gwylym a dangerous look.

'MI5, *obviously!* You don't really believe in ghosts do you? All those things running around outside are imperial agents in Halloween outfits – even the goblins.'

At his side, stood Gwylym's second-in-command, concentration creasing his well sloped forehead.

'But . . . how did they get inside those costumes? Some of the ones I saw couldn't have been more than three feet tall.'

Gwylym looked at his lieutenant sharply. '"They" . . . must be . . . using midgets,' he said with all the dignity he could muster, then, warming to the theme, elaborated: 'They've rounded up every dwarf from every circus in Europe to create a goblin effect!'

'What a load of old bollocks!' This from Crystal, who threw her raven-haired head back and laughed at the top of her well-padded lungs. When her air-raid siren of a voice had died away she swept the room with an intense gaze, and said: 'That old hag Megan was right all along. This is *the end.* We're all going to die!' She paused, and for a second it seemed as though bitter tears were welling in her eyes. She crushed them back with a growl of frustration. 'Men! It's all down to bloody men! The sooner this putrid male-dominated society is swept away by the fresh winds of change the sooner Mother Nature can start rebuilding things as they should have been all along. When She's wiped out the last pathetic snivelling male She'll create an Arcadian paradise here on earth for all her daughters.

You boys had your chance and you cocked it up!'

Hywell turned to his wife in amazement and muttered, 'I've been married to you for twenty years and I can't remember any male domination going on.'

'That's because you're the one that proves the rule.'

Suddenly, the cellar was rocked by a vast rolling detonation. Dust and startled earthworms cascaded from the ceiling.

Ivan was more than willing to accept Crystal's less than optimistic prediction. 'She's right! That bang was *them* breaking down the outer doors. If we don't get out now we're all doomed. Run for the hills! Run for the hills I say!'

'We're already in the bloody hills, idiot,' snarled Gwylym.

Then the aftershocks came, a series of ructions that seemed to carry on indefinitely throwing to the floor everyone who wasn't already prone, and anybody who was trying to get up again. Taking advantage of the confusion, Gwylym flung the remains of his corned beef aside to produce a weedy looking air pistol.

'Right – stop that screaming! I've had enough of this divisive bickering. I'm declaring martial law in the name of the newly formed Welsh Republic.'

Hywell glanced up from the spot where, his hands over his head, he was trying to be very flat indeed. 'Newly formed? Since when?'

Gwylym looked down in annoyance. 'Since I just said so. Anyone who panics is a traitor, liable to be shot without warning, so I suggest you all stop your whining and do exactly as I say.'

Crystal scoffed. 'If in doubt, shoot it. Don't you think there's been enough of that going on outside? You won't solve any of this with a gun.'

Gwylym was about to raise his voice a notch further to contend with the clamour of battle, but then stopped, the words half formed on his lips. With a mystified expression he slowly gazed up at the oak-beamed ceiling instead. He'd stopped because there was no longer any clamour of battle to shout above. The cramped basement fell silent as everyone gazed towards the heavily barricaded cellar door.

Hywell finally put their unspoken thoughts into words. 'Maybe,' he said climbing to his feet. 'Maybe it's stopped.'

We'll All Go Together When We Go

Up at Caer-Mathonwy Farm Mike had reached much the same conclusion. As he peered through his bunker's infrared observation periscope nothing moved amidst the scene of desolation below. With a confused frown he turned to Deborah.

'That last blast must have wiped them out. I . . . I think we might have survived this thing.'

Deborah pushed past the Professor to make sure for herself. After she'd scanned each direction, and double checked just to be on the safe side, a huge grin spread across her face. 'They've done each other in and passed us over. Let's get out there and take a look around.'

A worried frown creased Mike's brow. 'I wouldn't be in such a hurry, my dear. It may seem all quiet but there's bound to be something left alive, or as near alive as it ever was in the first place.'

'What makes you say that?'

Mike sighed. 'Well, this contest calls for a clear winner, not some indecisive compromise. Every authority I've ever come across agrees on the point. A draw isn't allowed.'

From across the bunker pathetic whimperings told them that Adam and Sid were slowly regaining consciousness. They had heroically fainted in each other's arms when the first bomb had gone off.

Mike turned back to the bank of controls built into the bunker's wall. 'I have to admit I don't know what this lull represents – though the radiation level from that last bomb seems to be falling rapidly. It should be safe out there sometime soon.'

Deborah and Aristotle had made their way to the stronghold's triple thickness blast doors. 'So what are we waiting for?' Why don't Aristo and I pop out to have a look around?'

Mike held up a hand. 'When I said "safe" I meant the background radiation has fallen to an acceptable level. There could be a hundred other dangers sat down a fox-hole just waiting for you to go wandering past. I'm not letting you out until I'm certain.'

Deborah's anger flared. 'Unless I missed something back there, you're the one who bought a house on the site of Armageddon to get away from it all. I'd hardly say your instincts are infallible, would you? If there's something worse on the way, this will be our last chance to see the outside world. Ever.'

The Professor sighed wearily. He didn't like being shut up underground any more than the rest of them. His first instinct was to have a safe line of retreat worked out in advance. 'I suppose we can't stay down here, ad infinitum. But no one leaves alone. If you insist on going, we all go.'

Deborah nodded, as by her side Aristotle quivered in anticipation. Mike turned to the command console and pressed a bewildering series of buttons, then stood up and straightened himself. With a quiet hiss the door seals were released and the first traces of smoke seeped into the bunker's stale air. Silently the huge blast doors swung open, revealing a debris-littered stairwell beyond. Mike gulped. 'Okay then. Let's find out what's left.'

Bring Your Daughter To The Slaughter

Aristotle was the first out, his mission to check the immediate vicinity for signs of trouble. Soon the cat was silently slipping between the smouldering girders and blackened bricks that were all that was left of the above-ground sections of Mike's home. A few tense minutes after leaving the others at the mouth of the tunnel he reported back.

Nothing except yesterday's leftovers. Wait a minute. There does seem to be something alive – that's if you could call it that. Though I don't think it represents any sort of threat.

Mike's mind conveyed impatience. No riddles now Aristo, please. What exactly are you on about?

Why don't you come up and see for yourselves?

Shortly Aristotle was joined by four cautious humans. The scene that met their eyes as they emerged from the hole they'd begun to call home could best have been described as impressive – at least it could have if you were impressed by boiling red sky, smoking cratered battlefields and whimpering black rune-swords embedded point-down in what was left of your front lawn. It seemed Soul Stealer had survived his master's recent explosive demise, as well as the nuclear blast that brought the battle to a close.

'Get me out of here!' the weapon yelped as it saw them approach. 'This is most undignified. I'll never get this soil out of my hilt if you don't do something quick.'

All eyes were fixed on the sleek black lines of the ancient weapon half buried in the earth. From a distance Mike studied the devilish runes that covered Soul Stealer's dark blade. To look at them hurt your eyes, to read them hurt your brain – and that was much, much worse.

'Pleeease get me out of here.' The sword sounded like Donald Duck on helium. 'Great riches and unearthly powers to whoever claims me as their prize! I'm also very good at getting the lids off paint tins.'

The three men stood deathly still. Mike knew full well the terrible fate that befell any mortal who had the temerity to lift the Sword of Lost Souls unprotected. For their part Adam and Sid had seen what Soul Stealer could do first hand, so weren't about to offer one of theirs. Next to them, however, a strange serene expression had crept over Deborah's face. Mechanically, as if driven by some exterior force, she took one step forward.

Mike grabbed for her but he was too slow. 'Wait Deborah! You don't understand – it's suicide!'

With two more steps she was there. Slowly she reached out one slender hand and grasped Soul Stealer by its carved hilt. Then, with no apparent effort, she drew the great sword from its resting place in the humming earth. To the sound of a damp frankfurter launched from the back of a daschund, the weapon slid free.

'Ooooh yeeeaah!' moaned the sword. 'That's better. I was beginning to think . . . Wait a minute . . . you're a girly! Put me down, put me *down* at once!'

'Better believe it BIC!'

'BIC? You compare me to a safety razor?'

Deborah hefted the six-foot sword over her head. Light didn't so much glint off the weapon as limp away hurt.

'This is most improper!' the sword squeaked petulantly. 'In all my aeons of existence I've never once been wielded by a . . . a . . . a WOMAN!'

'Shut it!' Deborah commanded, stunning the sword into submission by slamming it against a nearby rock. Soul Stealer's whining voice tailed off like a slow spinning record.

Mike looked on aghast. He'd never seen such a look of single-minded determination in his young friend's eyes before. It was that same look of menace that a peaceful snowdrift possesses before turning into an avalanche. With a backhanded practice swipe that would have impressed Richard the Lionheart, Deborah turned to her companions.

'Where's your sense of adventure, boys? Let's Rock and Roll!'

With that she bounded off towards the woods, in the general direction of the slowly smoking valley floor.

FOURTEEN

Sport is war without the shooting.
George Orwell

Dazed And Confused

At the epicentre of the twisted landscape, pockmarked by craters, punctuated by charcoaled woodland and scorched by the blackened scars of battle, two scarlet points of colour peeked gingerly over the rim of a particularly mangled crater edge. Closer inspection, had there been anyone with the eyesight or inclination, would have revealed these out-crops to be horns, surmounting a small delicately formed and similarly coloured head. Between these points rested a neatly combed head of slicked back black hair. Unusually for the individual beneath, several of the hairs seemed out of place. But seeing what he'd just lived through, perhaps that wasn't so surprising.

The owner of the head raised it above the crater rim with extreme care. He had good reason to be cautious. Not long ago he'd been doing more than his fair share to add to the maiming, rending, reaving and general all round slaughter that had so recently filled the secluded valley. For the first time in his long, long life Young Nick was scared.

It was too silent. For so long the sounds of conflict had seeped through his pointed ears . . . he'd begun to accept them as the norm. Now that it had stopped, the silence was awesome.

Slowly it all began to come back. The plan hastily

formed in the racing Cadillac, the traveller's N-bomb packed snug in the boot, the unexpected reunion with his two half-wit henchmen, and their pathetic last moments sobbing in the catapult's launch bucket. And then . . . the glorious heat and chaos he'd unleashed, sprung from the very lineless hands he now stared down at in terror. Then stillness had hijacked his world – until he'd come round, dazed and confused at the bottom of a deep hole.

With a flash almost as bright as the earlier atomic blast, Nick remembered just who, and what, he was. The significance of the battle and his place in it were quick to follow. With a dawning realization that would have eclipsed the brightest sunrise, the implications of the silence sank home.

The bomb had been for his enemies who had been ascendant on the field of battle. They were gone. But he had survived. The silent shadowy powers that be had preserved him to fulfil his destiny as master of all mankind. It was almost enough to make him laugh. It *was* enough to make him laugh. So he did, throwing his horned head back, and laughing to the top of his leathery lungs.

This went on for an embarrassing length of time, but there was none present to feel ashamed on his behalf. Even if there were, thought Nick to himself mirthfully, he was now king of all he surveyed. He could have them killed for listening without permission. Hey, he could have anyone killed. He could have *himself* killed if he wanted. He considered the various methods of execution available. Cheese wire was good. Forced suicide with a rusty stapler, better. The 24-hour inside-outer best of all. And now he was free to perfect them all in this land of opportunity. He laughed again, this time in unadulterated delight.

But in mid-howl he pulled up short. For standing on

the crater rim, looking down at him with one sparkling ancient eye, stood a wizened old hag. True, Mad Megan was hardly likely to win any beauty contests – not even if they were held in a gale-force wind in a leper colony – but there was no denying the weather-beaten face held an air of ageless wisdom.

'You!' spat Nick, his euphoria evaporating like the human race. 'What are you doing here? I've won fair and square, don't try telling me I haven't. Trust an old git to shuffle along and piss on my parade.'

'Don't see any processions passing by,' Megan said mildly.

Nick ignored her. 'I suppose you've got some sort of crown you want to bestow on me. Well, get on with it whore.'

Megan gazed down with a sly smile across her mahogany face. 'Have you quite finished sonny boy, because I've only just begun.'

Nick flared. If this was the start of his eternal sojourn as King of Man then being talked down to by an unkempt crone with a severe personal hygiene problem was not a good start. He'd been aware all along of this entity's special significance, but once the fight was won she was meant to fade away into her dim geriatric dotage. Not really knowing what to say next, Nick said nothing.

Megan seemed to read his thoughts. 'So you reckoned you had it won then, did you boy? Well, at least you've got one thing right – when it's over I'll be taking a back seat. Figure I've earned my retirement. But this ain't over, oh bless me no. The fat lady ain't even gargling yet.'

Nick put his hands on his hips. 'What on Earth are you nattering about? We blew 'em away, thanks to my cunning tactical ploy. It's clear I've won. Show me the creature that disputes my power!'

As if in answer Megan gave a theatrical flourish of her

moth-eaten shawl. From behind her, out of the shifting mists of battle, two columns crawled towards them.

Peace, Love, Understanding And Football

The two rows of shuffling figures approached from opposite sides of the narrow valley. From the right, the faintly glowing forms of bedraggled Assault Angels and the bowed and beaten figures of Lesser-Known Saints. From the left, the unmistakable outlines of giant demons, followed by a straggling selection of goblins, spirits and imps – all at the rank of private. When the two groups spotted each other across the shallow gully, Young Nick held his breath in anticipation of the deadly rain of gunfire that must ensue. To his great disappointment, nothing happened. The two groups simply eyed each other warily then continued on their way with their heads hung low. There were a few muttered curses from the back of the Hell's contingent, a muted growl, but nothing to suggest the pure instinctive animosity that should have prevailed.

What was the world coming to? Where were the baying psychopaths? He wanted froth-at-the-mouth hatred, and he wasn't getting it. It was enough to make Nick's green blood run colder than it already was. With a disgusted shiver, he clambered out of the crater and bellowed: 'Call yourselves evil? I've been more scared by a wasp! We've got this bunch of Christian cross-dressers whopped. One final push and we can wipe them out! . . . Watch. And learn.'

Nick grabbed an automatic rifle from a nearby goblin sniper and cradled it in his lithe arms. With a snarl he yanked back the weapon's bolt and pointed it at the heavenly throng. He slit his eyes and pulled the trigger.

Nothing happened. Just a dry grating noise.

'No ammo boss,' said the goblin dejectedly, from down at Nick's elbow.

Nick looked fit to burst. 'No ammo! What are these?'

He held his fists aloft. 'And these?' He pawed the ground with his hooves. 'Since when has that stopped my servants going about their work? A demon's reputation used to rise or fall on the strength of his fork work. Get over there the lot of you and stick your hob-nailed boots in!'

But Nick's impassioned rallying cry had little effect. To a demon they shuffled about nervously and took great pains in studying the charred earth at their feet. One granite-jawed Earth Elemental was the only creature brave enough to speak.

'I don't know Lord,' it muttered from between teeth that could have passed for a scale model of Stonehenge, 'there doesn't seem to be much point now does there? With so few of us left we might as well come to some civilized arrangement.'

'Civilized!' screamed Nick. The word was like a razor blade in his mouth. The Prince of Hell's fist impacted on the Earth Elemental's stony body and it shattered into a million tiny pieces. The elemental's colleagues picked off the shards from their infernal persons, while Nick ranted on.

'I just cannot believe it! We stand on the brink of our greatest victory and you can't be bothered to finish the job. I mean, look at them. Have you ever seen such a sorry excuse for an army? They're so out of it they don't even have the manners to run away!'

Indeed, what was left of the heavenly contingent did not bode well for an early return of *Songs on Sunday*. They had been burned, blackened, beaten and generally buggered-about with in every way possible. The Archangel Gabriel, who had somehow survived despite his pathological efforts to the contrary, had lost all the feathers from his once proud wings. Saint Gertrude, the frolicking nun of Fulham, would never frolic again – at least not without the aid of crutches. Those not bearing the physical scars of battle had the unmistakable haunted look that came from severe battle fatigue. Like their hellish foe the angels, saints and shell-shocked church members simply shifted around, bereft of hope, bereft of leadership. Until . . .

With a howl of derision Ted Trundell pushed his way to the front rank of what was left of the Forces of Light. 'Watch your mouth, donkey legs!'

The Church of the Eloquent Announcement's glorious leader looked terrible. His face was blackened with soot, his expensive Italian suit hung off him in shreds, and the entire left side of his body seemed to have a very bad case of sunburn. But when he spoke, out the corner of his mouth as if trying hard not to move his face, his words were full of passion.

'You don't speak to my crack troops like that. So we're a little shook up at present, but you just say the word. Whenever you want to kick off again, we're ready to get this ruck back on the road. Aren't we boys?'

The response from those around him was less than enthusiastic. Only Gabriel and some of the more gung-ho Assault Angels seemed keen to carry on where they had left off.

'MARTINI!' Nick spat, squaring up to the singed preacher.

'Whata you say to me boy?'

'Any time, any place, anywhere. We'll grind you into the gutter where you belong. '

'Oh yeah? You and whose army?' demanded Ted now eyeball to eyeball with Nick.

'Over that hill I've got five hundred mounted Pogo Stick Witches that I've been holding in reserve. When I give the signal you're finished.'

'Ha!' Ted scoffed. 'What a load of steaming bullcrap. You ain't got two Fire Elementals to rub together. If it weren't for that dirty trick you pulled with the nuke we'd be on our lap of honour by now. Face it, you're beat!'

A small cough interrupted their stand-off. Perched on a

low knoll nearby, Mad Megan sat patiently watching the confrontation. In her lap, half-finished knitting momentarily rested. None had noticed her quietly settling down as Ted and Nick squared up, or paid any heed to the rhythmic clickety-clack of her needles as they danced between her fingers. When she spoke it was with a tone of pained indulgence, like a kind old nanny scolding a pair of squabbling children.

'Now, now young sirs, let's see if we can't keep the noise down shall we? Carry on like this and I might have to insist you take your afternoon naps early today. When you two get tired you don't half come over all grizzly.'

'Ahhh, do you mind?' Nick said. 'We're having an adult tête-à-tête here. Future destiny of mankind and all that!'

Megan looked theatrically taken aback. 'I'm sorry young-fellow-me-jim, but it sounded just now like a couple of kiddies bawling over whose ball it was . . . Wait a second, that gives me an idea . . .'

Ooooh Aaaar Avatar

It wasn't a perfect solution but it would have to do. Finding something to use as the ball had been the tricky part, but then few had come prepared for a day at the beach. Despite the Chamber of Commerce's best efforts, there didn't seem to be any unmelted sports shops in the vicinity. So, not finding some-thing, they had to find some-one.

Horace the Helpful had been a Greater Swamp-Fiend of Fehnris, but now he was nothing but a bodiless head. Several well aimed anti-tank rockets fired at point-blank range had seen to that. There were a few bits left sticking out including three feet of twitching spinal column with more frayed nerve endings than at a trainee-dentist's first practical, but that was soon put right. Roger of Choppingham, Patron Saint of Cut-Price Butchers and part-time tree surgeon, had been called upon to oblige. Licking his lips in anticipation he'd produced a huge cleaver from his blood-stained apron and gone to work with relish. Five minutes of frenzied hacking had produced an item that, while not strictly spherical, was at least vaguely ball-shaped. Horace had been only too happy to oblige.

'Take some more off if you like. Don't mind me. I've always thought my chin jutted out too far. And what about that nose, have you ever seen such a thing? You can't expect me to roll true with a monstrous proboscis like that. Hack it off – hack it off I say!'

But by that stage both teams were too eager for the off to delay any longer. With all due ceremony Horace was left in a muddy puddle somewhere near the centre circle, as to the rear a pair of goals were quickly improvised. With cunning in their eyes and treachery in their festering black hearts each side retired for a final team talk.

Trundell was in fighting mood. 'Men, we may have lost our Commander-in-Chief to that nuke but that don't mean we can't still win this. I'm taking personal command as his designated son and heir, so what I say goes round here from now on. Is that clear?'

This sudden coup might have caused some raised eyebrows, particularly amongst the more senior Assault Angels, but due to recent events there wasn't much facial hair going spare. As it was, Gabriel and Raphael exchanged a knowing glance, as if to say, 'We don't follow no humie scum.' Not noticing celestial dissension in the ranks, Ted glowed in the warmth of Harvey's pledge of support.

'You bet-ya big fella! We'll follow ya till kingdom come.' There were nodded mutterings from the other church members and several of the surviving saints seemed amenable to the idea.

With a self-righteous smile, Trundell got down to business. 'Okay guys. Listen up and listen good, this here's our game-plan . . .'

Meanwhile, deep in his own half of the field, Young

Nick stood amidst a gaggle of his followers. He gnawed nervously at a long fingernail.

'It's at times like this that I wish I'd signed that karate-kicking Frenchman. He could have been ours at one stage but I let him slip through my fingers. Damn it to Heaven and back. Too late now, we'll have to go with what we've got.'

Which if Nick was being honest wasn't really very much. Jean-Paul, the mad Frenchman Nick did have and sole-surviving Masticating Monk, looked a bit tasty in midfield – a dishevelled Michele Platini with more than a dash of the Christopher Lee about him.

On balance the team's strengths probably lay in defence. At right back it would take a particularly tricky winger to get the better of Azantopeth, Nether-Demon of Slanesh. As for the centre half pairing of Scunthytiep, Elephant Warlord of Slumbering Mu and Beelzebub, Lord of the Flies, Nick felt certain nothing short of a tidal wave could get past them. On the left Srrggg-Dyrk, a centipede servant to the goddess of E-numbers, was an unknown quantity, but judging by his number of legs he promised at least to give a good account of himself. The rest of the team, however, were about as daunting as South Croydon Boys Second XI. A motley assortment of goblins, imps and quivering lesser-demons were all that remained to pad out the squad. The cream of Nick's forces had been wiped out by their sheer bravado, leaving him with nothing but the dregs. Which brought the Prince of Hell, not altogether neatly, back to a pair of old acquaintances.

Against All Odds

Guttlehog and Rubicante's suicide mission had only been partially successful. Successful in the sense that it had wiped out Heaven's High Command, but unsuccessful in that Nick's two hapless henchmen were still drawing breath. Against all the odds, as well as the laws of conventional physics, the two demons had survived. Well . . . not quite.

When a demon, a soulless being who is technically undead to begin with, gets itself killed it rotates another notch round the Great Wheel of Life that wobbles along on one corner of the Ford Cortina the Supreme Being joyrides across the multiverse. Guttlehog and Rubicante had recently been more thoroughly killed than most, so thoroughly killed in fact that they had gone full circle on the aforementioned wheel and come to rest 180° out of phase with themselves in the 'living zone'. What's the correct terminology for a living creature with no soul? Guttlehog and Rubicante had become nothing more than common-or-garden ghosts. This infuriating fickleness of sentient creatures to lie down and die when they should have known better would have been well known to any student of Murphy's Law, not to mention its little known corollary, Jenkins' Theorem.[1]

Whatever the reasons, a collection of cuts, bruises and a bit of a sore tummy was all the pair had to show for their recent close scrape with Einstein's uranium enema. Plus the fact you could now see right through them. Despite their less-than-physical appearance Guttlehog wasn't afraid to chip in with a few winning tactics. 'Excuse me sir, can I make a suggestion?'

On spotting them through his followers Nick's face crumpled. 'You are joking! No, you cannot make a suggestion. Just get yourselves up front – at least that way any damage you do might be to the Opposition.' Looking more bowed and beaten than ever before, Guttlehog and Rubicante scurried off to take their positions.

Nick looked over his pack. They had less chance than

---

1 If it can't go wrong, you're forgetting something important.

an ice lolly in Hell. With a desolate yet determined glint in his eye, Nick geed them up.

'Well, what are you waiting for people? Let's move like we've got a purpose. We've got a game to win.'

Some Multidimensional Entities Are On The Field . . .

As a contest it was always going to be more 1066 than 1966, but that was only to be expected. Up at the hastily traced halfway line Ted Trundell squared up to his opposite number.

'Okay, we play until sunset, first to score wins. Sudden death overtime.'

'It will be.' Nick smirked. 'But if for any reason one side can't continue then they've lost by default. Agreed?'

'Agreed!'

'No big guns and no magical intervention either. Let's keep this fair and square.'

'Okay by us.'

Both leaders paused for a moment, then looked for confirmation at Mad Megan, who had resumed her knitting while sat atop a nearby car wreck. The old crone stared back noncommittally.

'You'll have to sort out the winner by yourselves. I'm just here to see one of ya does win and there's no need for a replay. Get on with it then.'

Horace was only too pleased to offer his services. 'If you need a referee, I'm your demon. I'll always be close to the action and I'm guaranteed not to take my eyes off the ball.'

The only reply to Horace's brand of drivel was a swift hoof to the left ear, which Nick mercifully provided. With a loud yelp the head sailed majestically into the heavenly half of the field, all the while enquiring if he could be of any service at the post-game reception. With a wet thunk he was caught by Ted Trundell's second-in-command, the irrepressible Harvey T. Banger.

'We have a ball-possession situation sir! Am proceeding in a touchdown-scoring direction.' He began to charge up the field.

Harvey's survival was perhaps the most miraculous thing about that whole strange day. Over the course of the afternoon he'd personally led endless attacks on Hell's lines, often against odds which would have made the Light Brigade think twice. Despite always being in the thick of the fighting, and managing to get his entire command shot to pieces around him, Harvey had somehow made it through. His only battle scars were a splash of ectoplasm across his Gucci suit and a more than usually manic glint of righteous indignation in his eyes. But now someone meant to spoil his moment of glory.

'Hold on a minute!' screamed Nick from the other end of the field. 'That's hand ball! You can't carry it. Put it down an kick it.'

'Well gee,' Harvey called back, looking hurt. 'I played tight-end for Brigham Young University. I think I know my way round a football field.'

'I don't care if you played flapping-arsehole for Texas Polytechnic, you're not allowed to run with it. This is *foot*-ball, with the emphasis on the *foot* – which is where your teeth will be if you don't stop breaking the rules!'

Ted skidded to a halt beside his man. 'So this is that So-cher game then is it? Well why didn't you just say so? This puts a whole different twist on proceedings. I don't know if we can agree to take part now. Might have to call in my lawyers.'

Harvey was only too ready to agree. 'You said it, Boss. So-cher's a girl's game. I hope, Satan, you ain't implying we wear blouses?'

Being, as they now were, in close proximity, Harvey

was just about ready to take a swing at Nick, but suddenly he was held back by his more cunning leader, in whose eyes a dangerous glint had developed. Nevertheless Nick continued to goad the pair.

'It may have escaped your notice in North America, but we in the civilized world play a game called Association Football. I don't mean to get your goat, if you'll pardon the expression, but when we say football, that's what we mean.'

Giving Harvey a surreptitious wink, Ted showed Nick his sweetest smile. 'Well gee mister Lucifer sir, I guess you might have a point. I always do say that the first rule of good manners is 'When in Rome, wear a toga'.

'When in Rome, impale a Christian,' Nick muttered under his breath but Ted didn't appear to hear him.

'This ain't our patch, so we'll play by the local rules. It'll take a while to pick things up so bear with us. I'm sure you won't take advantage of our lack of skill, now will you?'

'Oh, absolutely not!' said Nick trying hard to suppress a giggle. 'We'll break you in gently, you just see if we don't.'

After giving his warmest thanks Ted motioned for his team to rejoin him in the huddle. Nick retired to his own half, all the while in conference with Jean-Paul, his designated vice-captain. 'I thought they were going to be stubborn back there, but my persistence paid off. This is going to be easier than I thought.'

Meanwhile, Ted's players were a little bemused by their captain's sudden change of heart. Harvey for one was looking decidedly crestfallen.

'So can we wear shoulder pads sir?'

Ted was adamant. 'Not even little ones.'

'Crash helmets?'

'*No*. But don't worry team. There's no sport on Earth more open to abuse than Association Football. I played it down in South America back when I was a struggling missionary. I picked up a trick or two, I can tell you. Some of the things them Injuns did to one another would make your toes curl.'

Harvey looked shocked. 'Are you suggesting we cheat sir?'

'No,' said Ted with a sly smile, 'I'm suggesting we don't get caught.'

They Thought It Was All Over . . .

The game recommenced under agreed rules. Ted's followers quickly picked up the unusual nuances, though their interpretation of the shoulder charge was a little on the harsh side. Whenever a dark minion found themselves in possession they were bundled off the ball with less ceremony than a Quaker Christmas party. Hellish calls for free kicks fell on deaf ears, though when the hugely fat Angel Branzith the Indigestible wiped out most of the hellish midfield a rare exception was made.

Although there were few scoring chances Nick's side was getting beaten and he knew it. It was only a matter of time before the holy midfield of Saint Peter, Harvey Banger and Bertrude The Ball-winning Bishop of Bath strung a few passes together to create an opening. In an attempt to spur his side on to greater efforts, the Prince of Hell jumped onto the roof of a burnt out delivery van and cried at the top of his lungs:

'A thousand nubile succubi slaves for the demon who wins us the match! Come on boys, where's your testosterone?'

Guttlehog, whose fighting spirit was on a cycling holiday somewhere in the South of France, looked up from the low wall behind which he cowered. From between chattering tusks the Boar Demon muttered to his insectoid companion.

'He's going to have to do better to tempt me out. Those Christians don't play fair.'

But one amongst the demonic host was inspired to lift his game, though his uses for a thousand sex slaves wasn't clear – apart perhaps as a light lunch. Srrggg-Dyrk was an entire book of revelations down the left wing. He began to rain in crosses with deadly accuracy, all the while leading the heavenly defence a merry dance. It was only down to Guttlehog and Rubicante's inexcusable lack of presence up front that Hell failed to take the lead.

With scant regard for the conventions of the beautiful game, Ted called a time-out. He could see the match was slipping back out of his oily fingers.

'So what's happening boys? We were screwing 'em over the barrel. Now we're under it.'

Harvey might have known less about soccer than he did about humility but even he could spot the thorn in their side. 'It's that multi-legged left winger of theirs, Boss! Each time we try to tackle the thing it switches feet. I didn't think passing to yourself was allowed.'

'Okay,' said Ted nodding his agreement, 'this is where we start playing dirty.' Several of his team exchanged the sorts of glances the Israelites must have swapped when Moses asked if they were prepared for a bit of a stroll. With a sneer Ted continued.

'Harvey ain't entirely perpendicular to the truth in his assessment. We've gotta take out that centipede critter – the thing's tearing us apart. Gabriel, I want you and Raphael to engineer a serious reduction in its mobility coefficient. Is that clear?'

Seeing Heaven's senior Assault Angels looking at him blankly, Ted explained further. 'Just break as many of its legs as you think y'all can manage. Don't make it too obvious, but don't dawdle neither.'

Now that it was put in language they could understand the angels gave well-disciplined salutes. Perhaps this pipsqueak humie wasn't so bad after all. At least he had plenty of fight in him. With a click of their heels they trotted off to take their positions.

Meanwhile, at the other end of the pitch, Nick had reached a similar conclusion. 'Srrggg-Dyrk is our one hope of winning this game. Get the ball to him at every opportunity. Once he's got it the rest of you can run around like gutless chickens to create a distraction – you seem to be very good at that. And as for you pair,' he spat, singling out Guttlehog and Rubicante, 'if I see you running away again I'll have your guts for athletic-supports, and I'll have what you keep in your athletic-supports for hood ornaments on the immense car I'm going to requisition to celebrate victory. Have I made myself clear?' With a crack of the long whip he'd pried from the claws of a fallen Flame Fiend, His Satanic Majesty sent them scurrying to their places.

Play was resumed by a drop ball on the halfway line. Horace's head was looking decidedly tatty, but that didn't stop him chipping in with a bit of helpful advice from between a mouthful of shattered teeth.

'Vat 'u vont ish to push vorward more. Get to the bye-line. Get behind the bugge-!'

His sentence was terminated by Harvey's boot. What was left of Horace sailed majestically over the upturned snouts of the hellish ranks.

And landed trapped beneath the cloven hoof of Azantopeth, the infernal right back. Azantopeth might not have been much of a ball player – the closest he'd ever come to Brazil was wearing a Carmen Miranda outfit to his department's annual fancy-dress – but he knew his skill limitations. With an aimless swipe as if trying to clear row Z, Azantopeth hacked the ball up the field like his life-force depended on it. Yet again Horace went ballistic, but this time at least he managed to keep his drivel to himself.

Waiting for the ball as it plummeted back to earth stood the stoical figure of Saint Peter. The famous fisherman had been a rock all afternoon on the holy right, putting in the sort of tackles that ended careers and brought tears to the eyes of men and demon alike. Now that he finally had time and space he resolved to show just what he could do. Setting off up field like an express train, Saint Pete began to dribble past demon after demon.

With an evil grin, Black Abbot Jean-Paul popped up from behind a crater. In his callused hands was a spike so sharp and so shiny that it threatened to puncture the very fabric of reality. If there'd been a dead chicken nearby it would have started to sweat, such was the implement's eye-watering possibilities. As there didn't appear to be much in the way of butchered poultry left around, Jean-Paul resigned himself to fresher meat – and that's where Saint Pete came in, or rather departed.

As Peter sped past, the Black Abbot took a two-handed swipe that hamstrung the waddling old gentleman with consummate ease. A blood-curdling scream and Saint Peter collapsed in a riot of thrashing limbs and flapping tendons, surrendering possession as he did so. So impressed was he with his spike-work, Jean-Paul was inspired to give himself a running commentary as he took control of the ball.

'And zo za gallant Gallic goal-maker once more comes to rescue! Wiz zkill 'e beats une . . . zen 'e beats deux . . . zurely nothing can be stopping 'im now az he 'eds for goal . . . THWACK!'

With breathtaking timing, Jean-Paul chose that moment to run straight into the man-mountain that had stepped out before him. As pureed Frenchman trickled down the front of Harvey T. Banger, the big American called out to his team captain with glee.

'We have a tackle situation in progress sir! Be advised I am initiating a ball-clearance initiative.'

Then, from over his shoulder came the sound of galloping hooves. King Arthur and Sir Gwal had been biding their time, doing their level best to work out what on earth was going on – and what their part in it should be. Jammed onto one seriously out-of-breath horse, the two plunged into the game.

Reaching for his jewel-encrusted scabbard, Arthur drew his ancient weapon and bellowed with rage. Excalibur seemed to spring from its sheath, so eager was it for the fray. But if swords could possess emotions, and after all some of them could, Excalibur might have been a little disappointed at the use to which it was now put.

'Simple really. Just like polo,' Arthur cried as he swung the weapon in a sweeping underarm stroke. With a loud clank, Excalibur zipped Horace down the touchline. Seeing an opening appear before his wind-swept eyes Arthur raced after the babbling ball. One more clean strike launched Horace past Hell's defence and into clear space waiting to be filled by a heavenly attacker. But out of the swirling mists of battle, a black shape reared its multi-hinged head. Srrggg-Dyrk came screaming in from the left, propelled by more legs than most football teams could muster. With a flick of its tail the giant centipede nudged the ball out of the path of the careering knights, and lined itself up for a run. Winding up its rear legs so they could keep up with their partners at the front, the giant centipede began his charge straight at the heart of the heavenly defence.

Remembering their leader's express orders the Archangels Gabriel and Raphael lumbered into position. With the previous attack much of Heaven's team had been drawn upfield, leaving the cherubs as the last line of defence. Angelic faces held rather less than angelic sneers as they glided to head off the centipede at the pass. Gabe and Ralph were to be the bread in a giant insectoid sandwich.

As Srrggg-Dyrk accelerated towards the gap the angels rushed to fill it. Something had to give, and it wasn't going to be pretty. In fact the situation was so ugly it could have lived under a bridge and made a good living bullying billy-goats.

But with an unexpected burst of frenzied motion the centipede's last set of legs cleared the killing zone, leaving the chunky angels charging together at breakneck speed – a phrase particularly apt in this case. Until now, no one had been sure if angels possessed bone structures in the traditional sense – the delicate wings, beautiful physique and ability to fly all lent itself to a rather idiosyncratic physiology.

But after the collision they did. And it wasn't pretty.

'I'm sure my leg shouldn't be wrapped around my wings like that,' moaned Gabriel, trying to get up and failing miserably.

'Errrrrg!' replied Ralph, turning blue as his halo slipped around his throat.

For once Srrggg-Dyrk was unconcerned with carrion – more important things were afeet. The final line of defence punctured like an out-of-date condom, the centipede raced in on goal, with only the keeper between it and eternal glory.

Saint Gertrude, Fulham's frolicking nun, had managed to improvise two crutches from a pair of badly damaged road signs Until now, her lack of agility in goal had not been a problem because of the ineptitude of Hell's forward line. But now she faced a far sterner test; one that, if it didn't end in tears, would at least finish with a severely trembling lower lip.

The giant centipede bore down on her with no pity and no change of course. Then suddenly, he stopped and wiggled his mandibles as if to chant, 'Come and take me on if you think you're mobile enough!' Gertrude spread her crutches wide, but she could not move. Srrggg-Dyrk waited until he could hear the first thundering of the heavenly opposition pouring back into their own half to dispossess him before nonchalantly flicking the ball into the air and swinging his entire rear-end to slam the ball past the convalescing nun.

For a second all was silent, then the remains of Hell erupted into great howls of ecstasy, punctuated with fountains of flame as the few remaining Fire Demons finally depleted their emergency reserves. To an imp, Nick's players started frenzied celebrations, chirping maniacally and rubbing strange body parts together at the risk of spontaneous combustion. Even Jean-Paul looked up from his semi-liquefied state and began to sing the Marseillaise.

Ted Trundell looked on in disbelief. 'Noooooo! This is not how it's meant to be.' Turning towards where Megan sat clacking away at her knitting he pointed at Nick and pleaded. 'Do something you mad crone. If he wins, the human race has had its fries! You can't let *him* win.'

'But he has,' Megan said simply. She sniffed and dropped a stitch. Beyond Ted's shaking finger, Young Nick lay on his leathery back laughing like a drain. With a side-splitting effort the Prince of Hell clambered to his hooves.

'Haahaahaaaaaaa!' he guffawed into Ted's drooping face. 'I've won by the rules and there's nothing you can do about it. I'm the king of the world so get down on your knees and grovel!'

Megan watched from a distance. 'I was rather afraid this might 'appen,' she muttered to no one in particular. Wincing at her arthritic limbs she creaked gingerly to her feet. 'Still, I suppose one of you had to go for good. Let's get it over with.'

. . . But It Wasn't Yet

Deborah was feeling decidedly strange. As the girl raced through the forest of shattered trees, with Soul Stealer clutched tightly in her hands and the warm breeze in her hair, she reflected that this was always meant to be. Somewhere behind her Mike and the others continued to call for her to stop, but she ran on, driven by some unearthly supernatural force, onwards towards her destiny. Deborah wasn't sure what it was, but she could sense it was near, and she could sense that it was soon.

In her sweatless palms the giant sword murmured back to life. 'Woooe is me, wooooe is meeeee! What has become of this realm when I am wielded by a wombed-one?' Deborah barely broke stride as she stunned the weapon on a barkless tree. She didn't seem to notice as it disintegrated into enough fire wood to power the very fires of Hell themselves.

Running through the forest, it seemed to Deborah that a strange mist appeared before her eyes. Keeping pace with her as she dodged between the trees, the fog flowed and eddied in a myriad of colours and hues. Over a period which could have been seconds but seemed to stretch for hours, the psychedelic haze formed into a friendly female face. Though they'd never met Deborah felt sure they knew each other.

The eyes were wise. Not young, yet not old. They were set in a kindly face that spoke of clean sheets and cool milk on warm summer nights, of waking to bird song on fresh spring mornings, of hot teacakes besides roaring winter fires. And when the newcomer spoke it was with a voice like rain on a still meadow.

'Be at peace, I mean you no harm. But be wary also, for those that do are close at hand.'

'I know,' replied Deborah flatly. 'I know what I must do.'

The face frowned faintly. 'The issue is not yet decided. I come to give you my blessings, not my assurances.'

'I know that too,' said Deborah with a grin, 'but then if it was all arranged beforehand it wouldn't be any fun now would it?'

The face smiled back, a look that sat far more comfortably. 'You are truly a worthy part of us. Know now that at your time of trial we will both be with you, giving you what aid we can. Our sister is already at the appointed place, though she knows not of your coming. Good speed and good luck.' By the time Deborah had given her thanks the face was gone, leaving nothing but the speeding blur of passing trunks between Deborah and her destiny.

As she reached the edge of the forest, an incredible sight unfolded before her eyes. Away to her right, beyond the shallow gully of a vaporized stream, stood a decidedly odd collection of figures. On one side, a whooping band of nightmare apparitions danced and frolicked, looking for all the world like their syndicate's numbers had just come up in the great lottery of life. On the other, a motley assortment of humans, cherubim and angels lolled with their heads, and in some cases steaming internal organs, in their hands. Between them stood three figures.

On his knees, Ted Trundell wept beyond control and pounded the ground with clenched fists. Next to him stood Noddegamra's very own witch, Old Mad Megan. The third figure, Deborah had not met, though she recognized him all the same. Horror movies, fairy tales and some of the more graphic stained-glass windows had prepared her for the favoured physical form of the creature known as Young Nick. He was preening his slick black hair and grinning like a bright red Cheshire cat.

In a shower of soot and ashes, Mike and the others skidded to a halt beside her. The Professor was badly out of breath but that didn't disguise the urgency in his voice.

'Do you want to get us all killed!'

Behind him Adam and Sid were pale and doubled-up, sucking hard on ozone air. Their frantic expressions showed they were both thinking along similar lines. Deborah said nothing, simply gazing down into the shallow valley with a faint smile on her dry lips. Slowly, Mike's eyes turned to match hers. When he saw what she had seen, all colour drained from his face.

'Oh my gods!' he muttered, beginning to tremble. 'What have we stumbled into? This is not our fight. We must leave. We must leave right now!'

But without another word Deborah bounded down the gravel-strewn slope. Mike gave a curse that would have made a pirate blush, then scrambled after her. Deborah, oblivious to his efforts, reached the bottom in a shower of chippings and set off purposefully towards the throng. Mike and the others floundered in her wake, descending the slope amidst an avalanche of debris.

Before them, upon the low mound where the crowning ceremony was about to begin, the day's protagonists were too rapt in their own concerns to spot the late arrivals.

In Which It Really Is All Over

Young Nick stood proudly with his cloven feet thrust apart and his boyish head craned up to the skies. He wore the sort of grin car salesmen pull when they smell restless money, his fangs shining in the low sun like one half of an antique ivory chess set. Beside him, lowered on bloodied knees, Ted Trundell banged his head repeatedly on the stony ground, muttering hoarsely over and over again: 'It could have been me, it could have been me. . .'

The appointed proclaimer did her duty stoically. Megan's face showed no emotion as she ran through the required ritual. Her hands theatrically held aloft, the old girl improvised up to her usual high standards.

'And so, by the power vested in me . . . by whoever it is that vests power round here – and whatever "round here" means anymore – I doth declare you the winner, able to go to bed when you like, answer back to your parents and eat as much as you want. In short, you are given *The Freedom of the World.* If any present doth know of any unjust cause or impediment why this should not be so, let them speak now or forever suck their gums in peace.'

For one hopeful second Ted looked up pleadingly, but the slightest shake of Megan's head reminded him that he'd had his chance and blown it.

Nick gazed around the assembled throng with that smug smile specially reserved for freshly installed tyrants and laughed from the bottom of his leathery lungs. 'Not so cocky now are we white meat,' he said with all the power of a new playground bully, as his steely hoof made loud contact with Trundell's exposed midriff.

Meanwhile, the demons and imps arrayed before the winning team captain maintained a respectful silence, while the vanquished foe continued to sob their eyes out and generally make babies of themselves. Just when none seemed ready to challenge Nick's awful authority, a clear voice rose from the back.

'I know of an impediment,' said Deborah, clearing the last few yards to stand at the foot of the mound.

Close behind Mike made one last bid to extricate them from the hole Deborah was fast digging. 'Have you lost your senses? For the sake of us all, leave while there's still time.' But Deborah could no longer hear him. She simply stood with a determined frown on her face and Soul Stealer clutched ever more securely between blood-drained knuckles.

Nick looked confused, glancing first right then left to spot who had interrupted his moment of triumph. When his burning red eyes came to rest on the delicate blonde head adjacent to his infernally curly belly-button, his laddish smile returned once more. Being, as he was, in the company of nine-foot-tall demons and towering Assault Angels, a five-foot-ten female was very easy to miss.

'Well, well, well. What do we have here? A little girly

all lost and alone. Good job you've got your nice Uncle Nick to take care of you, isn't it?'

Deborah jerked Soul Stealer upright, so that the tip of the great sword was just inches from Nick's throat. 'I've found tougher things than you clinging to the bottom of my shoe. Come one step closer and we'll see just what this sword can do.'

Nick looked up and down Soul Stealer's gleaming hilt and recognized the sword for the first time.

'I see you've managed to put in an appearance,' he commented drily. 'What happened to your master?'

Soul Stealer gave a choking sob. 'Muuuuuurdered. Slaaaaain by these treacherous humie dogs. They jumped us without a fair fight they did.'

'I might have known it,' sighed Nick, 'teaming Alastor up with those half-arsed assassins was as good as killing him myself. Still, you live and you learn or you don't live long. Now, where was I?'

'I know of an impediment!' insisted Deborah, her voice straining from the weight of the sword and the moment.

Next to Nick, Megan's weather-worn face had hung slack since Deborah's arrival. Now it came back to life like a spring sunrise. Wrinkles seemed to slip away, leaving a beaming expression of joyful surprise. As Deborah gave voice to her objections for a second time, Megan's face took on a knowing smile.

'You cannot be king of this world,' said Deborah with a dangerous calm.

Nick smiled down at her, humouring the little girl all lost in this wasteland. 'Why, pray? What is the precise nature of your objection?'

'*You!*' said Deborah, poking the Prince of Hell just above his chaotically hairy navel.

'What? Little old me?' Nick feigned a hurt look. 'I'm not perfect, granted, but the alternative? Do you actually like choral singing? Do you enjoy kneeling in a pew?

Do you want to be made to feel bad for all eternity about those naughty thoughts you have at night?' He gave her a knowing leer. 'If that bunch had won, that's what you'd have got. So, I ask again, how do I offend thee?'

With fluttering eyelashes, Deborah said: 'Because you're a bit of a git. You might be better than them but it's hardly straight "A"s on your report, is it? Cyanide pills might be better than being scalped, but I don't want to try either. Whoever said we had to put up with one or the other? We don't need either of you.'

Nick looked aghast. 'Okay, okay. So I might have munched a few babies in my time, but then that comes with the territory sweet-lumps. Just remember where I come from,' he said tapping his scabby cranium, 'straight out of the murkier parts of humanity's subconscious. I'm just a reflection of your own darker selves. Don't blame me, if you don't like what you see.'

Deborah advanced on him. 'Wrong! You don't come out of our subconscious, you come out of *theirs*.' She pointed at Ted and his followers. 'Once we've got rid of one mad bunch there's no need for the other. Who needs a counterbalance when the scales are empty!'

Nick spat dismissively, 'I am reeeeally scared – just look at me shake.' He held up one rock-steady talon as if to demonstrate. 'You might talk big, cutey-buns, but you're just like the rest of your snivelling sort – all mouth and no trousers. Come and have a go if you think you're hard enough!'

Well, he had invited her. She advanced up to the crest of the mound all the while pointing Soul Stealer's tip under Nick's chin. As she reached the top, a shining aura appeared about her dusty hair, and in the sky behind her an incredible image formed. At first it had the consistency and texture of wet lime jelly, but gradually it congealed into a shining female face. Reflected in Nick's terrified eyes Deborah recognized the stranger she'd met in the woods.

Nick looked up in awe, suddenly far less sure of himself. His clenched fangs begun to tremble like a malaria victim. But as with so many wild beasts the Prince of Hell was at his most dangerous with his back to the wall.

'Don't think you'll steal my prize so easily,' he snarled, crouching back on his furry haunches, 'You'll have to fight for it, like I did!' With a crazed leap he threw himself at the girl, claws and fangs flashing in the dying light.

Deborah was momentarily caught unawares. As Nick flew towards her, she struggled to bring her sword up in defence. Soul Stealer fought her efforts moving like a plate dragged face on in a stream.

From the foot of the mound Adam watched with mounting alarm. As Satan launched himself at his beloved, the reporter dived towards her. Just how he hoped to protect her armed with nothing more than a ball-point pen and his rapier he did not know. Fortunately for all, Mike reached Adam before he reached the girl. Wrestling the lovestruck reporter to the floor, Mike yelled in his ear. 'There's nothing we can do!'

Above them there was a deafening clatter as Nick's body hit the hard-packed dirt. Seeing there was no time to parry, Deborah had lithely side-stepped, leaving the raging demon clawing at empty air. The tactic had been a good one. Nick was left dazed, plus more than a little embarrassed as he sprawled in the dirt. Her enemy now lying amidst a tangle of scarlet limbs, Deborah rounded for the kill.

'This is for that stunt you pulled with the mad Austrian painter!' she cried, adrenaline strength forcing the massive sword high over her head, ready for a deadly downward strike.

He might have been strewn in a spaghetti-like confusion of arms and legs, but Satan had one last trick down his armour-plated pants. With a sound like steel rope unwinding, Nick's prehensile tail lashed out and grabbed

Deborah's legs. A sudden jerk with all his infernal might sent her reeling to the floor, and Soul Stealer tracing a graceful arc through the crackling air.

Now it was Nick's turn to look triumphant. Clambering to his hooves he towered above Deborah's prone form. 'Not so smart after all, are we my pretty one? I'll teach you to challenge my authority. Your death will be as lingering as it will be painful – *very*, on both counts.'

Mike had seen enough. Keeping out of things was all very well, but now his friend was defenceless. Yelling at the top of his lungs, the Professor charged towards the lumbering devil. 'Noooooo!'

He never made it to Nick's exposed flank. With a dismissive swipe of one huge-clawed hand Nick sent him flying at a tangent, to collide with an ominous thud against a charred tree stump. Mike slumped unconscious, blood trickling from the corner of his mouth. Nick resumed his advance.

'So you see my dear, not even your treacherous friends can save you now. I've waited to slime Nostrus for more years than you could imagine. Today is turning into a very good day indeed!'

But for Deborah the distraction Mike had caused had been enough. Scuttling desperately on all fours she made the last few yards to Soul Stealer, who was twitching in the smouldering earth. She grabbed it with inhuman ferocity and, in one movement, she swung the sword over her head and hurled it at her tormentor. Soul Stealer cartwheeled through the air, screaming as it did so in a frantic high-pitched voice, 'Look ooooooout!'

With a resounding thump the sword embedded itself hilt deep in Nick's heaving chest, there to judder and shake until the universe fell still.

'Ah,' said the Prince of Hell, 'the old sword-sticking-in-the-chest trick. Gets you every time . . . Suppose I'd better do the decent thing.'

With that, each of Lucifer's limbs started to tremble, slowly at first, but building until he seemed to be intimately involved in his very own personal earthquake. Next, green fire spewed from every orifice, all of his natural ones plus the rather larger fissure recently opened in his bosom. Soul Stealer too begun to shudder, as if attempting to be free from an infernal abode. Those close enough heard it wail, 'Noooo sooooul – noooo sooooul!' as a fissure coursed down its glistening black length.

Under such enormous pressures something had to give, and first to go was Nick's sweat-streaked skin. With a sound like ripping canvas, a small tear appeared just below his hairline, quickly spreading down his nose and along his barrelling chest. What came out wasn't pretty, but then the Prince of Hell had never been made of sugar and spice. Those creatures too close to the explosively expanding Dark Lord were treated to a heavy splattering of his idiosyncratic anatomy.

When the intestines, offal, and surprising amounts of blue nylon string finally stopped raining down, Adam looked up from the spot where he'd fallen. 'Bloody Hell,' he cursed. 'You've never got a camera when you need one.'

FIFTEEN

And look, an opened door in heaven. And the first voice was as of a trumpet, saying 'Come up here, and I shall show you the things that must take place.'
Revelations 4:1

A'rm-a-geddon Outa Here

They huddled in twos and threes, cautiously picking their way across the wreckage that had been their homes. Twisted black bodies littered the valley like the detritus of some grizzly flame-thrower accident. Dick squinted into the gathering gloom, at a confused tangle of corpses heaped into a makeshift pyre.

'Should there really be that number of legs with that number of bodies?' he asked with a rising note of panic.

Emmyr followed his gaze. 'Dunno mate. Reckon there were some strange creatures running around today. If I 'adn't seen 'em with me own eyes I wouldn't believe it.'

Dick gulped sickeningly. With a heroic effort he swallowed the hot bile that was threatening to add to the sorry condition of his home town.

Now it was Emmyr's turn to ask a question. 'Between them bodies, those box type thingummies – what do you suppose they are then?'

Now that he looked, Dick could see them too. They were everywhere – small black cubes, about six inches across, each sprouting a spider's-legs-worth of wires.

Before Dick could give his opinion Crystal came tottering

forwards, half supported by her husband Hywell. The landlord and his wife looked highly irate, perhaps more down to the wholesale squandering of their profits than the destruction of the village. The coven-mistress' temper was not improved by the unsuitability of her footwear – between black nail-varnished fingers she carried the snapped-off heel of one high-laced boot.

'What do you pissed pair think you're up to? We're never going to get out of this war zone if we keep stopping for tea breaks. This place gives me the creeps.'

Emmyr held up a pacifying hand. ''Ang on now Crystal luv. Don't go flying off the 'andle. We might have hit a snag.'

Crystal strained her heavily lashed eyes and peered over the gloomy plain before them. 'Nothing out there that I can see. Just a load of dead bodies and some small black lumps, probably the remains of the losing side.'

Emmyr gave a resigned shrug and started off over the open ground. The other villagers soon followed, weaving a meandering path between the littered corpses. Just as Emmyr's zigzag course was about to take him slap-bang onto one of the mysterious cubes, Gwylym proved that every idiot has a silver lining. His happened to be an anorak-level knowledge of military hardware. The only thing there was more of under his bed than toenail clippings were copies of *Big Guns Monthly* – and Gwylym was an avid reader.

'Don't take another step!' cried the rural commando freezing in mid-stumble. Without exception every head turned towards him.

Gwylym gulped. 'Those are . . . land mines.'

Emmyr's red-rimmed eyes went wide. 'Then this must be . . .'

'A minefield!'

Everything went quiet, apart from Emmyr's heart, which did its level best to make a run for it all by itself. The area of open ground had been scattered with self-arming land mines by one side or another. Now the battle was over they remained like discarded toys – and Emmyr had led the villagers plumb into their midst. Just when it seemed things couldn't get any worse, they had.

Twenty yards in front, the broken ground resumed once more. A smoking tangle of buildings had fallen in on themselves, providing a means of escape from the mines, but also cover for a potential attacker. Amidst the smoke and rubble something begun to stir, something big and something mean. Through the mists, an outline formed, rising slowly to rear up on hard and shiny legs. The villagers stood transfixed as the shadows of two enormous claws and a multitude of wobbling antennae towered over them.

A giant lobster, whose name was Pandrax Snappersnatch, clambered out from the ruins where it had been taking an afternoon nap and yawned the way only lobsters can. It had slipped into the inviting hole earlier that day, as soon as the battle had passed it by. Despite the annoyance of being woken from its blissful slumber, it was nonetheless pleased to find its afternoon snack presenting itself within such easy reach. With much crumbling of masonry, the lobster lumbered forward.

'Klak-klak clic-clic brrrrmph!' it said in its friendliest voice, the one it saved for initiating mating rituals and ordering take-away pizza.

'Run like shit!' cried Emmyr in his terrified voice, the one he saved for warning of giant lobsters who seemed in a mood to party.

Forgetting the minefield the villagers set off in a frenzy. By some miracle of agility, careful timing and very strong real ale none of the fleeing townsfolk set off a mine. Pandrax however was not so lucky. After two waddling steps an afternoon snack became the least of the lobster's concerns. Paying no heed to what got in its way, Pandrax flopped his massive mid-section down atop one of the hair-trigger mines. With a sound like an explosive pressure cooker left out in the sun, ten-and-a-half tons of lobster thermidor was blown nine hundred feet into the air.

The Whore Of Basildon Takes A Well-Earned Rest

Back at the centre of the desolation events had thrown many of those involved off balance. Following Nick's explosive demise the rest of his team stood around looking thoroughly dazed. They had seen ultimate victory dragged from the jaws of defeat, only to be tossed back into the waste-bin of hopeless surrender, then stamped upon by the jackboots of sneering contempt. Those capable of crying did so, their acidic tears forming foul puddles around their cloven feet.

At the foot of the blasted mound where she'd so recently faced her darkest hour Deborah cradled Mike in her arms. The Professor's colourless skin was drawn tight over his old bones, for once almost showing his true age. With a worried frown she gently dabbed the trickle of blood that seeped from his mouth, while nearby Aristotle sat thunking his tail irritably.

Will the old fool live? he asked, his harsh words belying the concern Deborah could sense in his mind.

'I don't know Aristo. He's taken an awful blow to the head.' Both cat and girl had been at Mike's side since he slipped from consciousness. Apart from a restless bout of mumbling he had shown no signs of recovery.

Overhead a crimson sky boiled and bubbled, as if it too were undergoing its own cathartic struggle. Across the valley floor the charred remains of battle stretched in a neverending sea. Over this scene of desolation gazed Adam and Sid, a look of glazed rejection of all that had happened clear on each tired face.

For one who had so recently taken a swan dive down the pit of despair, Ted had made a remarkable recovery.

Across the smoke-laced evening air the preacher's voice crescendoed.

'My children, my children this was always how it was meant to be – foretold in prophecy right here in the Good Book!' The big American thumped his ever-present Bible. 'Just when Satan's power seemed at its height, a treacherous worm in his very own camp laid him low! The avaricious Whore of Babylon could not let his strength rise unchecked. Now that the foul strumpet has done her dirty work we arise to claim our holy inheritance!'

Ted's survivors began to perk up. Their leader's words seemed to lift them, overcoming the effects of battle fatigue and the crippling trauma of defeat. Slowly, they gathered at the foot of the mound, gazing up with new hope brimming in their eyes.

'Trust me brethren, the kingdom is at hand. All the hymn singing and Bible recitals you could ever want will soon be ours, all the church picnics and Sunday school square dances that could take our fancy. Now is our chance to forge a new world, a world where decent God-fearing folk like you and me can walk safely down the main drag of our home town with our best girl on our arm and a 9mm semi-automatic at our hip – all without some whinging intellectual telling us what to do, what to think.

'And there'll be none of that rock'n'roll music neither. The devil's discos 'll be thrown on the scrap heap like the impure-thought-producing garbage they are. But we won't stop there, oh no! First chance we get we'll round up all the heavy metal fans, beatnik scroungers, college professors, gays, fags, hags, gooks, mics, spics, chincs and niggers, and put 'em in the biggest prison camp you've ever seen. We'll surround the place with guard dogs and a high wire fence, then just when they think we've left them to their own devices we'll bomb the bastards back to the stone age! Hall-elu-jaaaaaah!'

As Ted's sermon unfolded Old Mad Megan edged over to

where Deborah cradled the Professor in her arms. Aristotle and the girl were oblivious to Ted's rantings; they were more concerned with Mike's worrying condition than the fate of mankind. Megan, however, kept one eye on the preacher as she addressed Deborah's gently rocking form.

'Listen to me my sister, you cannot let this beast win. When I seen you slay 'is opposite number I realized there must be another way – a third way – neither of em have to come out on top. By intervening once, you've made us three a part of the struggle. Retake your sword and strike a blow for sense and decency. Slay Trundell.'

Deborah turned her eyes to the old woman. 'Megan, I can't do that. I have to tend Mike. He needs me more than ever right now. Besides, the sword is gone – and I'm glad it has. That thing was a part of it; it made me want to kill. I don't think I could do it again in cold blood.'

Megan was insistent. 'This ain't peanuts we're playing for now, me girl. This is the future destiny of the human race. If we don't do something it won't matter one jot whether the Professor lives or dies.'

But Deborah slowly shook her head. 'It's no longer my fight. I can't set myself up as a judge of what Ted *might* become, that way I'd be no better than him.'

Megan gave a heavy sigh. 'If that is your decision . . .' She inclined her head slightly, signalling acquiescence. 'Forgive me, I've come too close to this and let my impartiality slip. Going against your grain would only cause more trouble in the long run, and I think we're in for plenty of that soon enough. Listen to that nutter go . . .'

Up on the mound Ted was still in full flood. 'Sometimes you have to be cruel to be kind. But this is the only way we can separate the wheat from the chaff, the plump cornfields of Nevada from the sour sorghum of the Third World. Those not fit to enter the Kingdom of Heaven will be rounded up and shot – it's the only language they understand. We stand on the shores of eternal paradise, right here on Earth. All you have to do is join with me to smite the last few heathens that remain. Are you with me?'

'Yeeeeeeah!' they all roared.

With that affirmation, Ted was all set to lead his people on one final crusade of carnage, when suddenly he stopped in his tracks. His Christian army, on seeing their leader pause, did the same. The reason he'd pulled up short was slowly waddling towards him.

Megan's face wore the sort of look Noah's must have when God testily informed him he'd forgotten the softback armadillos. Resigned and world-weary, she halted twenty paces ahead of the leading fanatic and held up a tired hand. 'There'll be no need for any more killing today. Much as I'm loath to admit it you seem to have won. We'd better get on with the formalities, they may take some time.'

Ted eyed the unkempt hag suspiciously. He didn't trust her, but undeniably she kept turning up at crucial moments, always when events hung in the balance and always with fresh news. Reasoning that the Lord worked in mysterious ways, even if he had been blown to bits by a low-yield thermonuclear device, Ted halted his menacing advance and put on his best fundraising smile.

Winner Takes Whatever's Left

Ted and his followers stood in a rough semicircle round Megan's stooping form. None seemed sure what victory entailed. Only their leader was flushed with the thrill of success. Ted beamed like an overloaded light-bulb as he preened himself for coming glory. Megan wore a pained frown as she began the same tired ritual she'd started earlier that day.

'By the Power of Earth and Sun, by the wind and the rain, the moon and the stars . . . oh bollocks, I don't 'ave the stomach for this. I'm sure you're as impatient to begin your reign as I am to see the back of ya.'

'Sounds good to me!' cried Ted, grinning like a mad man.

'And so it goes,' Megan without enthusiasm, 'I declare Light and Law the winner, triumphant over the forces of Change.' With that she made a strange hand movement, halfway between a wave and a swipe for an imaginary wasp before her face.

For a split second all was still, then the universe seemed to hiccup and take a step to the left – not a new direction, simply a course parallel to the old. Those on their feet fought to retain their balance as their entire frame of reference shifted. Once the disturbance had passed it seemed little had changed.

'Is that all?' Ted asked, gawking down at his hands as if they'd been turned to solid gold. His followers glanced about hopefully, as if expecting the setting sun to reverse its course, or the first smattering of stars to rearrange themselves into a likeness of their leader.

Megan nodded. 'Yep. The Earth's yours. Try not to break it . . .'

'All-riiiiighty!' The preacher gasped, straightening his tie and smoothing down his hair. 'Let's get this show on the road! Which bit comes next?' Reaching into his jacket pocket Ted produced his tattered Bible. Turning the pages he quickly came to the infamous blood-and-thunder finale.

'Here we go, Revelations 11:12 – "And they heard a loud voice out of heaven, saying 'Come up here'. And they went up into the clouds with their enemies left behind." Sounds 'bout right to me – I can hardly wait!' Ted gazed at his followers in hope, as if expecting his entire flock to be a part of some jet-assisted takeoff. When it failed to materialize he began to lose patience faster than an impotent monk in a brothel.

'Well, you festering whore,' he shouted at Megan, 'when does it begin? We ain't got all day ya know. I've got a planet to run.'

Megan chewed her gums thoughtfully. 'Patience me boy. What you truly believe will be yours in good time,' she said, then added pointedly, 'have a little faith.'

Ted was about to warn her to watch her lip, when he was distracted by a movement away to his left. A hugely fat church member, who'd been clutching a crowbar in readiness for renewed hostilities, begun to wobble and sway alarmingly. With a frightened yelp his weight seemed to slip away as he slowly rose from the ground. When his scuffed cowboy boots hovered a good six inches in the air, the first of his wide-eyed comrades began to join him.

Ted gasped with glee. 'Then it's true – weeeeee're going to the shoooow!'

But his joy was short-lived. Within seconds the whole congregation was airborne, all except for their livid leader who stayed stubbornly rooted to the spot.

'Why ain't I going? I'm boss, I should be first, not left till last.'

Megan gave a heavy sigh. 'Nothing to do with me – it's all down to your own twisted expectations. When your time comes I'm sure you'll leave like a rocket.'

But suddenly Ted's lack of levitation became the least of his concerns. Overhead the seething clouds parted to reveal a breathtaking sun-drenched apparition. Floating high above the earth, seemingly suspended on dazzling rays of sunlight, rested a gigantic empty throne. At its base a host of hazy angelic figures gathered. The ghosts of Gabriel, Raphael and their brothers each held a burnished trumpet in their fast-healing hands. When they began to play the cacophony was deafening. The Final Trump was loud enough to wake the dead.

The faces of those around the grassless knoll looked up in wonder. Deborah gazed up from Mike's unconscious form as Adam and Sid cowered in terror. Only Megan seemed underawed by the sight. While all other eyes were on the sky, she watched as a double-glazed expression came over Ted. Next, a wide foolish grin broke over his sunburnt face. Pretty soon he bore close resemblance to a man suddenly recovering from a severe bout of constipation. The reason for his swift change of tune was that Ted had seen a vision.

A Paler Shade Of White

Around about him Ted's followers continued their ascension, but this was no localized phenomenon. All over the world those measuring up to Ted's stringent criteria found themselves doing just the same.

Back in Ted's home state, the local Grand High Wizard of the Ku Klux Klan and Emerald Dragon of the Knights of the True Cross, or Chuck as he was known to his friends, was busily ironing his favourite white sheet. He'd been particularly active recently, what with the widespread civil unrest sweeping the nation his lodge had felt duty-bound to reinstate its authority in the only way it knew how.

There'd been some mighty fine dust-ups lately and no mistake, he thought to himself warmly. Almost up to the standards of the good ol' days.

Their pristine robes had paid the price stain-wise for this festival of moral violence. Blood, sweat, smoke, peanut butter and jelly sandwich filling – all the usual hazards of modern life had been ground into the garments. But it had been a small sacrifice for a greater good. Rather than resort to fitted sheets, or suffer the indignity of Sesame Street duvet covers for their next outing, the God-fearing churchgoers who comprised Chuck's elite team had taken a break to spruce themselves up. Chuck's own garment had required several washes to restore it to glory, but at last it had come out whiter than his official family tree.

Chuck held up his favoured sheet to view his handiwork. But before he could check it for that special bluey whiteness, it wasn't just the linen that was held aloft. With a frightened squeal Chuck felt himself gripped by some unearthly force, and gently wafted out of the open window.

All Over The World

It was a scene repeated time and again all over the world. Wherever sad, mad, bigoted fanatics gathered the area would take on an unearthly Heathrow-like quality. They were the hypocrites, petty tyrants and small-minded bigots who made life a misery for those around them. Always convinced they served the best interests of their fellow man, they in fact served nothing but themselves. The world could have long done without them, and now it seemed the world wanted to try.

It wasn't an activity entered into by all Christians by any means. Many churches (which had been doing a roaring trade these last few weeks) remained thoroughly rooted to the ground. Here and there the odd Congregationalist found themselves slipping up into the heaving sky, often babbling incoherently about how this proved they'd been right all along, and that their neighbours should have listened when they'd tried to show them the error of their ways.

Neither was the great lift-off limited to the Christian world. Deep in the heart of the Middle East there were many individuals who shared Ted's outlook on life, if not agreeing on the finer details of worship. More than one ritual stoning was interrupted as right-minded citizens found themselves drifting skywards. And in the bomb-proof parliamentary chambers of a dozen governments, emergency sessions were cut short by a spate of nasty head wounds. Reinforced concrete bunkers, intended to provide protection, proved just as good at rendering their occupants unconscious.

Orange Crush

Ted saw none of this through his own tear-filled eyes. The vision unfolded before him on a personal cinema screen which seemed to be showing a private preview in his head. He sat back and watched as the ancient prophecies unfolded. With the sort of warm glow that normally only comes from taking a leak in a swimming pool, he knew that this was how it was always meant to be. On the subject of his late departure Ted need not have worried. He knew full well that he'd be first to those Pearly Gates. Now he came to notice, it seemed he was about to receive a vertical boost like he'd never dreamt possible.

'Yeeeeesss iiiindeedy. We have lift-off!' he cried, as beneath his feet the ground began to shift and splutter. Ted could almost hear the countdown in his head. He'd never been one to meekly wait his turn, and today was no exception. One by one he'd overtake the hand-picked few, to be at the front of the queue on reaching paradise. But just like the energy in such desperate need of release beneath his feet, before the huge flashing numbers in his mind could reach zero, Ted had one last speech bursting to get out.

'Hear me, fellow believers! We stand at the dawn of a Golden Age – an age of salvation for all right-thinking individuals. Gasoline 'll be free, there won't be no fornication out of wedlock, stores 'll shut on Sundays – and best of all, yours truly 'll be undisputed master of all mankind! If it ain't so, may the Lord strike me down where I stand!'

'Look out boss!' screamed Harvey, from the spot two hundred feet up where he hovered. Ted's second-in-command wasn't sure what he'd seen, but it had been big, it had been orange, it had been plummeting to earth and he could have sworn he caught a distinct whiff of partially cooked seafood.

Below him, Ted stood with his head thrown back and his arms raised to the sky in blissful rapture. He opened his eyes ecstatically – to see a thirty-foot lobster fast about to crush him. Moments before impact, Ted felt an invisible straitjacket tighten around him and, in a great ball of smoke, he began to accelerate skywards.

There, in the skies, they met.

With the central figure in the great planet-wide ascent stripped of one vital dimension – namely his height – the propects for Ted's multitude hung dangerously in the balance. For a breathless second all was still, white robes billowed, burning crosses burnt, somewhere a crow squawked. Then, far in excess of the normal force of gravity, the airborne armada began to cannonball back to earth.

Many ancient authorities had been specific about the worthy rising into the air at the Final Trump; those same authorities had been less specific about how they might return if they hit a snag. All told this was one air traffic control dispute which wouldn't be resolved by two per cent above the cost of living and free tea and biscuits in the staff rest room.

Back at sea level, it started to rain rats and false gods round the globe, as the world's most unworthy were briskly returned from whence they came. Within half a minute it was over, bar the cleaning up.

Deborah looked up from the spot where she'd fallen to protect Mike. Nearby Adam, Sid and Megan had taken shelter beneath the overhang of a small gully, their shadowy movements just visible as they gingerly peered outwards. Of Hell's team there was no sign. Perhaps, on seeing their foe's apparent triumph, they had retired to whichever foul dimension demons go when they're finished for good – some astral equivalent of Bournemouth perhaps.

The remains of Ted's team were unfortunately all the

more apparent. Scattered in a rough circle around her position, Deborah could clearly make out a fresh set of corpses adding to the general carnage on the valley floor. At the crest of the low mound where all the action had recently taken place the smoking shell of a giant burnt-out lobster gently steamed. Poking out from beneath its vast charred and blackened bulk were two carefully manicured hands and a pair of dusty cowboy boots. It seemed Ted Trundell had finally found a situation he couldn't talk himself out of. Turning away in disgust Deborah searched the surrounding wreckage for some sign of Aristotle.

No sooner had she begun to worry, than a furtive movement from beneath the shell of a badly singed bathtub caught her eye. A pair of white paws were quickly joined by a twitching nose, then a furry ginger face completed the cat's struggling form. Rushing to help him she received scant thanks for her efforts.

Yes, okay, okay. I'm all right. I managed to get under here on my own, I think I can get out by myself as well. Concern yourself with our patient. Looks like he's decided to put in an appearance after all.

Almost dropping the bathtub on the ungrateful feline, Deborah spun round and was at Mike's side instantly. But despite her best efforts there were no signs of life. Before she could question Aristotle as to what he thought he was playing at Deborah felt movement between her arms. With a weak cough Mike's eyes fluttered open, dazed at first, then clearing rapidly.

'Well my girl,' he said, carefully charting out the bumps beneath his thatch of thick hair, 'I have two questions. Did I miss much? And do you have any Nurofen?'

Keep On Running

Pausing briefly to check his bearings, Gwylym at last realized where he was. It was a far from simple task. If his guess was correct the slope to his left would bring him on to the Bala road – the quickest route out of the zone of desolation. It was not a difficult tactical choice. Pulling Ivan's limping form behind him, Gwylym started up the debris-strewn slope.

Reaching the top of the scree the pair received their first pleasant surprise of a long and painful day. Parked next to the rubble-covered roadway stood a massive eighteen-wheel chemical transporter, all fired up and ready to roll. Through the open doorway Gwylym could clearly make out the keys swinging in the ignition. It seemed their luck had changed at last. On this quiet country lane the perfect means of escape had somehow survived the maelstrom of destruction.

Gwylym was about to jump for joy when Ivan's bandaged hand caught his arm. 'I don't like this,' he muttered through tears of pain. 'What's it doing parked next to a battlefield? It might contain explosives, or . . . something worse.'

But Gwylym was past caring. It would have taken an ocean of steaming napalm to stop him. So, as was customary, he completely ignored his deputy and clambered in.

Start Her Up

'That should do it.' Rubicante grunted as he strained to tighten the last bolt. The demons-turned-mechanics had spent twenty frustrating minutes struggling with the complex reality engine that powered their stranded juggernaut. It was the same flying truck that the monks had arrived in earlier that day. On locating the damaged tanker the demons had embarked on a spree of intense celebration. But when they'd tried to start the motor all they'd got for their efforts had been an unhealthy rumble. Now, finally, Rubicante had finished the repairs.

'Right,' he called from his prone position under the

engine block, 'get in and start her up.' But before Guttlehog could clamber out from under the bonnet, the craft sprung to life, and lifted off the ground.

If the demons received a surprise, it was nothing compared to Gwylym and Ivan's.

'I only released the handbrake!' Gwylym screamed with mounting panic. 'I didn't know we'd take off!'

Not for the first time in his life Ivan was in no mood to be rational. 'Aaaaaaaaaaarrrrrgh! Make it stop – *make it stop!*'

But Gwylym was too busy taking a crash course in not crashing to pay much attention. With surprising skill he successfully negotiated the looming mass of the valley wall, piloting the craft up and around the first of a series of low hills. The immediate danger out of the way, Gwylym felt able to breathe easier and unpeel himself from the cab roof. Even Ivan joined in the general mood of optimism and stopped screaming long enough to draw breath. Gwylym gripped the massive steering wheel with new determination. His eyes still bulged as if they might pop from his head, but at least he was regaining control.

Between breathless pants the GPLA's brave leader stammered. 'We'll make for the coast. At least that way we'll have a softer landing.'

Ivan was about to point out that drowning held no more attraction than any other form of sudden death, when what was left of his mind was diverted from the subject. In fact it wasn't so much 'diverted', as sent the wrong way up a one-way street. The vehicle's cab was positioned just aft of a long and highly polished bonnet. Beneath this cover the engine thundered its deafening roar. Suddenly, with less warning than the Japanese Airforce's Christmas outing to Pearl Harbor, the clasps along its glistening length burst open.

As the lorry crossed the line of the silent Welsh coast 3000 feet below, man locked eyes with demon and demon locked eyes with man. All parties then engaged in a protracted 'see-who-can-scream-the-loudest-competition', in which the object was apparently to psyche your opponent more than he was psyching you. This high-volume, high-altitude contest was still heading for a high score draw as the contestants soared out over the surging Atlantic swell, and on towards the setting sun.

Later, authorities would agree that this was no great loss.

The End Of The World

Megan's cottage had remained an oasis of serenity amidst the carnage. The rambling rose bushes had seen better days, the whitewashed walls could have done with a fresh coat of paint, but the old place had stood up surprisingly well to The End of the World. As the small party of battered and bruised refugees made their way up the winding path towards Megan's home, Mike reflected that this ancient edifice had survived far better than his own custom built fortress.

Sid and Adam seemed the worst affected by the day's events. Their eyes held that stunned far away look that so often accompanies a close encounter of the occult kind. Aristotle, as usual, was his calm old self. Mike had only a hazy recollection of what Deborah must have been through, but from what he remembered, her quiet thoughtful mood seemed entirely appropriate.

As for himself, the Professor felt weary, and not just due to the day's awesome events. If ignorance was bliss then the opposite was also true. Mike had long been the sole custodian of a dangerous truth, and over the years it had taken its toll. It was going to be a major adjustment, not to have to shoulder that heavy burden. But it would be worth it.

Not long later, through the panes of the cobweb-laced

windows, warm light spilled into the desolate night. Megan was a good host, though she'd almost forgotten the art during her years of exile. As the last embers of the setting sun burned low in the west there came a gentle knock at the door. Mike and Deborah exchanged worried glances, but Megan seemed untroubled by this late arrival. 'I figured it'd be you,' she said creaking open the oak door. 'I suppose you wants to meet me guests? Come on then sis, you're letting the cold in.'

A regal figure glided in and regarded each of them in turn. Deborah recognized her at once; they'd met earlier in the woods. Mike seemed to see something deeper. He glanced from Deborah to the stranger, then back again. The similarities were astounding, once you allowed for the differences in age. At a guess he would have put the newcomer in her late thirties, though she exuded a sense of timeless wisdom that hinted at a much greater age. 'If I may venture Ma'am, would you be the one known as Mathonwy?' Mike asked courteously.

The stranger regarded him with kind eyes set beneath a neat head of strawberry blonde hair. 'That is correct Michael. I have borne many names, but that is the one I am known by in these parts. Some have called me Don, or Danu, but Mathonwy has always been my favourite.'

Mike looked humble, an expression which seemed to hurt his face. 'So you had more than a passing interest in today's events?'

Mathonwy smiled. 'Well, I *have* been watching each of you for many years, and I'm glad to see you've come through unscathed. The prophecies are fulfilled. What was separated has come together once more. The rift is healed.'

Mike was suddenly alert. 'Then my visions all those years, they were your doing?'

'I can't take that credit. The act of observation alters that which is observed – and in this case for the better.

We that have the power can only wield it with regard to a higher law. Warnings can only be given to those who will hear. You were one of my channels, a most successful one at that.'

'That's a matter of opinion,' Mike muttered dryly. 'But what about my recent dreams? You didn't expect me to spread the word at such a late date. I've been stung by trying to help the great unwashed before. You knew that this time I'd be looking out for number one.'

Faintly Mathonwy fluttered her lashes. 'I must confess to subtler motives. This time it was not your function to warn your fellow man. It was necessary for your companion to be here, so that she could perform her crucial tasks.'

Deborah looked alarmed. 'Me?'

Mathonwy nodded.

'You mean everything I did was preordained?'

'Tell me sister, don't you believe we tread our own paths?'

Deborah answered instantly. 'Of course. I don't know for sure, part of the plan might be to make us believe we're in control. But I've always thought – no, I've always *felt* that we take charge of our destiny. There are never any excuses. You take responsibility for what you do.'

Mike nodded vigorously. 'That's what makes me gag about those loopy cults, that abnegation of responsibility. Saying "It is God's will" is the ultimate cop out.'

'Good,' exclaimed Mathonwy. 'I knew you'd see things that way. Believe me Deborah, were never under the influence of an outside force. I simply orchestrated the scene, I did not write your script. Your own character was the only guide to what you would do. Are you happy with what you have done?'

Deborah thought for a moment. 'Yes. Though I'm only just beginning to realize it.'

Now it was Mike's turn to look thoughtful. 'I don't know whether to feel put out or not. It might take me a while to get used to playing second fiddle. But I'm glad to be shot of the responsibility. Congratulations Deborah, I've never sat close to a cosmic bigwig before.'

Mathonwy smiled indulgently. 'Now I must leave you, I have much to do. I can look forward to a busy spell, but I find creative work most worthwhile.'

'Don't we all sis,' Megan muttered as she showed Mathonwy to the door. 'I expect to see you tomorrow for breakfast. There ain't no reason to go shooting off without calling by.'

'I promise I'll drop in,' said Mathonwy, as she stooped to kiss the tiny witch. 'Sleep well, we shall meet again when I've begun the healing.'

After Mathonwy had departed, the cottage's occupants drifted slowly off to bed. Soon only the Professor and Megan remained. Staring into the hypnotic flames of the roaring fire, Mike said to the old woman. 'So my dear, what happens now?'

Megan looked thoughtful for a moment. 'Well, I'm staying here. There'll be plenty for me to do when the villagers return. In the olden days a woman with my talents could always make a living. I reckon we're in for a period of tolerance like we 'aven't seen in years.'

Mike nodded his agreement. 'Perhaps that's all this was. A great sorting out, calculated to clear away the dregs. It's happened in the past and I'm sure it'll happen again. But I believe you're right. This is going to be a more forgiving time. It'll make a welcome change.'

Megan slowly nodded. 'And what about you? What will you do now?'

Mike sighed. 'Oh, I think I might start travelling again. I've been tied to one place for way too long. There's always more to learn. I rather thought I might study flamingo dancing.'

'Don't you mean flamenco dancing?'

'No, flamingo dancing. It's like flamenco except you

hold a live flamingo in each hand then . . .'

The sound of Megan's snores cut him off.

I Feel Fine

Deborah slept soundly that night, and so did her companions. As the first light of dawn broke over the hillsides and spilled through the dusty windows, the girl woke gently from sleep and sat up in her bed. Despite her protests Mike had insisted she take the last remaining mattress, claiming that a night on the floor would do wonders for his back. Cursing his stubbornness, Deborah had at last given in. Now that she looked at him sleeping, it did indeed seem to have done Mike good. The troubles which had long weighed heavy on his brow seemed stripped away. And was she just imagining it or were the first traces of a smile forming across his ancient lips? Maybe he now dreamt brighter dreams.

The others in the guestroom looked equally serene. Sid no longer had that startled-bunny quality about him, as he snored peacefully, while beside him even Adam seemed to have lost his permanent leer. There had always been something odd about that pair, she thought, and it went beyond their glandular obsessions. It was some subtle link, and now that link was broken. Since the events of the previous afternoon Sid seemed, not to put too fine a point on it, blurry around the edges, while Adam was strangely subdued, not his old self at all.

Deborah silently got out of bed, padded across the flagstoned floor and made her way to the kitchen. As she poured herself a cup of Megan's oddly addictive herb tea, she felt a furry shape brush against her legs. Aristotle jumped onto the kitchen table and fixed her with his amber eyes.

So, you finally made it into daylight, I see. For a while I thought I was going to have to resort to my trusty feline arousal techniques.

Deborah winced. 'Be fair, we went through a lot yesterday. And we all need our beauty sleep after all – some more than others.'

Well, perhaps I'll let you off this once. Though yesterday you left it awfully late. For a while there I thought Nick had you beat. It would have been such a shame if all the training I'd invested in you had gone to waste.

Deborah was about to take issue, when she became aware of a figure standing at the doorway. Megan shuffled out of her bedroom and joined them. 'Morning dears. Have you noticed what's going on outside? It's spreading faster by the minute.'

Before Deborah could ask what 'it' was, Megan pulled her to the kitchen window.

'Been blooming since sun-up,' said Megan. Outside, lush vegetation was taking root before their eyes. 'Don't stop for nothing. Covered the remains of the village in no time flat. And see, it's almost reached the crater where the bomb went off.'

Deborah peered on in disbelief at a spot where a stand of ancient oaks had sprouted in a matter of seconds. Where Young Nick had met his end, a rowan tree stood in full blossom. Everywhere, life was digging its claws back into the landscape.

'It hardly seems possible. All that destruction. I never realized there was such power.'

Megan patted Deborah's shaking hand. 'This is just repair work. There are plenty of lands that need fixing right now, but repair they will, in time. Earth just needs folks to tend it. Appearances can be deceptive.'

Deborah looked deep into Megan's eyes, seeming to gain understanding of a fundamental truth for the first time. 'You choose to look that way, don't you? I don't mean to be rude but if there's an alternative, why not take it?'

Megan's smile revealed a vast expanse of gum. 'There's always an alternative. I think you know I'm not some mad old granny who chats to the birds – well, not only that anyway. I have . . . abilities that allow me to exercise a certain power. For example . . .'

Even allowing for recent events, what happened next was stunning. With what seemed like a weird wobble in the air Megan transformed from an ancient witch into a radiantly beautiful young woman. For half an instant, Deborah thought she was looking at a mirror, then her hostess coughed uneasily and scratched her perfect nose. Megan's younger self was Deborah's twin in every respect, except while Deborah's hair was blonde, Megan's was a fiery red.

'But we're . . .'

'Identical. But then we're sisters after all.'

'Sisters?'

'I know, I know. It's a long story, ask me when we're not so busy.'

Deborah fought a losing battle to regain her composure as Mike strolled into the room. The Professor looked from one to the other, then back again, finally breaking into a knowing grin. 'Morning Megan. Where do you keep that fantastic tea?'

'Am I missing something here?' Deborah demanded. 'Mike, how come you manage to take this in your stride?'

Mike looked pleased with himself, an expression that sat easily upon his craggy face. 'Come now,' he said smugly, though with warmth. 'I'm sure you're familiar with the triple aspect of the Earth Goddess – her maid, her matron, and her hag elements. Every human culture acknowledges it in some form or other.'

Adam and Sid stumbled in from the bedroom. Both seemed groggy from sleep and Sid seemed less distinct than ever, but on seeing Deborah's new-found twin they perked up with a jolt. Adam's eyes lit up like Blackpool illuminations as he sidled over to the kitchen table. Not taking his gaze off Megan for an instant he said, 'Deborah,

Deborah. You never told me you had a sister. Hello my dear, let me introduce myself, I'm Adam. We're going to be very good friends.'

Megan threw her twin a mischievous wink, then gazed up at Adam and fluttered her eyelashes, patting the seat beside her.

There's No Home Like Place

In the Dolman Corporation's Entertainment Debriefing Room aboard the Starcruiser *Globular Beach*, two figures sat across a floating two-dimensional light table.

'You have served your purposes,' Kwarmph-IV said, 'and served them well.' He indicated a smile in Andy's mind. 'Our takings are up threefold on the last trip. Your background info-bursts throughout the proceedings were entertaining, insightful and led directly to increased sales at our species counter. People liked you so much, you might even have started a craze.'

'Like, reearly, it was nothing,' Andy said bashfully.

Kwarmph-IV leaned back in his suspension cot, a picture of alien glee. 'Dolman are so impressed with how it's gone, I'm going to get a promotion. They're going to train me to be a pilot!'

There was a pause, which Andy suddenly realized he was expected to fill. 'I'm very pleased for you,' he said eventually.

'And I'm very pleased with you, Earthman Andy. So pleased in fact that I've decided to let you return home – a very rare privilege, I have to say. We'll be breaking orbit in . . . ten of your minutes, so off you pop now and pack your capsule.'

But Andy just stayed where he was, his elbows on the table pooling plasma.

'Off you pop now and pack your capsule,' Kwarmph-IV repeated.

'The thing is . . . I don't want to go back.'

There was a beat as Kwarmph-IV took in this information. 'But why ever not, Earthman Andy? All our abductees ever talk about when they're still alive is going home, going home, going home.'

Andy shook his head. How could he explain this to an alien with an IQ of 5000 but the empathy of a scorpion? 'It's not home anymore,' he said as directly as he could, staring into Kwarmph-IV's jade eye. 'I'm not sure it ever was . . . I don't think I fit in there.'

'And you do here?'

Andy smiled ruefully. 'Well, not here exactly. But one of the tourists . . . Shnnmfreh, I think her name was – she's been giving me amorous eyes. And that, like yah, doesn't happen to me, like . . . ever.'

'I see. And you'd like to go back with her, would you?'

'Yes. Yes I would, rather.'

'Most surprising . . . but it can be arranged. Got your passport?'

Andy's face fell. 'I . . . I didn't have time before you –'

'Just kidding,' Kwarmph-IV said tonelessly.

Andy relaxed a little. 'So . . . where does she come from?' he asked.

'Let me see.' Kwarmph-IV tapped the air and the cruiser's passenger registration files slinked into view. 'Now . . . Ahh, the small planet near Soil. Yes, you're compatible with the atmosphere, and biologically – just – with her.' Kwarmph-IV returned Andy's expectant gaze. 'She comes from Place.'

'Place.' Andy tested the word on his lips. 'Yes, I rather like the sound of that.'

Over The Rainbow

As a bright new dawn broke over the valley, the survivors gathered outside Megan's rose-covered cottage and looked down at the view. Mike held Deborah's slender hand in his, and Megan held Mike's, as beside them Adam and Sid looked on in wonder. As for Aristotle, on seeing the lush paradise right before his twitching nose, the cat had rushed off to explore, or as he had sternly put it, to gather reconnaissance data.

They stood there, taking it all in, breathing the newly fresh air and watching Mathonwy's stately figure gliding up the willow-shrouded path that led from the stream. Behind her, Noddegamra's villagers trooped at a respectful distance. Even at this range Mike could clearly see their arms weighed down with what looked like the contents of a small cash-and-carry. Wherever they were planning to hold it, it was going to be quite a party.

'Greetings, friends,' Mathonwy said, in her rich contralto as she reached them. 'My work here is almost done, there are many other places that need my aid, but one task remains.'

As Mike looked at her questioningly, Mathonwy turned to Sid. Adam's shady companion seemed to know what was coming. 'Time for me to go I take it?'

Mathonwy nodded her head. 'The other one has need of you no more. He has grown.'

'Like a fungus,' Deborah added bluntly.

Adam looked at Sid then to Mathonwy. 'Do you two know each other?'

Mathonwy shook her head. 'I knew about you, and what was happening to you.'

'Meaning?' Deborah asked.

'Sid is Adam. He's not your subconscious, Adam – he's what you will become if you don't change your ways. He was a warning. But as you can see, he's beginning to fade.'

'Does that mean you're going to stop being an arsehole now?' Deborah asked Adam.

He grinned, and it seemed that there was genuine warmth in it. 'Not completely. But you could say recent events have opened my eyes. Maybe it's a case of striking the right balance.' He paused, took a deep breath. 'I could start by apologizing to you for pestering you when clearly you weren't interested . . . Deborah, I'm sorry.'

All eyes turned to her. There was a delay, but eventually she said grudgingly, 'Accepted.'

At the sight, Sid tried to stick his fingers down his throat, but they were already disappearing. 'God, I'll be glad to go,' he said. 'He's been no fun recently. There's gotta be wilder stuff for me out there. See ya later folks.'

Waving his hand, and chuckling his hyena chuckle, Sid faded away until with a faint pop he was gone.

Megan pulled Adam to one side and started to lead him back towards the cottage. 'So Mathonwy reckons you've grown, huh?' she said suggestively. 'Maybe we could examine exactly how much in private?'

For the first time since that fateful day at the video store, Adam blushed.

Which left Deborah, Mathonwy and the Professor together in the cool morning sun, watching the preparations for Noddegamra's biggest ever party unfold.

'Won't you stay with us just a while – to celebrate?' Mike said. 'The view you created is spectacular. They'll all want to thank you.'

Mathonwy inclined her head. 'You flatter me Michael, as is your talent. I can always find time for you. Perhaps my duties can wait just a little longer.'

Nearby, Hywell set down two massive beer barrels he'd carried up from his deepest cellar, as Crystal started serving drinks. Dick and Emmyr were there too, along with the sorts of picnic hampers that could have fed the five thousand, though there was more on offer than the obligatory stale fish sandwiches. Even Purity Roberts had shown up, perhaps deciding that joining was better than beating after all.

Deborah leaned across to Mike and whispered, 'Adam's going to get such a shock when Megan reverts back to her true form. I just hope for his sake she's got her clothes on at the time.'

'I wouldn't bet on it,' Mike chuckled. 'Look at 'em go.'

He gestured over his shoulder, through the open door, to where Adam and Megan's newly youthful form sat close together. Grinning, Adam leaned forwards and whispered something saucy in her ear. Megan blushed pinkly and giggled like a schoolgirl, but didn't push him away as he edged closer.

Deborah smiled quizzically. 'Looks like Adam finally pulled after all. This is almost becoming sickening Mike. Is everybody happy?'

'Yep,' said the Professor with a grin, 'I'm rather afraid it looks that way. Though to be honest I do like a happy ending. What do you think Mathonwy, it's not every day I get to canvas the opinion of a real goddess.'

'I think,' she said looking far down the lush valley, 'that it's going to be a long and beautiful day.'

They all turned to follow her gaze. Down amongst the freshly sprouted foliage a large ginger cat was busy chasing butterflies.

AFTER

Emily pranced happily through the long grass, the morning dew prisming sunlight into tiny rainbows as it clung to her snowy fleece. Altogether it was the sort of morning only possible in shampoo adverts; the sort where flaxen-haired maidens rode bareback through sunlit meadows until, arriving at tumbling mountain streams, they washed their hair with the very latest in frequent-use, two-in-one, anti-dandruff concoctions. Perhaps later a strangely sideburned young man would turn up with a knowing twinkle in his eye and a straw between his lips, and the pair would wander off into the thicker parts of the woods to indulge in a spot of interactive evolution. Just what inbuilt advantages the offspring of this tryst would enjoy would not be apparent, though they'd certainly possess lovely shiny hair.

But Emily was unaware of any of this, because she was a young and happy sheep. In fact, these days, most sheep were happy sheep, their lot had improved considerably since the previous long and sultry summer.

True enough, Emily's sister Rosemary had gone missing in suspicious circumstances shortly before the Farmer's annual family barbecue. But then when you were a sheep you quickly developed a fatalistic outlook on the universe. All told, things were much better than they'd been in the bad old days. Sometimes on dark nights, when the elders sat around telling tall tales, one hardy soul might bleat stories of the 'Time of Detonations'. But Emily found them hard to believe.

As her frantic excursions brought Emily full circle to

where her mother stood placidly seeing to lunch, the lamb tottered breathlessly between its mother's legs. Across the gently rolling slope, down at the gate to the twisting valley road, movement caught her eye. Seeming to sense it too, Emily's mum looked up from her chlorophyll-based main course. Several humans seemed to be unpacking electrical equipment from a large and box-like truck. Printed onto its side brightly coloured lettering was clearly visible even at this range.

Emily's faltering voice held a note of wonder. 'Mummy, what does "BBC Outside Broadcast – One Man And His Dog" mean?'

'It means,' said Emily's mum wisely, as only a wise old sheep can, 'that things are back to normal.'

ACKNOWLEDGEMENTS

I'd like to thank all those people who read the early drafts of *Before & After* and gave me encouragement and/or abuse. I wouldn't have finished without them. In a sad attempt to persuade them and their friends and families to buy it, here's a list of some of their names. Tony Hossier, Barbara Thomas, Peter Reynolds, Matt Smith, Catherine Richards, Sara Ricketts, Robin Heydon, Georgina King, Olivia Thomas, Dave Proctor, Todd Gibbs, Dave Lomas, Kevin Bezant, Chris Ford, Helen Martin, Allan Duggan, Donna Jennett, Cath Bath, Claire Hopkins, Mad Julia, Russell Allcock, That girl on the train between Cardiff and Swindon, Laurie Dobson, Paul Martin, Simon Warner, Simon Hegarty, Andy Morgan, Andy's Wife, Nick Webber, Steve Powell, Julie Rutherford, Paul Vickers, Ioan Jones, Claire Jones, Mark Thomas, and of course, Lisa.